Forever Betrothed, Never the Bride

Forever Betrothed, Never the Bride

Christi Caldwell

For more information about the author:
christicaldwellauthor@gmail.com
www.christicaldwellauthor.com

ISBN: 194424008X
ISBN 13: 9781944240080

DEDIC

To my two baby girls: I can't wait to n
tremendous strength and power tha

To all my friends fighting for their
being with me on a very long journe

ACKNOWLEDGEMENTS

Tremendous thanks to my amazing critique partners who took me under their wings years ago. You have been my cheerleaders not only in my writing pursuits, but also in life. A special thanks to Aileen Fish and Samantha Grace. None of this could have happened without your support.

ONE

1817
London, England

Dearest Lord Drake,
Though you have never directly addressed me by name, I have decided I
am far too old to be called Em. I ask you to instead call me Emmaline...
that is, if you ever call upon me.
Ever Yours,
Emmaline

Two elegant phaetons barreled along Oxford Street, bearing down on an old woman peddling her goods. The merchant paled and tried to shove her cart up on the pavement. It tipped, swayed, and then careened into the street. Both men in their high fly-ers pulled sharp on the reins. Nearby, a passing gentleman pushed the lady on his arm away from certain calamity.

A vulgar shout and frightened screams split the cacophony of mundane street sounds.

Lady Emmaline Rose Fitzhugh paused on the pavement and raised a hand to shield her eyes against the sun's brightness. She frowned.

Lord Whitmore and Lord Cavenleigh. Two of Society's most dandi-fied fops.

Lord Whitmore tugged hard at the reigns and leapt from the still moving conveyance. "You filthy cow!" He raged at the poor woman in the street.

1

Lord Cavenleigh, jumped down from his carriage and muttered a string of curses.

Emmaline's skin heated at the rather descriptive obscenities they unleashed on the woman. Having an older brother, she'd heard her fair share of inappropriate words, but Cavenleigh's litany was rather original even on that score.

As the street erupted with the panicked cries of young ladies, the peddler bowed her head. Stringy gray hair straggled into her eyes. "Oi'm sorry, m-my lord."

Cavenleigh kicked a tomato at the old woman, and splattered her skirts with the ripened fruit.

Emmaline gasped.

Her maid, Grace, took her by the arm and attempted to steer her away. "Please, come away, my lady."

Emmaline ignored her efforts and rushed into the fray. "Cease, immediately." She stepped into the street just as the assailant launched another tomato at the peddler.

The projectile missed its intended mark and splattered onto the embroidered lace edging of Emmaline's ivory silk skirts.

Hands squared on her hips, she glared at the two men. "How dare you?"

Whitmore, with his slickly oiled and very deliberately curled red hair, stepped around Emmaline to launch a barrage of insults at the quaking woman. He brandished his riding crop. "Sorry? You're sorry? We could have been killed and for what? Your meaningless life and rotten vegetables?"

Emmaline threw herself in front of the aged peddler. "What manner of gentlemen would torment a defenseless woman?"

"No, my lady," Grace cried.

A tall figure stepped into the fray and positioned himself between Grace and the two assailants. Society knew the gentleman as the Marquess of Drake.

Emmaline knew him as her betrothed.

Lord Drake wrenched the whip from the cad's fingers, cracked the instrument in half, and tossed the two pieces aside.

Emmaline swallowed hard. Lord Drake stood more than a head taller than her and possessed the kind of hardened masculine perfection Michelangelo would have ached to memorialize in stone. The harsh angles of his face bespoke power and commanded notice. With rugged cheeks, aquiline nose, and squared jaw, he conveyed raw vitality. The hint of a curl to his unfashionably long golden hair seemed suited to this real life David.

"You clearly have very little value for your life," Drake said to the two fops who'd moments ago tormented the poor old woman.

Emmaline's stare collided with Drake's emerald eyes. The green irises pierced through her with heated intensity; robbed her of breath.

Get a hold of yourself, Em. He is just a man. A gloriously, stunning man—but that was neither here nor there.

She looked toward Whitmore and Cavenleigh. Cavenleigh had the good sense to stagger backwards and scurry from the incident like a rodent discovered by Cook in the kitchens.

Lord Drake returned his focus to the red-haired assailant who'd wielded the weapon. He grabbed him by the wrist and applied such pressure, the man gasped.

A hiss of pain whistled past Whitmore's lips. "For the love of God, man…" Whitmore pleaded.

"Had your whip hit its mark, you'd be facing me at dawn." Drake's voice was a silken promise. "What's your name, pup?"

Whitmore swallowed, as though he'd been forced to scrape up a rotten tomato from the grimy pavement and swallow it whole. "L-Lord W-Whitmore."

"Beg the lady's pardon, Witless."

A laugh escaped Emmaline.

Whitmore glared at her.

His actions did not escape Drake's astute gaze. Lord Drake tightened his grip and the dandy whimpered like a naughty child who'd just had a birch rod put to his person by a too stern nursemaid. "Apologize."

The young lord turned to Emmaline. "I-I'm sorry, my lady. M-my apologies," he croaked.

She folded her arms across her chest and nodded pointedly at the old woman. "I say, you rather owe the both of us an apology."

Whitmore's eyes rounded with shocked indignation. "You're mad."

Lord Drake squeezed again.

"M-My apologies, my lady."

Her betrothed jerked his chin in the peddler's direction. "Now, the woman."

Whitmore blinked; his pale white cheeks flamed a crimson red to match the bright hue of his hair. "Stupid old cow and her rotten vegetables nearly killed us." He motioned down the expanse of his peacock blue satin breeches. "And look at this stain. Why, Brummell himself would have been proud to wear these." The young man's whining tone indicated he considered the attack on his wardrobe to be an equally grave affront.

The peddler's chin fell to her chest as if she tried to make herself as small as possible.

Unable to remain silent any longer, Emmaline took a step toward the young fop. "Stupid, Lord Whitmore?" Passing a cursory glance over his frame, Emmaline shook her head. She nudged a tomato with the tip of her already ruined ivory satin slipper. "First of all, a tomato is a fruit, not a vegetable. Secondly," it was her turn to gesture at the garment in question. "those breeches were ruined long before this incident."

Whitmore frowned. "I don't understand, my lady."

Lord Drake's chuckle tugged her attention momentarily in his direction. His lips quirked upward in a devastating smile that quickened her heart's pace. "I believe that is the lady's point, Whitmore," Lord Drake drawled.

Whitmore's gasp forced Emmaline's attention away from her betrothed.

Enraged awareness dawned in the dandy's eyes. "You witch."

Emmaline took a step closer to Lord Drake.

A single black look from the marquess forced Whitmore to an ignoble halt. Drake leaned down close to the man and whispered something intended solely for the dandy's ears.

4

All color leached from the brute's cheeks. His head tipped up and down like a bobbing ship caught in a squall on the Channel. "M-my a-a-apologies, my lady."

Drake dropped Whitmore's wrist and wiped his hands back and forth as though he'd been sullied by the other man's skin. His lethal glare froze the coward in his spot.

Whitmore cleared his throat. "What I'd intended to say, my lady, is that your rich beauty robbed me of any sense." He looked to Lord Drake as he recited each word, indicating they were by no means original thoughts belonging to the jackanapes.

"One more thing," Drake said.

With obvious reluctance, the humiliated dandy reached into the front of his elaborate, violet-hued floral jacket. He withdrew a bag of coins, stared at it forlornly, and then offered it to the peddler. "Here."

The peddler's eyes widened.

"Take it," Drake said. There was an underlying warmth to his gruff tone.

With downcast eyes, the woman reached out and accepted the bag.

Drake returned his steely gaze to Whitmore. "I suggest you leave."

When the other man continued to eye the bag in the woman's hands with a blend of longing and bitter rage, Drake added, "Now."

Whitmore reached down, scooped up the remnants of his short whip, and then clambered into his phaeton. He shot one last black look at the peddler and Emmaline, before striking his white mount with a piece of his crop. His phaeton resumed its reckless path down the street. Emmaline stared after the carriage, glad to be free of Whitmore's loathsome company.

When Whitmore had gone, she turned back to the peddler. "Are you hurt?"

"No, my lady," the woman whispered. Fat teardrops filled her eyes and spilled over onto her cheeks. She sniffed and dashed a hand across her nose. "My lady, my lord, oi thank you."

Drake stepped out into the street. The heels of his gleaming black Hessian boots sank into a pile of rotten produce as he effortlessly righted the upended cart. Then, reaching into his jacket front, he pulled out a bag of coins, and returned to the old woman's side. "Here." He gently placed the bag in her dirt-encrusted fingers.

"Oi-Oi, thank you, my lord. Many blessings to you both." She dipped an awkward curtsy and pushed her nearly emptied cart down the road.

Emmaline watched after her until she'd disappeared from sight.

With the excitement now over, Oxford Street and its passersby returned to their daily humdrum. Lord Drake turned his focus to Emmaline. "Have you been hurt, Lady Emmaline?"

She blinked. Then sighed. Maybe not in that order. Her mind seemed a bit...muddled. Yes, it was muddled. And her heart beat an oddly rapid rhythm in her chest—*thumpthumpthumpthump*. She tried to catch her breath but failed miserably.

And then realized what had happened. "Oh dear," she said.

The earlier rage she'd seen in Lord Drake's jade eyes faded to warm concern. He took a step towards her and Emmaline backed up a step. "My lady?"

"Oh dear," she muttered beneath her breath. She'd read a fair number of poems and gothic novels to recognize certain telltale signs of that which ailed her. The books all indicated one's heart would race; one would be at a loss for words, and one would forget to breath. Yes, Emmaline knew what the onslaught of symptoms she'd been besieged by indicated—she'd gone and fallen in love.

"My lady?" Lord Drake and her maid repeated in unison.

Emmaline crashed back down to reality. The first thing she became aware of was that her toes were exceedingly chilly. She glanced down into the muddy puddle her slippers now called home and wrinkled her nose. A rather odd-smelling puddle of filthy water, crushed tomatoes, cabbage, and Lord knew what else.

With the tip of her right foot, she pushed aside the stray purple leaf clinging to her other slipper.

"My lady?" Lord Drake interrupted her musings.

Her head snapped up. *What did he say?* Her mind tried to drag up his recent question so she might form a suitable reply.

"Just splendid." There, that seemed like a perfectly, *splendid* response.

A smile pulled at the corners of his lips. "Uh, well you may find the stench of that puddle splendid but I must insist it is foul. Regardless of who is correct, might I offer you my arm?"

Emmaline wished said puddle were about five-feet-one inch deeper so she could sink beneath its surface.

She stared at his outstretched hand until her maid cleared her throat, and jerked her back to the moment. Emmaline placed her fingers in his. He tucked them into the fold of his elbow and carefully guided her away from the remnants of the cart.

"Thank you, my lord."

That was the best I could come up with—just thank you? She grimaced and stole a peek from the corner of her eye to gauge his reaction to her less than stimulating repartee. Couldn't she have offered some witty banter, as so many other ladies would have managed?

His expression may as well have been carved from granite.

Emmaline had never been a flirt, so she settled for honesty. "What you did for that peddler...and me, was—heroic."

If she hadn't raised her gaze at that precise moment, she would have missed the way his strong, square jaw tightened.

"I would hardly call it heroic, my lady." His words sounded curiously flat.

Emmaline dug her heels in, and forced him to stop. She motioned to the sea of preoccupied lords and ladies. "Look around, my lord. Look how busy the street is. There are ladies and gentlemen rushing about, and not one of them stepped forward."

He gently steered her ahead. "That isn't quite true."

Emmaline looked at him askance.

"You placed yourself between the peddler and the dandies," he said.

She beamed.

"What would possess you to do something so reckless?"

An errant lock of hair escaped her chignon and fell across her eye. She blew it back, but it fell right back into place. Forgetting the

CHRISTI CALDWELL

recalcitrant strand, she again dug her heels in and forced him to a stop.

Emmaline looked up at Lord Drake. "What would you have had me do? Allow them to beat the poor woman?"

A growl lodged in his throat. "I would rather you hadn't placed yourself in harm's way."

If he hadn't sounded so surly about it, Emmaline would have sighed like a debutante at her first ball. Instead, "I couldn't just let them hurt her. What kind of person would I be if I'd allowed that?"

The corner of his lips lifted ever so slightly. He motioned for Emmaline to continue walking. "A safe one."

"Ahh, but what is safety without honor?"

He looked at a point over her shoulder. "Honor is an oftentimes overestimated word with little meaning, my lady."

A frisson of distress traveled along Emmaline's spine, and in spite of the unseasonable warmth of the day, gooseflesh dotted her arms. She hadn't failed to miss the bleakness in Lord Drake's distracted stare, and found herself, yet again, at a loss.

"Might I see you home, Lady Emmaline?"

A cowardly sense of relief that she'd been saved from replying to his previous, baleful statement assailed her. Lord Drake wanted to escort her home? Had he asked, she would have taken tea in the muddy puddle he'd rescued her from. Still, it wouldn't do to come across as too eager. "I would be grateful, my lord."

They walked along in silence and Emmaline mourned the passing of each block that brought her closer to home.

She caught her lower lip between her teeth and searched her mind for something to discuss. The weather...? What clever young lady would discuss something as mundane as the weather?

"Your earlier actions were brave, Lady Emmaline—and I respect them."

She blinked. "Well, I really hadn't been expecting that from you, my lord."

He continued as though she hadn't spoken. "But still foolish."

"Now, *that* I expected."

A deep laugh rumbled up from his chest. "I've been boorish today. Forgive me."

"Yes, yes, I say you have," she said, under her breath.

He raised a single brow. "I beg your pardon?"

Emmaline nodded. "Very well, since you are begging." His brow furrowed. "I'm teasing, my lord," she said. She shook her head. "You've been nothing but honorable, brave, and heroic—a true gentleman." The effusive praise spilled from her lips with all sincerity and she willed herself to silence. Alas, she'd never been one to dissemble.

"We've arrived," he said.

Emmaline shook her head, but Lord Drake gave a slight nod.

She looked up at the white finish of her brother's townhouse and groaned.

Lord Drake's gaze snapped to her. "Are you certain you were not injured earlier? Did you turn your ankle?"

He had a look as if he were about to draw her skirts back and peek for himself, which sent her heart sputtering wildly.

If she'd been brazen or clever, she would have feigned an injury blocks ago. But alas…"No, no. I assure you, I'm fine."

Her brother's aging butler pulled open the front door. Emmaline jumped, and pressed a hand to her breast. Goodness, the man could shock a ghost.

Lord Drake took a step away from her and offered a deep bow. "I am glad you were uninjured. I bid you good day, my lady."

Without awaiting a response, he turned on his heel and continued down the street. Emmaline stared after him until his figure faded from sight, and then entered the townhouse.

She'd been betrothed to Lord Drake for fifteen years. In that time, their contact had been limited to passing greetings and letters she'd written to him—letters which she'd never bothered sending. This, could therefore, be considered the first real interaction she'd had with him…and in a heroic fashion, he'd come to her aid. Perhaps he'd been so captivated by her act of *bravery*, as he'd called it, that he, too, had fallen madly in love with her. Even now, he might very well be strolling down the streets, unable to formulate a coherent thought, unable to think about anything other than the sight of her.

Emmaline sniffed. "What is that smell?" She looked down and her nose scrunched at the stench clinging to her skirts. Why, he surely failed to even note the rotten fruit smattered all over her beautiful ivory gown.

Yes, she was certain Lord Drake would begin courting her.

Any day.

TWO

My Dearest Lord Drake,
I am perturbed with you. You should have informed me that once I
indulged in Father's brandy, it would hardly be a secret. I was sick for
two whole days....and in no small amount of trouble.
Ever Yours,
Emmaline

Drake weaved in and out of the tables at White's. He didn't return the waves or greetings thrown his way. His gaze was trained on one particular spot in the far corner.

He drew to a halt in front of Lord Sinclair.

"What do you know about Lord Whitmore?" Drake said in the same commanding voice that had served him well during his time in the military.

Lord Sinclair glanced up. He had the distinction of being the one person Drake considered a friend. "Well, good to see you, too. I've only been waiting here an hour for your always agreeable company."

Without preamble, Drake tugged out a chair and sat. Reaching across the table for the bottle, he poured himself a glass of whiskey, and took a long sip. He relished the trail the hot liquid burned down his throat.

"Whitmore," Drake repeated. "What do you know of him?"

Sinclair raised a brow. "My, what a foul mood you're in."

"Sinclair?"

"Very well. Other than the fact that he dresses like an ass?"

Drake drummed his fingers along the tabletop. "Don't state the obvious."

Sin's brow furrowed. "Overly fond of the gaming tables and rumored to have a hot temper. Also known as something of a mother's boy. Why?"

Drake stared into the contents of his drink. "What do you know about Lady Emmaline Fitzhugh?" He looked up when Sin remained silent.

Sin blinked. "Uh-I, do you mean your betrothed?"

Drake waved his hand. "Is there another Lady Emmaline Fitzhugh?"

"Not that I'm aware of," Sin answered with a tad too much humor.

Drake kicked him under the table.

"Ouch," Sin muttered. His lips pulled in a tight grimace. "What is that God awful smell?"

"My boots."

"Why do—"

"Enough about my boots, Sin. What do you know of her?"

"Rather unremarkable. She's never been considered a diamond of the first water. She's barely an inch beyond five feet and is remarkably un-curved in all the areas a lady should be curved."

Drake opened his mouth to protest but Sin continued. "Her plain, dull brown coloring has never attracted any notice. Her lips are too full for..."

"Enough," Drake snapped. He fought back an overwhelming urge to drag his friend across the table and plant him a facer.

Sin frowned. "But I thought you wanted to know about her."

"I know what she bloody well looks like." Drake heard the frosty bite to his own tone but couldn't stifle it. Christ, how could Sin and Society be so very wrong about Emmaline? Her brown hair put him in mind of deep chocolate. And she had the most interesting dusting of freckles along the tip of her nose. His lips twitched. He'd never known anyone with dark hair to suffer from the blemishes and found it, well, rather endearing. And her lips, too full for fashion's dictates put Drake in mind of wicked thoughts.

12

Sin picked up his drink and downed a long, slow swallow. "So then what would you like to know?" He reached for the bottle, poured himself another, and swirled the contents of the glass. "I'm afraid I'm going to have to know more."

Drake forced himself to take a casual sip. He thought about his chance encounter with Lady Emmaline. Since he'd returned from the Peninsula three years ago, hailed in the papers as some kind of war hero, he'd gone out of his way to avoid his betrothed. He'd been tied to Lady Emmaline for more than half of his life, and yet knew next to nothing about her. As much as he wanted to find out more about the intriguing creature, he was loathe to show any outward interest, even to his friend. Oh, the fun Sin would have at his expense. "I happened to come upon Lady Emmaline this afternoon."

Sinclair arched a dark brow. "Oh?"

Since the moment Drake had witnessed Emmaline place herself between the old peddler woman and a gentleman's riding crop, aside from concern for her well-being, he'd been unable to think of anything but his betrothed. Before that moment, if you'd asked him if a lady of Quality would ever risk her own safety for a common woman on the street, he'd have scoffed at the ludicrousness of such a notion. Now, the image of Lady Emmaline, like some kind of warrior princess defending her keep, would be an image forever emblazoned on his mind.

Drake shifted uncomfortably. "For the last time, what do you know about the lady?"

Sin shrugged. "I don't know much about her."

"Not much? You know next to everything about everyone."

"I know she's a wallflower."

Drake sat back in his chair, flummoxed. "Impossible." A woman whose eyes could blaze with such life while challenging two men could never be a wallflower. Wallflowers were content to be dull creatures seated on the sidelines, escaping any notice. They were not clever young ladies with cheeky retorts.

Sinclair leaned forward in his chair. "Oh?"

13

Drake's skin heated. Good God, he couldn't be embarrassed. He tugged uncomfortably at his cravat. No, surely it was just that his cravat was too tight. "I had an encounter with Lady Emmaline a short while ago."

When Sinclair's brows shot up to his hairline, Drake realized his words could be mistaken for something more lascivious in nature.

"Don't be ridiculous," he snapped.

Like a babe looking for a story from his nursemaid, Sin propped his arms on the table and stared at Drake with impatient eyes.

Drake sighed, and then proceeded to recount the events he'd witnessed. When he concluded his story, Sin sat back heavily in his chair, with arms folded across his chest. "Humph."

"That's it? Just 'humph'?"

Sinclair raised one brow. "What would you have me say? Sounds like a rather dangerous thing for the lady to do."

Discounting the fact that Drake had the very same reaction with Lady Emmaline, he took a long swallow of whiskey. "You are missing the point, Sin."

"Oh? And what is the point?"

Drake dragged a hand through his hair. Was the point that his betrothed had bewildered him? Or was the point that he hadn't been able to stop thinking about her since the moment he'd seen her challenging Whitmore and his crony?

The irony wasn't lost on him. For the past three years, he'd forced thoughts of Lady Emmaline from his mind. He'd ignored the contract between them. If he'd returned from the Peninsula as the same man he'd been before the war, fulfilling his duty to her would have been somewhat easier. Not palatable but an obligation he would have fulfilled, nonetheless.

"If you admire her, perhaps you should claim her."

Drake grunted.

Sin raised his tumbler in mock salute. "I imagine marriage based on mutual admiration is a good deal more than most unions are built from."

Drake thought about his feisty intended, her eyes sparkling with flashes of defiance and courage, her rose hued lips made for sinning, pursed tight with fury. He silently tacked desire to Sin's components of a successful marriage.

Drake picked up his glass and drained the remaining contents. At this rate, he'd be drunk before supper. "There is no mutual admiration."

His friend scoffed. "No? Are you really so modest to believe she couldn't admire you?"

Drake set his tumbler down hard enough to rattle the table. "For what? I'm…"

A madman. A monster. A beast. If he were less of a coward he'd come right out and share the truth with Sinclair. Consumed by restive energy, his gaze skimmed the club. Some gentlemen laughed uproariously while others chatted with friends and acquaintances. Once upon a lifetime ago, he'd been at ease around other people, too.

Sin didn't press his line of questioning, and for that Drake was grateful. Instead, his friend reached for the bottle of whiskey and poured himself another glass. Then, he leaned over and filled Drake's glass. "I'm assuming it was quite a sight seeing Lady Emmaline challenge a gentleman." He paused. "As much as one can consider Whitmore a gentleman."

Drake smiled and toyed with the rim of his glass. "I thought I could no longer be surprised by a woman. I learned otherwise, today."

"Sounds like marriage to the lady might not be the worst of fates."

Drake made an impatient sound. "Marriage to me isn't in her best interest."

"You are the most honorable man I know," Sin said.

There it was again. That word he loathed with every fiber of his *honorable* being. Emmaline had described his actions as honorable, had looked at him as some kind of hero. He managed a half grin for his friend. "That isn't saying much about the men you know.

Sin shook his head but didn't press the point. "Sooner or later, you are going to have to do right by the young lady."

Great. First his father, now his best friend.

But that was the rub of it all. Sin merely spoke the truth. Fact: a betrothal contract had been signed between his family and Emmaline's.

Fact: the young lady was past her twentieth year and required a husband. Fact: Drake just couldn't bring himself to commit to a wife. He could not subject any woman to the madness that plagued him.

He picked up his glass and rolled it between his fingers, studying the shimmering gold of the brew. The shade reminded him of the glint in her eyes when—he shook his head forcefully. "I need a mistress."

Sinclair snorted. "You need a wife."

Drake ignored him. He needed a woman who was safe, a woman who wouldn't look at him with any kind of adoration, and wouldn't desire anything from him, other than his prowess in the bedroom. These were the kind of entanglements that were safe, devoid of any emotional connection.

Yet why did the thought of setting up a mistress seem like a chore?

THREE

Dearest Lord Drake,
What I am about to write is exceedingly intimate. I pray you will not
judge but I can no longer keep silent.
    I must confess my deep, adoring love—for gardening.
Ever Yours,
Emmaline

Emmaline couldn't sleep.

Even if she could, she most assuredly would still be awake. Unlike the majority of the *ton*, she loved mornings because she appreciated any and all time away from the smug, condescending members of Society.

It had been three weeks since the incident with Lord Whitmore. And in three weeks she hadn't heard word from Lord Drake. Following the encounter with her betrothed, Emmaline had believed she'd finally garnered his notice and a real courtship was imminent.

She snorted. So much for love.

Or admiration.

Or childish dreams.

With her maid trailing at a distance, Emmaline marched through the western part of Hyde Park, until she came upon Kensington Gardens. The fiery sun peeked just over the horizon, dousing the dawn sky in ethereal hues of burnt flame. She paused to appreciate the light playing off the abundant foliage of the cascading elm. A faint breeze caught hold, stirring the long row of horse chestnut trees. She glanced up and briefly closed her eyes on a smile, as a handful of white leaves sprinkled with red dots fluttered down to the earth. They tickled her skin, and then continued their path to the pavement.

God bless Queen Caroline for having been an avid gardener with the good sense to celebrate the beauty of the land. Men might own the land, but women rejoiced in its splendor.

At last, Grace caught up, her round, girlish cheeks red from her efforts. "My lady, would you like…?"

Emmaline held a hand up. "Did you hear that?"

"Hear what, my lady?"

Her ears pricked up. "There. A faint whistling."

Grace fought back a yawn and lifted her shoulders in a small shrug. "I don't hear anything, my lady."

Emmaline cocked her head, and listened. There it was again. Almost like the sound of a whipcord slicing through the air. "That." She started off in the direction of the odd noise.

Grace groaned. "My lady, can't we just…" Her words were lost as Emmaline's quick steps put space between them.

Emmaline's chest rose and fell from the rapid pace she'd set. She chewed her lip and surveyed the area.

Nothing.

Her maid finally caught up, wheezing slightly. She bent over and placed her hands upon her knees, taking in several deep breaths. "My lady, please, stop. I'm sure it's nothing."

"Just rest a moment, Grace. I'll take a short turnabout. I'll not go far."

A flash of gratitude lit the maid's hazel eyes, and she nodded, brushing away a stray lock of brown hair.

Emmaline hurried down the meticulous stone path that emptied out into one of the many private floral gardens. The collective beauty of the bright array brought her up short. For Christmas, her brother had given her the oddest contrivance. A tube containing loose pieces of glass inside and clever little configurations. He'd told her it was called a kaleidoscope; explaining that "kalos" was the Greek word for beautiful and "scopos" for watcher. All winter Emmaline had pointed the apparatus up at the light and peered through the tube, admiring the shifting patterns of color. Kensington Gardens never ceased to stun her with its vital beauty. With the pale pink of the spotted orchid, the effervescent hue of the violet bluebells interspersed with the lilac-white of the cuckooflower; it was like its own kaleidoscope of nature's beauty.

She searched the area and her gaze settled on a lone gentleman with his back to her, swinging his walking stick. His fluid movements cut a swath through a blanket of pale blue forget-me-nots, as he severed the heads off the buds.

Emmaline gasped. She raced over. "Whatever are you doing?"

Startled, the tall stranger spun around. *Lord Avondale.*

His ornate stick soared through the air, and landed with a soft thump amidst the blue blooms. He folded his arms across his chest and peered down his long nose. "I assure you, I've not come for company."

If her brother Sebastian, the powerful Duke of Mallen didn't intimidate her, this reed-thin fellow with his elfin-pointed ears and mottled skin certainly wasn't going to, either. "And I assure you, sir, the forget-me-nots had far grander hopes than decapitation by your stick on this glorious day."

The man angled his head. "They're just plants."

Emmaline's eyes slid closed. Whitmore and the fruit. This idiot and flowers. It was a wonder men held the power they did.

"They are flowers," a deep voice said dryly.

Emmaline spun on her heel so quickly, her foot slid. She fought to maintain her balance.

Lord Drake.

Their gazes caught and held. Emmaline's heart fluttered in her chest.

Then she remembered Drake's blatant disregard since their meeting three weeks prior. Her mouth tightened. The bounder had better have some choice words for Avondale's treatment of the flowers to redeem himself.

Drake shifted his attention to Lord Avondale.

"Avondale."

"Drake."

19

They exchanged bows.

Emmaline folded her arms across her chest and tapped her foot. Drake's pleasant greeting of Lord I-Kill-Poor-Defenseless-Flowers was certainly not the fierce rebuke she'd hoped. "Ahem."

Drake sighed. "My apologies. Avondale and I go back to university days. Avondale, may I present Lady Emmaline Fitzhugh? Lady Emmaline, Lord Avondale."

Her toe ceased tapping mid-movement and hovered a hairsbreadth above the ground. "I don't want an introduction."

Avondale straightened the lapels of his maroon jacket. "Well, I say—"

Emmaline spun to face him. "You'll say what? You had no business destroying the flowers."

Avondale blinked. "They are just..."

She looked back just in time to see Drake shake his head and realized...he didn't understand, either.

They weren't just flowers. Considered small and fragile by most, they were a good deal more resilient and important. They could survive an unexpected frost or chilling deluge and remain unscathed. In spite of their gentle strength, they were viewed as nothing more than a thing of beauty set aside for Society's pleasure, subject to the whim and fancy of a cruel world that held them in little esteem. When in reality they were so much more. They were the lifeblood of human existence. In that regard, they were not unlike women, which is what made the men's dismissal so infuriating. It only served as a reminder of Drake's disinterest, his total lack of caring for her. Why, she was not very different from the bud, trampled beneath man's place in Society.

Drake said something to Avondale. Her eyes narrowed. She took a step forward. "They are just what?" Emmaline said with lethal calm.

The two men fell silent and eyed her. Avondale had the good sense to be alarmed by her expression. He took a step back and looked to Drake, a helpless gleam in his eyes.

Apparently taking pity on the other man, Drake inserted himself between Emmaline and Lord Avondale. "I'm sure you have pressing business to attend to."

Avondale nodded vigorously and turned back to the cluster of flowers.

Emmaline gasped. "What do you think you're doing?"

He scratched his head. "Collecting my cane?"

"Are they really so unimportant that you would grind them beneath the heel of your boots?" *Or fail to call for years and years?*

"I—"

She pointed a finger at him. "Do not answer that question. You most certainly are not trampling through this garden to retain your weapon."

A chuckle escaped Drake.

Emmaline speared him with a look, and then returned her attention to Avondale. "I will not allow you to—"

Drake interceded. "Why don't I purchase you a new walking stick?"

The man gave another tug at his lapels. "That won't be necessary. I've plenty of others."

Just as Drake most assuredly has other women.

Avondale gave a perfunctory bow and made his good-byes. Leaving her alone with Drake.

"Coward," she muttered, though the rebuke wasn't solely reserved for Lord Avondale.

"My lady—"

Emmaline swiveled on her heel and planted her hands on hips. "How could you let him leave after what he did?"

A swift surge of icy fury filled his eyes and an animalistic groan gurgled up from his throat. Emmaline froze. She'd never borne witness to such emotion and her mind numbingly tried to process what words or actions had triggered his response. She took a step back and quickly looked around for the hint of danger that had unleashed this savage creature.

"Did he hurt you?"

His words brought her up short. She cocked her head. "Hurt me? No." She gestured dumbly to the fragile blue flowers, besieged by a sudden wave of hot embarrassment. "He hurt the forget-me-nots."

The tension remained in Drake's stiffly held frame. "He forgot what?"

Emmaline briefly closed her eyes, and shook her head. "The forget-me-nots."

When he continued to eye her with puzzlement, she dropped her hand, and gestured to the ground. "The flowers."

Drake laughed and pressed the heel of his palm against his forehead as though he were trying to rid himself of a devilish headache. "What would you have me do? Make Avondale plant new ones?"

This was all a game to him. He would no more do right by those ruined flowers than he would by her. She squared her jaw. "Do you find this amusing?"

"I should think by my reaction you can deduce I'm not amused," he said.

Emmaline bristled at the condescending edge to his words. "You did just laugh."

Drake took a step toward her and she retreated. He continued to advance, and this time she held her ground. He leaned down, his lips inches from her ear. The faint hint of coffee lingered on his breath, tickled her senses. The rising sun played with the strands of his flaxen hair, and created a pallet of golden hues and a memory intruded.

He was thirteen and she five. With his blonde crown of curls, he looked like a prince. Her innocent heart had danced with excitement at the prospect, and she had wanted to ask him if it were true. Even back then, his lips had been bent in a serious frown as he ignored her completely, and the question had died on her lips.

"Is this to become commonplace, my lady?"

She gave her head a shake. "I'm sorry?"

"As you should be. Interrupting a gentleman's solitude."

She ground her teeth.

Drake touched the line of her jaw. "If you continue to grit your teeth so hard you are going to give yourself a megrim."

Under most any other circumstances she'd have delighted in her betrothed's touch. Not, however, on this occasion. His insolence stirred her blood. She removed his finger from her person. "I was *not* apologizing."

"You said 'I'm sorry.'"

"For not understanding your question," she snapped. "You asked if this was to become commonplace."

A lull of silence descended. Drake eyed her with an unfathomable expression. "Is this to be the rest of my life? Am I to constantly be rescuing you from a series of scrapes?"

Emmaline fought back a wave of indignation. "I didn't ask or need to be rescued by you."

"My lady?" a voice called softly.

Emmaline and Drake spun to face her startled maid at the entrance of the gardens.

"We are leaving, Grace." She gave a toss of her head. "And you, my lord, can return to, whatever consumed your thoughts before you came to my rescue." She executed a perfectly respectable, deep curtsy. "You clearly need to work toward developing a greater appreciation for all life."

The air left Drake's lungs on a sudden exhale. "You are indeed correct, my lady."

His agreement brought her up short. She quickly recovered. Giving a toss of her head, she nodded. "I bid you good day, my lord."

FOUR

Dearest Lord Drake,

I attended my first play. I informed my mother and father that if I hadn't been born the daughter of a duke, I would have had a career on the stage. Of course, that would have required I be a competent actress and singer—which sadly, I am neither. Still, I enjoy the stage tremendously. Perhaps we will one day attend the theatre together.

Ever Yours,

Emmaline

One hour and twenty-five minutes, and one long walk later, Emmaline's fury was still a palpable force with life energy. The rub of it all was that she couldn't single out what had left her most infuriated.

Drake's disregard for the flowers.

Or Drake's disregard for her.

No, that wasn't true. She knew very well the reason for her upset.

She stomped up the steps of her brother's townhouse. Carmichael, the family butler with his uncanny ability to know when visitors had arrived, pulled open front doors and she sailed through the entrance.

"My lady, Miss Winters is here. I took the liberty of having her wait in the Yellow Parlor."

That brought Emmaline up short. She looked at the butler and smiled her first smile since...since...

Two very arrogant males had shattered her attempt at solitude. Her smile fell.

"Thank you, Carmichael." She marched to the parlor. A visit with Sophie Winters was just the thing she needed.

Emmaline entered the room.

Her friend sat on the sofa, covetously eyeing an array of pastries and various other confections Cook had prepared.

The tray rested beside an unopened copy of the *London Times*.

"Hullo, Sophie."

Sophie looked up. A smile wreathed her full, heart-shaped cheeks. "Em, I hope you don't mind my early...." Her brow furrowed. "What is it?"

Emmaline plopped into the seat beside Sophie. She drummed her fingernails on the arm of the chair. She could say with a great degree of certainty that in her twenty years she'd been wrong on many scores.

At this precise moment, some things stood out more than others.

She'd been confident that upon reaching the advanced age of twenty she would have at least three things settled.

Firstly, she would have a home of her own.

Secondly, there would be a dog to cuddle with on cold days.

And, lastly, a husband to also cuddle with on cold days.

As it was, sitting on the chintz sofa in her *brother's* parlor, she did not have a home of her own. Nor, for that matter did she have a dog. And most of all, she unequivocally did not have a husband. What she did have, as she had for the better part of her life, was a betrothed.

"Em?"

Emmaline shook her head. "I came upon a brute cutting the heads off a bed of forget-me-nots."

Sophie wrinkled her nose. "What cad would do such a thing?"

Finally, a rational person.

"Lord Avondale." She chose not to mention Lord Drake's involvement. Giving her fingers something to do, she snapped up the copy of the *Times*.

"Avondale," Sophie muttered. "He was one of the gentlemen Mother hoped I'd make a match with in my first Season."

25

"Consider yourself spared." Emmaline scanned the front of the London Times before flipping to the next story. Her eyes snagged on a name at the center of the page and she bolted upright.

It appeared a certain Marquess of D had secured the affections of the recent Opera sensation from Italy, Signora Nicolleli. The papers reported her to be talented, vivacious, and stunningly elegant. etcetera, etcetera...

Emmaline tossed the paper aside, her eyes boring into the offensive sheets.

Thinking on it, she picked up the paper and crushed it into a sloppy ball and threw it to the floor. Since it did not make her feel better, she reached for it again.

Sophie snatched the copy, intercepting Emmaline's efforts. "I'll take that." She unwrinkled the ball and ran a smoothing hand over the surface several times and read for herself. She muttered something a lady of good Quality should never think, let alone breathe aloud. "I've seen her. She really isn't that beautiful." She smiled unconvincingly at Emmaline.

Emmaline's eyes narrowed. "Liar." There was something disheartening in going through life being considered *tolerably pleasing*, as the papers had labeled Emmaline in her first Season. She waved a hand over herself. "It is no wonder he has no interest in marrying me." That, and as he'd pointed out, the fact he'd had to rescue her on two separate occasions. She snorted. As though she needed rescuing. Why, with his scandalous pursuits and history, he probably needed rescuing a good deal more than Emmaline ever had or would.

Emmaline sighed. "Thank you for your support, Sophie, but it isn't necessary. I know what I look like."

"Don't be ridiculous, Em. You are utterly lovely." Sophie spoke with such stringent confidence, had Emmaline been anyone else, she might have believed her.

Emmaline pointed her eyes to the ceiling. "Come, Sophie. I've already come to terms with the fact I will never be considered a great beauty."

"Why, you have the most beautiful eyes I've ever seen."

Leave it to Sophie to remind her of the one attribute she could not find *much* fault with. For all her plainness, Emmaline's eyes were pleasing. Her father used to say they were the color of warmed chocolate, and through them, her every emotion could be revealed. As a girl, it had sounded so poetic. Now, grown up, she'd come to find such transparency was anything but positive amidst the gossiping *ton*.

At thoughts of her father, she sighed. He'd been gone now three years and the pain of that loss still hurt.

As she and Sophie nibbled at their pastries, Emmaline contemplated her circumstances.

Her frustration stemmed from so much more than Lord Drake's avoidance of her. Somewhere along the way, she had begun to question her late Father's manipulation of her future. At some moment, a time she couldn't pinpoint, she'd grown resentful that the decision to marry had been wrested from her hands when she'd been a mere child. And yet, whether Lord Drake had been short with a baldpate or whether he was a specimen of male perfection, Emmaline felt obligated to make a go out of her circumstances. For Father.

"It's hardly fair he should be so blasted perfect," Emmaline muttered. "Can't he have a flaw? A high-forehead, jiggling jowls? A paunch? Something."

Sophie laughed. "You are the only person to complain that her betrothed is too handsome."

"You are not helping."

"He does seem very severe whenever I see him," Sophie offered obligingly.

Emmaline thought to their recent exchange in Kensington Gardens and sighed. Yes, that was Lord Drake's flaw. Except it seemed to only garner further notice from the ladies.

"And he's a war hero to boot, Sophie. What is my great accomplishment?"

"You are a wonder in the gardens."

Emmaline snorted. Considering Drake's regard for flowers, that great talent would hardly bring him up to scratch. "You and I both know it's a skill no one but my family can appreciate." The only efforts at gardening acceptable for a young lady were the flowers she stitched on the fabric in her embroidery frame.

To the *ton*, Emmaline remained largely—unremarkable. Which most likely explained the efforts Lord Drake went through to avoid her.

Her betrothed may have had a grand time since he'd returned from the Peninsula three years ago, but he'd consigned her to an odd position in Society. She'd become a bit of a conundrum. Emmaline was attached but unattached, forever betrothed but never married. For these reasons, honor dictated no other gentleman could pay her court.

"Do you know, Sophie, there are times I think I might prefer being wanted by a young lord for the size of my dowry. Then at least I would be wanted for something, which is vastly better, than not being wanted at all."

Sophie looked up from the wrinkled paper she'd resumed reading. "You're mad! Your betrothal is the only reason you have not been pursued. Any gentleman would be honored to wed you."

Emmaline ignored Sophie's defense. With a sigh, she opened her clenched fist and studied the bisecting lines traversing her palm. She ran a distracted little path over the surface of her skin. She may be betrothed, but she was not unlike Sophie, who also remained unmarried. Emmaline's betrothal to the Marquess of Drake had always been common knowledge to the *ton*. Nothing more than a piece of gossip dragged out by old dowagers whenever there was a dearth of more current on dits. Neither Emmaline nor Sophie were truly sought after or cared about by any gentleman. The one difference between them being Emmaline had a scrap of paper saying someone had claims to her.

Well, that was no longer enough.

"Do you know, as much as I resent the Marquess of Drake's deplorable treatment, I cannot help but empathize with why he's made the decisions he has?"

Sophie sputtered around a mouthful of tart. "That is far too generous of you, Em."

Emmaline chose not to respond to Sophie's unspoken censure and instead grabbed another pastry and nibbled the corner. She couldn't expect Sophie to understand, and to say as much would merely come across as insulting.

Yet, Emmaline did, to some extent, recognize the reason for Drake's annoyance. She suspected his decision to enlist had been borne of resentment that his fate had been decided for him when he'd been a mere boy. Perhaps he'd wanted a say in the person he would wed and spend the rest of his days with. Perhaps he'd wanted a great beauty to arouse grand passions—like his opera singer.

Perhaps he'd felt those things because she herself felt them. Well, all those things except for the opera singer, of course.

She yearned for some control in her life, ached to know love and grand passion, too. But it was gauche to even think such thoughts.

Over her long walk home from Kensington Gardens, she'd put a great deal of consideration into her circumstances. In spite of her dreams and wishes, Emmaline had made a commitment to her father. And blast it all, she would try to make something of this betrothal—whether Lord Drake wanted it or not.

"Whatever it is the Marquess of Drake feels, I no longer care. It is time for him to grow up and honor his obligations." She flinched at thinking of herself as an obligation, and then shoved away any self-pity. The days of woe-is-me were officially at an end. It was time for the Marquess of Drake to be brought up to snuff, and she was just the woman to do it.

"What are you thinking?"

Emmaline's jaw set. "I am done waiting for the Marquess of Drake. I want a real marriage or nothing at all." Emmaline ticked on her fingers. "I want to be courted. I want him to take me riding in the park. I want him to escort me to the opera." She grimaced at the thought of Signora Nicolleli. "Mayhap not the opera, but perhaps Covent Garden for a play," she amended. "And I want him to waltz with me. That's not much to ask, is it?"

Sophie shook her head with such force she dislodged a golden curl from her chignon. "Hardly, the man is after all your betrothed."

Emmaline gave an emphatic nod. "His days of bowing over my hand and beating a hasty retreat are at an end. I'm going to bring him up to scratch and if I can't..." She paused. "I haven't determined all the details, but what I do know is I will be speaking to my brother about this farce of a betrothal."

Sophie gasped.

Emmaline well knew it was one thing to be displeased with the Marquess of Drake's lack of attention, it was quite another to speak of severing the legal contract between their families. She folded her arms. "I'm not getting any younger. Why I'm already twenty years old."

Lord Drake may be a war hero, but Emmaline was prepared to fight some battles of her own. She reached over and seized the paper that had pushed her to her limits. Taking great care, she ripped out a neat square and studied it. She clenched her lips into a hard line.

Sophie had been about to take another bite from her tart. The partially bitten pastry dangled, forgotten between her fingers. With her mouth hanging open and her wide, unblinking cornflower eyes, she rather had the look of an owl. She set the treat aside, and leaned forward. "What are you going to do, Em?"

Emmaline smiled, and if her mother had been present she would have known to be alarmed. "Why, we're going to the opera."

Sophie blinked. "The opera..." Her mouth widened and her eyes dawned with understanding. "Ohhhh, the opera."

Emmaline gave a tight nod. "Yes, by God, Lord Drake will notice me whether he likes it or not. There will be no more opera singers, ballet dancers, young widows, none of it. His days of carefree debauchery are officially at an end. He just doesn't know it yet, but he will, beginning tonight. If your mother will have me, I will be joining your family in their box this evening."

A laugh bubbled up from Sophie's throat. "Mother will be thrilled to have the Duke of Mallen's sister." It was no secret Sophie's mother, Viscountess Redbrooke, all but drooled like a pug in summer with any mention of the Mallen title.

Just then, there was only one gentleman whose marital status Emmaline cared about...and it most definitely was not her brother's.

Sophie nodded. "I will let Mother know upon my return."

Emmaline's jaw hardened in anticipation of seeing Drake's face that evening.

Lord Drake, I hope you haven't put away your uniform, for you, sir, are headed back into battle.

FIVE

My Dearest Lord Drake,
For the first time in my life, I am grateful you are not here. I spent hours
in the gardens and am bright as a beet. I am not a sight fit for good
company. At least that is what my brother said.
Ever Yours,
Emmaline

Signora Valentina Nicolleli, an accomplished mezzo-soprano, had a voice with a deep, rich sultry tone that twined around each note she sang like a sea nymph clinging to the hull of a ship. The sensual quality could be felt from her soaring E sharp to her A flat, which resonated off the theatre walls. The Italian opera sensation's musical talents, however, had not been what had attracted Drake's notice.

Studying her from his theatre box, Drake recalled how they'd spent last evening, and his gaze narrowed. Valentina was an inventive, nubile woman, endowed in all the places a man hoped his woman would be generously curved. And yet, he watched disinterestedly as she pranced about the stage.

"I still don't see why we have to sit through the blasted show," Sin muttered. He occupied the seat next to Drake. "It hardly seems fair you're the one who gets to bed the creature and I'm the one who has to sit through her infernal caterwauling." His bored gaze surveyed the crowd, then paused, and narrowed ever so imperceptibly.

Drake didn't bother looking to see what drew his friend's attention. "Come, come, Sin, you'd have me believe you'd rather be escorting your mother and dear sister to some other infernal event?"

Sin gave a visible shudder. "No, no, you have the right of it. At least when this blasted opera is over I can head to the tables. Will you be joining me later this evening?"

Drake gave a short nod. What else was there to do? Lord knew he didn't want to return to the damned townhouse and deal with his father. Or the nightmares. Restful sleep did not await him at the Duke of Hawkridge's townhouse. Peaceful nights had eluded him since...

He shook his head, willing thoughts of war into the deep corners in which they refused to stay banished. When he'd been a young man, war had seemed like the logical escape from the stringent expectations placed on him by the Duke of Hawkridge. Drake's life had been planned out for him since the moment of his birth. It had been ordained by his father where he would attend school, who he would wed, and Drake had chafed at the rigid order imposed upon him.

His time fighting Boney had proven there was nothing logical about war. The day he'd left the Peninsula, he'd longed to return to normalcy. He'd returned to England with a desperate urgency to slip back into the life he'd been familiar with. Consequently, he'd never given much thought to the impossibility of such a feat.

Three years ago, he'd come back from battle, a returned *hero*, greeted with parades and lavish balls; the recipient of public praise and countless honors. All of it had meant nothing to him. All the fanfare had served to do was emphasize his despair. It had served as a stark reminder of the lives he'd taken and the horrors that would haunt him for the rest of his days.

The sound of applause interrupted Drake's dark musings. Act I had concluded.

"Are you certain you wouldn't prefer to join me in a game of Hazard right now?" Sin asked.

Drake passed an absent gaze over the theatre that swarmed with bodies. The hand of a silent specter gripped his throat and squeezed, making breathing difficult. Vivid, unflappable memories and images of friends in arms swept past the floodgates of his mind, flooded him with their overwhelming intensity.

He jerked as the crowd's murmurs gave way to the agonized cries of his men as they were cut down around him until he wanted to clamp his hands over his ears and drown out the remembrances. Except there was no escaping his loyal horse, Midnight's tortured last whinny as the faithful creature was shot out from under him. Or the men, screaming for a God who didn't exist, as the physician sawed their limbs from their person.

He needed out. Black remembrances of the war had crept in, and if he left the theatre, perhaps he could also leave the memories behind...just for the night, anyway. "Let's go," Drake growled.

He bolted from his seat just as the curtains of his box were thrown open.

And a hand slipped through, hitting him in the face. "Oomph!" he barked around a mouthful of the billowing, red velvet fabric. The curtains fell neatly back to their respective place, revealing the identities of the intruders.

"My Lord, how good to see you!" One young lady greeted, her voice dripping with effortful charm, either unmindful, or uncaring, that he had been hit square in the face.

Drake froze, a prickle of unease traveled up his nape. After the weeks he'd spent trying to banish thoughts of the lady's impressive showing from each corner of his mind, all his efforts were ground to dust in this instant.

Lady Emmaline Fitzhugh stood before him, her spine erect, a determined glint in her eyes.

Emmaline's smile stretched so taut she thought it might crumple and shatter if somebody didn't fill the void of silence following her unexpected intrusion of Lord Drake's private box.

Almost as one, the two gentlemen seemed to remember their manners, bowing deeply. "My Lady, Miss Winters," Lord Sinclair murmured, claiming first her hand, and then her companion's for a chaste kiss.

Respectful was the word tantamount to the exchange.

Stiff, formal, respectful deference.

It made Emmaline want to stamp her foot. Drat, the man was her intended. And he hadn't exchanged so much as a word with her. Well, that was if one didn't count the startled exclamation he'd let out when she'd hit him in the face with the curtains.

Thank Heavens for Sophie. Sophie dipped a curtsy. "Lord Drake, Lord Sinclair." She smiled and then proceeded to do one of the things Emmaline dearly loved about her—she filled the awkward silence.

She waved her hand about, like a small hurricane, gesturing animatedly to the crowd milling about the Opera House. "My father's box is very nearly opposite your box, my lord, and it was of course Lady Emmaline who mentioned this."

Three sets of eyes swiveled to look at Emmaline.

Loved in the past tense, Sophie's uncanny ability to fill voids was one of the things she *had* loved about her.

Emmaline cleared her throat, flushing under the veiled scrutiny she received from her betrothed and the hint of smile his friend, Lord Sinclair favored her with.

"Yes, Viscount Redbrooke's box is located just over there." She gestured vaguely; glad when the three sets of eyes in unison moved in the direction she was motioning.

She did not go out of her way to point out that the box in question was in fact situated a good deal farther to the left and significantly lower than Lord Drake's box.

"But I saw you, my lord, and….and," Words fled. His jade-black gaze pierced her, probing, as though he knew her every secret. *Blast him and his arrogance*, she thought, finding the courage to finish her sentence. "Well, I would have been remiss if I failed to greet you."

Drake blinked and Emmaline knew he recognized that he'd just been delivered a set-down. She rushed on. "I felt compelled to visit your box and discuss your thoughts on the opera. It has come to my attention from the papers that you have a great affinity for the opera, in particular the capable Mezzo-Soprano Signora Nicolleli." She furrowed her brow, feigning deep contemplation. "In my honest opinion, I have a preference for the light, airy quality of a lyrical soprano."

She detected Lord Sinclair's shoulders rising and falling in what, she felt safe to assume, was mirth, while poor Sophie scoured the theatre.

To Lord Drake's credit, or perhaps the better word would be discredit, he did not so much as flinch. His only telltale reaction was a slight arching of a golden brow as he met her stare. Emmaline glanced away.

"My dear, Lady Emmaline," In Emmaline's honest estimation, the words hardly sounded like an endearment. "I hadn't taken you for a gossip."

A subtle reproach coated his hard words. Double blast the man. How dare he make her feel uncomfortable? He was after all the one who'd abandoned her for two—approaching three—years. And that wasn't counting the fifteen years that had lapsed in their near lifelong betrothal.

Her lips set tightly. "La, sir, but how else am I to find out about my betrothed's likes and dislikes? But I do know you have a preference for mezzo-sopranos, so that is something, no? I look forward to meeting the great Signora Nicolleli and securing an autograph for you. I will be sure to tell her you are an ardent admirer, my lord. We'll call it something of a wedding gift."

The lights dimmed and the crowd bustled about, returning to their seats.

Sophie cleared her throat. "Em, I rather think we should return, lest mother worry about our absence."

Emmaline smiled and favored Lord Drake with an impudent wave. "I'm certain she won't fret when she learns we were with my intended. You would hardly allow harm to befall us, my lord? I've heard such stories of your heroics on the Peninsula, I could hardly feel anything but safe in your company."

His eyes grew shuttered. "You should never let your guard down regardless of whose company you are in, Lady Emmaline."

"You are far too modest, my lord. Alas, I must bid you good evening and await our next meeting." She favored Lord Sinclair with a smile. "A pleasure, my lord."

"Likewise, Lady Emmaline, Miss Winters." He bowed and nudged Drake until he followed suit.

"Now we must return to our box," Emmaline said. "If you'll excuse us." She gave a jaunty wave and quite deliberately shoved the curtains back with enough force to send them flapping, and took her leave.

War had been declared.

SIX

Dearest Lord Drake,
My brother has been most stringently critiquing my efforts at painting.
He has informed me of the following: I'm terrible at watercolor, awful
with pastels, and deplorable with oils. I've taken to addressing him as
Your Grace. To my amusement, it annoys him quite a bit.
Ever Yours,
Emmaline

Drake sputtered around another mouthful of red velvet curtains as Lady Emmaline made her dramatic exit from his opera box. Cursing under his breath, he violently slammed the drapes down, back into place.

He wanted to throttle her. Nay, he was going to throttle her. He counted to three. When he still felt the same way, he counted to ten, and because he couldn't direct his anger at Lady Emmaline, who'd since taken her leave, he leveled a black glare at Sin, whose broad smile indicated he was far too amused by the turn of events.

"Stuff it," Drake said.

Sin blinked. "I didn't say anything."

"This does not bode well."

"No, it certainly doesn't," Sin concurred.

With the intrusive eyes of the *ton* on them, Drake and Sin could not comfortably escape the theatre without Society taking note. To do so would only fuel gossip about what had transpired in the box, which would result in a lengthy write up in the gossip columns.

They reclaimed their seats.

Drake fixed his gaze on the stage below. He'd be damned if he fed any more into the rabid curiosity of the *ton* who continued to stare at him.

The little termagant. How dare she corner him in his box, and call him out for his behavior? They were not married. It made his cravat tighten painfully around his neck just imagining what married life would be like with Lady Emmaline Fitzhugh. Over the years he'd avoided run-ins with his betrothed. He'd taken deliberate pleasure in refusing to attend any and every formal function his father had requested he attend. The last event he'd gone to at his father's entreaty had been more than seven years ago, when Emmaline had been a bright-eyed girl.

Scanning the crowd for the now bright-eyed woman, he gave thanks for small favors. It had been good for the both of them no one had been privy to the exchange, for the gossip fodders would be reeling with the set down the little imp had delivered. He thought back to the incident with the old peddler three weeks ago. He'd heard the commotion, and then spied Lady Emmaline as she'd jumped into the fray in order to protect the woman. Before the cowardly dandy had even raised his whip, Drake had known with a soldier's intuition what the man's next actions would be.

This evening had proved, in addition to being brave, Emmaline was far bolder than he'd ever imagined. Not that he'd had many imaginings of her—that was, until recently.

He continued his search for one particular lady clad in a fashionable emerald green silk piece, trimmed in white Italian lace. He grimaced. Where had *that* detail come from? Then his gaze landed on his quarry.

His eyes narrowed. "The little liar is hardly opposite this box," he hissed.

The meddling gazes of the *ton* swiveled his way.

Sin shoved an elbow into Drake's side "Shh."

"Why, she is a good deal to the left and much farther below." And as though Sin couldn't ascertain exactly where he meant, he boldly gestured towards his betrothed.

39

His actions earned a murmur from the crowd and must have captured Emmaline's attention. She tilted her head up, and rewarded him with a beatific smile and a cheeky wave.

He growled low in his throat, and nodded for the benefit of the watchful crowd. He could imagine tomorrow's gossip column if he failed to return his betrothed's salutation in the over-flowing Royal Opera House. The wiser course would be to acknowledge the impertinent bit of baggage, rather than have to deal with the consequences of slighting her.

"You might want to smile. You look bloody terrifying," Sin said beneath his breath, passing a hand over his mouth to shield his lips. He gave a shake of his head at Drake's attempt. "Looks more like a grimace."

Drake ignored his friend and directed his attentions to the stage where Valentina was prancing about. Unbidden, Lady Emmaline's words came taunting the edges of this thoughts and, God help him, he couldn't look at his bloody mistress, at least not while knowing Emmaline was there studying him.

He turned his eyes in his betrothed's direction, expecting to see her teasing brown eyes, but instead found her to be engrossed in the performance on the stage below. Perched at the edge of her seat, her fingertips gripped the edge of the box, her head cocked at an endearing little angle.

He studied her. Normally he preferred women with generous curves, rounded in all the right places, but Drake found Emmaline's litheness oddly appealing. Unbidden, his eyes fell to her lips. As he was being objective, he could say definitively that those ruby-red, full lips were lips a man dreamt of, imagined suckling, tasting. He could imagine them passing over his body, trailing lower, and swallowing him—all of him.

Christ, where had that thought come from? He gave his head a violent shake and jumped to his feet, startling Sinclair.

"Let's go," he said.

Sin's gaze shifted momentarily to a box a good deal left and much farther below. "If it's all the same to you, I'd like to remain." He acknowledged with a sheepish smile.

Drake spared another glare for the minx who'd upset his plans for the evening and found her watching his exchange with Sin's; a wide, knowing smile on her face. "Fine," he grumbled, knowing his tone was more fitting of a small child, but too incensed to care.

Without a backwards glance, he turned on his heel, and set the curtains fluttering.

SEVEN

My Dearest Lord Drake,

Feeling confident you can keep a secret, I can admit my insatiable curiosity. Father and Sebastian are often availing themselves to brandy. I wonder…what is the appeal? I am therefore planning my own secret experiment…

Ever Yours,

Emmaline

"Well, this has been a disaster," Emmaline groused beneath her breath.

She slipped out of the Viscount Redbrooke's box. Sophie trailed along at her side. This time a diligent maid followed right on their heels.

The thrum of the orchestra blended with the chorus filled the auditorium. The haunting melody echoed throughout the theatre and lent a dramatic feel to their movements.

The high E belonging to a particular soprano, Emmaline decided, was largely flat. It rent the opera house, muffled only slightly by the chatter of the *ton*. Her opinion had nothing, absolutely nothing to do with the fact that the high E came from the mouth of her betrothed's mistress.

Sophie's brow furrowed. She glanced over her shoulder toward her brother's box. "Mother is going to be livid."

The Viscountess had not made one mention of the ladies' visit to Lord Drake's box. Her erect form and snapping eyes had conveyed the

42

extent of her displeasure. It also explained why Sophie's maid dogged their movements.

Beset by an onset of guilt, Emmaline bit the inside of her lip. "She might not have noticed."

Sophie wrung her hands. "She would be the only one in the theatre, then."

On the heels of that statement, Emmaline imagined Sebastian and Mother's displeasure the following morning. She groaned aloud. In the end, it would appear the first battle had been won by Lord Drake.

"I do believe I have lost the first round, Sophie." It chafed to admit defeat of any kind. To be defeated by Lord Drake, however was not to be countenanced.

Sophie paused and directed her attention to her maid. "Leave us." The maid's mouth set in a mutinous line, but one more look from Sophie and she slipped away.

When the maid was no longer in sight, Sophie returned her attention to Emmaline. "You couldn't have expected it would be easy?"

Emmaline's gaze wandered to a point over Sophie's shoulder. "No, I didn't, but I…I…"

Apparently she took pity on her friend. Sophie claimed Emmaline's hands in hers and gave a gentle squeeze. "From what you told me, Lord Drake had been so impressed by your showing with Whitmore. I just don't understand." Sophie tugged her hand. "Now, come."

Emmaline allowed her friend to drag her forward. She didn't understand it, herself. Any of it. She could only speculate as to Lord Drake's disinterest in her over the years. "Mayhap I was wrong. Mayhap I was ruminating fantasies about what Lord Drake felt that day. He is such a gentleman, he would have come to any lady's rescue."

A tall, solid figure stepped into their path. Sophie managed to step out of the way even as Emmaline collided into a hard muscled chest. She gasped. She might as well have hit a wall—a large, immoveable wall.

Emmaline faltered, and would have fallen if Sophie didn't grab her arm just as the gentleman reached out to steady her.

"My lady, Miss Winters," Lord Sinclair said.

"Goodness, you startled me, my lord." Sophie nudged her in the side. Emmaline frowned. "He did startle me."

Sophie rolled her eyes. "You shouldn't say as much in front of him."

The gentleman's lips twitched with what was assuredly amusement.

Emmaline glanced over his shoulder, seeking out…

"He left," Lord Sinclair said.

Emmaline's eyes snapped forward. "I don't know whom you are talking about," she said, a touch too quickly.

"I'd say it is rather obvious," Sophie muttered.

Emmaline gave a pointed nod in Sinclair's direction. "You still shouldn't say as much."

"'Tis no different than you stating how startled you were when Lord Sinclair gracelessly bowled you over."

Lord Sinclair bristled. "I beg your pardon?"

Emmaline and Sophie promptly fell silent.

"Our apologies," Emmaline said. This time it was she who nudged Sophie.

"Uh, yes, our apologies, my lord."

He bowed his head. "Think nothing of it."

They each dipped a curtsy and made to move around him, but he held up a hand. "Might I beg a word alone with you, my lady?" He extended his arm to Emmaline.

Sophie's shocked gasp split the awkward silence.

Emmaline traced her lower lip with the tip of her tongue. After a momentary pause, she tucked her hand into the fold of his arm, and allowed him to lead her several paces ahead. Sophie trotted along at a discreet distance, muttering loud enough for the both of them to hear just what she thought about the impropriety of their actions.

"I must admit, my lord, I'm intrigued." She stole a peek up at him from the corner of her eye.

Sin's lips twitched. "I would like to speak to you about Lord Drake."

Emmaline missed a step, and with his assistance, righted her footing.

Sinclair led them to a vacant alcove and drew back the curtain. She hesitated for the slightest moment, and then followed him inside. He dropped the curtain into place and turned to face her.

He spoke without preamble. "I want you to marry Drake."

She smothered a laugh with her hand. "Well, then that makes two of us, my lord. If only the decision was yours to make."

The curtains rustled at Lord Sinclair's back and Emmaline would wager her entire dowry that Sophie had her ear pressed to the fabric.

He folded his arms across his chest. "How well do you know Drake?"

Silence stretched between them. Unbidden, her mind tripped along a forgotten memory. She was five. Seated in her father's library. An angry little boy had stared mutinously across at her.

Lord Sinclair cleared his throat. "Uh-my lady?"

Emmaline gave her head a shake. "We've been betrothed since we were children, my lord," she said with deliberate vagueness.

His gaze skimmed a path across her face. "Do you know much about him?"

Emmaline arched a brow.

"I am not saying you should not desire a marriage to Lord Drake. I'm...I'm..."

"Just what are you saying?" The recipient of enough discomfort this evening, it was someone else's turn to grapple with the emotion.

An awkward stretch of silence descended like a funeral pall, but Emmaline wouldn't feel guilty for it.

She didn't know Lord Sinclair enough to confess the particular details of her relationship with Drake. Why, Sophie wasn't even privy to half the memories she'd buried in her heart. Sinclair may be close friends with her intended, it did not, however, grant him carte blanche to ask intimate questions and expect answers. Nor for that matter would she ever reveal just how she'd come by her knowledge of Lord Drake. To do so would open her to pity, and she was not keen on the rather useless sentiment.

"My lady, forgive me. I know this questioning is far from conventional," he said, filling the void of quiet. He tugged his ear. "Were you aware I've been friends with Drake since we were just thirteen?"

She started at the admission. "I wasn't aware." She should have known that. How strange to think two of Drake's most significant relationships had been cemented when he'd been a boy of thirteen.

Sinclair continued. "He'd always been a fun boy, though angry when I met him because..." A dull flush stained his cheeks, "Because...."

"Because?" It didn't take much to gather thirteen-year-old Drake had assuredly been upset because of his betrothal to her five-year-old self.

Sinclair rocked back and forth on the balls of his feet, looking himself like a thirteen-year-old boy who'd been caught pouring ink in his tutor's tea. "Any young boy would be less than thrilled at being betrothed to a young girl."

She decided in that moment she liked Lord Sinclair a great deal. He did not feel inclined to mince words, and for that she respected him.

"We don't have much time, so might I be candid, my lady?"

Emmaline giggled. She raised a hand to muffle the sound. "Oh dear, you haven't been up to this point?"

Sinclair ignored the question. "May I ask if you are interested in marriage to Lord Drake because he is heir to a dukedom?"

If she weren't so amused by the question, she was certain she'd have been insulted. "Are you asking whether I am interested in his fortunes? Whether I aspire to the role of duchess?"

He didn't back down under the directness of her question. "My lady, Drake has been pursued the better part of his life for his title. Forgive me for being leery of any woman's intentions."

She sighed. "My lord, my life has been dictated for me since the moment I was born. Yes, Lord Drake was betrothed to me when he was thirteen, but might I remind you, I was only five. A mere babe. I have been as trapped by this betrothal as Lord Drake." She paused, biting her lower lip. "I don't aspire to a status, Lord Sinclair, I aspire to happiness."

Sinclair ran a probing, hazel-green stare over her.

"Do you believe Drake can bring you happiness?" he asked with a bluntness that made her flinch.

46

Emmaline forced a smile. "I certainly hope so." All Emmaline knew was she'd waited years for Drake. Had attended more balls and soirees than she could count, and even several masquerades. It had always been known that she was unmarriageable. During her first Season, she'd sat on the fringe watching all the young ladies who'd had their Come Out being courted, the recipients of poetry and flowers. Emmaline had received nary a flower. Not even one sonnet praising the hue of her hair or the glow in her eyes. She would have settled for even a poorly written poem.

Emmaline didn't long for marriage because she desired a suitable match that would raise her status in Society. She wanted what all young women did, and yet would never admit—to be loved. She ached to know true love. She wanted a man to love her so helplessly, so desperately that he cared for nothing in the world but her.

Was it a fairytale she dreamed of? Perhaps. But it was what she yearned for. If it weren't for it being her late father's grandest wish that she wed Lord Drake, Emmaline would have tired of Drake's disinterest years ago.

Well, the time of waiting for Drake to come up to scratch was at an end. She needed to determine if he was the man who could give her all those things she yearned for…and if not, well then she needed to move on.

Lord Sinclair didn't say another word. Instead, he reached into the front of his black jacket and fished out a small parchment of paper. He handed the folded sheet to her.

Emmaline took it and opened the note. She glimpsed at it puzzled, and then looked up at him.

"They are the events Lord Drake is planning on attending for the next several nights."

Emmaline's mind was slow to process his words. Sinclair couldn't possibly have known her intentions to pursue Drake. The only soul who knew of her plans was Sophie, and Sophie would never have betrayed her confidence.

"Should you choose to attend the events, I'm sure Lord Drake would be elated to see you." He proceeded to fill in the details of his plan. "It is my hope that Drake can finally honor your betrothal, my lady. I believe should he take the time to know you, he will then cease...." His philandering ways. The indelicate words did not need to be spoken.

Her gaze dropped to the list. "Why are you doing this?" She raised her eyes to his.

Lord Sinclair's expression grew veiled. "I can't imagine you like existing in this suspended universe, my lady. You are neither wed nor pursued."

Emmaline's brow wrinkled. It hardly sounded flattering when stated in such a way.

"My lady, I meant no offense. I am simply providing—"

"The reason I should go along with your plans," she finished for him. "I understand."

A swell of applause resonated throughout the theatre, and from the other side of the curtain, Sophie nervously cleared her throat.

Lord Sinclair did not seem at all alarmed by the threat of discovery. "Lord Drake is a very different man from the boy you once knew. He has not been the same since..."

"Emmaline," Sophie said. "Hurry."

Emmaline wanted to curse at the interruption. Instead she dipped a hasty curtsy. It wouldn't do to be seen emerging from a hidden alcove with her betrothed's closest friend. "My lord, I thank you for your assistance."

He sketched a short bow. "We shall see you tomorrow evening?"

"Emmaline," Sophie again urged, this time her tone frantic.

She cast one more look down at the scrap in her hands, then folded it and stuffed it into the reticule dangling from her wrist. "You shall."

He held up a staying hand. "Oh, my lady, one more thing. I thought you should know, Lord Drake was most impressed by your showing with Lord Whitmore."

Emmaline smiled as she slipped from behind the curtain.

EIGHT

Dear Lord Drake,
I'm beginning to suspect you are avoiding me.
Ever Yours,
Emmaline

Drake filled a dish with several pieces of toast from the sideboard, and sat down across from his father at the long dining table. "Good morning," he murmured.

His father lowered the paper he'd been reading. He appeared startled by the salutation. "Uh-good morning, Drake."

He raised the paper back into place.

Drake picked up the silver knife beside his plate and proceeded to spread blackberry preserves upon his toast.

He looked up at the shuffling form in the doorway. The old butler, Winchester, who'd been around as long as Drake had been alive, entered. He stopped in front of Drake and held out a small, silver platter.

Drake ignored his father, who had set aside his paper, and now stared at him with blatant curiosity. Drake put his knife down and lifted both the sealed envelope and the blade presented by Winchester.

The faint scent of lemons wafted from the thick ivory envelope. Drake inserted the blade under the seal and withdrew two slips of parchment.

One was an autograph.

The other a note.

Dearest Lord Drake,

What kind of intended would I be if I didn't keep to my word, honor a promise, and present to you that which I offered—a signature from the great Signora Nicolleli?

Ever Yours,

Emmaline

He laughed.

Who knew? His betrothed had a sense of humor.

NINE

My Dearest Lord Drake,
How odd you are traveling the world when I've hardly been anywhere
at all. With this in mind, I packed up several dresses and provisions
and took a very long journey about our Leeds estate. My parents raised
a hue and cry when they discovered I'd gone missing. Needless to say,
I have been punished and forbidden from going anywhere for the next
five years. I say that seems a rather harsh sentence.
Ever Yours,
Emmaline

In May of 1811, at the Battle of Fuentes de Onoro, Marshall Massena had retreated back to Spain to find Wellington had already effectively blockaded Almeida. Though Wellington had been surpassed in manpower, he'd outnumbered the French in artillery. With the French failure at Fuentes de Onoro, Massena had been unwilling to attack because of Wellington's strong position. Subsequently, Wellington had made the assumption that the French army of Portugal had been sufficiently weakened and discounted his enemy. The end result had been Wellington's retreat.

Both, Wellington and Drake, had learned something very important at Fuentes de Onoro—never underestimate one's enemy.

In this case, it wasn't an enemy per se...but an opponent, whom he happened to be betrothed to.

No place was safe from Lady Emmaline. There was no sanctuary. When staring down the inevitable face of defeat, the only logical option had been retreat.

Drake scanned Lord and Lady Wilcox' ballroom for the woman who'd occupied his thoughts for the better part of the evening.

From the time their betrothal contract had been signed, Drake had tried his damnedest to avoid any interaction with Lady Emmaline. Instead, he'd relegated her to the role of un-aging child, thus preventing her from becoming a woman to whom he had obligations.

As a result, he knew next to nothing about her. He didn't know her likes or dislikes. He didn't know what made her laugh, what she read, or even if she enjoyed reading. He didn't know if she had a personality. Until now.

Drake discovered Lady Emmaline was called Em by those closest to her. He learned her only real friend was Miss Sophie Winters. He noted Emmaline sat with Miss Winters at most events, smiling and chatting, all the while seeming oblivious to the pitying stares directed her way.

And she had a sense of humor. He thought about the note she'd sent round—the same note that had put an immediate end to his affair with the lovely Signora Valentina Nicolleli. Following the whole peculiar exchange with Emmaline, he would never have been able to carry on with the voluptuous mezzo-soprano without hearing his intended's teasing voice.

Just then, Drake spied the brown coiffure of a young lady moving through a sea of guests. He held his breath, waiting for her to turn, then realized, upon closer inspection, that her hair did not possess the same deep chocolate hues.

"Are you looking for someone in particular, my lord?" An amused voice drawled over his shoulder.

He started, and swung around.

"Lady Emmaline."

Emmaline expected to see vexation in her betrothed's jade eyes, which is why she was struck breathless by the flash of amusement in their fathomless depths.

Her heart quickened.

"I was looking for someone, my lady." He winked.

Winked! Oh, the insufferable bounder!

Emmaline's heart resumed its normal cadence.

Her lips formed a moue of displeasure. She glanced around. "I see." Her gaze locked on the imposing figure striding across the ball-room dance-floor. She cocked her head to the side. "Perhaps it is my brother?"

Drake groaned aloud as her brother, the Duke of Mallen, came to a stop before them. Sebastian's foreboding black glare teemed with fury.

Sebastian bowed, the gesture a smidgeon shy of disrespect. "Lord Drake, so good to see you."

Drake returned the bow. "Your Grace," he said flatly.

She studied them as they eyed one another like small boys fighting over the last pastry.

Over the years, she had learned there was no love lost between her betrothed and brother. She strongly suspected she was the cause of their animosity toward one another.

"Quite the surprise, seeing you with my sister." A frosty bite under-lined Sebastian's words.

Emmaline wanted to groan at his less than subtle reprimand. Dead. She was going to kill him dead that evening.

Drake's jaw clenched. "Why should it be a surprise? She is, after all, my betrothed."

Sebastian's hand landed with a resounding thud upon his chest. "Shocking you should even remember that detail."

Drake's shoulders stiffened. His gaze went positively glacial, and he gave a dismissive nod in her direction. "Not of late. If you'd paid attention to your sister's goings-on, I think you would have noted we've been in each other's company a great deal." There was the slightest hint of something suggestive in Drake's words that seemed to get Sebastian's hackles up.

Sebastian took another step forward.

Emmaline placed a hand on his shoulder. "Lord Drake has requested the next set. Can you conclude this at a later time?" She removed her fingers and placed them on Drake's sleeve. The hard muscles of his arm tightened convulsively beneath her touch, and he allowed Emmaline to lead him to the dance-floor.

The current partners were taking their places, and the thrum of the orchestra indicated they were to dance a waltz. Drake brusquely grabbed her hand. He set his other hand at her waist, all the while glaring down at her. "I didn't need to be rescued from your brother," he said.

She squared her chin. "What makes you believe I was rescuing you? Perhaps I did it for myself. Do you always believe everything revolves around you?"

His grip tightened on her waist and his words came out on a whisper she had to strain to hear. "I have known since I was a boy the obligations and responsibilities that belong to me as the heir of a dukedom. I do not believe the world revolves around me. I'm relatively powerless in this well-ordered world."

A harsh sincerity underlined his words; it chilled Emmaline. Drake's hard coiled muscles bunched tightly beneath the fine line of his expertly tailored black evening coat. "Have you ever considered… others…might feel the same?"

Those emerald eyes passed over her face, penetrating.

Emmaline did not give him an opportunity to respond. "Do you believe this is the life I want for myself? Do you believe I'd rather know this formal aloofness, than…?" love or passion? She bit her lip hard to keep from humiliating herself. Silence stretched between them punctuated by the strings of the orchestra's violins.

Studying Emmaline's emotion-laden eyes, Drake was humbled by a dawning realization—he hadn't been the only one wronged by their childhood betrothal. How odd he'd spent the past fifteen years angry with her, when she'd been just as much the victim. They'd both been robbed of choice and chance and…destiny. Listening to the words she spoke, he found Emmaline, not unlike him, yearned for what he'd been searching for since he was a boy of thirteen—the power of choice.

It felt like he was seeing her for the first time. Truly seeing her. "What do you dream of?"

Emmaline's gaze skittered off to a point beyond his shoulder. He studied her mouth; the way her teeth worried that plump, lower fleshy fold. She bit her lip when she was concentrating or when she was embarrassed. He found it, with no small measure of surprise, captivating.

She looked back at him. "This is the first time in my entire life anyone has asked me about my dreams and wishes. None of my family asked that question of me. Not even Sophie, my dearest friend in the world. It has seemed since I was a small girl, there was an understanding that I am the privileged daughter of a powerful duke, who wanted for nothing, and therefore could possibly have no need for anything."

Her words were a mirror into his soul. "The world couldn't have been more wrong could it, my lady?"

An ironic smile turned her lips. "No, it couldn't. As silly as it was, I dreamt of more than a cold emotionless entanglement signed by my father to further grow our estates and riches."

Somewhere along the path of life Emmaline had consigned herself to the obligations thrust upon her as a young, unmarried lady. He didn't know why that thought should surprise him. Simply put, it was the way of their world. It seemed, however, at odds with the woman who would boldly challenge gentlemen with little regard for her safety.

Guiding her graceful form through the steps of the waltz, he came to find he shared a special connection with Emmaline. Though she'd been born a female, Emmaline's life had not been very different from his. They were, in a way, kindred spirits.

It didn't escape his notice that she'd failed to answer his earlier question.

"So then tell me, Emmaline. What do you wish for?" Her name slipped from his lips as easily as the next breath he took.

Emmaline's gaze dropped to the simple folds of his snowy white cravat. "I want to be loved. I want a family of my own." The words emerged haltingly.

"You want to be loved?" He couldn't hold back the derisive question. The word love was so foreign to Society that there was something crass and vulgar in simply thinking it to oneself, let alone speaking it aloud.

Her body stiffened beneath his touch. A dull flush stained her cheeks. "Yes, my lord, I want to be loved."

Drake's lips twitched. "Ours is hardly a love match."

Based on the hurt little expression she wore, he thought she might have preferred his laughter.

"Though we'd hardly know if it could be a love match," she pointed out.

"If it is love and flowery poems you seek, my lady, be forewarned, you will not find it from me."

She blinked several times. "You don't believe in love?"

He shook his head. "I didn't say that."

"So, you do believe in love?"

Drake arched a brow. The lady was persistent. "Though never the recipient of such an insipid emotion, I understand my parents were in love. So I do believe some people capable of it."

Everyone in Society knew the history of Lord Drake's mother. The Duchess of Hawkridge had died giving birth to her son. He'd never known his mother. Drake wondered if perhaps the absence of a maternal figure in his life had resulted in the jaded man he'd become. That, and the hellish things he'd done on the battlefield, of course.

A liveried servant at the edge of the dance-floor stumbled. His lofty tray of champagne flutes tilted, sending the crystal glasses tumbling to the floor. There were gasps of horror and shrieks of surprise as the guests on the side were sprayed with tiny bits of glass and French vintage champagne.

"Fire towards the ground," Drake commanded. The 31st Regiment of Foot was low on artillery and had to improvise their canister shot with nails and scrap iron.

The lieutenant loaded the canister into the cannon and prepared to fire at the relentless French army on foot.

The canon failed.

The canister shot did not. The closed cylindrical metal canister intended for the advancing enemy troops skipped a path, twenty-five, thirty-yards, across the ground.

Then an explosion rent the world around them. Shrapnel flew. Men were screaming. His men were screaming...

"But you are not capable of it?" Emmaline's question interrupted his momentary lapse in sanity.

Drake swallowed convulsively. He would never escape the war. His mind would forever remain on the bloody fields of battle.

"My lord?" she asked, confused eyes studying the lines of his face.

Drake forced himself to relax his tightly clenched jaw. Emmaline clearly couldn't detect the hell that gripped him. Nor, for that matter, did she seem aware of the drama at the edge of the dance-floor.

"My lady, I'm not certain I'm capable of marriage."

Emmaline blinked several times. "Well, of course you'll marry. You have to marry me," she blurted. Her cheeks turned a bright shade of pink. "Uh, that is, I mean—" She dropped her gaze to his cravat.

Drake grinned. "Do I?" he teased. He applied a subtle pressure to where his hand gripped her waist, encouraging her to look at him. He found something soothing in her brown eyes. They reminded him of deep, rich Belgian chocolate warmed in the hot summer sun.

"So we've been told," she muttered.

A bark of laughter escaped him. It came out rusty from ill use, and appeared to startle her.

She glanced up, their stares locked, and held.

Then she began to study his face. He knew the moment she noted the faint scar that started at his temple and traversed a parallel path to his jaw. Many of the women he'd bedded had assessed the mark with a kind of fascinated horror.

Emmaline reached up a hand as if to touch it, and then seemed to remember where they were. She drew her hand back but her gaze did not leave his scar.

Her interest triggered a vulnerability he'd thought dead. The sight of her; unsullied and pure and him, brutal and vile, made him feel like the devil dancing in church. She'd been untouched by hands of evil, when his had wrought death and destruction.

He waited for her to ask the blunt question most ladies of his acquaintance asked. A kind of perverted glee that they'd dared to touch a blood-thirsty warrior.

Except she didn't ask the question, didn't beg to know how he'd come by the mark.

She was different than any other woman he'd ever known...and it scared the hell out of him.

Damn her for making him feel things he didn't want to feel. A little too forcefully, he angled her body close to his—closer than was fashionably appropriate.

"Do you look at all gentlemen like this?" he asked, his voice hard. His vulnerability robbed him of both reason and the more than twenty-eight years of gentlemanly behavior that had been ingrained into him.

"Like what?"

"Like you have wicked thoughts in your innocent head."

Emmaline's breath caught and she opened then shut her mouth several times, as if she were trying to formulate a suitable response to his insult. It would seem Emmaline could be flummoxed.

He was a complete and utter bastard.

And, as though Drake needed further affirmation of that truth, his mind traveled a path of silken kisses and seductive caresses. He became aware of the feel of her delicate waist under his hand. The fine satin russet gown did little to veil the warmth of her skin. He yearned to strip the fabric from her body and run explorative hands along her satiny flesh. He wanted to move his hand lower, tug her skirts up, and caress her.

Emmaline winced and he realized he'd unconsciously gripped her hand too tight. He flexed his fingers, forcing himself to relax his hold. He studied her hand using it as a lifeline back from the path his mind had wandered.

Except...

They really were lovely fingers. He imagined them wrapped about his length, stroking, squeezing, teasing...His breath came hoarse. Where had that thought come from? But it was too late. The forbidden thoughts were there as he held her in his arms.

Had he thought her figureless? Her breasts, though not large, were the size of small, firm apples. God, if he didn't have a taste for the forbidden fruit. Now he knew the trial Adam had been presented with in that garden of temptation, understood why he'd thrown away Paradise. The curve of her waist flared nicely under his fingers, and he wanted to reach lower, grasp her buttocks, and tug her to his center. Drake gave himself an invisible shake, reminding himself where in hell they were.

Emmaline licked her lower lip. "My lord?" she whispered.

Drake's eyes fell to those full red lips that haunted his dreams and he dipped his head, a hairsbreadth from capturing them. He was going to kiss her, right there, in the midst of the dance-floor and he gave not one damn that every last peer present would bear witness.

"The dance has ended." Emmaline brought Drake's forbidden musings to a staggering halt. He became aware of the fact they were standing in the middle of an emptying dance-floor.

Drake's body jerked and he set Emmaline from him as though he'd been speared with a bayonet. When had he looked at Emmaline and seen beauty instead of obligation and responsibility? His heart raced with panic.

He dipped a mocking bow and clapped his hands in a deriding fashion. "Brava, my girl. You have gotten what you wanted. How neatly you've inserted yourself into my life." With that, he spun on his heel, and abandoned her amidst the emptied dance floor.

He truly was a bastard.

TEN

Dearest Lord Drake,
I have begun keeping a journal on your efforts on the Peninsula. I am
amazed by your bravery and courage. It is an honor being betrothed to
such a noble man.
Ever Yours,
Emmaline

"What was that about?"
Emmaline started even as Sophie reached out and gripped her arm. She gave silent thanks as her friend steered her from the dance-floor.

Words lodged in Emmaline's throat. She feared with one wrong word uttered, she might splinter into a thousand shards across the ball-room floor, and disintegrate beneath the heels of the lords and ladies witnessing her humiliation. How, in a matter of minutes had she gone from feeling a sense of connection with Drake to being the recipient of his condescending ire?

She told herself not to look for him, but for the life of her couldn't prevent her gaze from searching the crowd for a hint of him. It wasn't difficult to locate his tall, strong figure in the crowded ballroom.

And then wished she hadn't.

He stood beside a stunningly beautiful woman with midnight black curls artfully arranged in an elegant upsweep. One loose strand, twisted in a clever curl, gave the illusion the silken waves could tumble free at any moment.

A pained sound lodged in Emmaline's throat. If she couldn't have been born with the preferred fair coloring, couldn't she have at least had the other woman's splendid locks? How terribly unfair.

The woman was none other than Lady Smythe, a notorious widow. In Emmaline's estimation, Lady Smythe was far too young and far too beautiful to be a widow. Widows were supposed to be old harridans in a perpetual state of sorrow. They were not meant to be clad in indecent dark sapphire gowns with an overlay of French lace, cut scandalously low and displaying an abundant décolletage. And they most certainly were not supposed to have that décolletage one small breath away from exposure.

As if ample attention wasn't being drawn to her *ample* endowments, an enormous teardrop sapphire necklace encircled her neck. It was cut in a teardrop design and provocatively pointed down to those *attributes*. Lady Smythe snapped a fan open and fluttered it flirtatiously in front of her mouth, obscuring her rouged lips from the *tons* interested eyes. If possible, the lady sidled even closer. She layered her form indecently against Drake. He dipped his head down, and the woman tilted her head up, whispering something.

Then he laughed.

Even with the span of the dance-floor separating them, the deep, rich sound reached Emmaline's ears. She thought his laughter should have cut her to the quick and braced for the additional bite of pain.

It didn't come.

During the waltz they'd shared, Emmaline had experienced Drake's laughter. It had startled both of them. That laugh he'd been unable to contain during their set was different from the practiced one she heard now. The one he spared for the lovely creature at his side was disingenuous and Emmaline found that somehow—soothing.

Drake reached for a flute of champagne from a passing servant.

Seeming to feel Emmaline's stare, he looked directly at her with a veiled, faintly mocking expression. He raised his glass in her direction and downed the contents, before he again directed his attention to Lady Smythe.

The earlier solace she'd found was crushed in his deliberate attempt to humiliate her. This time, Emmaline couldn't stifle the ball of anguish that crept steadily up her throat, the pain so overwhelmingly sharp it nearly choked her. She could feel the lords and ladies gawking at her, the snickering harpies, the pitying looks. Suddenly it was too much.

"Get me out," Emmaline pleaded, fumbling for Sophie's hand. If she didn't leave, she thought she would crumple in a heap. How the *ton* would love that. She wouldn't give them, or him, the satisfaction.

"Hush, silly! We hardly need His Lordship thinking he's won this battle." Sophie's stern reprimand steadied Emmaline.

"They are watching me," Emmaline whispered. She stole a quick peek around and noted the stares directed her way.

Her humiliation gave way to blinding rage.

"Yes, they are." Sophie guided Emmaline from the ballroom to an empty withdrawing room. Closing the door behind them, Sophie directed her attention to Emmaline. "We need to freshen you up." She pinched Emmaline's cheeks—hard.

"Ouch!" Emmaline yelped at the firm pressure.

"Sorry, you were looking pale," Sophie explained, not sounding at all apologetic.

On a sigh, Emmaline dropped unceremoniously into a King Louis gold-painted seat. She stretched her legs out in an undignified fashion, closed her eyes, and wished when she opened them to be anywhere other than where she currently sat. Nay, that wasn't altogether true...she'd prefer the seclusion of the retiring room to that infernal ballroom. At least in here she was spared from hearing the *tons* snickering remarks.

Sophie sunk to the floor and rested her cheek on Emmaline's soft silk skirts. "I think this is going to be more difficult than you or I expected," Sophie conceded. "I mean, what other peer of the realm would shirk his responsibilities all these years and carry on so under your nose?"

Emmaline flinched. "I don't want to be his responsibility, Sophie."

Sophie hesitated. "What do you want, Em?"

And for the second time that night, and in her life, Emmaline had been asked what it was she wanted.

What do you want? A voice silently jeered. Do you want him to love you? Court you? Whyever would he do something so foolish when he could and did have any number of beautiful ladies? No, Emmaline had been a fool on many scores. She couldn't even speak those words to her dearest friend.

Sophie was kind enough not to press Emmaline. She picked her head up and angled a glance at Emmaline. She spoke haltingly. "You couldn't believe after just a few exchanges, Lord Drake would change his opinion?"

Emmaline chewed her lip. "No—no. I-I had hoped…" Her words trailed off. Because, naively, that had been what she'd hoped. Hearing it from Sophie's lips indicated it had been no more than a fairytale constructed from balderdash.

She thought about Drake standing beside Lady Smythe, flirting shamelessly with the voluptuous widow. Emmaline glanced down at her own, less than stellar attributes, and wrinkled her nose. "It's hardly fair," she muttered.

"What is?"

"Lady Smythe should be so generously endowed while I, while I…" Emmaline made a vague gesture over her own less than impressive décolletage. Leaning forward, she puffed her chest out and then, realizing how ridiculous she must look, lolled back against the cushions of the chair, throwing a dejected hand across her eyes.

A bark of laughter escaped Sophie. "Ah, here. These are just the thing!"

Emmaline dropped her hand from her eyes and watched her friend reach onto a nearby table for a stack of linens, wrinkle them into a sizeable ball, and thrust them at her.

Emmaline reached for them and made quick work of stuffing them into the front of her gown. The two women glanced down at Emmaline's new endowments and promptly burst into laughter.

After their giggles had abated, Sophie glanced up. "You know," she began hesitantly. "It really is a shame you're hiding in here. He is, after all, the one who has behaved like an absolute cad."

Emmaline blinked several times. "You know, you are right. Why should I cower behind closed doors while he enjoys a grand evening?"

Sophie shook her head. "You shouldn't."

Tugging the balls of linen from the front of her gown, she set them on Lady Wilcox' table and took to her feet. "I am not going to hide."

Sophie popped right up beside her. "Brava, my dear!"

The more Emmaline thought about Drake, the more infuriated she became. "His interest in Lady Smythe stemmed from nothing other than his desire to lash out at me." She lifted her hand up, mimicking her betrothed's movements. "And his mocking salute with that champagne flute. Why, he may as well have shouted 'victory' from across the ballroom."

Sophie gave a perfunctory nod. "This battle has gone to Lord Drake, but it is just one battle."

The two women marched arm in arm, through the antechamber, until Sophie placed a staying hand on Emmaline's arm. She looked at her with somber eyes. "You must promise me something, Em."

Emmaline inclined her head.

"The moment you feel any sadness in Lady Wilcox' ballroom, the moment you feel the desire to flee—you simply must think of how outlandish you looked with our hostesses fine linens stuffed in your chemise."

They erupted into laughter and then prepared to face the elegantly clad pariahs swarming the ballroom with a taste for blood. With heads held high they moved across the ballroom. Emmaline caught sight of her brother weaving through the crowd, his expression thunderous. "Great, my brother," she muttered. She really didn't need him to make this evening any more difficult than it had already become. "Come, this way." She tried steering Sophie to the far left corner of the ballroom.

"I think we've lost him," Sophie said, looking around.

"Lost who?"

Sophie shrieked and dropped Emmaline's arm. "Y-your Grace."

Sebastian sketched a bow and claimed Sophie's hand for an absent, perfunctory kiss.

"I'll kill him," he muttered beneath his breath. He obviously wasn't concerned that Sophie was privy to the conversation. Sebastian knew Sophie's loyalty to Emmaline and was not inclined to shield his anger. He held out his arm.

Emmaline turned to Sophie, who waved her on. "Go ahead, I'll be over there." Sophie hurried off to claim a seat amidst the other wallflowers.

Emmaline returned her attention to Sebastian. "You most certainly will not kill him," she admonished as he led her into the next set. They took their place in line for the quadrille. The orchestra began playing and they moved through the intricate steps of the lively dance.

"Whatever are you doing fawning over him?" His censure was tangible. "Mother is furious."

Emmaline's gaze sought out her mother, engaged in conversation with their hostess. Mother caught Emmaline's eyes and frowned.

Emmaline tried not to feel hurt at her mother and brother's obvious disappointment. Emmaline and Sebastian were parted, and she was saved from responding, until they came together.

"I am not fawning. He is my betrothed. What would you have me do? Exist in this false world for the remainder of my life? I am already twenty."

Sebastian opened his mouth to say something but was prevented from speaking by the steps of the dance that once again separated them.

Her brother remained silent when next they came together in the line; his ducal stare quickly surveyed the room. Emmaline knew beyond a doubt who he sought out. She also knew the moment his gaze collided with Lord Drake beside Lady Perfection.

She tapped Sebastian on the arm. "Do you trust me?"

He appeared startled by the question and redirected his attention to Emmaline.

"Do I trust you?" He seemed bemused by her question. "I must be honest, Em, I've never given it much thought. You've always been my baby sister. I haven't really seen you as anyone other than the little girl who used to dog my every step."

Emmaline rolled her eyes and waited until they came together. "I'm no longer the child who cried in your arms when my pony fell ill and had to be put down."

There was something melancholy in Sebastian's eyes, as if he'd just realized Emmaline had grown up, that she was no longer a child, and, in fact, a woman. "Of course I trust you. Now, whether Mother trusts you is another story," he said teasingly.

"I need you not to interfere, Sebastian."

She knew if Drake felt compelled where their betrothal was concerned, then nothing would come of it. And foolish as it was, there was a part of her, deep inside that longed for more. She wasn't willing to let go of the dream that was Lord Drake. Though common sense told her that her pursuit was futile, she could not relinquish the dream she carried in her heart.

The quadrille came to an end, and the dancers clapped. Sebastian raked a frustrated hand through tousled dark locks, and directed one last black look in the Marquess of Drake's direction. "Just say the word and you shall be freed," Sebastian promised Emmaline, and then guided her to the seat beside Sophie.

Sebastian sketched a bow for Sophie's benefit and took his leave.

Any feelings of relief at being alone with Sophie were immediately quashed by an unexpected intrusion.

"My, my, my, how lovely seeing you here, Emmaline." Except the statement laced with gleeful malice lacked all sincerity.

Emmaline looked up and resisted the urge to shield her eyes from the offensively bright glare of the gentleman's abundantly greased red hair. With the evening she'd had thus far, why should she be surprised?

She wrinkled her nose in distaste. "Witless, I don't remember giving you leave to address me so familiarly."

Lord Whitmore closed the small distance between them with a violent lunge. He faltered and seemed to remember where they were. He grasped the lapels of his fuchsia silk embroidered evening coat and preened. He gave a cocky little nod across the room. "Seems your hero has directed his attention elsewhere."

Sophie gasped and slipped her hand encouragingly in Emmaline's.

Unwilling to let him see the impact of his words, Emmaline jutted her chin out. "Tell me, Whitmore, are you simply here because you've run out of old women to beat and horses to whip this evening?"

Like a setting sun, Whitmore's brows lowered. "How confident you pretend to be. But tell me, my lady, how confident can you truly be when the man you're betrothed to is sniffing the skirts of another woman right under your nose? How confident can you be seated with the other wallflowers? Why you," he paused and gave a cocky smile, "should thank me for merely acknowledging you by name."

Oh God, forget a whipped horse…Whitmore had landed a solid blow, right in her gut. His victorious expression said he knew it.

Sophie clamored to her feet. "You odious little creature. How dare you come over here? Why, do you know who Lady Emmaline's brother is?"

Whitmore ignored Sophie.

"What do you want, Whitmore?" Emmaline drawled. She'd run out of patience for the "odious little creature," as Sophie had dubbed him.

He turned blood-shot eyes to Emmaline. "Why, I would like an apology of course."

Emmaline blinked. "That is all you want? An apology?"

He nodded like a chicken pecking at feed.

"Well then, sir, if that is what you are waiting for you can hold your hand over your heart until Lord Wellington makes friends with Napoleon himself."

ELEVEN

Dearest Lord Drake,
My brother has informed me that though I'm no great beauty I'm a
woman of character, which is more important than anything else. I
solemnly reassured him that even though he is not the most intelligent
gentleman, he is certainly the most pompous.
Ever Yours,
Emmaline

Drake was bored.
And frustrated.

And annoyed.

With himself, and the woman prattling on and on at his arm. If he'd been paying an iota of attention to whatever she was saying, he was certain there were a number of sexual innuendos buried within her words.

His eyes caught Sin's form cutting a path through the crowd, and sighed.

He owed Sin.

Sin stopped before them, and bowed to the widow. "Lady Smythe, stunning as always!"

Her ice blue eyes, flashed with annoyance. "My lord."

Sin smiled, clearly immune to her displeasure. "Lord Thurmond has been looking for you. I did him the courtesy of letting him know where you were. Ahh, here he comes, now," he said with a wide smile and for good measure, nodded in the direction of the furious gentleman crossing the length of the ballroom.

Withholding any hint of society niceties for Sinclair, Lady Smythe gave him an elegant shoulder, and directed her attention to Drake. "My lord, I'm eager to continue our discussion," she purred.

Drake offered a non-committal response and sketched a bow. The young widow gave him one last heated look. She shot a black look at Sin, and then sauntered away.

Sin rolled his shoulders in a mock shudder. "Egads, that scowl makes her hideous."

Drake grinned. "Many thanks."

Sin waved him off. "Think nothing of it." He retrieved a champagne flute from a passing tray, and took a long sip. "What you should be thinking about, however, is the gossip you've created."

Drake didn't pretend to misunderstand. Instead, he surreptitiously watched Emmaline, seated at the outskirts of the dance floor, engrossed in conversation with Miss Winters, her hands spiraling animatedly, like two little tornadoes. All the hurt she'd worn earlier for the world to see, now gone. Instead, she fairly beamed. A vibrant sparkle glimmered in her eyes, like a beacon. The desire to go and bask in her unabashed joy hit him with a physical intensity so strong, he nearly staggered under the weight of it.

Then Drake became aware of certain other things. With any hint of scandal now gone, the *ton* had lost interest in gawking at Emmaline. And that was when he made the shocking realization—Lady Emmaline *had been* relegated to the inglorious fate of wallflower.

One month ago, such a revelation would have been no revelation at all. Yet having seen her challenge Whitmore, and then himself being the recipient of her saucy boldness, it baffled him that she was not sought after. The hair he'd once thought mousy was really a pleasing shade of deep, rich brown hues, which made Drake imagine just-melted chocolate cascading in rippling waves. Before the end of each night, one errant strand always managed to escape its coif, as stubborn as the lady herself. He found himself giving a very stern, albeit silent, command to his feet to stay planted and not cross the room so he could brush back that lock.

He took a step forward, then froze.

Sinclair wore a puzzled expression. "Uh…are you all right, Drake?" Drake ignored the question.

Either he'd been staring so long it was inevitable, or she'd felt his eyes trained on her because, just then, she looked up and the glimmer he'd spied flickered out. The distance separating them could not dim the hurt in those amber depths, and he felt like the worst sort of bastard. She wrenched her gaze away.

"Go to her."

Drake wasn't sure whether the words had been uttered aloud by Sinclair or were trapped in his mind. The seductive strands of a waltz teased his consciousness. The urge to close the distance between them, draw her close into the folds of his arms, and breathe of her oddly alluring crisp lemon scent was a tangible force.

He ignored Sinclair's stare. Though truth be told, the only way he'd be able to move his gaze from her delectable form was if somebody were to move him by sheer force. Emmaline's sinfully delicious lips turned up at the corners, but oddly, in the course of a short time, he'd come to know what each tilt of her lips meant. He'd come to know her smile enough to know this particular one she wore for the *ton* was a façade—and knew he was responsible for the false show of joy she put on.

Sinclair seemed to read Drake's disordered thoughts. "You can make it right," he said quietly.

"Sin," he bit out. "I'm not your business."

Sin bristled. "No, Drake. You aren't my business. You are my friend. Do you even know what that means?" The stinging words made Drake wince.

It wasn't the first time that evening Drake had been appalled by his own words and actions. "My apologies," he said gruffly.

Sin shook his head. "Don't give it another thought."

How could he not? Drake wondered at what point he'd lost the veneer of humanity that had once allowed him to fit in this world. What had happened those four years on the Peninsula that he now didn't know how to be civil to his betrothed or best friend? Emmaline's and Sin's glaring disappointment in him was just one more stark reminder that he no longer fit in with civilized society—that he was better with vipers like Lady Smythe.

His gaze swallowed Emmaline. But, if he didn't crave an emotional entanglement, why couldn't he look away from her?

She desired love. She spoke of a family. God help him, when she'd spoken of her desires in that far-away husky whisper, she made him want to scale the walls, climb through a window, into the sky and retrieve the moon and a handful of stars for her.

Unlike him, Emmaline remained unscathed by the ugliness of life. The center of her existence was still their betrothal…that hadn't been the case for him in years and years. At one time the obligations of his betrothal had seemed like the worst fate. What a fool he'd been.

Sin looked from Drake to Emmaline. "Her hair is merely brown, you know?"

Drake gave his head a shake. "It's like the color of Belgian chocolate, you fool."

"Same with her eyes, just brown," Sinclair pointed out.

"They are not brown. Why, they are more of a whiskey hue with a hint of…"

God, what was happening to him?

His friend gave him a triumphant look and with steely determination, Drake resolved to cease staring at his betrothed.

Sin opened his mouth to speak and Drake glared him into silence.

Regardless of the length of their friendship, Drake neither wanted nor needed Sin interfering with his betrothal agreement.

"So you do not have feelings for the young lady?"

Drake sipped his champagne. "None at all."

"Which would probably mean you wouldn't care if she has to deal with the likes of Whitmore, again?" Sin dangled.

Drake's gaze flew across the room. His hands balled into tight fists. Whitmore and Emmaline. Without a word, Drake strode toward his betrothed. By god, that cowardly fop had better not cause her any distress or he'd end him right there with Society as his witness.

"Well, I guess I have my answer," Sin called after him.

Rage dripped from Lord Whitmore with such ferocity he put Emmaline in mind of one of her brother's hunting dogs who'd gotten so ill he'd frothed at the mouth. "You little fool," Whitmore bit out.

Emmaline's hand flew to her breast at the vulgar declaration. "Whitmore, as crass as usual."

She spun around and discovered Drake at her shoulder. The lines of his face were set in a hard mask. A slight tick at the corner of his eye, the only indication of his fury. He offered a perfunctory bow to both her and Sophie, and then turned his attention to Whitmore.

The young dandy's cheeks turned an unhealthy shade of white.

Throwing an arm around Whitmore with enough force to nearly drop the man to his knees, Drake proceeded to give him a slight shake. To those observing the scene, Drake's mannerisms could be construed as male jocundity.

A mottled shade of red restored color to Whitmore's cheeks. "M-my l-lord, I-I'm surprised to find you here. Why Lady Smythe and all, you know?"

Emmaline flinched. Apparently the young dandy had far more temerity than she'd credited him with.

The moments ticked by with an exaggerated slowness. Drake still hadn't spoken, which added a marked intensity to the exchange.

Stupid as he was, Whitmore had the sense to know he'd said something unpardonable, something which had only served to raise the Marquess of Drake's ire. He took a step away from Drake.

Her betrothed pinned a glacial stare on Whitmore, his mouth set in a firm, unrelenting line. "Why don't I join you? But first, make your apologies." Her betrothed's words were as silken as the edge of a blade.

"M-my apologies, ladies." Whitmore bowed so low he nearly toppled over his feet.

"Tsk, tsk...I'm beginning to notice a rather unseemly trend, Whitmore," Emmaline said.

Drake inclined his head. "I believe the young man needs to inform his mother of how callously he's been treating young ladies."

Whitmore sputtered and he gripped Drake's arm. "Please, I implore you. Do not let my mother know," he said, his gaze skittered off to land on the rotund, graying woman conversing with the host and hostess.

"What do you think, my lady? Miss Winters? Do you think I should inform Lady Whitmore?" Drake asked.

Whitmore's eyes bulged. "Have a heart."

Sophie tapped her chin. "I don't know. What do you think, Em?"

Drake arched a golden brow in Emmaline's direction. "Yes, what do you think, my lady?"

What did she think? She actually had very little thought reserved for Lord Whitmore. She was still trying to grapple with the warring personalities Drake presented to her. One moment he was the aloof, indifferent bounder, the next he was a champion charging over on his white steed, defending her from miscreants.

"My lady?" Drake pressed.

Emmaline returned her attention to the matter at hand. She studied the little toad quivering before them. She almost felt bad for him. Until she recalled the old peddler woman and Whitmore's poor battered horse. "No, I think Lady Whitmore would definitely want to know about her son's proclivity for rudeness."

Drake turned to the cowering dandy. "How about a round in the ring, tomorrow, as well, Whitmore?"

Words eluded Whitmore who continued to rapidly shake his head back and forth in a way that nearly made Emmaline ill.

Her gaze locked with Drake's and it appeared there was something more he wished to say, but the presence of Sophie and Whitmore prevented it. "My apologies, my lady," he said. "I have a meeting with this pup's mother, isn't that right, Whitmore?"

Emmaline watched him go with his *pup* in tow, knowing there were many layers to that apology.

"Indifferent, Em." Sophie snorted. "I think not."

TWELVE

My Dearest Lord Drake,
I begged Sebastian to allow me to accompany him to London Hospital.
The visit was nothing short of remarkable.
Ever Yours,
Emmaline

Sebastian pulled his watch fob from the front pocket of his jacket and proceeded to check the time. "I am going to visit London Hospital. Are you—?"

Emmaline set aside the book she'd been reading and clambered up from the window-seat that overlooked the gardens below. "I'm coming! Give me a moment."

Sebastian had been a board member at London Hospital since their father had died. Three years ago, when Sebastian had been planning his first visit to the hospital, a teary-eyed Emmaline had begged to go along with him.

Her brother had insisted London Hospital was no place for a seventeen-year old, genteel, young lady but, Sebastian had eventually been worn down. Ultimately, the older brother of a young grieving sister had been wont to deny her anything.

When Sebastian attended London Hospital's monthly board meetings, Emmaline accompanied him and visited with the soldiers who'd fought Boney's forces. In addition, she spent one day each week reading to the soldiers.

"I have a meeting with the Board. I told you to be ready by—"

"Just a moment!" Emmaline grabbed her stack of books, and handed her burden over to him. "Here." She looped her arm through his and they made their way to the foyer.

A servant assisted Emmaline into her burnt orange taffeta cloak. She smiled. "Did Cook have that basket readied?"

She'd not even finished her question when a maid rushed forward with the basket outstretched. "Here it is, my lady."

"Thank you," she murmured as Sebastian relieved the maid of her burden. Emmaline followed Sebastian to the carriage.

After he placed the basket on the opposite seat, he sprawled into the red velvet squabs of the carriage bench.

Emmaline nudged him in the side. "Slide over. You are crowding me."

"I'm insulted, Em. This carriage is enormous and..."

She rapped his fingers. "Just move over."

"You'd never know I was a duke," he muttered and moved over to the other bench.

Emmaline's lips twitched.

Sebastian reached over and snagged the stack of books she'd brought with her. He shuffled through the pile and then set them aside. "Byron? Coleridge? Blake?" He arched a brow. "Are you certain this is what the men prefer to hear?" He dropped the books down on the opposite seat with a condescending thump.

Emmaline bristled. "Who wouldn't want to read Byron, Coleridge, or Blake?"

Sebastian gave his head a shake as if to say, *I'm more than certain I'm right and you're wrong.* He at least had sense enough not to say as much, aloud.

Instead, he flipped open the lid of the basket. "What do we have?"

Emmaline leaned over and slammed the top down on his fingers. "*We* have nothing."

"Ouch." He popped the smarting digits into his mouth.

"Really, Sebastian," she chided, and slapped his other hand for good measure. "You can avail yourself to Cook's pastries any time you want. These are for the soldiers."

"I wasn't going to eat anything."

"Liar." Emmaline ignored his response and turned her attention out the windowpane as the London scenery passed by.

"So, Em, what's the story with Drake?"

Her eyes snapped back toward Sebastian and she felt a warm flush climb her neck and heat her cheeks. For the better part of the month, Sebastian had made it clear he did not approve of her efforts to secure Drake's affections.

"What do you mean?"

Hazel-brown eyes narrowed. "You asked me if I trusted you. I responded yes. I am, however, the Duke of Mallen and your guardian. I need to ensure your protection."

"What rubbish." She puffed out her chest and threw her chin back in her best impression of a duke. "I'm the very powerful Duke of Mallen and want to know just what my little sister is up to."

Sebastian folded his arms across his chest. "I don't sound like that."

"No, you sound like that."

His brow wrinkled as if in annoyance. "Oh, and just what *that* are you referring to?"

"You sound like my older brother who is trying to find out what I'm up to."

Sebastian sat back in the squabs of his seat. He drummed a finger on his leg. "Is there something wrong with me wanting to protect you?"

A swell of emotion climbed up Emmaline's throat and made it difficult for her to reply. For all the responsibilities he'd inherited, and all the obligations that went with being the Duke of Mallen, occasionally there were moments when Sebastian was not the all-powerful peer and simply was her brother.

Emmaline leaned over and took his hand in hers. She gave it a light squeeze. "Of course not. But that is all you needed to say, brother."

He cleared his throat, noticeably uncomfortable with her show of emotion. "So?" he urged.

He was like a dog with a bone with this one.

She sighed, letting his hand go. "I want a decision from Drake. I want a courtship and a true marriage. He is no longer allowed to run from me."

Sebastian's jaw set. "No."

Emmaline's lips twitched. "I wasn't asking you."

He scowled. "I still feel as though I should tell you how I'm feeling."

"Fair enough," she said with mock solemnity.

He opened his mouth to add something when the carriage drew to a halt.

"We're here!" she called cheerily. Before the groom had even reached the side of the carriage, she leaned across Sebastian and thrust the door open, effectively squashing the remainder of the discussion.

Emmaline accepted the hand from the groom. "Thank you, Charles."

She accepted Sebastian's arm and allowed him to escort her up the column of stone steps into London Hospital. The hospital faced White-Chapel Road and was divided by a carriageway. The main entrance led into a receiving room where they were always greeted, before heading to the ward.

Emmaline walked down the stark white halls, and greeted the fifty-five soldiers who now made London Hospital their home.

"My lady, so good to see you," one soldier called. "Your Grace," he added, almost as an afterthought.

Emmaline waved to the soldier. She stopped at his bedside. "Lieutenant Woods, how have you been this fine week?"

The burly red-haired soldier grinned a nearly toothless smile. "Better, now, my lady. Better now!"

Emmaline waggled a brow. "I'm certain you are simply referring to my arrival with Cook's latest creation. Though I must tell you," she dropped her voice to a conspiratorial whisper, "it was all I could do to defend the basket from His Grace. I had to slap his fingers in the carriage ride over."

Woods guffawed with laughter. It blended with the echoing chuckles from the men in nearby hospital beds.

Looking around at her growing audience, she nodded for good measure. "No, truthfully, I gave them a little slap." She teasingly demonstrated said slap on Sebastian's fingers, and earned another round of laughter.

Sebastian pointed his eyes towards the ceiling and shook his head. "I will return after my meeting," he muttered. His response only fueled the soldiers' amusement. He turned to the nurse who'd followed them into the ward and handed, Emmaline's books over to her.

Emmaline gave him a quick buss on the check and then he left. She returned her attention to the basket. "Ahh, let us see…what have we here?" She extracted a raspberry scone and handed the confection to Woods.

He accepted it as though he'd been offered the King's crown. "My lady," he said in solemn thanks and then took a wide bite of the treat.

Emmaline sat beside him for a short while, reading some of Byron's work before she moved on down the rows of beds. She stopped to inquire after each of the soldiers, occasionally reading to those who asked her for a poem.

Then she reached the last bed in the ward.

No buoyant grin met her at this particular bedside. No warmth. Nor amusement. As long as Emmaline had been visiting London Hospital, this bed had been devoid of any trace of cheer.

Emmaline turned to the nurse who'd accompanied her. "Nurse Whiting, I will just be reading here. You can see to the other soldiers."

"You are always so kind, my lady." Nurse Whiting dropped a curtsy and turned her attention to a soldier at the far end of the room, calling out for assistance.

With the woman gone, Emmaline shifted her focus to the soldier. "Lieutenant Jones," she greeted with the same smile she had for each man.

Jones, whose bed was situated at one of the back windows, had his eyes closed and his head directed toward the window. It was much the same every time she visited. Sometimes his closed eyes would be pointed to the end of the room and sometimes out the window.

They very rarely fell on her. They were never open.

Lieutenant Jones had lost an arm in the war. He had been gaunt three years ago. A skeleton of a human being. Since then, he'd gained weight, but seemed trapped within the hell of his experience fighting Boney's forces.

Emmaline had committed to never abandoning Jones.

She waved one of her copies beneath his nose, so close it wafted his skin with the movement of air.

"Coleridge," she said.

She waved another.

"Byron?"

And a final copy. "Or Blake?"

She waited.

As usual, there was no answer. "You are always so kind to let me decide. I choose..." She thumbed through the volumes, "...Coleridge today." She scanned several pages. "Would you know, Lieutenant Jones, my brother had the audacity to tell me you are assuredly disappointed in my reading selection. He called poetry frivolous. Can you imagine that?" There was no outward reaction from Jones. "I told him, with utmost confidence, I was sure you approved of my selection. But," she leaned close and whispered, "upon careful consideration I was forced to wonder if you ignore me because of the poetry."

For the first time in three years, Lieutenant Jones opened his eyes. They were a startling shade of grey; like a summer sky right before a turbulent lightning storm.

Emmaline gasped, and dropped the volume at his bedside.

Lieutenant Jones continued to stare.

Emmaline smiled. Tears stung her eyes but she blinked them back. The last thing this man needed to see was her weak display of emotion. "Should I take that as a yes or no, Lieutenant? You just let me know. I assure you I shan't be offended." Her hand shook as she turned the page and began to read.

A long while later, she glanced up when the soldiers at the front of the ward called out greetings to the Duke of Mallen. She snapped the book of poems closed.

"I must tell you one of my favorite things about you, Lieutenant, is that you are the only gentleman here I am certain isn't fond of me simply for the treats I bring from Cook."

She gasped when his hand shot out and wrapped around her wrist. For all his years of confinement and his lack of physical exertion, his hold felt like a weighted chain on her person. Emmaline stared down at the strong hand that gripped hers. She supposed she should feel some sense of alarm—and yet, she didn't. Deep inside, Emmaline knew he wouldn't hurt her.

"Why do you persist?" His voice came out rusty from ill use. "Why do you not go away? Why can you not let me be?"

Emmaline met his steely grey-eyed gaze square on. "I don't think you want me to go away, Lieutenant. I think, whether you'll admit it or not, you like me. And for whatever reason, I have grown to like you. Though, I must say you have proven far more amicable when you don't say anything at all."

His eyes narrowed, passed over her face, as if he sought the answer to some question she wasn't privy. He abruptly released her wrist. Then, for the first time in three years—smiled.

THIRTEEN

My Dearest Drake,
After scaling down one of the ancient trees outside my bedroom window,
I found my mother and father waiting for me at the bottom. They
forbade me from climbing that tree ever again. I solemnly assured them
I would respect their orders. So I have taken to climbing the trees far
away from view of the house!
Ever Yours,
Emmaline

For the better part of a fortnight, Lady Emmaline had been there. By *there* Drake meant, in attendance at every event he attended. With her ability to ferret out his plans, she'd have made a hell of a spy for Wellington.

It begged the question why, at that precise moment, as Emmaline, her friend Miss Winters, and a maid snuck into a bookshop on the corner, did he not want to remain hidden in the confines of his black lacquer carriage? He didn't pause to pay the silent question rolling around his mind much thought. Drake rapped on the roof of the carriage which came to an immediate halt.

Drake jumped down, and crossed the bustling street to the Old Corner Bookshop. He entered through the single door that set a tinny bell a-jingle and did a quick survey of the establishment.

The adage "Old" seemed rather generous. With an overwhelming scent of stale must, the inside of the establishment was ancient... and that too, might have been magnanimous. The rows and rows of books held a pungent odor of aged leather. Drake ruffled his nose and quelled the urge to sneeze. Clearly, the Old Corner Bookshop was not the most thriving of establishments.

"My lady, Miss Winters, so good to see you both." The boisterous greeting caught Drake's ear and propelled him deeper into the shop.

The ladies' murmured response was lost in the rows of shelving.

"Why yes, yes I do in fact have the very novel." The shopkeeper's voice had dropped to a clear attempt at conspiratorial whisper, a feat Drake was sure the other man hadn't exhibited in at least two decades.

Drake's ears perked up. His betrothed enjoyed literature. What were Emmaline's reading preferences? Poetry. She struck him as a romantic. The thought summoned a memory from long ago. He was kneeling down beside a five-year-old Emmaline. She'd fallen and he'd helped her to her feet. *"Are you a prince?"*

He started. He'd all but forgotten that moment in time. It wasn't particularly something a boy of thirteen would remark upon, let alone remember. But in his mind he could clearly see the five-year old girl's brown eyes pooled with tears of pain. He remembered the way they'd widened in wonder at the sight of him.

The muffled sound of Emmaline's whisper brought Drake's attention back to her circumspect efforts. With a sure-step, he moved deeper into the shop, closer to the voices in discussion, and peered around the edge of the shelf.

Emmaline's smile stretched wide, as she displayed a row of pearl-white teeth and one slightly angled, yet highly endearing front left tooth. She accepted the work proffered by the rotund little man as gingerly as if the Archbishop of Canterbury had offered her the Holy Grail. Turning it in her hands, she studied the cover, and said something to Miss Winters, who laughed, and accepted a second copy from the shopkeeper.

The man bowed and continued down the aisle, leaving the ladies alone.

The furtive glances his betrothed continued to steal only heightened Drake's intrigue. What could she be up to?

Battlefield experience had shown him the importance of having the upper hand.

"Lady Emmaline, Miss Winters, what a pleasure seeing you both!" he called out.

A squeal of surprise rent the quiet hum of the empty bookshop followed by a thump as the book Emmaline had been holding fell to the floor. The novel tumbled open, and landed indignantly upon its spine, the title still concealed.

✐

Blast and double blast!

She'd rather have ripped her hair out one strand at a time than have him find her here. After all her chance-meetings with Drake, this would be when he happened upon her.

"Lord Drake, what a pleasure to see you," she lied.

Emmaline saw his lips moving but didn't pay attention to his response. All her focus remained on the book at her feet. She peeked out the corner of her eye at Sophie. She dared hope Sophie had formulated a plan to recover the volume without attracting Drake's notice, for Emmaline was stymied.

In an attempt to distract him, Emmaline favored Drake with her most winning smile and stuck the tip of her satin slipper out as she tried to drag the leather volume toward her.

Drake's jade eyes fell to her extended foot.

So much for her winningest smile.

"Please, allow me," he insisted.

Like hell, she silently fumed. She made one last valiant attempt to collect the novel but he bent down to rescue the source of her quandary.

"No need. I have it, my lord." She bent over just as Drake did. Their heads met with a loud crack.

"Oomph," Emmaline gasped. The world rocked from under her and she would have splayed in an inelegant heap at his feet, but Drake's arms were already out. He expertly righted her, rescuing her before she crashed to the floor and cradled her slender frame against his sculpted chest.

CHRISTI CALDWELL

Emmaline's breath caught. The press of his body against hers left her incapable of formulating one coherent thought. All she could comprehend was the absolute and total heat of his touch, the scent of sandalwood clinging to his person, tantalizing her senses.

Sophie sighed.

It would appear Drake heard it, too. As though Emmaline had spiked thorns along her forearms, he set her from him with alacrity.

She hated that her whole body should go on alert the moment he entered the same room, when he remained impervious to her. She might as well be a matronly relative. No...he probably would treat matronly relatives with far more regard than he showed her.

Sophie stammered her pardon and scurried down another aisle. Emmaline wasn't certain if her friend was either: one, allowing her time alone with her betrothed or whether two, she sought escape before he discovered their scandalous reading habits. Which reminded her...

Emmaline made one more attempt to retrieve the work, but alas her betrothed had the reflexes of a lightning strike. He intercepted her efforts, and rescued the volume, holding it aloft, well beyond her reach.

A single, strand had escaped Emmaline's neat chignon during her exertions and hung over her brow. She blew the lock back and folded her arms across her chest. "I would like my book back, my lord."

Her eyes were drawn to the slow smile that quirked one corner of his lips. Drat the man. He seemed far too amused by this exchange. She briefly contemplated snatching the volume from his hand and dismissing him without a further word. Based on his earlier speed, any effort she made to retrieve it would prove ineffectual.

"Hmmm, what have we here?" he wondered, and lowered the book to eye level. His smile widened and he revealed a row of perfectly white even teeth.

Of course he would have perfect teeth, she thought, promptly snapping her mouth shut. She'd not allow him to see her own imperfect row, the way her front left tooth angled slightly over its right counterpart. Her brother had forever teased her over it, and it had always been a source of insecurity. She could only imagine what her betrothed would think about it.

Drake glanced at the title.

At any other place, at any other time, Emmaline would relish the levity of their exchange. Not, however, at this particular moment. Her reading preferences were an exceedingly intimate part of herself that she did not want to share. He very well may be her betrothed, but he was still a veritable stranger.

He blinked several times. "*This* is what you're reading?"

Emmaline did not like his emphasis on the word, this. "I'll take it now, my lord," she said. She held her hand out, and waited for him to turn it over.

Drake ignored her and opened the front flap of the book. His eyes scanned the words, and then snapped in her direction "This is what you are reading?" There was a measure of haughty disdain in his words.

Annoyance blossomed inside her chest at the way Drake kept repeating himself. "You needn't sound so...so...incredulous."

Drake closed the book and shook his head. "Gothic novels. This is where your interests lie."

Rules of etiquette be demmed, Emmaline snatched the volume from his hands. "I do not appreciate your condescension. Nor do I care for the way you keep repeating yourself." Somewhere along the way his words had ceased to be a question and had become a statement.

Drake opened his mouth to speak but Emmaline continued before he had the chance. "How terribly stuffy of you, my lord. It is difficult to imagine that you, who've had scores of mistresses littering the better part of England, should be so scandalized by a mere piece of literature. Your reaction is simply staggering."

Drake advanced a step in her direction and Emmaline took a step back. There was something overwhelmingly masculine and at the same time predatory in his hooded expression.

"Stuffy?"

His words washed over her like a silken caress. She told her brain to remind her head to nod. "Yes, stuffy."

85

Before she even suspected his intentions, he again relieved her of her copy.

The work under his scrutiny was *Glenarvon* by Caroline Lamb. Emmaline had always had a love for Gothic novels; however, this one was even more intriguing than most, for it told the story of doomed love between a married Lady Calantha and a dashing Irish Revolutionary. The work was not even a thinly veiled disguise of Lady Caroline Lamb's own tempestuous love affair with Lord Byron, and that, combined with her rather unflattering satire of leading members of Society, had set the *ton* abuzz.

"Are you mad, reading this?" His voice was a harsh whisper. He stuffed the volume on the shelf behind him, and cast a glance about as though discovery were imminent.

Emmaline tugged the volume out from the spot where he'd haphazardly deposited it. "First, that is not where this book goes," she reprimanded. "Second—"

"I don't care where the bloody book goes as long as it is not in your hands," he bit out. He wrested it from her grip, returning it yet again to the wrong shelf.

Emmaline directed her eyes to the ceiling. Who'd have imagined Lord Drake would be squeamish when it came to a gothic novel?

"I am purchasing it, my lord." She snatched it back from the shelf and held it protectively to her chest. She hadn't had a say in the man she would wed, not one aspect of her future. She would be damned if she would be denied a say in her reading choice.

"I should have expected you would be interested in one of the most controversial novels, and one about a great love affair." His words fairly dripped with condescending irony.

Her eyes narrowed. "I beg your pardon?"

"I said, you're filling your head with extreme nonsense. You'd be better served by reading the classics." He paused. "I do not want to see you suffer, Lady Emmaline." Drake's usual jade eyes had lightened to a gentle moss shade, and Emmaline read something warmly protective in his expression.

And she realized—*he's concerned about me.* The realization nearly bowled her over. For years he'd been indifferent but now, he seemed utterly panicked on her behalf. Warmth filled her.

"I'm concerned about you," he said, as if he'd read her thoughts.

There was something seductive about his softly spoken words. Emmaline swayed toward him.

"I say, are you all right?" His hand shot out to steady her.

She gave her head a small shake. "Fine."

Drake swiftly dropped his hands from her person and redirected his attention to the volume held against her bosom. "Of all the silly, nonsensical things to read."

So they were back to that, were they? "You sound like my brother."

A sound caught in his throat. "Don't ever say that."

Emmaline crossed her arms at her chest. "Well, you do. He's so hidebound when it comes to what I read, so very ducal. And you, you aren't a duke, but..." She gave an exaggerated sigh. "You will step neatly into the role, I imagine."

"You're an impertinent thing." He took another step toward her and her arms fell back to her sides. She took yet another step back. "And I will say just one more time, enough comparing me to Sebastian."

A palpable tension radiated from his person, as he eyed her with a hard glint in his eyes, and she knew better than to debate the point.

"Have you ever read a Gothic novel, my lord?"

Drake snorted. "I would never waste my time with such drivel."

His reaction killed any of the earlier warmth she'd felt toward him.

"By your own admission, you've never so much as read a Gothic novel." She clicked her tongue. "Tsk, tsk, I would have never thought you were so stodgy and judgmental to develop such an uninformed opinion."

Drake's shoulders drew back. Emmaline wasn't certain if he had taken particular offense at being called stodgy or judgmental. Or perhaps both.

"Lady Emmaline, that book," he jabbed a finger in the direction of the offending work, "has set Society on its ear. Every lord and lady named in that work is outraged. They are shunning anyone who reads or supports the cowardly author who wrote it."

An inelegant snort escaped her. "I assure you, no one gives a fig what novel I'm reading." *Even if it is one of the most scandalous works of the Season*, she silently added. "Not to mention, with the exception of you and Sophie, no one else knows."

"That does not condone it." His jaw hardened.

And because she knew it would infuriate him…she laughed in his face. "You're acting like an old, strait-laced gentleman." She waved her hand. "I would never have taken you as one who feared Society's ridicule. Nor, for that matter, would I believe you naïve. Do you truly believe the entire *ton* isn't scrambling to secure a copy?"

Drake growled low in his throat and for the first time since he'd come upon her in the bookshop, Emmaline became truly nervous. She took a tentative step away from him, having forgotten she'd run out of backward steps, until she collided with the shelving. She sidled to the left of him. Perhaps she had gone a touch too far.

"I'll just be going," Emmaline said, as though she'd not just offended a lord who was not used to being offended, insulted, or anything else she'd done to him that day. She would have stepped around Drake but his arm again shot out, and he pulled her close, his lips a hairsbreadth from her own.

"Doddering old man?" His hot, softly spoken words whispered against her lips, tickling them.

Emmaline licked her lips. Even through the silk fabric of her gown, her skin heated where he touched her waist. "I didn't call you doddering…" Her words trailed off when Drake's eyes dropped to her lips.

Before she could form another coherent thought, his mouth was on hers, hot, intent, with purpose.

Emmaline froze, stunned by the unexpectedness of her first kiss, then her body weakened as she curled against Drake, and she who had never before been kissed, kissed him back, eagerly.

She had often dreamed of what her first kiss would be like…had always assumed it would be with her betrothed, but this, this she had not been prepared for, nay, could never have prepared for. His lips were firm and when a sigh escaped her, his tongue took advantage and slipped inside, plundering, devouring, tasting.

Emmaline moaned and she reached up to tangle in the silk strands of his longer than fashionable golden mane.

She moaned. "Drake." The breathy entreaty obviously jolted him; his body jerked as if he'd been struck.

He set her from him with such alacrity she almost lost her footing. Ever the gentleman, his hands shot out to steady her. Drake scanned the area around them, as if to ascertain whether or not they'd been discovered.

Emmaline tried to fight a stab of hurt. "You don't have to look so relieved," she said, hating the way her words broke, wishing she could remain composed.

Drake dragged a hand through his hair. What the hell had he done here? Then his eyes took in Emmaline's swollen lips, the loose brown strands that had come down around her shoulders—and he knew exactly what had overcome him. A sweet fire had glinted in her eyes as she'd challenged him and Drake had needed to taste that passion on her lips. It was vastly easier to focus on the flare of desire between them than on the tumult of emotions that he couldn't explain.

He cleared his throat. "You should be relieved you haven't been discovered with that book."

"So we are back to that again, my lord? Very well, I'd like to issue you a challenge."

"I'm sorry?"

She sighed. "Perhaps your age has affected your ability to hear, my lord."

His eyes narrowed. "I'm not old."

"A challenge, then my lord."

Drake's mind went down a whole series of seductive, sexual paths, that all ended with Emmaline on her back, silken waves fanned out upon his pillow, arms outstretched, legs parted...

"A challenge?" His words came out gravelly to his own ears. He shifted to ease the ache that had settled in his groin, praying his betrothed didn't glance down and see the large bulge at the front of his breeches.

She held the volume of *Glenarvon* out to Drake.

He took it and she continued. "We will each purchase a copy and read it. Whoever finishes the book first may call in whichever demand they want from the losing party."

Drake fought down another rush of images; Emmaline on her knees, taking his length between her lips, sucking him…"And what will those terms be, Lady Emmaline?" he asked hoarsely.

She gave a toss of her head, apparently having no idea that her every movement enflamed his passions. "Why, I would like to be taken on a picnic. What do *you* desire, my lord?"

A sound, very near a groan, lodged in his throat. He gave his head a violent shake.

Emmaline's brow furrowed. "You must want something." Her eyes went wide and she up held a finger. "I have it, my lord. If *you* win, I shall make it a point to avoid whichever event you attend for an entire week."

Drake froze; his tongue could not move to form words.

If he won this silly wager, she would cease pestering him? He should leap at the opportunity. Why then did the thought of not seeing her rest like a pit in his stomach? He told himself it was because he welcomed the diversion she presented. It was nothing more than that. He'd begun to enjoy their subtle repartee.

"A week," he said. He hated the sadness that clouded her eyes, and felt like a bastard who'd kicked a kitten. It was on the tip of his tongue to argue the terms were not his, but rather her own. He held out his hand.

Emmaline hesitated, then reached out and placed her small white gloved fingers in his. "How will we know whether the other is being truthful?"

A smile tugged at his lips. "In other words, my lady, how will you know if I've actually held my word? Tsk, tsk. I'm insulted. What about a test of sorts? Whoever completes the reading first will have to answer a series of questions about the book."

Emmaline nodded and gave a slight but firm shake. She had a stronger grip than most gentlemen he knew.

"I bid you good day, my lord. Oh, and one more thing." She plucked the copy of *Glenarvon* from his free hand. She turned dismissively to go and pay for her volume.

Drake frowned. "What about my copy?"

Emmaline continued down the long aisle. "That is not my problem." She tossed over her shoulder, and then disappeared around the shelf at the front of the establishment.

Her victorious giggle echoed throughout the store.

Drake grinned. The little minx.

The gauntlet had been thrown.

FOURTEEN

My Dearest Lord Drake,
I sometimes wonder if we had not been betrothed, would Fate have
intervened to see us wed anyway? I like to believe so.
Ever Yours,
Emmaline

Drake stared up at the canopy above his bed. Eerie shadows, cast by the small fire in the hearth danced off the fabric and walls of his room.

The memories were worse at night. In the late hours, when the inky black fingers of the evening sky had stolen the last of daylight, Drake heard things; sounds, people. The hum was sometimes so deafening he would clamp his hands tightly over his ears and rock back and forth on the edge of the bed, willing the ghosts of fallen friends to release him, forgive him for living when they remained forever on the battlefields.

The irony didn't escape him—the decision to enlist had been entirely his own. He'd been motivated by resentment for his father's high-handed manipulation of his life. Drake hadn't even been allowed the opportunity to decide which university he would attend. Instead, it had been stated in no uncertain terms he would attend Eton and Oxford, just as his father had, and his father's father, etcetera, etcetera...

Drake had known early on all the responsibilities that went with being the only son and heir to the powerful Duke of Hawkridge. He'd even had a clear idea he would be expected to one day marry for his title. What Drake had resented was being robbed of the choice as a mere boy.

The day Drake had coolly informed his father of his enlistment, the Duke of Hawkridge had slammed his fist onto his desk and threatened to have the King strip him of his commission. When all was said and done, his father hadn't interfered.

He'd imagined nothing could be more horrendous than the Duke of Hawkridge's controlling influence. He shook his head.

The time he'd spent fighting had proven just how naïve he'd been. Amidst the battering cold of icy rain, clad in a mud-drenched uniform, he'd dreamed of the day he'd return to White's and Brook's, Gentleman Jackson's, and all his other frequent haunts.

The day he'd returned from the Peninsula, he'd wanted nothing more than the easy comfort of his former life.

Society had different plans for the returned *hero*.

The only way Drake had managed to retain his grasp on sanity had been to bury himself in drink, women, and any other mindless pursuits. He'd made it a point to ignore his father's silent censure.

Drake forced his attention away from dark remembrances and to the novel he'd thrown haphazardly to the bed where it lay untouched… staring mockingly up at him.

Just the thought of his exchange with Emmaline at the Old Corner Bookstore chased away the demons dancing about his haunted mind.

Before she'd taken her leave from the bookshop, Emmaline had wished him luck.

It had turned out he would need it. The shopkeeper had looked visibly distressed that his only two copies of *Glenarvon* had walked out the door with his two loyal customers, leaving Drake copy-less. So had begun Drake's quest for the sought after, scandalous novel all the *ton* was fascinated by.

He'd spent hours scouring bookshops without success. He'd known whom to blame for his inability to attain a copy. At each respective establishment he'd visited, a note had been left with the shopkeeper for Lord Drake. It had contained one line. "Happy Hunting!"

Drake laughed at the memory of it and shook his head. What was it about her? She possessed a buoyant spirit that energized him in a way that reminded him he was very much alive.

In the end, Drake had prevailed and found a copy of the book. To prevent rumor of his reading-search from being bandied about Town, Drake had paid every shopkeeper a small fortune to keep his selection private.

He picked up the volume of *Glenarvon* and scoffed. What utter rubbish. Why the pages would be better served as kindling for a fire. He thumbed through the book, unable to stifle a smile at the caricatures of some of the *tons* leading members; Lady Jersey, there, plain for all to see. The patroness of Almack's fury had been so great, she'd banished the author from the hallowed assembly hall.

Lying down, he dragged another pillow under his head and opened the book.

Only because the minx had a significant lead on him.

Drake gave his head a shake. "I cannot believe I'm reading this." He fanned the pages, his eyes landing at a random point and read.

"She is even dangerously ill."
"And pray may I ask of what malady?" he replied, with a smile of scorn."
"Of one, Lord Glenarvon," she answered with equal irony," which will never endanger your health—of a broken heart."

Drake snorted. "What rubbish." He intended to tell his betrothed the next time he saw her.

He turned to the first chapter and began to read.

"Wake up, son. Wake up!"

Drake lunged up. Beads of sweat fell from his brow. He threw off his father's grip and the energy seeped from his tightly coiled body. He studied the room through a clouded haze of horror, as he tried to sort out where his physical body was.

His gaze collided with his father's. The Duke of Hawkridge said nothing. He never did after Drake recovered from one of his terrors.

Drake raked a hand across his face, and scrubbed it back and forth, with deliberate roughness. "I had a dream," he said.

The Duke of Hawkridge nodded somberly. "I know."

None would dare to believe that this man with his dressing gown rucked about his legs, kneeling at Drake's side with tears in his eyes was in fact the Duke of Hawkridge.

Drake took care to avoid his father's eyes. "I fell asleep. I shouldn't have." The last time he'd awakened from a nightmare to find his father next to him, he'd looked into the duke's eyes and found them filled with pity, guilt, and regret—it had been too much for Drake.

"You have to sleep." His father awkwardly patted Drake's hand.

This is how it went when the nightmares came. Afterwards, neither of them knew what to say.

Hawkridge began slowly. "About your betrothal…"

Drake's eyes slid closed. He braced for the lecture. His father was choosing this moment to speak to him about his responsibilities?

"I want you to know, I…I want you to be happy. I will…" the Duke of Hawkridge fumbled, seeming to search for the right word, "terminate the terms of the agreement, if that is what you so wish."

Drake didn't say anything. The irony of the duke's offer was not lost on him. If those words had been spoken eight years earlier, how different would his life be? His rash decision to enlist would never have come to pass.

Oddly, the offer now left Drake with a feeling of emptiness inside. *Take it, accept his offer and sever the contract.* It would be the ultimate victory over his father's will.

He opened his mouth to speak.

Then tried again.

But the words wouldn't come.

It may have had something to do with the fact that for the first time since he'd returned from the Peninsula, he felt blessedly alive. Lying in the arms of stunningly beautiful courtesans, playing at the gaming tables, none of it had elicited anything from Drake.

Somehow Lady Emmaline had succeeded where nothing else had—she'd made him feel human again. When he was with her, he laughed, made jests. She made him feel a whole host of emotions he'd never thought to experience again.

And Drake was loath to lose the thin grasp on humanity she provided.

He scrubbed the back of his hand over his eyes. "I'm tired."

Hawkridge stood a little too quickly, a demonstration of his discomfort with the state of his son's well-being. "Yes, yes, then. Please think about what I've said." He held a hand up, reached out, and then swiftly dropped it back to his side.

Drake watched him leave, thinking about what his father had said, and even more, thinking about why it was so hard to consider accepting the offer.

FIFTEEN

My Dearest Drake,
I have a confession. I am lonely. How odd, to have a mother, a father, a
brother and frequent visitors, and yet still be lonely…I wish you'd come
home soon and take me away from it all.
Ever Yours,
Emmaline

S omewhere amidst the crush of people who had shown up for the musical event of the Season, Lord Drake was present.

The Earl and Countess of Cranford had all daughters; five of them to be exact, which provided a sufficient number for a whole evening's worth of musical entertainment. The young ladies, ranging from seventeen to two and twenty, were as gifted musically as they were stunning examples of golden, blue-eyed, English beauty. Each lady possessed a crystal-clear tone and broad range that would make a choir of angels green with envy. And thus, the event had become the only musicale that members of the *ton* looked forward to.

Emmaline scanned the hall.

Lord Sinclair had sent around a note indicating Lord Drake would be in attendance. She glanced over at her mother, engrossed in conversation with Lady Bloom, who therefore couldn't notice Emmaline's pointed search for Lord Drake. It was bad enough Emmaline had to deal with Sebastian's censure over her pursuit of her betrothed. She didn't relish the prospect of having to fend off Mother's disapproval, as well.

Emmaline caught her lower lip between her teeth. Lord Sinclair had insisted Drake would be present and yet...this wasn't her betrothed's usual entertainment. No, he'd far prefer balls where he could receive the attentions of scandalous, voluptuous widows. She could not even begin to speculate as to Drake's motives in attending the annual musicale. There must be some woman in attendance who'd captured his interest.

Her mother touched the small of her back and Emmaline started. She'd not realized Lady Bloom had taken her leave.

"Your brother is speaking to Lord Waxham," her mother said.

Emmaline followed her mother's gaze to the opposite end of the hall, to where Sebastian conversed with Lord Waxham. The two men had been close friends for longer than she could remember. The relationship had begun at Eton, and over the years Waxham had been a frequent visitor to their London townhouse.

Of late, Sebastian had begun to mention Lord Waxham with an increasing frequency. Emmaline could only take that to mean Sebastian had despaired of anything truly coming of her betrothal to Drake.

Emmaline sighed. 'Twas a dark day indeed when one's brother angled to secure a suitor for his still-betrothed sister.

Sebastian slapped Waxham on the back and the two gentlemen started in Emmaline and her mother's direction.

Emmaline groaned.

Mother's sharp gaze of disapproval snapped in her direction. Her mouth flattened in a tight line. "Emmaline, be polite," she reprimanded, and then seemed to remember her own manners, for she presented a smile for anyone who happened to notice.

"I cannot survive Sebastian's tactless attempt at matchmaking. For the love of God, I'm betrothed, Mother."

"Don't be silly. He is not..."

Emmaline didn't pay attention to what her mother thought Sebastian was up to. Instead she scoured the room for an escape.

As if sensing her daughter's intentions, she gripped Emmaline's hand and effectively halted her retreat.

"My dear sister and mother! Don't they look beautiful?" Sebastian asked loud enough for those around to hear.

Emmaline winced. If she could throttle her brother for his less-than-tactful approach, she'd do it right there.

Her mother's brows narrowed.

Emmaline dipped a curtsy and greeted him. "Lord Waxham."

"Two very beautiful ladies," Waxham said. His deep baritone was both masculine and pleasant. But he was not Drake. He bowed and flashed Emmaline a smile.

A tide of guilt swept over her. It was hardly Waxham's fault that her brother was...well, her brother. "How are you this evening, my lord?"

He grinned. "Better now."

A wave of heat flooded her cheeks.

From an objective point of view, she could admit Waxham was a handsome gentleman, even if he was Drake's counter-opposite. Though both gentlemen stood a good several inches past six feet, Waxham was still a smidgeon shy of Drake's towering frame. With Waxham's dark, almost Gypsy-like coloring hinting at his Roman ancestry, he was Lucifer to Drake's Michael the Archangel. Still, Waxham happened to be in possession of the most magnificent dark curls Emmaline would have traded her left pinky for.

The dark devil captured her hand for a kiss, his eyes sparkling at Emmaline's perusal and she scrunched her toes in embarrassment at being caught.

"Lady Emmaline, will you be regaling us with a song, following the scheduled performances of Lord Cranford's daughters?" Waxham asked.

An inelegant snort escaped Emmaline. She covered her mouth with a gloved hand. "I'm not foolish enough to follow such lovely voices, particularly when my pitch is as flat as my—"

Her mother's eyes shot up to her hairline. "Emmaline, why isn't that Miss Winters?" Her question emerged as a high-pitched squeak.

Truly, did her mother think Emmaline would be so inappropriate as to mention her attributes in the midst of Lord and Lady Cranford's music hall? One side glance in her mother's direction, indicated that very thing.

"I was going to say my fresh pressed gloves." Emmaline added with a teasing smile. She wiggled a glove about for Waxham's inspection.

He laughed, earning an audience of curious stares from the surrounding *ton*.

His unrestrained mirth was infectious. Emmaline joined him laughing. "No, no I don't see her, Mother." Her eyes narrowed.

The Marquess of Drake stood conversing with Lord Sinclair and Lady Smythe. The cad didn't even notice Emmaline standing at the opposite side of the hall.

Literally, the opposite side of the hall. Why, if she held her arm perfectly straight and followed it one hundred paces, she'd jab him in the chest with her fist…which was certainly no less than he deserved.

The audacity of the man, carrying on with that woman right under her nose. Oh, this would not do.

"I do see her after all, Mother. If you will excuse me, Lord Waxham." She dipped a hasty curtsy and set out to greet Sophie and if along the way she happened to bump into Drake, well, then that couldn't be helped.

In the end, she settled for running into Lady Smythe, garbed in a gown so fine it was almost sheer, made of the reddest satin and trimmed in black Italian lace. The satin had been purposefully dampened so it clung to each curve of her body. Could she be any more garish? *For the love of God, the woman had only recently been widowed. She might as well dance a merry jig on her poor late husband's grave.*

Emmaline raised a hand to her mouth. "Oh, my lady, my deepest apologies. Imagine me stepping where I shouldn't have. It is just a reminder that one must tread carefully."

The widow's mouth fluttered in a way reminiscent of a rainbow trout Emmaline had once caught. The poor thing had flapped about helplessly on the shore, before she'd taken pity on it, removed her hook, and set him free. She still remembered how graceful the fish had been as it leapt into the air, his body twisting, relishing in his release, before disappearing below the water's surface.

Lady Smythe, however, was no fish. Instead, she was the one with her hook sunk deep where it didn't belong.

Emmaline directed her attention to Lord Sinclair before the widow could speak. She dipped a deep curtsy and smiled. "Lord Sinclair, ever a pleasure."

Sinclair bowed, a conspiratorial smile on his lips. "Likewise, my lady."

"Lady Emmaline," Lady Smythe said frostily. "I believe your mother is beckoning, my dear." A mocking edge danced on those words in clear reminder that as a widow she was afforded luxuries that Emmaline herself was not.

Emmaline called on every ladylike lesson that had been drummed into her since birth to keep from slapping the other woman. "I assure you, I'm a woman and don't need to be beckoned like a child, Lady Smythe. Though I do see Lord Thurmond beckoning *you*." Every single member of the *ton* knew whose bed the indiscreet widow was warming.

An unbecoming red mottled the pale creature's cheeks. She gave a flounce of her black curls and then left on a huff.

Sinclair coughed, in a clear attempt to cover a laugh. Emmaline gave him a sly wink.

Drake's glower was black enough to smite a weaker person on the spot.

"I do believe Lord Drake has been delivered a slight by Lady Smythe. His ego is surely smarting from the insult," she whispered conspiratorially. She looked in the direction of Lady Smythe and Lord Thurmond, and studied the couple in a dramatically overlong fashion. She tapped a finger along her jaw. "I do say they make a striking pair, don't you agree?"

Fury fairly oozed from Drake's form. His jaw was set tight at a steely angle. "Have you had your ego bruised, my lord?" She made a pitying sound.

Sinclair leaned close and whispered back. "He does appear bothered."

Drake took Emmaline's forearm in a firm grasp and determinedly steered her away. She cast her gaze sideways. With his amicable smile and the seeming gentlemanliness of his arm looped through hers, the crowd would be wont to notice anything untoward in his reaction.

His manacle like hold on her person was unrelenting. He drew to an abrupt stop beside an alcove in the corner of the auditorium, sending Emmaline's still moving form pitching forward. "Oomph," she breathed.

His hands came up to steady her shoulders...until he seemed to remember his fury. "Are you done, Lady Emmaline?" he said, his tone frosty.

She schooled her expression. "Whatever do you mean, my lord?" If he'd expected or hoped for a meek debutante, well, he was destined for disappointment. Emmaline hadn't been a girl for a very long time. It was time he realized that. "I'm sorry. Have I embarrassed you in front of your friends and members of Society? How terribly insensitive."

Drake's mouth set in a hard, flat line. "You are making a fool of yourself, Lady Emmaline."

Her body jerked as though she'd been physically struck, and she felt the color drain from her cheeks. "Perhaps. But you *are* a fool, my lord."

His turbulent jade-green stare slid away but not before she detected a trace of something that resembled guilt, in his eyes.

No words he uttered could ever be adequate and yet she silently counted to ten, waiting for his apologies. When she reached fifteen, it became clear that he didn't intend to break his silence and her hurt gave way to rage. *The lout!*

She found solace in her anger; it strengthened her, drove away the humiliation. Emmaline shook out her skirts and made to step around him. His arm shot out in front of her. He pressed his hand against the opposite wall, effectively cutting off her escape.

"Move," she snapped.

Damn him.

Drake looked down at Emmaline through flinty eyes. He leaned close so his lips were scant inches apart from hers. "What is this game you play, Emmaline?"

And because Emmaline couldn't formulate one suitable response, she leaned up and kissed him.

He stiffened at the feel of her lips pressed to his. But then it was as though he was unable to fight the baser masculine urgency that demanded more. He took Emmaline in his arms and with only a flimsy satin curtain between them and Society, his mouth ravaged hers, his ministrations hard and demanding.

The hot taste of him, tinged with whiskey, sapped the strength from her muscles. Drake guided her hands up around his neck, and then anchored her against the hard wall of his chest. She clung to him. Then his hands were about her, gripping her buttocks, pulling her even closer against the hard length of his shaft.

Her moan was lost in his hot, skillful mouth.

It was that same moan that seemed to pierce Drake's desire. He jerked away from her with a hoarse groan. Horror flooded his eyes. His arms fell useless to his side.

Emmaline touched her fingers to her lips. In all the dreams she'd carried in her heart, in all her girlish yearnings of her betrothed, she had imagined his kiss. This passion, overwhelming in its power, moved beyond even what they'd shared in the Old Corner Bookshop. It made her ache to know more.

And yet...he was so coolly aloof, she could read nothing in him.

The detachedness of his response threatened to shatter her composure. How could he kiss her with such fever and then withdraw into this shell of a man? Something must have shaped him into a detached person incapable of warmth and affection.

The alcove curtain stirred.

"Emmaline?"

The sound of Emmaline's name being called from behind the fabric had the same effect as a bucket of freezing Thames water being dumped over her. She went motionless. Her gaze darted around the cloaked alcove, and collided with Drake's. "My brother," she mouthed.

He held a finger to his lips.

"Emmaline," Sebastian called in a faint whisper so as to not risk discovery.

She waited with breath held for him to continue on his way—all the while knowing with one word, one whisper, even so much as a sigh, her and Drake's intimate position would be revealed, and both of them would be forced into a union.

A marriage based on a compromising position was not what Emmaline dreamed of for herself. Other young ladies might only care about an advantageous match but Emmaline wanted more.

What might have been seconds or minutes felt like an endless stretch of time. They waited. And waited.

The soft tread of Hessian boots moved on and indicated that Sebastian had left.

"Emmaline," Drake whispered.

She slipped out of his arms and darted out from behind the curtains, leaving him alone.

Drake dropped his head against the wall and shook it back and forth. For one, inexplicable moment he'd wished Mallen had thrown back the curtain and discovered him and Emmaline. It would have meant her ruin and Drake would have been forced to do right by her.

Such senseless thinking would have only resulted in a miserable existence for Lady Emmaline Fitzhugh; uncertainty, fear, danger. Drake had committed enough wrongs in his life that he wasn't willing to add this unpardonable sin—even if he did desire her and the peace she managed to somehow bring him.

"Emmaline! Where were you?" A voice hissed.

Drake picked his head up.

He strained to hear Emmaline's muffled response.

"I assured Mother you knew what you were about but you are making a fool of yourself over Drake. You must have some pride," Mallen chided.

Drake's hands curled into fists at his side. How dare Mallen speak in that haughty tone to Emmaline? Just once he wanted to plant a left-handed jab into the other man's face, just bury a fist into his nose.

"This is neither the time nor the place, Sebastian."

Drake envisioned her with hands planted atop her gently-curved hips, a becoming flush on her cheeks, and all the desire he'd quashed earlier, came rushing back.

"You walked off on Waxham," Mallen charged. "It was rude of you. He's always been..."

The wicked trail Drake's thoughts had been meandering down, meandered right over the edge of a steep cliff. *Waxham?* What was this about?

"Enough, Sebastian," she bit out.

For once, Drake wanted Mallen to continue running his mouth because he wanted to know why, exactly, it should matter that Emmaline had walked off on Waxham and what Waxham had always been. Had Waxham always been like a brother to her? In love with her? What the hell had Waxham been? The unspoken words were perhaps worse than the not knowing. They made him gnash his teeth and want to bloody Waxham senseless.

"You need to be prepared, that is all I'm saying. Come. We'll discuss this on the way to London Hospital tomorrow." Mallen effectively ended the conversation.

Drake listened to the click of Mallen's boot steps in harmony with the pad of her soft silk slippers, until they were no more. Long after they'd gone, when the concert had already begun, Drake finally moved out from behind the spot, tormented by the bloody niggling question; what the hell was Emmaline's relationship with Lord Waxham?

He knew of the other man. Waxham was deep in the pockets, fond of the tables but not overly fond. Kept one mistress but didn't frequent houses of ill-repute. Had respectable stables of horseflesh, which he bred and raced. Sparred regularly at Gentleman's Jackson's and was quite good at it.

In sum, the other man was a bloody paragon.

And suddenly, Drake hated him for it.

He moved into view of the concert, filled with a restless fury. With the exception of a lovely lyrical soprano voice, the auditorium was silent. He spied Sinclair seated at the back of the room, the end seat next to him open and made his way over.

"There you are. Where the hell were you off to?" Sin whispered as Drake slid into the vacant seat. "It's bad enough I'm attending these events with you, quite another to be abandoned amidst match-making mamas."

He ignored Sinclair. From his vantage, he could appraise the entire hall. Where the hell was she?

Then he spotted brown tresses he'd recognize amidst any crowd. He pointedly ignored Sin's knowing chuckle. What had happened this evening? Whatever had transpired had been significant. For the life of him, he was incapable of looking at anyone but her.

He did not know what had compelled him to return her kiss and in nearly full view of the *ton*. And God help him, he could not rid himself of the taste of her lips or the eager way she'd sought his tutelage.

Drake tried to account for his fascination with Lady Emmaline, a woman he'd steered clear of for the better part of fifteen years. She was unlike every lady of his acquaintance. Those other women had perfected the art of coquetry. They fluttered their fans exactly the same, wore the same serene expressions.

On the contrary, Emmaline possessed a spirit that seemed indomitable. There was no mask where she was concerned. She made it quite clear exactly how she felt and made no apologies for it.

His eyes remained fixed on her.

And he became aware of something else.

"Waxham."

Sin cast a sideways look in his direction. "What?"

The gentleman seated beside Emmaline leaned down and whispered something into her ear. With a smile, she tipped her head up, and appeared to whisper something back before redirecting her attention to their host's eldest daughter, who'd just launched into an aria.

Mallen and Emmaline's discussion a short while ago replayed in Drake's mind. His gut tightened as an emotion that felt remarkably like jealousy reared its head. Just seeing Waxham seated beside Emmaline did something to Drake; something he did not like at all. He wanted to storm the room, drag Waxham up by the lapels of his jacket, and throw him out of the bloody recital hall.

It felt—primal.

Why should he care that Emmaline's smile was far too warm or her proximity to Waxham too close? Drake's hands balled into tight fists as he took in the overt glances the interloper directed toward Emmaline's too low décolletage.

How dare she flaunt herself so freely under his nose, in front of the *ton*, no less! His first order of business in the morning would be to pay a call on her and demand more appropriateness when they were amidst Society.

Drake focused on her flagrant display with Waxham and his own indignation at being made a fool of in front of the lords and ladies in attendance. His ferocity had absolutely *nothing* to do with the fact that he'd come to care for Emmaline.

Nothing at all...

Except...

Waxham whispered something else close to Emmaline's ear.

And the feeling of wanting to tear the man apart did not feel like nothing at all.

SIXTEEN

My Dearest Drake,
When I tend the gardens, I talk to my plants. Do you find that odd?
Sebastian does. He teases me mercilessly about it. I told him my plants
make for far better company than him.
Ever Yours,
Emmaline

"**Y**ou have a visitor, my lady."

Emmaline sat back on her heels so abruptly her elbow knocked the collection of gardening equipment she'd set haphazardly against the wrought iron bench. The array of metal shovels and hoes shifted, but managed to remain fixed to their spot.

Emmaline rubbed her injured elbow. "Can you direct my caller here?"

When the servant had left, she tugged the straw bonnet off her head, swiped her forearm across the sheen of perspiration that dampened her brow.

She'd not been expecting Sophie, and had planned on dedicating her day to cleaning up the weeds that had decided to infiltrate her London haven. They both had a mutual love for gardening and Sophie was usually eager to help. Emmaline set her bonnet back on and tied the ribbons underneath her chin.

Emmaline returned her attention to the lilies of the valley. She'd cultivated the sweet-smelling woodland plant several years ago. According to legend, the small, pure white buds represented a return to happiness and therefore, it was one of the flowers she liked to share with the soldiers who resided in London Hospital.

She trimmed back some of the buds, set the delicate ivory bellflowers into the basket next to her, and returned her attention to the next dainty row that needed rescuing from a cluster of weeds.

"I'm sorry I've been so neglectful, my dears. I've been busy in pursuit of my betrothed, and I feel my efforts in that score have only resulted in my neglect of you. It is unpardonable and I shan't let it happen again." She tugged a particularly stubborn weed that had wrapped around the base of the plant. She twisted it first left, then right, before yanking it straight up. "You are a tenacious one," she muttered.

"I would say the same of you, Lady Emmaline," a masculine voice drawled.

Emmaline careened backwards and landed in an inelegant heap upon her derriere at Drake's feet. She stared overly long at the tips of his perfectly shined black Hessian boots and gave thanks for the wide brim of her flat-brimmed hat that shielded the stain of mortification that warmed her cheeks.

Sebastian had forever mocked the bonnet, but now, more than ever, Emmaline had a deep appreciation for it. The brim kept Lord Drake blessedly out of view. When her face had cooled, she tilted it back. "You are not Sophie." The words came out faintly accusing.

Drake's firm lips twitched at the corners. "No, I am certainly not Miss Winters."

Emmaline toyed with the weed she still held in her hand. She could only imagine what Lord Drake thought about his betrothed working in a garden like any common servant. If he'd been scandalized by her preference for a gothic novel, well then this offense was surely tantamount to treason in his pompous eyes.

He continued to study her with that unreadable expression. The man must be a marvel at the gaming tables. She dropped the weed and scooped up a small bit of warm, moist soil, and sifted it through her fingers. A thin, slimy worm became caught between her fingers.

She released the creature. It slithered off, deeper into a safe patch of ground away from prying hands—out of sight.

A sigh of envy escaped her. *Lucky creature.* What she wouldn't herself give to have the ground open and swallow her deep into its hold of invisibility. She cast a hopeful gaze to the sky, willing the Good Lord to assist with a miracle.

Several moments later, Drake cleared his throat.

Emmaline sighed. Apparently the Lord was attending to more important miracles than rescuing one peculiar young lady from a healthy bout of humiliation.

She dusted her hands together. "Lord Drake."

Drake held out a hand.

Emmaline glanced down at her mud-spattered fingernails, and then placed it in Drake's, marveling at the strength of his long fingers wrapped so securely about hers. He effortlessly guided her to her feet, and she wondered that he should be so unaffected by the feel of their joined hands when it had sent her heart racing.

"Thank you, my lord," she murmured, bemoaning the loss of contact when he removed his hand from her grasp. She dusted off her hands upon the chintz apron she'd donned for gardening. Her small shovel and spade jangled in her front pockets.

"You garden."

"I am surprised to see you."

They spoke in unison.

"Yes, I garden." She frowned at the pile of weeds at their feet. "Though I fear I've been neglecting these far too long this Season."

A full smile turned Drake's lips. This wasn't the mocking grin she'd come to expect from him.

Her heart leapt erratically beneath her breast.

"Uh, yes, I overheard that as well," Drake said.

Her toes curled with mortification. Of course he'd heard that. And of course the day he chose to pay his first visit, she would be less than presentable. She grimaced. With her stained skirts, 'less than presentable' was being magnanimous.

To top off this splendidly disastrous day, he'd discovered her talking to plants...about him no less.

"I have a tendency to talk to my plants."

He said nothing and Emmaline felt all the more humiliated for the admission. *Stop talking, Em.*

Over Drake's shoulder, she caught sight of Grace as she entered the gardens. The maid sat on a bench near the entrance of the portcullis.

Emmaline waited for Drake to fill the void. She'd learned over the years; nothing her betrothed did was without careful deliberation. Something had brought him round to visit today...and she didn't think it had a jot to do with her stimulating company.

"I've come by for a reason."

And direct. Lord Drake was direct.

Well, they may as well get to the heart of it. Oh, but how nice it would have been if he'd merely come for a visit. She sighed. "What brings you here, my lord?"

"About last evening," he began. "I saw you and I must inquire as to your flirtation last evening."

In the full light of day, memories of her brazen kiss from the evening prior made her cringe. She toed the ground with the tip of her black boot, kicking aside a soft patch of mud. Oh, if she could just dig a hole and bury herself. "I-ah—it was merely a kiss." But it hadn't been just a kiss. In fact, it felt blasphemous to so slight that magical union of their lips.

A vein bulged at the left corner of his neck, the only indication of his tightly suppressed control. "Just a kiss?" he asked silkily.

Now she'd gone and done it. She'd offended his male pride. Emmaline waved her hand breezily, or rather gave her best attempt at breezy. "La, sir. You've kissed so many ladies. I cannot imagine my kissing one gentleman would rouse such a stuffy reaction." She cringed. *Had she really just said, La sir?*

"You kissed him, too?"

She scratched her forehead. "I kissed who, too?"

"Him," he growled.

"Do you mean, you?" His convoluted questioning was beginning to give her a megrim. "And I would hardly call it a flirtation," she added.

His eyes narrowed, the emerald deepening to a jade hue, as they were wont to do when he was irate. Emmaline had come to know Drake enough to recognize that telling reaction.

She placed her hands on her hips and glowered back at him. "How cowardly of you to blame me. I daresay you are of equal blame for what transpired last evening."

He took a step towards her and she scrambled away from him. She didn't believe he'd hurt her but still, gentlemen fought duels for lesser charges against one's character.

Drake's lip pulled back in a sneer. "Are you saying I'm at fault for what transpired between you and Waxham?"

Emmaline placed her foot on a moist patch of ground and felt her boots sink into the earth. She tried to tug it free, when his words registered. "Waxham?"

"Yes, Waxham," he bit out.

"Waxham?" *Whatever was he talking about?*

"You kissed him."

What?! "I kissed Waxham?"

His nostrils flared, and she realized he'd construed her question as a statement. "You think I kissed him." Emmaline snorted, and then she howled with laughter, hilarity shaking her frame until she doubled over with a stitch in her side. Tears of mirth smarted from behind her eyes. "A-are you d-daft?" She struggled to breathe. "I didn't kiss him."

Drake cocked his head to the side. "You didn't kiss him?"

She dashed a hand over her eyes. "No, you silly man. I kissed you."

He made a show of dusting the impeccable sleeve of his sapphire coat. "I saw you tilt your head, whisper, and smile up at him. I daresay I've engaged in enough flirtations to know the nuances of one. And I will not allow such flirtations to continue so long as we are betrothed."

Emmaline shook her head. "Oh, you are daft."

Had she been made of less stern stuff, the flinty gleam in his eyes would have caused her trepidation. But it would take more than that to make her run.

As if remembering they were not alone, Drake glanced over in Grace's direction. He lowered his voice to a near whisper. "I saw you with Waxham. After shamelessly kissing me, you hurried over to flirt with him. Mayhap you have set your cap on him if you can't bring me up to scratch."

Emmaline's hand flew out and she slapped him soundly on the cheek.

His head jerked back under the ferocity of the movement. He cradled his sore cheek. "Damn. For one so small, you can deliver quite the wallop."

He deserved more than that slap and still, guilt filled her at the crimson stain her fingers had left on his scarred cheek. "Uh, why thank you."

"It wasn't a compliment," he mumbled, his words somewhat muffled by the edge of his palm as he still held his cheek.

She jabbed him in the chest with her pointer finger.

"Ouch!"

"How dare you?" she demanded. "You come here." Another jab that forced him backwards. "And reprimand, me?" Another jab. This time he flinched. *Good!* "You, who have forgotten for the better part of fifteen years that I so much as exist," A fourth jab drove him back another step. "dare to address *my* behavior?"

"Grace, will you excuse us?" She ordered, not even bothering to look back at her maid.

"Very well, my lady," Grace called. The young woman's tone indicated she approved of Emmaline's outrage.

Emmaline redirected her attention on her betrothed. "How dare...?"

"I will not be subjected to another of your rants," he muttered.

He kissed her.

Drake tugged the silly, too-large bonnet from Emmaline's head. The hasty movement unsettled the precarious chignon in which her silken brown tresses had been arranged, and sent the chocolate waves tumbling to her waist. Had he really ever thought the color mousy? He tangled his fingers in the luxurious strands, angling his head to better avail himself to her mouth.

She whimpered, and her body melted against his like a Gunther's ice on a summer day. He held tight to her so she didn't dissolve into a puddle at his feet. Filling his hands with her gently rounded buttocks, he anchored her against his center.

"Drake," she moaned against his lips.

Another groan tore from his chest and he stroked her tongue with his. He ran his hands over her body in an attempt to explore the subtly seductive flare of her hips, the delicate swell of her buttocks.

He cupped her breast in his hand.

"Ohhh," she gasped.

The husky timbre of her voice drove him wild, and he ached to slide between her moist folds and stroke her with his length.

He wanted to take her here and now, right on the garden floor. He sat down on the bench and adjusted her on his lap which set the gardening tools clattering. That small tinkling of metal meeting metal penetrated his consciousness. Drake pulled away with infinite slowness. He placed one more lingering, kiss upon her swollen lips and rested his brow atop hers. His breathing labored and harsh blended with the loud beat of his heart and made thinking difficult.

What hold did Lady Emmaline Fitzhugh have over him? When he was with her all logic and reason fled. Enough of his life was riddled with bouts of lost control. But she was like a tonic he could not live without, and whether he liked it or not, whether he wanted it or not, he craved her with an intensity that bordered on physical pain.

Emmaline's breathing settled into a normal cadence. He stroked the small of her back, grateful at the time she took regaining her composure for it afforded him the same opportunity.

She spoke first. "Waxham is a friend of my brother's."

Apparently his kiss wasn't as powerful as he liked to think. She hadn't forgotten the reason for his earlier upset, the reason he'd kissed her into silence.

She went on. "Waxham has been like a brother to me."

In spite of her words, Drake felt that awful emotion, he was beginning to recognize all too well as jealousy, rise in his throat, and nearly choke him. Emmaline might view Waxham as a brother but Drake had recognized the very appreciative male gleam in Waxham's eyes. There had been nothing brotherly in the way he'd eyed Emmaline. "I don't care about your relationship with him. I worry about how it reflects on our betrothal," he lied. A bloody pathetic lie.

That callously insensitive remark drove Emmaline from him and replaced all warmth in her eyes with a sheen of coolness. Drake regretted the transformation even as he knew he was the cause of it.

"You're worried about our betrothal, my lord?" She mocked. "Now? After all these years? After three Seasons? *Now*, it bothers you who I converse with?"

Drake braced himself for another assault from her finger.

Then the fight seemed to go out of her. The sparks glimmered, flickered, and finally dimmed. She hugged her arms across her stomach. "I am tired of this."

Drake's brows dropped.

"I don't want to do this anymore," she whispered.

"Then stop dogging my every step."

As soon as the harsh words left his mouth, he wanted to call them back.

The sad, detached expression she wore tugged somewhere in the vicinity of his chest and filled him with panic, a fear that he had said something irrevocable. He fished for another rejoinder, to rouse some other emotion than the defeated one she now wore. He wanted to redirect her thoughts away from...from...

From what?

Giving him exactly what he wanted?

Except of a sudden he realized he didn't know exactly what it was he wanted anymore. He'd spent nearly fifteen years lashing out over the betrothal he'd been committed to as a child. It had redefined his relationship with his father, had resulted in Drake fleeing to fight on the Peninsula. He'd built up years and years of resentment toward Lady Emmaline, who'd herself been a victim of their circumstances.

In a short span of time, he'd come to the realization that nothing was or had been as it seemed for perhaps, ever—and it left him feeling off-balance. It was as if the world had been flipped upside down and he was hanging on by his fingernails.

Crash!

Drake flung himself on top of Emmaline, and knocked her to the ground, burying her body beneath his.

His breath came fast as he waited for the crack of the gunshots, the ensuing cries and screams. They never came. His mind remained embroiled in the hellish world of roaring cannon fire and the blinding thickness of gunpowder smoke.

"Drake."

Drake's heart hammered wildly in his chest and under any other circumstance he would have luxuriated in the feel of Emmaline's lean, lithe body under his. In that particular moment, however, mind-numbing terror gripped him in a tight vise. It sucked the air from his lungs.

Emmaline wrestled a hand from between them stroked back the hair that had tumbled across his brow. "It was just the tools," she whispered, as though speaking to a fractious mare. "They fell. All is well," she assured him.

It wasn't Emmaline's words that reached through his tortured remembrances and wrenched him back to reality, but the soft, soothing cadence of her voice that penetrated the devil's unyielding hold.

She stroked his cheek. Drake leaned into her touch. His eyes slid closed, needing her touch. It was like a balm on his wounded soul.

Please, don't stop touching me. In Emmaline's embrace he felt... whole. Drake swallowed painfully and through sheer will forced himself to pick up his head. Emmaline's troubled eyes caught and lingered on the vivid scar traversing his cheek. He flinched under her scrutiny.

She spoke again. "Are you all right?"

His mind conjured a trail of blood beneath her fingertips as she traced the mark.

"I-I am sorry," he stuttered and climbed to his feet. He helped her up from the ground. "Have I hurt you?" *Of course you hurt her, you bloody monster.*

Emmaline shook her head. "No, no, I'm not—"

"Please, forgive me." In his haste to be free of the nightmare unfolding before him, he stumbled backwards, and tripped over the metal gardening tools.

Emmaline reached for him but he recoiled.

He mustered a hasty, distracted bow and fled.

SEVENTEEN

My Dearest Drake,
I had a nightmare last night. I dreamt the war had ended and you
forgot to come home. You were wandering about an empty field. If you
forget how, promise you will write me...I will help you.
Ever Yours,
Emmaline

Emmaline sat on the window-seat in the Floral Parlor. Her copy
of *Glenarvon* rested haphazardly upon her lap. She surveyed the
gardens below.

On any other day, the small patch of nature, awash in the glow of
the sun's bright slanting rays, would have soothed her. She pressed her
forehead against the cool pane and stared down. Not this day.

With all of the hurts Drake had unknowingly inflicted, it should be
easy for her to go to Sebastian and request he terminate the betrothal
contract.

Except this morning in the gardens with Drake changed everything.

Resting her chin on her knees, she rubbed it back and forth over
the smooth fabric of her dress. Funny, the greatest concern she'd had
upon waking had been the neglect she'd shown toward the gardens.

How could so much change in the span of a few hours? Her earlier
concerns about the weeds and her garden sanctuary now seemed so
trivial. She didn't think she would ever be able to see her garden as
any sort of refuge again. Not when it had revealed the inner Hell that
gripped Drake.

When Drake had been on the Peninsula, she had penned him a note each day he'd been gone. She'd signed every letter. Sealed them. And stuffed them into the bottom of her trunk.

Reflecting back on the contents of the notes, she cringed. In her unsent letters she'd blathered to him about the mundane. She'd gone on and on about her aggravation with her brother and lamented the boredom she felt in the country. There had never been a moment when she'd truly stopped to think about Drake's time on the Peninsula. She hadn't stopped to consider that Drake had been a young man who would be irrevocably changed by his experience.

That wasn't to say she hadn't worried over his safety or thought about what he was seeing and doing—she had, every day. But she hadn't thought about war in the graphic sense. Instead, she'd seen it as more of a grand adventure. Why, he'd had the opportunity to travel and see different landscapes and meet exotic individuals, who were most definitely not the prim, proper members of English society.

She hadn't been able to think about the violence and death that went with war...until she'd confronted the soldiers who'd returned to London Hospital. Still, even visiting the wounded soldiers, Drake had somehow seemed removed from those men who'd lost limbs and eyes. The physical scars they bore were very obvious. Drake however, had returned physically intact and yet, how hard it must be for him to move about Society scarred, but in ways that only he knew. How very lonely for him.

Her fingers distractedly toyed with the copy of *Glenarvon* in her lap, fanning the pages, and absently thinking about her unsent notes. All those years ago, she'd written letters but had been too much of a coward to send. After all, why would a man who'd sought out a war to avoid her, ever welcome any words from her?

Now she wished she'd sent them. Perhaps she would have made a fool of herself and he would have continued to view her as an empty-minded young child, but it might have brought him some comfort to receive a note from the world he'd left behind. Instead, she'd waited for him to return, so selfishly focused on what his arrival meant for her life and her happiness that she hadn't thought about his happiness—or worse, his lack of happiness.

She'd only been capable of a girlish self-centeredness. It hadn't been until mere hours ago that she'd truly understood Drake was no longer the boy who'd sat across from her when their betrothal documents had been signed.

She snorted. No wonder he hadn't wanted a thing to do with her then, or even now. To Drake, she had been a child with childish interests.

The realization shamed her. She was humbled with the extent of her self-absorption.

Emmaline laid her cheek on her emerald muslin skirts, staring unseeing out the window. The fabric's deep rich hue bore a similarity to the color of his eyes. She had never before seen eyes as haunted as Drake's had been that morning—and with the time she'd spent in London Hospital she'd seen her fair share of misery.

A spasm wracked her heart and she took a deep, shuddery breath. She yearned to hold him close, soothe his hurt.

A warm drop landed on her hand, then two, and absently she realized she was crying. She swiped her hand across her cheeks. Emmaline cast a despondent stare up toward the sky. She squinted under the brightness of the sun's rays that reflected off the glass panels and shot prisms of light around the parlor walls.

If today Drake had walked away from her the same man she'd come to know these many years, detached and indifferent, then it would have been easy to march into Sebastian's office and request that he dissolve the betrothal contract.

Drake, however, was far more complicated than she'd ever known. He was scarred, hurting, and it surely explained much of his distantness. She could no sooner walk away from her lifelong commitment to him than she could cut off her own arm.

It wasn't pity that held her to him. It was something more, something deep that defied years of bitterness and resentment. When she'd witnessed him reduced to a near shell of the man he was, she had wanted nothing more than to cradle him in her arms and take away his fear, make it her own.

"You were missed at breakfast, my dear."

Emmaline started at the intrusion. She sat up and swiped her hand discreetly across her cheeks. "Mother," she murmured, keeping her eyes averted.

The robin's-egg blue seat cushion dipped under her mother's slight weight. "I understand you had a visitor this morning."

Emmaline again rested her ear upon the cradle of her knees.

"And that he left rather hastily and seemed to be quite upset."

Emmaline chewed her lip, her heart tripping painfully at the horror Drake had worn blanketed across every crease, every line of his face. The horrified jade pools of his eyes were testament to the fact he'd stared down the bowels of Hell and lived to speak of it.

Except he didn't speak of it.

Society had no idea that the carefree, elegant lord sought after by every lady, was in fact tortured, and battling demons no one could ever suspect.

"Emmaline, my dear. What happened today?"

Emmaline opened her mouth to speak but nothing came out. This was her mother. The woman who had given her life, who'd cradled her close after numerous scrapes. She wanted to discuss the scene in the gardens, but even as the words were poised on the tip of her tongue, she bit them back. To air Drake's secrets would be a betrayal. He'd spent these past years cultivating an image of himself for Society, and she'd not rob him of that—not even for her mother.

Her mother wrinkled her brow. "Emmaline?"

Emmaline settled for a meager explanation. "I believe there is more to Lord Drake than anyone truly sees."

Her mother's probing stare bore into Emmaline and she resisted the urge to fidget like a little girl who'd been caught sneaking away from her governess.

"Does this—" her mother paused, "more, merit your waiting for him to finally make you his wife?" Her mother continued. "I spoke to Sebastian. He only wants you to be happy. I am of like mind."

Surely her mother wasn't saying what she thought she was? "Mother?"

Her mother stroked the crown of her head. "You know my dear, even as I respected your father's commitment to the betrothal contract, there has always been a part of me that has ached for all the opportunities you missed."

Emmaline made a dismissive sound. "I haven't missed anything." She strove to reassure her mother, but they both knew Emmaline wasn't being truthful.

Mother went on like Emmaline hadn't spoken. "Oh, at the time, the arrangement between our families made tremendous sense, and I respected your father's meticulous planning of your future. It had seemed right at the time, safe…" She paused. A sigh escaped her. "I have watched as the years slipped away, Emmaline. Watched you grow and mature and have felt a longing for you to have a real, un-entangled Season. I've wanted the pleasure of seeing you courted, of seeing suitors arrive with bouquets of flowers, and penning sonnets lauding your beauty. How selfish is that of me, my dear?"

A wave of guilt swept over Emmaline for silently agreeing with her mother's words. Nonetheless, she shook her head emphatically. "You have never been selfish."

Mother's throat worked, bobbing up and down.

Oh, please don't cry. I cannot bear it when you cry.

"I have deprived you of those experiences that by rights should have been yours. And should you so desire them, I will see that they are made available to you."

In other words—her mother would support a termination of the contract. The thought of her betrothal being severed caused Emmaline's chest to constrict painfully in a way that made breathing difficult. "Thank you, Mother. I—I am not yet certain."

Her mind steeped in logic told her to simply state the words her mother had given her leave to speak. Her heart, at that precise moment, called them back, froze them on the tip of her tongue.

Soft hazel eyes caressed her face. "Just say the words. You will be freed." She pressed a kiss to Emmaline's brow, stroking back the tendril that had escaped its chignon and dangled over her eye. "Shall I remain with you?" The strand again sprung loose.

Emmaline shook her head, brushing it back behind her ear. "I am fine, Mother." The last thing she wanted was company.

So of course at that moment Sebastian strolled into the room.

"What's going on here?" he drawled lazily. He dropped into the mahogany rose-velvet sofa adorned with winged lions and stretched his legs out in front of him.

God, she hated that sofa; those nasty lions were all the rage. The beastly piece of decor rather ruined her favorite room in the house. In fact, she might have sought out another room, if it weren't for the view of the gardens.

"Are you almost ready? We'll be late to the hospital." she asked, desperate for escape. Scrambling to her feet, she tried to hurry him out. "Let's go."

"We were discussing Lord Drake," their mother explained.

Emmaline wanted to stamp her foot. She handled them quite well on her own but when Mother and Sebastian were together, they were quite grating. "Can we do this later?"

Sebastian's dark green eyes narrowed to unreadable black slits. "What about him? What is there to discuss, other than whether or not you want to end this farce of a betrothal?"

She probably had the only guardian in the entire Kingdom this eager to sever ties with one of the most powerful titles simply because his sister was not happy. Sebastian seemed to take Drake's disinterest as a personal slight. And Emmaline loved him for that.

Mother's gaze alternated between Emmaline and Sebastian. "I've already spoken with Emmaline on the matter, Sebastian."

They both ignored her.

"I asked you to trust me," Emmaline snapped at her brother.

He sprung from his leisurely pose; his spine stiffened as all feigned attempts at nonchalance disappeared. "And I told you yes, but with limits. You have been making a fool of yourself, Em. This is what you expect me to trust? You want me to blindly look away while you arrange your schedule to—"

This time she couldn't help it...she stamped her foot. "I certainly don't want you confronting him and trying to force his hand!"

A slight knock and the sudden appearance of a servant at the door cut off Sebastian's diatribe. Emmaline was never more grateful for the sudden appearance of another person in her life.

A liveried servant came forth with a silver tray bearing an envelope. He cleared his throat. "Pardon, the interruption. You have a note, my lady."

She accepted the envelope, aware of her mother and brother intently studying the parchment in her hands.

Recognizing the dark, strong scrawl at the front as distinctly different from Sophie's wide, flowing letters, Emmaline turned the thick ivory envelope over in her hands. She noted the lion-emblazoned gold seal and trailed a fingertip along the raised surface. She hesitated and lifted the blade from the servant's tray. Her fingers trembled as she slid the tip under the seal and withdrew the note.

"My Dear Lady,
I cannot believe you enjoy reading this drivel. I am writing to inquire as to your progress with your copy. And of course, to ask after your well-being.
—Drake

All day she'd been consumed with anxiety of how Drake would address what had transpired in the gardens. Her greatest fear had been that he would humble himself with an apology he need not make.

A burst of relieved laughter escaped her.

Sebastian had been the Duke of Mallen for almost three years, and most of the time epitomized the role to perfection. This time was not one of them. In his haste to sit up, he almost slipped off the sofa. "What does it say?"

Maybe if she'd been weaker she would have given him the information he sought. But this was still the same brother whose steps she'd dogged, the same brother she'd played pranks on as a young girl, and to her, he would always fit that role.

She waved the note in the air. "It says you're a nosy busy-body who can't mind his business."

The Duchess of Mallen looked to Sebastian. "Perhaps he has finally come to his senses?"

Sebastian snorted. "I'll believe it when she's marching down the aisle on my arm," he said.

A smile played about Emmaline's lips. If she had her way that was just how it would be.

EIGHTEEN

Dearest Drake,
I wonder if you even know my middle name. As my betrothed, I rather
feel you should. It is Rose. I'm not much of a rose. Sebastian forever tells
me I'm more of a thorn upon the rose. I would like to tell you what I call
him, but that wouldn't be ladylike.
Ever Yours,
Emmaline

Drake had convinced himself to send 'round a note to the Earl
and Countess of Mooring, offering up his regrets for their
annual ball. After what had transpired earlier that morn, coward that
he was, Drake had wanted to avoid his betrothed.

He'd sat down to dash a note to the Earl and Countess of Mooring,
making his excuses. For the better part of an hour, he'd stared down
at a blank piece of parchment. In the end, all he'd done was drip black
all over his desk.

Lady Emmaline was some kind of enchantress who'd managed to
weave a magical spell over him, depleting him of his wisdom, leaving
him well and truly—bewitched. For at that moment, in spite of his
intentions to avoid her, Drake stood behind the Earl of Mooring's pink
marble pillars and studied Emmaline.

He'd known Emmaline since she was a small girl and had only ever
seen her as a bothersome child, the daughter of his father's very good
friend. Then she had become a responsibility...well, a future responsibility, anyway. But sometime, Drake didn't know when, she'd changed

from the little girl who'd been perched on the chair opposite him in her father's library to a headily desirable woman.

He hadn't thought of her as a responsibility in a long time. Instead, she'd become a mischievous young woman who defended those in need of defending, who talked to her plants...and of course, liked a good Gothic novel.

And he had fast become enraptured.

The irony was not lost on him; he'd gone to bloody war to avoid the very woman he now so desperately ached for but couldn't have. This morning's episode only cemented that truth.

Someone in the ballroom stepped between Drake and his direct line of vision, temporarily blocking Emmaline from sight. "Move," he whispered, willing the matron away. Drake sidled to the left and peered around the pillar just in time to see Emmaline throw her head back and laugh at whatever Miss Winters had said.

Her smile transformed her.

Then, as if she felt his gaze caressing her, she froze and surveyed the room, until her eyes landed on the pillar that hid his frame. She tilted her neck to the side and her lips turned up in secretive smile as if she knew he was there.

He needed to see her. Not in this clandestine manner, but up close. Suddenly, of their own volition, his feet were leading him from his spot behind the column and carrying him over to her seat.

All day he'd debated what he would say to explain the incident in the gardens. Even as his long strides carried him across the ballroom and to her, he realized he'd run out of time to come up with excuses, but didn't care. All he cared about was being with her.

"Lady Emmaline, may I have the next set?"

Emmaline's mouth formed a small moue of surprise and Miss Winters nudged her in the side.

"Ouch," Emmaline exclaimed.

Miss Winters colored and grasped her elbow. "Oh, dear. I fear I must have done something to my elbow. It seems to be moving erratically."

Drake arched an amused brow at the young lady, who must have felt she needed to throw in further proof for good measure, because her elbow jerked again.

"See? Why, there it goes again."

Emmaline glanced down at the card hanging from a string on her wrist. "Although hesitant to leave Sophie in her present condition, I will make an exception and abandon her to accompany you in the next set, my lord."

She shivered when his hand touched hers.

They took their place at the dance floor for the next set.

The musicians began to play a waltz.

Now that he held her, Drake, who was usually so urbane, didn't know what to say.

"My lord, are you well?" she inquired haltingly.

He could have pleaded ignorance to what she actually referenced, but he wasn't that much of a coward.

"I wanted to apologize for…for what happened," he fumbled, faltered through the apology. "I do not know what overcame me," he lied. He did know exactly what had overcome him. "I have worried over your welfare."

Emmaline caught her lower lip between her teeth and worried the flesh. "There is nothing to apologize for," she said. "You forget I have an older brother."

Drake would wager that her older brother had never put his hands on her and if said older brother did, then Drake would beat him within an inch of his life.

Emmaline said nothing else for a moment. "Does…this…happen to you frequently?"

Drake swallowed, and wished for the first time that they'd danced anything other than a waltz, because then there would be a natural separation, and he'd have time to craft a vague response. He fixed his gaze over her shoulder. "It has gotten better, though there are moments when I am…when, it still occurs." Surprisingly, he felt oddly freed by the admission.

"Do certain things trigger these episodes?"

For the first time in three years, Drake wanted to confide in another human being. He hadn't shared any part of his transformation with his father or Sin, partly out of embarrassment and partly out of fear that they would realize he had a touch of madness. Something about this small slip of a woman, made him want to share this part of himself with her. "Certain noises startle me. The sound of a gun will sometimes trigger a reminder of the war." He smiled wryly. "Needless to say, I no longer attend hunting parties." He shrugged. "That is all."

That is all.

Oh, Drake. Her heart bled. How had he dealt with this alone for all these years? *Why didn't you come back to me? Why didn't you let me be your wife, and help you heal?*

But he was here before her now. And that was enough. She wanted to remind him life could be uncomplicated and peaceful.

"It is nothing to be ashamed of."

The muscles beneath his midnight black jacket tightened under her hands. "No, of course not. Every gentleman has bouts of madness," he replied sardonically, an edge to his words.

"You are not mad," she said vehemently.

"How do you know? How do you know the man you have made it a point of pursuing this Season, the man who is to be your husband, is not a madman? How can you trust I won't hurt you?"

"You would never hurt me."

"Never intentionally. But what if I didn't realize what I was doing? Like….like…" The incident in the gardens.

Silence descended between them and Emmaline's mind turned over any possible response that would bring solace, only to find there was nothing she could say. No words could chase away the demons he faced. The reality of it crippled her with a sense of hopelessness.

Emmaline would not allow him to look like this defeated man before her. This was not the time or place for him to bare his soul. "How have you been enjoying your reading?" she asked.

His brow furrowed at the unexpected shift in conversation. "I think you can gather from the note I sent that it leaves much to be desired."

She gave a little toss of her head. "You should be warned, my lord, I am nearly through my copy. You had better devote some time to your reading if you have any hope of winning our challenge."

"I fear I have lost already," he said cryptically.

"Tsk, tsk." She tapped him with the fan hanging from her wrist. "You so readily admit defeat. I thought you would have put greater effort into your readings, as it would mean I would no longer bother you for a week."

The chords of the waltz drew to a halt, and they came to a reluctant stop on the dance floor, standing there amidst clapping couples.

Drake's emerald gaze seared her with its intensity. "How did I ever think you a bother?"

Emmaline blinked. "My lord?"

Drake shook his head. "Uh, I said, I think I see your brother."

Emmaline followed the direction of Drake's stare and felt her skin smart with embarrassment. Nothing could kill a romantic moment more than the glowering figure crossing the ballroom, to intercept their movements.

"I think your brother would want to see us make a match of it," he mumbled under his breath.

Emmaline laughed. "All Sebastian knows is that for the past three years he has had to escort me to more events than he would ever want because I'm unwed. He is therefore a tad resentful where you're concerned," she explained, as her brother drew to a halt before them.

Both men sketched respectful bows.

"So good to see you are finally doing the honorable thing and attending your obligations, my lord. Though a waltz is hardly tantamount to a formal declaration for my sister." For appearances sake, Sebastian at least had the good sense to smile at Drake.

Whatever fleeting connection she'd shared with Drake vanished like a chord struck on the pianoforte.

Drake stiffened at her elbow.

She was going to kill Sebastian for calling out Drake before a crowded ballroom. It was all she could do to keep from throttling her brother there on the spot.

Sebastian took her hand from where it rested on Drake's elbow and placed it in the crook of his arm.

Drake's eyes narrowed at the subtle gesture of possessiveness.

Emmaline didn't answer to anyone. She tugged her hand free.

Her betrothed raised a brow. "I would have never taken you for one to make a public scene. Yet this is the second such time you have attempted to create a scandal. How very un-duke-like of you, Your Grace. If I didn't know better, I'd say you are attempting to sever the connection between Lady Emmaline and me." The bite to Drake's words were belied by the strained, albeit congenial smile he wore.

Emmaline couldn't help the sound of skepticism that escaped her. She spoke before Sebastian could formulate a response. "That's preposterous, Drake. Why would my brother want to dissolve the contract?"

A stony, telling silence met Emmaline's question. Her shoulders stiffened. Mindful of where she was, she plastered a smile to her face and directed her attention to Sebastian. "Tell him that's foolish."

Sebastian's façade of civility slipped and his only response was a flinty-eyed glare for Drake.

Panic caused her heart to speed up. Emmaline wet her lips. *He will not end this betrothal. Not now. Not when I've finally come to know him.* A very thin grasp on reason reminded her of where they were.

Sebastian's jaw set, he surveyed the room to verify the exchange went unnoticed. He returned his attention to Emmaline and Drake. "I've tired of this farce between the two of you. I want a decision soon, Drake."

"Remember where you are," Emmaline cautioned. Oh, how the scandal sheets would love to plaster this meeting on their front pages.

Drake folded his arms over the hard-muscled wall of his chest. "My, if you don't epitomize the role of arrogant, commanding duke."

Emmaline mustered another weak attempt at a laugh. The sound emitted was more that of a bull-frog who'd downed a stone instead of a fly. She closed her mouth.

Oh dear, this had gone from bad to worse.

"I urge you to remember to whom you are speaking," Sebastian said between clenched teeth.

Drake squared his shoulders. "Oh? And who am I speaking to?"

Sebastian's words emerged as a silken threat. "Who am I? Why, I'm the lady's guardian, of course. One word from me and this," he gave a wave of his hand, "game you are playing with my sister is at an end."

Emmaline gasped. Before she could muster a response, Sebastian neatly took her hand, and steered her from the dance-floor.

NINETEEN

My Dearest Drake,
Forgive me for not writing. I fell from a tree and my arm was dislocated.
It was dreadfully painful. I now understand why mother said ladies
should not climb trees. So, I have climbed my last tree.
Ever Yours,
Emmaline

S he wished it were raining.

And she hated the rain.

But today the sun's bright rays were so abundantly, well, *bright*, and it was making it difficult for her to remain buried in her cocoon of covers, pretending it was still time to be abed.

Anything so she didn't have to face the inevitable confrontation with her brother.

After the tumultuous exchange between Drake and Sebastian that previous evening, Sebastian had chosen to let the matter rest. Emmaline had been dealt a reprieve. Alas, today was the day she visited London Hospital.

Emmaline sighed.

The last thing she wanted to endure was a closed carriage ride with Sebastian. She considered postponing her trip until tomorrow. That would allow her a brief reprieve from—

"My lady?"

Her maid, Grace, hovered in the doorway.

Emmaline waved her in.

Grace hurried over to Emmaline's armoire. "His Grace wanted me to remind you of your visit to London Hospital."

Emmaline scrubbed her hand across her eyes. "Was that all?" If she knew her brother as well as she believed she did, then there was certainly more.

Grace's hand, which had been ruffling through Emmaline's row of day gowns, paused. "He also instructed me to tell you—" she cleared her throat, "—that you couldn't hide in your room forever. His Grace's, words, of course."

"Of course."

Grace returned her focus to her efforts at hand. She apparently would rather choose to ignore Emmaline's stinging sarcasm.

Oh, he was an insufferable bother.

Tossing the covers aside, she flung her feet over the side of the bed and jumped to the floor. "Help me dress, Grace."

The ever diligent Grace was already crossing the room with an ivory silk organza creation draped over her arms.

Emmaline allowed her maid to assist her out of her nightgown and into the lovely gown. She stood in front of the floor-length ornate silver mirror, trimmed in roses not really seeing Grace's final efforts.

What could she possibly say to Sebastian that would make any sense? How could she brush aside his very legitimate concerns of her betrothal, when she herself saw merit in them? In four months she would be one and twenty, and another year would be behind her, leaving her still unwed.

Grace cleared her throat. "My lady?"

Emmaline jumped. "Ah, yes, thank you, Grace."

And because Sebastian was correct and she couldn't stay in her room forever, she left the sanctuary of her chambers.

She found him waiting for her at the base of the stairs with a book tucked under one arm, and checking his timepiece.

He spied her coming and slipped the piece back into his jacket. "I took the liberty of selecting your reading selection for the men today," he said by way of greeting.

He held up the maroon leather volume up for her inspection.

She read the title. "Byron," she murmured. "I thought you found all poetry to be rubbish."

She accepted his arm and accompanied him to the carriage. He waved off the groom and handed her up himself.

"I decided to delve a bit deeper to see what it was that so fascinates you…about poetry, that is. I maintain my earlier position. Most of the stuff is useless drivel." Emmaline was astute enough to detect the subtle nuances of her brother's casual conversation. She remained silent. "But then there is Byron. Rather smart, if not an odd fellow. Do you know what he once said?" Sebastian didn't wait for Emmaline to answer. "I do detest everything which is not perfectly mutual."

Emmaline's gaze snapped out the window.

Folding her arms, she braced for the onslaught of his lecture. She waited. And waited….

But he didn't add anything further.

Nary a word.

Somehow that unspoken disappointment was far greater than if he'd come out and reprimanded her.

Sebastian earned points for not making any mention of Lord Drake on their carriage ride to London Hospital. He even dutifully carried the basket and books into the ward without being asked, pausing beside various hospital beds to speak with the soldiers.

He took his leave, and Emmaline finally settled into her comfortable seat beside Lieutenant Jones.

"My lady," Jones greeted her with a slight inclination of his head. He motioned to the empty spot beside his bed. "What have you brought this day?" He nodded to the bundle in her hands.

Emmaline flashed him a smile. She found peace in being with the men here who were a bit rough around the edges and had the false edge of Society's veneer dusted free. It was refreshing.

"Byron?" She opened the volume and fanned through several pages before settling on, "The Lady".

"Are you anyone's lady, my lady?" Jones interrupted.

The brazen question caused Emmaline to stumble in her recitation.

Jones smiled broadly, displaying a row of crooked teeth. It had been three weeks since he'd first smiled and spoken to her, and yet Emmaline was still startled by the transformation of the soldier she'd known for three years.

"Easy enough question," he teased.

Emmaline troubled her lower lip. Yes, for most it was an easy enough question. She chose to break with the strictures on what merited appropriate discussion. "I'm betrothed," she said at last.

His brow wrinkled and he shoved himself up with his only elbow. "So you've got yourself a gentleman?"

She managed a small smile. "I've got myself a gentleman." Unused to speaking freely about her betrothal to Lord Drake, she hesitated. "He was a soldier. He also fought on the Peninsula."

Jones' eyes widened the same way she imagined they would if she'd proclaimed diamonds were falling from the sky.

"You're marrying yourself a soldier?"

"I am." Or she was supposed to. She couldn't go and explain the complicated aspects of her and Drake's relationship.

Jones gave an approving nod. It seemed she'd risen even more in the man's estimation.

He whistled between his teeth. "You found yourself a fancy bloke who fought in the war, too? Not many lords were giving their lives, my lady."

Not many of them had been running away from a childhood betrothal, either. "No, no they weren't."

Sensing Jones was far more curious than any time in the three years she'd known him, she decided to share this personal piece of herself. "He is the Marquess of Drake, he fought—"

The man's shocked gasp cut into her words. "Lord Drake is your gentleman?"

Emmaline blinked, unprepared that this man should know him. She leaned forward in her chair. "Did you know of him?"

"Know of him? I served under him," he said, his eyes round with amazement. "My battalion was hit hard. We lost our commanding officer. The captain was given control of our battalion." His eyes took on a far-off quality that suggested he was seeing things Emmaline didn't want to see. "He's a hero."

Yes, Drake was a hero. She'd read that in every last smattering of articles she'd collected on his accomplishments. How funny this stranger should truly know, firsthand, what Drake had seen and done.

She continued to aggravate her lower lip. "W-what was he like?"

Jones didn't respond right away. Instead he studied Emmaline with a near overwhelming intensity.

This time it was her turn to try and tamp down the awkwardness brought on by the conversation.

How odd to finally realize the discomfiture she must have caused Jones with her probing questions these past years.

"He's a good man," Jones said quietly.

"Yes." That wasn't really the bit of undisclosed information she'd been seeking from Lieutenant Jones.

He must have suspected as much. "After the Battle of Salamanca, the French left Madrid and Wellington marched us into the city." Lieutenant Jones glanced down at his hands. "He left three divisions to guard the capital and then marched the rest of us to Burgos. The captain led us in that march. We came to a scorched field. There was this mangy pup. Emaciated thing. All bones. Whimpering. A step from death. Literally." He tried to grin but it failed, resembling more of a twisted grimace.

Emmaline thought to the well-nourished, loving hunting dogs and pugs her family had over the years. Then she tried to envision the poor, neglected creature described by Jones. Her heart hurt for the poor little fellow.

"As we marched, that mangy dog followed the captain's horse until the captain drew his horse to a halt, and scooped up the flea-ridden creature. He nursed that old dog back to health. He would give the dog half of his own rations." A wry smile turned the man's lips up at the corners. "That dog even ate from the captain's plate. Drank his water." He shook his head, as if still dumbfounded. "I've never known a lord who would share food from his own plate with a filthy dog. He named him Valiant. That dog followed him everywhere. There wasn't much to laugh about then, but we used to laugh about it."

Emmaline's heart hitched.

God help her, she loved Drake. She loved him with a desperation that made her want to fling down the book and run out of the hospital and find him.

She tried to imagine Drake riding beside some of the men here in the hospital, bantering back and forth. He was such a proud man. So very serious. Emmaline couldn't reconcile the Drake she'd come to know with the one being described by Jones. "I imagine Lord Drake was not pleased with the ribbing he received?"

Jones slashed his one hand through the air. "Aww, he took it all in good humor. Men respected him for that. You know, being able to laugh at himself and all."

Emmaline sat back in her chair. "I don't understand why he didn't return with Valiant...." Her words trailed off when Jones looked away.

"Lieutenant?" she asked hesitantly.

Jones remained silent.

Don't do it, she willed herself. *Don't ask.*

She had to know what happened to Valiant. It was a piece that explained what had transformed Drake into the very serious man who was now unable to laugh with ease or sincerity. "What happened to Valiant?"

Jones looked away with a sad shake of his head. "Not a story fit for a lady's ears." He also clearly respected Lady Emmaline too much not to share with her what he knew, because he sighed and continued. "After we were forced into retreat, Wellington spent the winter reorganizing the forces. Whenever there was a battle, Captain Drake would find a tree far from the battle, and tie that dog up. Battle of Vitoria was a big one." It had been the one that ultimately crumpled Napoleon's forces in Spain. "We were in some serious hand-to-hand combat with the Frenchies. That dog, my lady, must have known his master was going to need him, because he gnawed through those ropes and wandered amidst the battlefield with that chewed rope still bound around his neck, searching everywhere for the Cap'n."

Emmaline's eyes slid closed as she battled back a wave of pain. She loathed the question stuck on the tip of her tongue. "Did he find him?"

Intuitively she knew that he had.

Jones nodded again. "Found him fighting two Frenchie bastards. Pardon, my lady," he hurried. Red infused his cheeks.

"Fine, fine." She felt the same way about the men who'd tried to kill Drake. She urged him on, needing to hear, needing to know.

Jones went on. "That dog,"

Valiant, she silently corrected. His name was Valiant.

"Launched himself at one of the bas—uh, Frenchies, who had his knife at the captain's throat. Grabbed onto his leg and bit, tearing at the man's breeches. It allowed Captain Drake to…, to…take care of the other man. But the other fellow, well, he grabbed that rope and wrenched that dog's neck. Broke it just like that." He snapped his fingers.

Emmaline's eyes slid closed as she imagined Drake standing there, fighting for his life, and seeing his faithful companion killed in front of him.

Just like that.

TWENTY

My Dearest Drake,
I think it unfair I cannot have a dog of my choice. When we are
married, you have to promise me we might have a dog and that I may
choose its breed. I think I should like a Shetland Sheepdog....perhaps
we can even have some sheep.
Ever Yours,
Emmaline

Drake strode down the pavement ignoring the curious stares and whispers being directed his way by the lords and ladies who strolled down the street. His Hessian boots drew to an immediate, jarring halt when he reached his destination. With purpose, he stomped up the townhouse steps, and tucked the wriggling bundle of fur into the crook of his left elbow.

He slammed the knocker with his right hand, while holding onto the four-pound devil in his opposite arm. The pup sunk razor like teeth into the flesh of his fingers until Drake winced as a hot trickle of blood dotted his flesh.

Drake raised his fist to again pound the wood panel when the door opened.

He fished a calling card out of his pocket around the squirming mass and handed it to the blank-faced butler. "Lord Drake to see His Grace."

The staid man studied the card, and then peered down a hawk-like nose at the yapping pup. He wrinkled his nose disapprovingly. "Right this way." He turned, as if expecting Drake to follow.

Drake was ushered into the Duke of Mallen's library.

Mallen lifted his eyes from the papers he had been studying but didn't bother to rise. "Drake, this is a surprise." His tone said it was not a happy one.

"Mallen." He set the pup on the floor and the little beast set to work chewing the edge of Drake's boots. He winced. "Your sister sent me a dog."

Mallen's head quirked to the side. "A dog?"

Said dog scrambled up onto one of the two leather-winged chairs facing the Duke of Mallen's enormous desk, and yapped at the befuddled peer.

"The pup seems to be a good judge of character," Drake drawled beneath his breath.

Mallen's brows converged in one, annoyed line. "Your dog is going to destroy my chair."

Drake glanced down to see the mangy beast was using all his energy to dig a hole through the surface of the leather. "It's not my dog."

Mallen shoved his seat back, scraping the dark wood of the floor, and stood. "You barge into my home with…"

The door opened and the Duchess of Mallen sailed into the room which sliced into Mallen's scathing diatribe. "Lord Drake, how very good to see you." A smile wreathed her ageless face.

"Always a pleasure and honor." Drake's attempt at politeness was ruined by the dog that jumped off the chair and ambled back over to him. The mangy thing stood on hind legs and began to scratch at the fabric of Drake's breeches.

"If that were true, I'd imagine we'd see you more frequently, Drake." She glanced down at the puppy and let out a sound of happy surprise. "Oh, you've brought your dog."

Drake sighed. "He's not my dog."

She either failed to hear him or chose to ignore his response, for in a very un-duchess-like move, the Duchess of Mallen went down on a knee and called the scruffy black dog over. The puppy yapped, and proceeded to run in circles around her. "My, you are full of energy," she cooed, occasionally landing a pat.

The pup eventually tired of his game, and instead of sitting for the duchess, returned to Drake and plopped down atop his boots. The creature's eyes fluttered heavily, before he emitted a contented sigh, and fell into a deep, snoring slumber.

The duchess gracefully rose and crossed over to Drake. She claimed his hands in hers and leaned up to kiss him on each cheek. "It really is wonderful to see you, Drake. How is your father?"

Drake had been raised a gentleman and was therefore able to momentarily forget the four-pound reason for his visit.

"He is well, Your Grace, thank you for asking."

She rang for refreshments. "I must say, I'm thrilled to see you, but surely there must be some other reason for your visit?" She softened the searching question with a wide smile.

Drake started. It was Emmaline's smile.

Mallen reclaimed his leather seat and motioned to the puppy. "He's come to tattle on Emmaline."

The duchess blinked in confusion, wide hazel eyes moving from her son to Drake.

"I did not come to tattle." Drake shuffled on his feet, momentarily displacing the pup. The beast was a resolute one, for he climbed right back up onto his perch and gave what Drake swore was a disapproving look. *Great now the dog is put out with me as well.*

Mallen smiled. "Oh good, then. He came to thank Emmaline."

Before Drake could disabuse him of the notion, Mallen rang again. "Have Lady Emmaline summoned immediately," he said to the servant who entered the room.

The servant bowed and hurried to do the duke's bidding.

"Of all the preposterous things," Drake said under his breath, shifting the dog from his feet.

The pup's eyes flew open at being jarred, but then he gave a high-pitched yap and found a renewed burst of energy. He began running circles around Drake, who momentarily followed him with his eyes before getting dizzy, and forced himself to look away from the pup's display.

"Did you call me preposterous?" Mallen snapped.

"Why yes, I did."

Mallen's chest puffed out. "Don't call me preposterous."

"I'll not take orders from…"

The Duchess of Mallen clapped her hands together once, then twice. "Gentlemen, please. Remember you are men." She focused an overly long, disapproving look on Drake.

He resented being made to feel in the wrong. Noble young ladies did not, under any circumstances, send gifts to unmarried gentlemen—even if they were betrothed to the gentleman. It simply wasn't done. This, however, hadn't simply been a gift. Why, she'd sent round a dog.

You didn't send someone a dog. You just…well, you just didn't do it.

Emmaline sailed into the room. "You wanted m—" Her glance alighted on Drake and an enchanting smile wreathed her face. "Oh, hello, my lord!"

He bowed. "My lady."

She wore that same silly, wide brimmed straw hat she had worn in the gardens. The same one he'd torn from her head and tossed to the ground before he…

Her whiskey-colored eyes fell to the black pup. The little devil jumped at Drake's legs again, clearly asking to be picked up.

"You've met him! Isn't he precious? Aren't you precious?" she said in a high singsong voice. She gracefully sank to her knees, sending her pale blue skirts fluttering, similar to the way the duchess had moments ago.

Only this time, thank God, the infernal beast went gladly over. Emmaline scooped him up and allowed him to lap her face with his rough, pink tongue. *Lucky fellow.*

"Aren't you sweet? Do you like your new master? I'm sure he's taking wonderful care of you."

Drake blinked several times. Why did he feel as though he'd stepped on the stage of a great farcical comedy of which he was the lead actor but didn't know his lines?

"Lord Drake has come to say thank you, Emmaline," Mallen called from behind his desk. His expression indicated he was enjoying the exchange far more than Drake.

"No, I haven't. I have come to return him," Drake bit out. As if understanding those hurtful words, the black puppy whimpered and flipped onto his back, sidling back and forth on the Aubusson carpet.

"Never say you are displeased with the little fellow." Mallen pressed a hand to his chest in feigned astonishment.

"I wouldn't say I *am* pleased with him," Drake snapped.

Emmaline's smile faded like the sun dropping from the horizon to usher in the night sky. "You cannot return Sir Faithful. Poor Sir Faithful." She went over to the crestfallen pup and scratched his tummy. "Mean Lord Drake has hurt your feelings. Nasty, nasty man."

Just then a tray of refreshments was delivered and set on the table at the corner of the room. Mallen chuckled. "Ahh, perfect! Refreshments to accompany this show."

Drake glared at the other man and then Emmaline's words registered. A loud guffaw sprung from his lips. "Sir Faithful? Surely you jest? You have named the creature Sir Faithful?"

Emmaline climbed to her feet and planted her hands on her hips. "There is nothing funny about his name."

Drake took a step forward. "No, there is nothing funny about his name. There is *everything* funny about his name."

Drake rolled his shoulders and looked helplessly to the duchess and Mallen. Finding no help there, he jabbed a finger in Emmaline's direction. "Nor for that matter can you go about simply naming other people's dogs."

"I thought you weren't keeping him," Mallen pointed out.

"Be quiet."

Drake, Emmaline, and the Duchess of Mallen ordered in unison.

Mallen crossed the room and scanned the array of sweets artfully arranged on the tray, before settling on a cherry tart. He took two bites and then popped the remainder into his mouth. "So much for being one of the most powerful peers in the realm. I don't even have power in my own library," he muttered around a mouthful of treat.

The duchess folded her hands and looked from Emmaline to Lord Drake, a contemplative gleam in her eyes that Drake didn't like in the least. Apparently smoothing over conflict was inherent in a mother's nature.

"Emmaline, my dear, I'm afraid Lord Drake is correct. You cannot simply give him a dog. Especially if he doesn't want it."

Emmaline shot a look of hurt betrayal at the duchess, and Drake thought she might stick her tongue out at him.

The duchess turned to Drake. "And you, Lord Drake, it is hardly gentlemanly to return a gift."

Emmaline's expression turned victorious, and he gritted his teeth.

Drake could handle one small duchess. He inclined his head, his tone solemn. "Your Grace, you are indeed correct. It is an unpardonable affront to reject any gift. That was never my intention. I simply cannot bring this dog into my home."

Emmaline and Mallen emitted matching snorts at his flowery speech.

The Duchess glared at the both of her children and returned her attention to Drake. "I'm sure there is a solution so no one's sensibilities are hurt."

"Yes, there is. Lord Drake can keep Sir Faithful and say thank you," Emmaline volunteered. She crossed the room and selected a cherry tart before Mallen could finish off that particular flavor.

"I am not keeping him and that is final."

Emmaline gave a flounce of her head.

Drake shot a hopeful glance in the duchess' direction but it would appear her efforts at restoring civility had collapsed.

Carrying the tart on an embroidered napkin, Emmaline crossed to Sir Faithful and offered the pastry to the little black pup.

Drake's eyes slid closed. "You cannot feed a dog cherry tarts."

Emmaline paused mid-motion. Sir Faithful scratched at her hand, and she shifted her attention back to the pup. She popped a piece of the treat into his mouth and patted him on the head. "For someone who does not want him, you are fairly well-versed in how to handle his care."

He took a step in her direction. "Anyone would know not to feed him dessert treats."

"Anyone would know Sir Faithful is a perfect name for a faithful dog." She took a step closer to him until they were a hands-length apart, both breathing heavily, the spectators in the room, once again, irrelevant to their exchange.

Emmaline's lips parted. Drake's emerald gaze dropped to those lips and he forgot whatever words he'd intended to speak.

He studied Emmaline's flushed cheeks. She really was—lovely.

Even in her ridiculous, oversized hat.

Especially in that silly bonnet. It put wicked thoughts into Drake's mind; he and Emmaline in an open field on a hot summer day. He would tug the article from her head and release the luxurious brown locks so they fanned about them...

A stream of something warm and wet snapped him from his reverie.

"Your dog is pissing on my carpet, Drake," Mallen drawled.

Drake glared at him. "My dog is pissing on my *boot*."

"Gentlemen, language," the duchess scolded.

Emmaline clasped her hands to her chest and favored Drake with a radiant smile. "So, you are keeping him?"

Drake gave his clouded head a shake. He'd never said that.

The duchess gave a little clap of her hands. "Lovely news! Then it is settled!"

And just like that it was settled.

He had a dog.

A dog named Sir Faithful.

Whether he liked it or not.

And since he was only admitting it to himself, he could secretly acknowledge, he wasn't altogether displeased with Emmaline's gift.

TWENTY-ONE

My Dearest Drake,
I am never going hunting again. It is cruel and awful. I feel as though
I lost the wager after all. Sebastian felt so bad about my tears, he
promised never to go hunting again.
Ever Yours,
Emmaline

For all intents and purposes, it was late in the evening.
Or early in the morning. Most of the civilized members of the *ton* had abandoned the evening's revelries and were safely ensconced in their beds, sleeping away too much drink and overly rich food.

Drake walked at a brisk pace through Hyde Parke, the little black pup admirably keeping stride with his steps.

Sleep—a fickle friend—eluded Drake. He supposed he should be thankful for it. At times like this, when his nerves were frayed, when his mind was exhausted, the nightmares came in their worst form.

In his dreams, he would see things: fallen friends, fellow soldiers, images of men wandering through battlefields dazed, severed limbs held in their hands.

He drew to a sudden halt and fixed his gaze out at the gardens before him. Sir Faithful, tired from his efforts, sat dutifully beside Drake's feet.

On nights such as these, Drake often walked through the emptied streets and visited an eerily silent Hyde Park. He always managed to find some small measure of solace in the gardens. The smell of the fragrant flowers served as a reminder that he had survived.

But now, they reminded him of more than just that. Now they reminded him of Emmaline. The sight of the flowers and climbing ivy, put him in mind of Emmaline at work in her own garden. This image of her was always in stark contrast to the remembrance of charred, barren wasteland scorched by man and by war.

Sir Faithful scratched his leg and whined at him.

This time, Drake was not alone.

He bent down and scratched Sir Faithful between his ears. "She did you a great disservice, my friend," he murmured to the black pup. "Sir Faithful, she dubbed thee, and forever you shall be."

The pup's tongue lolled out and he gave a happy little yelp, as if in approval of Lady Emmaline's selection.

Drake stared out at the expanse of night sky as the creeping fingers of dawn's purple hues edged across the horizon and pushed back the darkness. As lovely as the morning sky was, the beauty was that much greater in the country, where the air wasn't heavy with dirt and grime.

Drake reflected on Mallen's growing impatience with Emmaline's unmarried state.

Mallen had gone so far as to demand Drake commit to Emmaline or else. The duke had issued the command as though it were the simplest thing in the world.

But then, perhaps to the other man, it was.

How could Mallen, or anyone for that matter, ever know what held Drake back? What would Mallen say if he knew Drake would not wed Emmaline for fear of her safety? Mallen certainly wouldn't want an answer. Instead, he'd end the betrothal without another word and have Emmaline neatly tied to Waxham. His gut clenched at the thought of it.

He thought back to his most recent episode in Emmaline's garden.

It had been several months since he'd last lost control as he had with Emmaline. He'd begun to believe, nay hope, that he'd put those moments behind him. He'd fooled himself into thinking that he was like any other gentleman. That afternoon with Emmaline, he'd physically assaulted her and proved he was nothing more than an animal better off committed to Bedlam.

It had been his greatest fear realized.

No waltz and a simple apology could pardon such an affront. He was foolish to think it could have.

Drake lived through too many sleepless nights, too many hellish nightmares, and too many bouts of lost self-control to ever trust that he was a good candidate for marriage.

Ultimately he would have to marry. As the only heir to the Duke of Hawkridge, Drake was aware of his obligations. It had, however, been his hope that the demons he continued to battle would diminish over the years; that time would, as they say, heal all wounds.

He now realized he'd clung to foolish optimism. This hell would always enshroud his existence. How could he marry and expose Emmaline to that.

Sir Faithful ears pricked up and he looked around as if he'd detected an interloper. The dog gave an excited barking yelp and bounded off to greet their guest.

"Drake," Emmaline murmured softly.

Drake started at the unexpectedness of the interruption. Every muscle in his body went tight at the feel of her presence.

He no longer wondered about her uncanny ability to determine his whereabouts.

Drake turned and dipped a respectful bow. "Emmaline."

Emmaline tapped her copy of *Glenarvon* against her thigh. "You can leave us, Grace," she instructed her maid.

Grace nodded and then took her leave.

Emmaline bit the inside of her lower lip, the soft thread of her maid's footsteps echoed in the quiet until they faded to silence. Emmaline and Drake were left cloaked in the privacy the shrubbery.

She took a deep breath, wishing she were more poised to hide her uncertainty from this man she'd been connected to since she'd been a babe.

Emmaline crouched down and caressed Sir Faithful.

"I've finished…"

"You are walking rather…"

They both stumbled to an awkward, halting conclusion, their words unfinished.

He helped her to her feet.

Silence again descended.

Emmaline drew a distracted circle upon the ground with the tip of her slipper.

Drake studied the movement. "Are you visiting the park at this ungodly hour to merely draw artwork with your slipper?" he teased.

Emmaline's foot paused mid-circle and she grinned. "You've found me out, sir. I spend a great deal of time gallivanting over Hyde Park completing very fine slipper-art. It is all the thing."

His eyes smiled at her inane response. Funny that. She'd never known one could smile with their eyes.

"I must say, completing slipper art in public is not the action befitting a future duchess," he said solemnly.

Emmaline made an X over her heart. "I pledge to abandon the activity when we are wed, my lord."

Nothing could kill the shared levity of the moment swifter than mention of their betrothal.

Drake's eyes darkened and he directed his focus to the book in her hands.

Her heart twisted painfully in her chest as he regarded her the way he might a stranger.

"Have you come here this morning to read?"

She hated that his words came out clipped and cool. Yearned for the light, teasing warmth she'd come to know from him.

She waved her copy of *Glenarvon* about. "As I started to say, I have finished my copy. I am here to complete our challenge."

His face, an otherwise blank mask, revealed a flash of surprise. Wordlessly, he held a hand out.

She gave him the novel, and watched as he thumbed through the pages. Neither of them said anything as he perused the copy, searching for his questions.

She resumed her slipper art.

Suddenly his fingers stilled and he looked at Emmaline with piercing jade green eyes.

"Calantha marries one man but is seduced by another. Who is her seducer?"

Emmaline's foot drew to a sudden halt and she cocked her head to the side. "That is one of your questions?" She pressed a hand to her mouth to stifle her laughter. Surely Drake could have found something a good deal more challenging.

"I say, answer the question. That is, if you know it," he challenged.

"If this is one of your questions, you do not stand a chance."

He bristled. "If you do not answer the question on a count of three, I will determine that you do not know."

"*Glenarvon*," she answered, a smile twitching at the corner of her lips. "Tsk, tsk, my lord...I'm afraid you are going to have to do better than that, or you are surely going to lose the challenge."

Drake opened his mouth to speak, but then his eyes dipped to her mouth and whatever he'd been about to say remained unspoken. He groaned.

"Drake, are you all right?"

He cleared his throat. "Fine, fine."

Drake returned his attention to the book in his hands. He perused a passage. "Calantha speaks of losing all. Who does she blame?"

Emmaline tapped a finger along her jaw. In the work, Calantha was frequently alternating between a sense of guilt and no regrets for her great affair. "Can you read me the passage?"

It was Drake's turn to issue a tsking sound. "Come, come, my lady. Who does she blame?"

Emmaline thought about it a moment, thought of her relationship with Drake. As a woman, who did she usually blame for Drake's lack of regard?

"Herself, my lord. She blames herself."

He nodded, before concentrating his efforts once more on the book. He leafed through the pages.

A loose strand of hair fell across her eyes. She blew it back. "Have you found your next question, my lord?" she pressed after several long moments of silence.

He didn't bother picking his head up to look at her. "Eager thing, aren't you?"

She smiled. This light side of Drake was the one Lieutenant Jones had spoken of...and was one she'd come to love. Until just recently, he'd always been the phantom handsome figure who issued her a respectful bow and then beat a hasty retreat. To have him tease her, to furrow his brow as he rustled through a Gothic novel, was something she couldn't have conjured in her wildest imaginings.

"Ahh," he said, glancing up. He wore a triumphant expression. "Complete this sentence from the passage—"

"That is hardly fair," she protested. "A question is far different from memorizing the work."

"We did not stipulate terms of the questions, my lady."

Emmaline folded her arms. Drat, if he wasn't right.

"Fine," she muttered. "What is the passage?"

"That which causes the tragic end of a woman's life is often but a moment of amusement and folly in the history of..."

Emmaline's chest tightened. "A man."

Drake snapped the work shut, holding it out to her, and took a step forward.

He was so close his breath, laced with a hint of coffee, fanned her lips.

"Calantha argues Glenarvon has seduced her with what?"

Her body swayed closer to him. "The power of attraction," she whispered.

The book slid from her fingers, to the ground where it fell indignantly open on its spine.

Then he was taking her in his arms, folding her close, covering her mouth with his, parting her lips and tasting her. She moaned, a low, husky purr that sounded wanton to her own ears.

Emmaline twined her hands about his neck and pressed her body close to his. His manhood prodded hard and angry against her belly, and her body flared with the swift, hot flood of desire. It overtook her, nearly brought her to her knees.

"Please, Drake," she pleaded against his lips.

Drake lowered her to the ground and knelt with her cradled against the hard-muscled wall of his chest. There was something both erotic and yet sweetly beautiful, kneeling in the gardens as though they were Adam and Eve partaking in their first sinful taste of the forbidden fruit.

Through the thick haze of desire, Sir Faithful's bark cut into their embrace. The dog hurled himself atop them and licked Emmaline's face.

She turned away from the eager pup and laughed.

Drake paused. "Sit." He issued the order with the same authority she was sure he had used to command his men in battle. At the brisk tone, Sir Faithful promptly laid down. He lowered his head dejectedly on his paws.

Drake returned his attention to her. "Where was I?" he asked hoarsely.

"You were touching me," she said breathlessly.

"Was I?" He kissed the corner of her lip.

She moaned. "Yes."

"Yes, like this or yes, you like it?"

Her head thrashed back and forth. "Stop teasing me."

Strong fingers traced a knowing path over her body, and grasping her buttocks in his palms, he urged her closer to the length of him.

Emmaline gasped. She was going to catch fire from her need and set Hyde Park ablaze.

Her head fell back when his lips left hers. He nipped the corner of her lips, her cheek, and then he caressed her neck with his lips. The unshaven scruff of his beard tickled her skin. She giggled.

Drake didn't even break his ministrations, his hands releasing her breasts from the bodice of her gown. The peak of her nipples hardened under his stare. "Is there something that amuses you, my lady?" he asked huskily, not waiting for a reply as his mouth lowered to her breast. With deliberate slowness he drew the ripened bud into his mouth. He gently suckled, laving the peak, and then flicked it teasingly with his tongue.

Emmaline's head fell back.

Drake switched his attention to the tip of her other, neglected pale white mound.

Emmaline gasped aloud. She twisted her fingers into the silk strands of his golden hair. "Drake, show me more."

The cool of the morning air slammed into her bare legs, as he slid her skirts up, higher, and higher, to her knees. His fingers skimmed over her belly, and then before she could comprehend what he was doing, his hand delved between her legs.

It was as though every last vestige of energy was sapped from her. Emmaline collapsed in his arms. He sat down, atop a bed of white cerastium, and moved her onto his lap while his expert fingers continued to work her.

Drake slipped another finger into her and began to move them; in, then out, in then out, until she bucked under his hand. "Yes," she cried softly.

He continued to stroke her, playing with the pliable nub of her center. Emmaline supposed she should feel a sense of shame but couldn't drum up one single rational thought about the indecency of what they were doing and where they were doing it.

All she knew was him.

She closed her eyes and undulated beneath him, searching for more.

His lips reclaimed hers. "Come for me, love," he urged, his voice a husky command.

Come? What on earth did he mean? Pressure built inside her, unfurling like a rapidly growing weed, taking over everything. Her cry was lost in his mouth. She frantically arched her hips as he rung every last bit of pleasure from her.

And then she collapsed, replete with the gift he'd given her.

So that was what he'd meant. She laid her cheek alongside his and felt her breath fanning his.

Drake's fingers played with the tresses that had tumbled from her knot and covered them like a blanket. "So beautiful," he whispered.

Emmaline's throat worked. She knew she was no great beauty but when he said it like that, in those emotion-laden words, she believed him.

He kissed the slight birthmark just below her temple.

"What an interesting spot for a birthmark. Rather unique...just like you."

He brought her skirts down and she finally, reluctantly, pulled back.

She looked at him through heavy eyes. "I won the challenge, my lord," she reminded him huskily.

He laughed and kissed her once again for good measure. "Yes, my lady. You certainly did win."

TWENTY-TWO

My Dearest Drake,
Does a man who is betrothed still propose to the lady he is betrothed to?
I would imagine it would be more romantic if he did.
Ever Yours,
Emmaline

He was going to marry her.

Drake expected to be consumed by anxiety at the thought of relinquishing bachelorhood. He'd always believed marriage symbolized the death of a gentleman's freedom.

Yet oddly today, he had no reservations. It wasn't obligation that drove his decision. Nor his responsibilities to the ducal line. Somewhere along the way, it had become about him and Emmaline—as it should have been.

Sir Faithful barked.

He glanced down apologetically at the pup. "No, you cannot come, my friend." Sir Faithful dropped his head back between his paws and gave him a long, sad look.

"I'll tell you what, Sir. Soon I'll bring her back here as your mistress, then you can see the both of us."

That was apparently too much for the pup to understand. He just cocked his head sideways, tongue lolling out, and continued to study Drake.

Drake returned his attention to his plans for the morning, feeling once again like a soldier about to embark upon a decisive battle. Why had he fought this? He thought of all the time he'd wasted, thought of his leaving to fight on the Peninsula, when what he'd been fleeing had turned out to be a person who made him smile more than he had in years.

He glanced down at the ring resting on the bureau top. The eight carat emerald nestled amidst a cluster of diamonds, glittered in the morning light. It had belonged to his mother, and the duchess before her, and the duchess before her. And it would be Emmaline's. He picked it up, studied it, and then placed it in the inner fold of his midnight jacket.

His valet appeared in the doorway. "My lord, as requested, your mount has been readied."

Drake nodded and made his way below stairs, to the foyer.

He was met by the usually staid, butler, Winchester.

This time Winchester's weathered face was wreathed in a smile that went from one ear to the next. As if he knew Drake's special business. Which shouldn't really surprise him. Winchester had always managed to glean Drake's intentions before he himself even really knew.

"My lord!"

Drake grinned back. "Winchester."

Since he'd lain Emmaline down on the garden floor and pleasured her, he'd worn a perpetual smile. To be more precise, he'd seemed to be in a state of happiness since she'd come into his life. Emmaline's joy had been infectious and he'd been her willing victim.

A startled shriek rent the air, punctuated by a resounding metallic crash. Servants seemed to materialize out of nowhere and hurried to the mishap. A two foot silver vase lay on its side amidst a cluster of white flowers. The young maid who'd dropped the floral arrangement wept into her hands.

Her blubbering blended with the cacophony of sound as servants rushed to clean the mess.

Drake's eyes remained riveted on the glint of the metal urn. The maid's cries wavered in and out of focus, until they were replaced with the agonizing shouts of his fallen men.

As if slammed by a cannon ball to the stomach, Drake's body jerked. With a bellowing roar wrenched from deep inside his soul, he

157

dropped to his knees and covered his ears, in an attempt to blot out the deafening sound of grapeshot ricocheting off each corner of his mind.

Drake's eyes flitted around like that of a cornered animal. His horrified gaze landed on the earth strewn with destroyed flowers, and waited. When no bodies fell, in an attempt to flee, he darted past the horrified men around him. He willed his legs to pump faster, lest he be caught in the thick of the battle.

A powerful hand snaked around Drake's arm. He cried out. Thrashing violently, he leveled his opponent with an elbow that caught the man in the ribs. The hiss of exhaled breath fired like kindling just about to catch. The man held onto Drake with fierce determination, but Drake refused to surrender because if he did, he'd be at the mercy of the French bastards.

"No, no, no!" Drake roared.

"Drake, I won't hurt you. Nobody is going to hurt you."

Drake stilled. When the man's grip lightened, Drake wrested his arm free, and beat a hasty retreat up the stairwell.

The Frenchie was on him again. He knocked Drake's knees out from under him, tackling him to the ground. The action knocked the breath from Drake with a powerful whoosh, and something flew out from his jacket front. He heard the soft ping, ping, ping, as it skidded across the white Italian marble floor.

White Italian marble floor?

"Drake? Drake?"

"My lord?"

Drake struggled beneath the weight of the bodies that pressed him down.

Bodies. There were more than two.

Drake? My lord?

His breath was coming hard and fast on deep gulping gasps for air.

Think, Drake. Why would the French be calling me by my name? Think. Where were the echoing shots? He waited for the sounds that never came.

All energy drained from him and he rested his forehead upon the hard cool surface of the marble, which penetrated his haze of horror.

It had struck again.

He blinked down at the floor but his vision blurred, blending the surface. He wanted to cry. A trickle of wetness trailed a path from his cheek and fell upon his lips.

Nay, he was crying.

He became aware of his father helping him up, gathering him in his arms as if he were no more than a boy.

Except he wasn't a boy. He was a battle-scarred man who would never be normal again.

His whole frame shuddered with the jarring return to reality.

"It's fine, Drake," his father whispered. He stroked his back. "You can leave, Winchester."

It wasn't fine. In fact, Drake wanted to toss his head back and rail at a non-existent God.

He stiffened and took a staggering step away from his father and remembered. Remembered this humiliation had been witnessed by a host of servants, servants who would surely talk. Then the entire *ton* would know. She would know. His gut churned. He was going to be ill.

"Not one member of this household will speak on what happened here," his father said, correctly interpreting the direction of Drake's thoughts. There was an air of ducal confidence to the promise.

Drake took another step backward, placing much needed distance between them.

His father's throat bobbed up and down, displaying his unease. He held an outstretched hand toward Drake. "Don't, Drake. Don't turn from me." It was an order. It was not a ducal order, but rather the words of a father demanding his child not shut him out.

Drake ignored him and, without another word, turned on his heel and climbed the last stairwell. He walked at a brisk pace down the long hall and finally reached his chambers. He shoved the door back with an aggravated force and entered, shutting the door behind him with a decisive click.

Drake leaned against the closed hard panels of the oak door, borrowing the strength to stand. The hum of the room's quiet fell in cadence with the heavy sound of his breathing.

When he thought he could move again without collapsing into a heap of shame, he dropped to the floor and sat with his body flush against the door.

Sir Faithful bounded across the room, and ran excitedly about Drake's feet. The dog climbed up in his lap, and favored Drake's face with a coarse, pink-tipped lick.

A bitter laugh escaped Drake, which he buried in Sir Faithful's neck. "I should have known better."

Instead, he had deluded himself into believing this defect in him, this tendency to lose control, would not prevent him from finding happiness with Emmaline. The memory of her, the taste of her lips, the sweet sounds he had swallowed within his own mouth, had all allowed him to pretend he could be more than he was. A monster bound for Bedlam.

It hadn't been enough that he'd lost control in front of her. Hell, that time should have been the first and last he'd allowed himself to be in her presence. But he'd persisted—because he was a selfish, filthy bastard who'd cared more about how she made him feel, how she made him forget.

Drake should be grateful this had happened. Now he could at least spare her hurt. He could take it on as his own. In fact, Drake should be glad for it.

So why wasn't he? Why did he wish the day had continued along as he'd imagined.

He would have marched up Mallen's steps with an armful of the white flowers he and Emmaline had lain amidst and then asked for her hand.

Her endless brown eyes would have sparkled with merriment and shock when he told her he wanted to make her his wife.

Mallen would bang his fist on his desk and glower at Drake with displeasure.

Drake dropped his head into his hands and pressed his fingers against throbbing temples, and continued to cradle Sir Faithful close. Excruciating headaches usually followed the episodes. He welcomed the pain this time for it helped dull the agonizing feeling of his heart being ripped piece by piece from his body.

The pain prevented him from thinking about how close he'd come to having it all.

TWENTY-THREE

My Dearest Drake,
Is it silly that, when you return, I want you to court me?
Ever Yours,
Emmaline

Emmaline fairly raced through Hyde Park in a manner that would have earned gasps of disapproval from Society members—if they'd been present, of course. She had sent Drake a note, claiming her picnic as the prize for their *Glenarvon* challenge.

That had been a week ago. Well, six days to be precise, which to Emmaline may as well have constituted a week.

In that time, there had been no acknowledgement, no return note, no teasing banter, no sudden appearance at a ball or musicale. Nothing. It had been as though everything she'd shared with Drake had been nothing more than a fleeting fantasy.

Emmaline had begun to think he'd never again contact her.

Until yesterday.

At last, Drake had replied to her request.

"My lady, can you please slow down?" her maid called out in a panting gasp. The sound of gravel kicking up furiously punctuated her breathless request.

Emmaline glanced over her shoulder. A twinge of guilt hit her. She sighed and slowed her steps. The ivory drawstring bag dotted with blue beads she held in her right hand swung against her side.

"My lady, would you like to rest soon," Grace suggested.

Emmaline drew to a full stop on the Serpentine Bridge, which marked the boundary between Hyde Gardens and Kensington Gardens. Her abrupt movements sent Grace stumbling against her.

"Beg pardon, my lady."

Emmaline glanced down at the parchment in her hands. "Fine, fine," Emmaline said. She studied the note.

My Dearest Emmaline,
Would you do me the honor of meeting me in Hyde Park at Kensington
Gardens? I shall be there at five o'clock in the morning. That is if it
isn't too early.
Yours,
Drake

Emmaline squinted off into the distance. A lone figure stood with his back to her and Grace. Attired entirely in black, there was something ominously dark about him.

Emmaline turned to Grace. "Please, wait here."

Emmaline didn't wait to see if Grace did as she was ordered. Instead, she hurried toward her betrothed.

Drake stood with his back to her. His gaze trained on the indigo and pale lavender hues traipsing across the early morning sky.

It was Sir Faithful who gave her a barking greeting. Drake's broad frame stiffened as she approached but he didn't so much as turn to look at her.

She fell to her knee. "Hello, Sir Faithful. How have you been, my boy?" She rubbed the spot between his eyes and he leaned into her touch.

"Emmaline," Drake greeted, his tone deadened.

Emmaline stood, her pale blue muslin day gown rustling on a wisp of wind. "Why have you not returned my notes?" She heard the edge of hurt betrayal underlining her words. "I don't understand. One moment, you seem to enjoy my company and then you disappear. It is as though you are two people."

He stiffened.

"I believed you had come to care for me," she whispered. "Can't you even look at me?"

Drake spun around; his flat emerald eyes leveled her. She took a faltering step backwards, unprepared for the cold gaze he passed over her. He arched an icy, indifferent brow.

"I really don't have anything to say to you." His voice was as frigid as a January freeze.

One hand attempted to smother a gasp wrenched from inside her heart while the other dropped the bag she'd carried with her.

It hit the gravel path with a soft thud.

She angled her chin up and refused to be cowed. She didn't know where she found the courage for the next words. "I've waited fifteen long years for you. I'm no longer a girl. I can't continue as we are." She held an outstretched hand towards him. "It's breaking my heart." The words stripped her of her remaining pride.

He dragged a hand through his hair and cursed. It was a foul curse she'd only heard uttered by her brother once, and that had been the day their father died.

"Emmaline, I believe you have made too much of—of," his hand slashed the air, "this." He motioned between them.

"I believed you had come to care for me, Drake. Would you have me believe that you do not?" She reached for him and he flinched. A laugh that sounded half-mad to her own ears escaped her. "Have I been so wrong about us?"

He didn't respond.

"You can't even have the decency to answer me that?" The words were desperate. "What game do you play? Why would you send round a note and ask me to meet you here if—?"

There was a flash of surprise in Drake's expression. "What note?"

And then she knew. Her breath whistled between her teeth. "Oh God, you didn't send it."

A dull, throbbing pain came from somewhere in the vicinity of her heart, a heart she was certain had already withered inside her.

Her hand went to her chest. The organ continued to beat. Odd, the rhythm seemed too steady and strong for someone dying.

She dropped to a knee and with fingers that quivered, fished an envelope from the drawstring bag. Her hands shook so badly she clumsily dropped the note. The scrap fluttered forlornly to the ground.

Drake bent down and swiftly rescued it. He perused the note he'd been purported to have written.

His brow furrowed while he scanned the parchment and then his eyes glazed over with a haze of fury. And she had her confirmation.

She wanted to flee, turn on her heel and be spared this humiliation.

Wordlessly, he stuffed the note back into its envelope and handed it back to her. On legs that trembled, she rose without assistance. Dazed eyes remained focused on her name scrawled across the thick ivory vellum, because then she didn't have to look at the black rage in his expression.

Emmaline was possessed of a violent urge to tear up the piece. She wanted to rail at herself for not recognizing the scrawl as similar to other notes she'd received these past weeks from Lord Sinclair. Hated herself for seeing only that which she'd wanted to see.

"I—I allowed myself to hope." And hope had clouded her reason.

"Sinclair?" he asked tersely.

Emmaline looked away.

Drake cursed.

He would bloody murder Sinclair.

"Why ever would he send that note?" Then it hit him with all the force of a bayonet to the gut. All along it had been Sinclair. "It all makes sense."

She blinked at him with soulful brown eyes. "What makes sense?"

A cynical laugh burst from his chest. "Don't play coy with me. You schemed with Sinclair. It was he who informed you of my whereabouts this Season." He'd been betrayed by his closest friend and his betrothed.

"I assure you I couldn't manage coy if I tried," she snapped.

"But you could manage deceitful."

Her delicate palms curled into little fists at her side and he thought she might hit him which really would be no less than he deserved.

She sucked in a deep breath. "Really, Drake? Is that how you see me? As some kind of maniacal scheming debutante?"

An image of Sinclair and Emmaline closeted away trickled into his consciousness. He imagined them laughing while they planned to trap him. The idea of them, plotting behind his back, sent rage spiraling. He was besieged by a tumult of emotions and couldn't sort whether it was jealousy of her closeness with Sin or anger at the good laugh they'd had behind his back.

"What fun you must have had at my expense." Filled with a restive energy he presented her with his back and stepped away.

"Has it really been so awful being in my company?"

He ran a hand across his face and swung back around. "So you enlisted Sin's aid to ascertain my plans each evening. I understand your means of conspiring against me. Your intention was to force my hand, but Sinclair?"

"Bah. Why can't you believe Sin was just trying to help you because he believes we belong together?"

He arched a brow. "I am rather surprised he accepted your appeal for support. Subterfuge is not really one of Sin's traits."

Emmaline folded her arms indignantly across her chest. "But it is one of mine? My, what a low opinion you have of me. I suggest you speak to Lord Sinclair for the answers to your questions." She tilted her chin at a mutinous little angle. "You are a beast," she spat.

He tipped his head in assent. "Truer words were never spoken."

A near hysterical hiccough of laughter burst from her lips. "Did you ever really care for me?"

Drake studied Emmaline. The tightness around her mouth, her lips dipped down at the corners indicated that she was wavering between fury and despair. How dare she take on the role of the offended party? She had, after all, been duplicitous. He owed her no apologies.

Yet still...when her lush red lips trembled in that forlorn way, he wanted to knock himself out for being the cause of her pain. He hated himself for hurting her, even if ultimately it would be best for Emmaline. Then all false illusions she carried of him being an honorable gentleman deserving of her love could be at last squashed.

He closed the short distance between them with long, determined strides. Emmaline backed away. "Come Emmaline, am I to believe this plan you crafted was designed out of love for me? That it had nothing to do with your ultimate goal of marriage?"

"How little you think of me," she snapped and then took a bold step toward him, so only a hand of distance remained between them.

They were toe-to-toe, breath coming fast from the force of their emotions.

"What do you want from me?" The words wrenched from deep within him.

"I want to be your wife," she whispered.

Drake looked away, unable to see the love pouring from her. God, when she said it like that, he was wont to deny her anything. She at least deserved some element of truth from him. "I am not ready to marry you."

Her response came out wobbly. "Why?"

He knew how much that question cost her and just added one more thing to the list of all the reasons he hated himself.

"I'm not ready to be a husband."

There it was. To him, the truth—a silent acknowledgement that he was defective and not good enough for her. She, however, would see it as nothing more than a rejection.

"You're not ready to be a husband? Or you're not ready to be my husband?" He said nothing and she squared her shoulders. "I see."

No, Emmaline. No, you cannot possibly see. Because if you did, then you would know right now I feel as though I'm being run through, over and over with a rusty bayonet.

Drake stared out into the horizon at the fading purple hues rolling back, as they ceded the spot to the full morning sky. "I should never have touched you." Even if it had felt like the only thing perfect in his life.

Emmaline laughed bitterly. "I don't imagine many of the ladies you've been intimate with have heard those words from the great Lord Drake." She reached down and rescued the forgotten bag at their feet. She thrust it into his hands. "These were yours. I wrote them, to you… for you…when you were…gone…" She fumbled about, seeming to search for the right words. "I am freeing you," she breathed the words into existence. She jerked as if startled by her own declaration, but then resolutely met his gaze. "I am no longer your responsibility."

Drake's heart thumped, once, twice, then froze. He gave his head a firm shake, in an attempt to make sense of what Emmaline had said but the loud buzzing in his ears overpowered his ability to reason.

Perhaps he had misheard her.

"I am freeing you," she repeated. "I cannot do this any longer. You don't love me. Even as I…love you. I cannot bear to be a responsibility you do not want, nor for that matter have ever wanted in your life. I want to be courted. I want someone to bring me flowers and write me poems. More than anything, I want to be loved. And do you know, Drake? I deserve to be loved."

Yes, she did. Except, Emmaline could walk from one corner of the earth to the next, and never find a man who cared for her as he did. It was that regard for her which allowed him to set her free, in spite of his selfish yearnings. A ball of pain lodge in Drake's chest.

Odd, he'd been stabbed, had taken more bullets than a living body was ever meant to take and yet the ache of losing Emmaline, was somehow greater than all those hellish wartime moments combined.

God help him. He was a selfish fiend after all. He wasn't ready to lose her.

"What if I don't want to be free?" The words ripped from a place deep within his soul, a place where the last vestige of humanity he'd returned from the war with, still resided. If Emmaline walked out of his life; she'd snuff out the sole flicker of light that existed within him.

Emmaline gave him a sad little smile. "Come Drake, you don't want me. You have never wanted me. Even this Season." Her hand fluttered about. "I've followed you from event to event, but I've never really been anything more than a nuisance. So I am freeing you as much for me, as it is for you."

She stepped close to him. The crisp citrusy scent of lemons tickled his senses. His eyes slid closed. He would never know if it was the scent of her soap or a dash of perfume dabbed behind her ears, because she would be gone to him, and he would lose the right to know all those intimate things he yearned to know.

Through a surreal fog, he was dimly aware of her taking his hands. She gave them a gentle squeeze and picked up her chocolate gaze to meet his. "You have had the opportunity to make at least some decisions of your own. You went to war. I've never had that. Let me have this. Let me have my Season."

Drake's throat worked painfully. If only he could tell her the decision he'd made, his one reckless grasp at independence, had been the most horrendous mistake he had ever made. It had cost him everything: his sanity, his happiness. Her.

"I have never said I wanted to be freed of you."

Why couldn't he call forth the words to keep her?

Because you don't deserve her, a silent voice jeered.

Emmaline smiled sadly. "But you never said you wanted me either." She reached out a trembling hand to his jaw and rubbed the cleft there. "When my father died, I was devastated. I never thought I'd smile again."

Drake tried to slog through the the unexpected shift in conversation.

"I waited for you, but you never came." Emmaline swallowed, her throat working. "I still remember the chaos. There were so many cries and screams. I still cannot sort whether it was mine, Mother's, or the maids'." A small shudder racked her frame and she crossed her arms, as if to ward off a chill. "Countless peers came to pay their respects, but I really only wanted to see one person walk through the door." Her lips tipped up in a sad rendition of a smile. "You were the only one I longed to see. I waited for you to come to me…but you never came."

Drake's stare wandered away from her precious face as his mind tripped down a path of remembrance. In spite of how it had appeared to Emmaline, he had indeed cared about the loss she'd suffered. He had meant to go to her.

It was that moment when he realized with certainty—he could not fight for her. The great hurt she still carried with her, a hurt she was more than entitled to, symbolized a divide that would forever keep him from being worthy of her. He had failed her too many times.

"I am sorrier for that than you can ever know," he said. He flinched when her soft, delicate fingers caressed his cheek.

Hesitating just a moment, she reached up on tiptoe and placed a sweet, lingering kiss on his lips.

It tasted like good-bye.

Without a word, she turned on her heel, and left.

TWENTY-FOUR

My Dearest Drake,
I have just returned from London, where I found the most delightful
straw bonnet for my gardening! I shall never be beet red again!
Ever Yours,
Emmaline

Drake stood rooted to his spot. The scent of Emmaline seemed to linger and he feared if he so much as moved, he'd waft the citrus scent of her off into nothing more than a memory. He stood so still his shoulders ached.

Time passed at an interminable crawl.

Sir Faithful nudged him in the leg until he looked down. The loyal fellow favored Drake with a sad, accusing brown-eyed stare. "I'm a fool, Sir."

Sir Faithful yapped in agreement.

The irony wasn't lost on him. He hadn't felt anything in the three years since he'd returned and now he should feel it all: pain, happiness, despair. He hated the swell of emotion that threatened to carry him away.

Over the past three years Drake had constructed a wall around himself; a barrier against the outside world. In a few short months, Emmaline had taken it down brick by brick until she'd exposed him as a scared and hurt man.

Even as he cared for Emmaline, in that moment, Drake hated her for forcing him to face the lie he'd been living. He'd tried his damnedest to bury himself in empty pursuits, whoring and gaming. And those were no longer enough and would never be enough.

Now the only thing he longed for, craved like air he breathed, was her.

And she was gone.

He wanted to slam his fist into something. There was no one to release his pent up fury on…except…

Drake turned on his heel.

He retrieved his mount and headed to the home of the one person he could direct his wrath upon.

When he arrived at his destination, he flung the reins to a waiting boy and threw him a sovereign and promised another when he returned. Drake strode up the townhouse steps and banged his fist on the door.

A wide-eyed butler opened it. "My lord, I shall…"

Drake stormed past the servant and started up the stairway. "Where is he?"

The graying butler's skin turned ashen. "My lord," he squeaked, and hurried up the steps, two at a time. "He is still abed, if you…"

Drake's long legs had already outdistanced the butler, and the other man's words trailed off. Drake continued on down the hall.

Having, of course, never visited Sin in his bedchambers, he wasn't entirely certain which rooms the bastard occupied.

It did, however, give Drake some matter of satisfaction to kick in each closed doorway, sending them bouncing off the wall with a resounding boom.

Half-way down the hall, he kicked in one more door, and heard an answering groan.

"Get up," Drake thundered, entering the chambers. He crossed over to the bed and tugged down the mound of blankets. He tossed them to the floor.

Sin draped an arm across his eyes seeming to care more about the intrusion of light than his naked form which had been exposed. "What has you in such a foul temper?" he groused, and dragged a pillow over his eyes.

Drake fished the note from his pocket and flung it at his friend. He began to pace. "What is this about? Where are your loyalties, that you would assist Emmaline in her maneuverings?"

Sin tossed aside the pillow and sat up slowly. He reached over the side of the bed and picked up his robe. "Whatever are you talking about?" Sin asked as he jammed his arms within the sleeves. He reached for the note, read it, and set it aside. "Oh, this."

Drake's movements were drawn to a jerky halt. He fixed a glare on his traitorous friend. "Oh, this? That is all you have to say?" Anyone else would have been terrified by the bloody calm in Drake's words.

As if to show Drake how *terrified* he in fact was, Sin stifled a yawn with the back of his hand. He stood and belted his robe at the waist. "You were in need of a push," he said matter-of-factly. His bare feet padded across the plush Aubusson carpet.

Unmindful of the early hour, Sin strode over to the drink cart situated against the curtained window, and poured a healthy glass of whiskey. Very deliberately, he swirled the contents of the glass and then took a long, slow swallow, until he'd polished off the brew. He set the empty glass down.

Drake clenched his fists at his side, knowing his friend was trying to stir his ire. He took a deep breath. "It isn't your place to meddle in my life. I neither want, nor need your interference. I've had to deal with my father's maneuverings. I don't need yours as well."

Sinclair picked up his glass and refilled it. He studied Drake almost quizzically. "Are you sure of that?" He took a sip of whiskey. "Can you honestly say you've been happy since you returned from the war? For the love of God, Drake, you've gamed and whored more than even I can keep up with. And tell me? Has it brought you happiness?"

Drake had to restrain himself from hurting his friend. "What do you know of it?" He seethed. "Who are you to judge and condemn? You carry on as you please." Drake reached for a glass and the decanter of whiskey and sloshed the brew into his glass.

Sinclair held his glass up in mock salute. "Yes, but I am not betrothed,"

Drake opened his mouth to speak and then promptly shut it. He stared blankly at the gold damask curtains behind Sin's shoulder.

Except, neither was he. With just a few words, the betrothal contract, which had bound them since childhood, had been snipped like a stray thread on a piece of fabric.

"It still was not your place to assist her. As my friend, you should have come to me the minute she proposed her scheme." He finished his drink and set the glass down hard on the table.

Drake wanted to be well and truly drunk by the time he left this room.

Sin scratched his forehead. "Proposed...? She did not tell you." A knowing light flickered to life in Sin's eyes. "You believe Lady Emmaline approached me? You believe she enlisted my support? She did not tell you it was I who approached her?"

TWENTY-FIVE

My Dearest Drake,
I have learned you are in London. I know it is not ladylike to admit
this but…I am excited to see you.
Ever Yours,
Emmaline

Emmaline sat on the wrought iron bench in the gardens. She tugged the wide brim of her bonnet lower to conceal the extent of her grief from her maid, and hugged the small spade close to her stomach. She welcomed the sharp sting of the metal biting into her flesh, because it momentarily dulled the pain of her broken heart.

She had ended it.

Even thinking it now, it seemed surreal.

Since she'd been a mere girl her life had been seamlessly entwined with Lord Drake's. She'd come to know him as her future. After years of waiting for him to finally come up to scratch, she should welcome the liberty of finally being free. Now she would have a real Season, an opportunity to pursue what she yearned for most in life—love.

Yet, why did she feel as though she'd had everything she ever dreamed of and had lost it?

She turned to her maid. "Will you fetch the duke?"

Grace rose and rushed to do Emmaline's bidding. "Yes, my lady."

Emmaline stood up from the bench and paced the gardens, failing to see the flowers. Then she made the mistake of stealing a glance at the cerastium covering the ground and it was too much.

She sank to her knees and lovingly stroked the silk of the tiny, fragile bloom. She dropped her face in her hands and shook her head back and forth, trying to tamp out the feel of Drake's touch, the memories of how he'd made her body unfurl like petals opening up in the early spring.

A shadow fell over her and blotted out the nauseating sweetness of the sun's rays.

Sebastian's concerned voice interrupted her musings. "Em? Are you all right?"

She didn't stand up. Didn't look at him. "It is done. I have freed him."

How did she manage to keep her words so steady?

Sebastian fell silent.

Emmaline didn't know what she'd expected. Perhaps a bit of gloating on his part. After all, how many times over the past months had he insisted she break it off with Drake?

Sebastian sat onto the wrought iron bench. He rested a hand on her shoulder.

She leaned into him much as she had when she'd been a small girl who'd tumbled down the stairs. He'd scooped her up and held her until he'd driven away all the hurt. Oh, why couldn't she be a small child again, back when life was so very simple?

"You know I just want to see you happy?"

Emmaline gave a jerky nod.

"So why do I feel you are still not?"

She rested her chin on Sebastian's knee, and looked up at him. "I love him. Of all the mad, foolish, awful things to do…I went and fell in love with him."

Her brother said nothing for a long moment. Finally, he removed her broad straw bonnet, and gave it his utmost concentration. "Do you know Em, I still remember the day you were born. You were red-faced, screaming. Tears were dripping down your chubby cheeks. The nurse was desperately trying to soothe you. I leaned over the crib, and just like that, miracle of miracles, you ceased crying. I hadn't given much thought to what being an older brother meant. I realized in that moment I wanted to protect you from any and every hurt."

"Some things are beyond even your control, Sebastian."

"Unfortunately, I know that." He redirected his attention to the hat in his hands. "You know I think this bonnet is ridiculous."

She wrinkled her nose and swatted him on the arm. "I love that bonnet."

He spared a disparaging look for the item in question. "I would never, ever pick this hat for you. I have teased you time and time again. But you insist on wearing this one. There's no explaining it, is there, Em?" He directed his attention to Emmaline. "Simply a matter of... taste, I guess you could say."

Emmaline swallowed. "It is that," she whispered.

Sebastian tugged at the fraying blue satin ribbons. "See how it's fraying here? Even the straw is starting to tear." He dragged a finger along the areas in question.

"Seb—"

He continued. "Someday you are going to need a new hat. You will find the hat, and it will be perfect for you."

Emmaline chewed her lip. "I will never, ever feel this way—about another, hat." Her words were strong with conviction.

"No, no you may not. But nonetheless, you will find one and you will learn to love it. Do you understand?"

She nodded against his knee, again feeling like a little girl.

Sebastian set the hat down on the bench beside him. During her childhood, he used to tease her mercilessly about her concerns over Lord Drake's devotion. As the years passed and it became clear that there was credence to her fears, he'd ceased tormenting her. He then became the protective one. The brother who assured her that she was, indeed, wanted. Now, he was the brother who was being truthful. She loved him even more for that.

"I'm never going to be happy again," she said, nearly choking on the words.

A hoarse sound lodged in Sebastian's throat, and he dragged her unceremoniously off the ground into his arms. He took her by the shoulders and gave her a slight shake. "Listen to me. You are beautiful and kind and smart. Someday you will find a gentlemen deserving of your love and it will be Drake's loss. He made a foolish mistake and someday I'm certain he'll realize that."

Emmaline buried a gasping sob in his jacket front. "For all the consolation that is. Oh God, I've become a watering pot."

He tugged out a kerchief and wiped her nose. "A rather messy one at that."

She claimed the kerchief and held it to her face while she wept. "He never wanted our betrothal. Why?"

Sebastian cursed and took her by the shoulders. "Look at me. He is flawed."

Emmaline bit her lip. In spite of what had come to pass between her and Drake, in spite of his unwillingness to commit, not defending him felt like a betrayal. She thought about his loss of control in the gardens and felt an urge to defend him. Sebastian would call her all kinds the fool for trying to disabuse him of his notions.

Yes, Drake was scarred. But that had nothing to do with why he didn't want her.

Sebastian folded an arm over Emmaline's shoulders and gave a gentle squeeze. He waited until her tears abated to a watery hiccough. "Better?" he asked.

Oh Sebastian, I'm not a child anymore. One good, healthy cry could not erase the waves of hurt cascading over her. She didn't have the heart to tell him that she'd never be better, that this hurt would always be there. "Better," she lied.

Sebastian brightened and dropped a kiss on the top of her head. He picked up her hat and set it atop her head. "I'm serious. I am getting you a new hat, whether you like it or not."

Emmaline managed a laugh. "Someday you'll realize, you can't just find the perfect hat, anywhere."

Sebastian winked at her. "We shall see about that."

TWENTY-SIX

Dearest Drake,
Do you ever find it odd we've been betrothed for eleven years and yet
have only met a handful of times?
Ever Yours,
Emmaline

From where Drake stood at the edge of the ballroom, a sea of dancers swirled by him. A champagne flute dangled between his fingers.

He ignored the merriment; the gay laughter, the *ton* gossiping about the latest *on dit*—all of it.

Emmaline occupied every corner of his mind, in the same way she occupied every corner of his heart.

Since he'd stormed out of Sin's townhouse, Drake could not rid himself of a ravaging guilt over the insults he'd leveled at her.

It turned out she'd not enlisted Sinclair's aid. In spite of his ugly accusations, Emmaline possessed too much integrity and honor to betray Sin.

Should he really be surprised? She was, after all, the same woman who'd used her own body to shield an old peddler in the streets.

He could live ten lifetimes and never find another woman he'd rather wed.

Drake took a sip of champagne. He had returned home and awaited a summons from the Duke of Mallen. His mouth hardened. He knew the other man would delight in ending the agreement between their families.

CHRISTI CALDWELL

He'd spent the day seated in his father's library, his copy of *Glenarvon* on his lap. Memories had consumed him; the moment he'd seen her standing in a pile of refuse, the day he'd startled her at the Old Corner Bookshop. Memory after memory filled him, and he forced himself into a painful recollection of each one.

Drake recognized Emmaline's decision was for the best. And yet, with each tick of the clock, dread had filled him as he awaited a letter from the Duke of Mallen.

The day had come and gone. Strangely, it was as though nothing had changed. Drake even convinced himself that mayhap he'd imagined the whole blasted exchange with Emmaline.

He perused the crowded ballroom, longing for just one glimpse of her impish smile. Except when last she'd left him, she hadn't been smiling. He remembered the circumstances of their last meeting and lashed himself with the painful memory of her request to be free.

He tossed back the last of his champagne.

She didn't know which event he was attending and God knew she certainly wouldn't be approaching him with a smile. Which was the reason he'd taken pains to send a servant around from his household to the Duke of Mallen's household to ascertain Lady Emmaline's plans for the evening.

A slight flutter in the doorway caught his attention, and then his breath left on a hiss.

Had there ever been a woman more stunning? A sea-foam silk and organza creation clung to her delicate form. Her suggestive décolletage, trimmed with crystal beading caught the light of the chandeliers and radiated rainbow hues out into the hall. The rich fabric of the gown clung to her hips and swayed with any hint of movement. She was a siren. She beckoned to him.

He willed her to look at him. To forgive him.

Then she did. He knew the moment his presence registered. Her eyes lit with joy that was all too fleeting, only to be replaced by an aching sadness. It tore at his insides.

In a protective manner, the Duke of Mallen's tall frame moved closer to Emmaline and impinged on Drake's view of her. The duke

180

leaned down and whispered something in her ear. Emmaline's lips lifted ever so slightly, in rendition of an amused smile. Drake wondered if he were the only man present who recognized the gesture as forced.

She looped her arm in Mallen's and discreetly pinched him. If Drake hadn't been attending so closely, he would have missed the slight movement.

Drake stepped forward. He took two more steps and then had to use sheer will to halt his movements.

Mallen said a quick word to the Duchess of Mallen, and then ushered Emmaline to the opposite side of the room. He deposited her along the wall next to Miss Winters.

Drake cursed blackly, earning curious and shocked stares from the lords and ladies around him. He ignored them. If Drake had a sister, he would do far better. He wouldn't abandon her amidst a row of wallflowers.

Though was it really Mallen who was responsible for that, a silent voice jeered? *Aren't you the one truly responsible?*

A servant came by to relieve Drake of his empty champagne flute. He deposited it on the tray and continued his study of Emmaline. Emmaline's fair cheeks glowed as she spoke. She gestured wildly with her hands and Drake wondered what the young women discussed.

Sin sidled up next to him. "What's caught your attention, Drake?" he drawled.

"Stuff it, Sin." Drake motioned for another flute of champagne and proceeded to ignore his friend.

Not one to be easily intimidated, Sin accepted a flute for himself and looked across the ballroom. "Ahh, Lady Emmaline. Imagine finding her here even though she was unaware of your plans for the evening. How fortuitous for you."

Drake ignored the mocking edge in Sin's words.

"She looks rather well, considering."

Goddamn Sinclair for dangling that last word.

Drake told himself not to give in to the temptation of asking. Forced himself to count to ten.

He got to nine. "Considering what, Sin?"

Sin feigned wide-eyed surprise. "Why, you haven't heard? There is talk among the *ton* of a row between you and Lady Emmaline." Sin lowered his voice so Drake had to strain to hear. "Apparently she was seen running through Hyde Park, in tears. You were seen departing shortly thereafter."

Drake shuttered his expression, and even though he told himself not to look at her, he could not prevent himself from stealing one more glance. He recognized that forced dazzling smile for what it was; a brittle attempt at lightheartedness. Even with the distance and crowd between them, he could see her fingers curled tightly in her lap, blood-white.

"Mallen looks like he wants your blood," Sin murmured.

Without a word for Sinclair, Drake started across the room.

"Of all events for him to attend," Emmaline muttered. She twisted her hands anxiously in her lap, grateful for Sophie's calming presence. "Now, when I have no desire to see him, this is where he is?"

A frantic laugh bubbled from her throat.

Sophie reached for Emmaline's hand. "Oh, Em." She glanced across the ballroom floor. "He is looking this way," she said in a frantic whisper.

"Who?"

Sophie pointed her eyes toward the ceiling. "Who do you think? The Marquess of Drake."

Emmaline fought the urge to spin in his direction. She hated that even after his callous dismissal, she still longed to see him. She clasped Sophie's hand. "I want to leave," she said.

"Shh, they are staring. What has he done that makes you want to flee?"

Emmaline picked up her fan. She snapped it open in attempt to conceal her lips. "He sent a note requesting I meet him in the park. I showed up like a love-struck fool, and in the end, the note wasn't even from him, Sophie. It was Lord Sinclair's ploy to throw us together. Needless to say it ended in disaster."

Sophie's eyes went round. "Oh, Em."

Emmaline snapped her fan shut. "I broke off the betrothal."

If possible, Sophie's eyes widened even more. "You what?"

Emmaline scrunched her fingers into the folds of her gown, crushing the lovely sea-foam creation. Madame Touseou would be livid if she saw how callously Emmaline handled one of her finest gowns.

"I ended it. Lord Drake does not care for me. He never did. So in the end, I gave him his freedom."

Sophie's brow furrowed. "I have to believe he cares for you, Em."

A snort escaped Emmaline. "What makes you say that?"

Sophie stole another peek across the room. "He hasn't taken his eyes off you since the moment you arrived." She tapped her chin. "And he doesn't appear disinterested. No man can look at a woman the way he has looked at you all night and not feel something." Sophie sighed. "I'd give my last eye-tooth to have a man stare at me the way the Marquess of Drake stares at you."

Emmaline followed Sophie's focus. Why was Sophie staring at Sebastian? Her friend must have taken note of Sebastian's lethal black stare.

The urge was even stronger to find Drake in the crowd, but Emmaline continued to resist. "I assure you Drake is merely annoyed by my presence." Emmaline remembered his detachedness in Hyde Park earlier that day. He might as well have been one of the stone statues that graced her mother's gardens. Anything else her friend read in his response was fanciful thinking.

"Are you certain of that?" Sophie's question jerked Emmaline back to the moment.

"I couldn't be more…"

"Because he is headed this way."

Against better judgment, she sought him out. Drake cut a swath across the room, right to the seat she occupied.

Oh God, why is he doing this? Didn't he know she was going to collapse in a heap of despair at the feet of Society?

She and Sophie scrambled to their feet and dipped matching curtsies.

Drake bowed. "Lady Emmaline," he said without even the pretense of niceties for Sophie's sake. "I would like to request the next set."

Emmaline swallowed and attempted to muster her earlier indignation. "I'm afraid my card is full, my lord," she lied. She clutched her card close so he couldn't see the void of names.

He held out his arm, as if daring her to refuse. "I am certain some gentleman would be more than willing to forgive my boldness in stealing his set."

What kind of weak ninny was she that she wanted to take his arm and grant his request? For in spite of what had come to pass, she wanted to be in his arms.

A booming voice laden with false sincerity interrupted Emmaline's musings. "Lord Drake, so good to see you."

Emmaline and Drake turned in unison.

Sophie jumped up.

Drake passed a black glare over her brother. "Mallen."

Sophie shifted on her feet. "Your Grace." She remembered to dip a curtsy.

Sebastian paused and then seemed to remember the years of gentlemanly behavior drilled into him. He bowed. "How are you this evening, Miss Winters?"

"I'm—."

He didn't wait for an answer as he slung an arm around Drake's shoulder, neatly steering him from Emmaline.

"Well," Sophie muttered in his wake.

Emmaline hurried after the two gentlemen, fearing they would come to blows.

Drake shrugged off Sebastian good-naturedly and spoke through his teeth. "If you put a hand on me again, Mallen, by God, I swear I will lay you out in front of this entire room."

"Sebastian, do not cause a scene," Emmaline hissed.

Sebastian hesitated momentarily, seeming to consider the measure of Drake's threat and Emmaline's words. "I want you to stay away from my sister."

Drake's jaw hardened. "She is no longer a girl. She hardly needs you to dictate her actions—"

For the *tons* benefit, she playfully tapped Sebastian on the arm with her fan. "I'm standing right here, gentlemen."

Sebastian ignored her. "Ahh, but I'm not dictating her actions. I'm dictating yours. I said stay away from her."

"Mallen, I faced down a squadron of soldiers firing at me. It will take a great deal more than you to intimidate me," Drake drawled lazily. This time he thumped Sebastian between the shoulder blades. "I bid you good evening, Mallen." He turned his attention to Emmaline as he favored her with a last, hot, lingering look.

Emmaline's breath caught. She would always love him.

The moment was shattered by Sebastian. "Oh, Drake, one more thing?"

No, Emmaline screamed silently. She wanted to take back what she'd said to both Drake and Sebastian. She wanted to find a way to start again.

Drake raised a single, insolent golden brow.

"I'd like to request a meeting tomorrow morning, at nine o'clock. I'm sure you have an idea as to what it's about."

Emmaline's eyes slid closed on a wave of pain and when she opened them, Drake had already left.

TWENTY-SEVEN

My Dearest Drake,
I have begun to fear there was merit to my parents' suspicions that you
left because of our betrothal. My brother used to tell me such thoughts
were foolish. He has since stopped protesting. Regardless...I hope you
do not come to harm because of me.
Ever Yours,
Emmaline

Emmaline stood hidden by an enormous Doric column in her
brother's foyer. She rested her forehead against the hard, cool
stone and trailed a finger over the ridges. How long had she been waiting? Minutes? Hours? Days? Years?

A loud resounding knock bounced off the front doors. Even
though she'd been expecting it, she jumped. Her heart thumped
wildly and she folded her arms to her chest, making herself as small
as possible.

From her hiding spot, she peeked out from behind the structure.

The expressionless butler, Carmichael, opened the door and
admitted an ever regal, handsome Lord Drake. The black flowing fabric of his elegant cloak swirled around his legs.

Drake handed the servant a card. "His Grace is expecting me."

Carmichael assisted him out of his cloak and handed it to a nearby
servant.

The butler motioned for Lord Drake to follow. "Right this way, my
lord." Emmaline watched him go. His boots tapped methodically on
the marble floor. Then he froze, and suddenly whipped back around.

She pressed tight against the other side of the column, furtively studying his actions.

His unreadable jade stare quickly panned the foyer, before swiveling back and settling on the column that served as her hiding place.

Emmaline smothered a gasp with her hand, torn between laughter and tears. Drake had a way of doing that. Of somehow, knowing just where she was.

"My lord? This way, if you please," Carmichael prompted.

He inclined his head and then continued on to Sebastian's office.

When she was certain he'd gone, Emmaline dashed from behind her hiding place, and raced to her brother's office.

Once upon a lifetime ago, Emmaline had been a little girl seated in her father's office swinging her legs to and fro, opposite a young boy. She'd been unaware of the goings on across the room. Fifteen years later, the little girl had been replaced by a woman, now barred from that very same room. Now she stood at the fringe of a closed door.

Unlike that time from her girlhood past, Emmaline knew exactly what was being discussed between the present duke and her betrothed. And found she preferred the not knowing.

The large paneled oak door muted the voices closeted away in the office.

"Come away from that door, Emmaline," her mother hissed from the hall.

Emmaline ignored her. Even if Emmaline was eavesdropping like a small girl, she was in fact a grown woman.

"Emmaline."

Emmaline leveled her mother with a forceful stare. "No," she mouthed silently.

When her mother took several steps closer, Emmaline held up a staying hand.

"By God. Mother, everything has been dictated to me since I was five years old. I'm telling you now, I need to be here. Please go, lest I be discovered."

For the first time in her entire life, the usually eloquent Duchess of Mallen appeared speechless. With great gentleness, she took

Emmaline's face between her hands and dropped a kiss upon her forehead.

"You are right, my dear. I have imposed enough of my will on your life." She spared another glance at the door. "Find me when it's done."

The seconds ticked by and the muffled sound of speaking grabbed her. "Mother," Emmaline said urgently.

"Right, right," she whispered and with obvious hesitancy, left Emmaline alone.

Emmaline shifted her focus to the heavy oak door, wishing it was instead a mere slip of a curtain so the exchange could be unfiltered. On the heels of that thought came a startling realization. It hit her with all the force of an unexpected summer lightning storm; the implication of the momentous proceedings on the other side of the door managed to suck all strength from her limbs.

The stoic force she'd found to face down her mother left her on a silent breath and she realized this would be the last time Drake ever entered her home. Never again would he tease her. Or stroke her body like a virtuoso, who'd been gifted a new instrument. For when Drake exited Sebastian's library, he would cease to be a part of her life. All they'd shared, from teeth-gritting annoyance to easy companionability would fade into nothing more than a fleeting memory of a brief time she'd been close to complete and utter rapture.

After a copious amount of tears shed for her betrothed, Emmaline had risen that morning certain she couldn't manage one more salty drop for Drake.

A tear slipped down her cheek and she swiped at it with an aggravated hand. Apparently she'd been wrong.

"A drink?" Mallen offered. He gestured to the open bottle of brandy.

Drake gave a curt shake. "A bit early for a drink, no?"

One of Mallen's dark brows arched. "Not one for social niceties, are you?"

Drake's jaw hardened. He forced himself to unfurl his tightly clenched fist.

He would be damned if he gave in to Mallen's attempt to draw him into a row. He'd caused Emmaline enough hurt and wouldn't further add to it by beating her brother to a bloody pulp in her home.

Mimicking the pompous duke, Drake arched a cool, mocking brow. "Is this why you asked me here? For a social visit?"

"Sit, sit!" Mallen urged and reclaimed the seat behind his desk.

Drake settled into one of the leather winged-back chairs and stretched his legs out in front of him.

Mallen propped his chin on steepled fingers and drummed them together. "You know why you're here," he said at last.

Drake gritted his teeth. "Have out with it already."

Mallen leaned forward and reached for a leather folio. He pulled out several documents, appeared to review them, and then reached for his pen. The duke dipped it in ink and scratched his signature on a series of pages.

He signed the final document and settled the pen back into its crystal well with a decisive click. "I am severing the contract between you and Emmaline." Mallen shoved the open portfolio across the surface of his otherwise immaculate desk.

Drake had known this exchange was coming, and yet his stomach twisted with an agonized pain.

A contract.

Over the past few months, Emmaline had become so very much more than a contract. She'd become the sole reason for Drake's every happiness. She represented all that was courageous and strong. And the bloody scraps of parchment would erase all of that from his life.

His heartbeat increased, forcing him to draw a deep, shaky breath.

Mallen's eyes narrowed. "Let's get on with it."

Drake reached for the damned documents. He proceeded to read them with deliberate slowness. He turned the pages with such jerky movements he ripped one of the sheets. When he finished reading them, he set them aside.

189

Mallen spoke. "I'm perplexed. Based on your previous sentiments, I should think you'd be very eager to put your signature to the documents."

Drake growled. "Sod off."

Still, he didn't pick up the pen. His gaze wandered off to the sconce of lit candles throughout the room. How easy it would be to cross to one of those small torches and carry it back to the bloody document and set the whole foul piece ablaze.

Mallen leaned across his desk and tapped the parchment. "Your signature, Drake."

Drake lunged to his feet. He wrenched the pen from its crystal container, held it aloft, so that ink smattered the duke's desk and paper. He glowered at Mallen. "You are enjoying this, aren't you?"

"Shouldn't you be enjoying it?" Mallen drawled.

Rage filled Drake. He scribbled his name hastily, and again dipped the pen in the inkwell. "You have never liked me." He could not bite back the seething hatred he felt for the other man.

"Oh, come. We both know the sentiments have been mutual."

Drake scratched his signature on another parchment. "Wholeheartedly."

"Can you answer me this, Drake?"

Drake paused and glanced up.

"You ignored Emmaline for fifteen years. You ran off to fight a war, and left your responsibilities behind. You've made it clear to Society how you felt about your betrothal. You returned and carried on with a whole host of women, you drink, you gamble." Mallen paused, probing eyes, seemed to search out answers. "And yet, you don't strike me as a man eager to sign the severance document. Why is that?"

Drake set the pen down, and leveling his palms on the desktop, leaned forward. "You are not betrothed to anyone, Your Grace. Why is that?" He didn't allow Mallen to answer. "It is because you made that choice. Had you been a boy of three and ten and had that very important decision taken away from you, well, then I'm sure then you might understand some of my rationale."

Mallen inclined his head. "You might be right. That is neither here nor there," he said with a wave of his hand. "What matters is Emmaline is still my sister, and I would see her cared for." He motioned to the documents. "Get on with it."

Drake dropped his stare to the parchment. With the black ink, he'd made a mess of one of the sheets. He wondered if the document would even be considered legal.

"You did not answer my question," the duke said.

Drake would be damned if he fed the other man's curiosity. He signed the final sheet. Straightening, he threw the pen onto the desk where it landed with a thunk. "No, no I am not."

Silence descended.

It is done.

Mallen reached his hand across the desk, and Drake stared at it blankly. He wanted to snarl at him. Tell him to go to the Devil. Sebastian shook his hand. They were after all, gentlemen.

He turned to leave.

"Drake?"

He froze, keeping his back to the other man.

"In spite of what you believe, I don't hate you."

Drake managed a dry laugh but didn't answer; because if he did all he'd end up saying was he couldn't care less about what Mallen felt for him. Instead he nodded.

"Do you know why we've never gotten along, Drake?"

God, the man was a termagant. Tenacious.

Like his sister. *Oh God, why did that thought hurt so bloody much?* Drake turned around. "You aren't going to let this go, are you?" he bit out.

Mallen smiled. "We never got along because we resented each other. You resent me because I love her. And I resent you because you do not."

He measured Mallen's words for a long moment.

"One more thing."

Drake froze. Waited.

"Can I ask why you didn't want to marry her?"

He swallowed once. Twice. Then gave a jerky shake of his head.

"That is not something I'm willing to share with you, Mallen." With a curt bow, Drake did what he'd been longing to do since he'd gotten there—he left.

He stormed out quickly and nearly stumbled upon the young woman hovering against the wall.

He froze. He eyed her, beset by a range of different emotions; agony, regret, hopelessness. She'd been the last thread holding him to humanity. *What am I without you?*

The moment seemed to stretch into forever.

"Goodbye, Emmaline," he said hoarsely. "It was never my intention to hurt you. Please know that."

Emmaline's expressive brown eyes pooled with tears. "Goodbye, Drake."

Then he left, knowing until he drew his last breath, he'd be haunted by the sorrowful image of her standing there.

Emmaline sank against the wall. She pressed a hand against her mouth to stifle a sob.

Sebastian opened the office door and tugged her into the room away from any potential gossipy servants and when he'd closed the door, promptly pulled her into his arms. "Shh," he murmured against the crown of her hair.

She wept against his shirtfront. She had wanted this. So why did it hurt so much?

"I asked him, Em."

"I-I know." She'd heard the whole exchange.

"I'm sorry you didn't get your answers."

Not as sorry as I am.

TWENTY-EIGHT

Dearest Lord Drake,
I know young ladies ought to be demure and proper. Yet upon reading
your name next to a very notable widow in the scandal sheets, I feel
anything but ladylike.
Ever Yours,
Emmaline

Drake strode down St. James Street, through the black iron fence, and up the famous steps of White's. A uniformed butler opened the door, granting him admittance.

News of his broken betrothal had found its way into the scandal sheets not even one day after Drake's meeting with Mallen. Since then, he'd been plagued with a flea-like tenacity by curious looks and bold questions from the *ton*.

The bustling activity, the card games in progress all ground to a jarring halt as every pair of eyes swiveled in his direction. Christ, you'd think he was suspected of a bloody murder for all the scrutiny his movements garnered.

Drake's jaw twitched. Apparently not even his club would serve as a sanctuary. He looked straight ahead, pointedly ignoring the gentlemen who were as eager as the matrons at Almack's for a juicy morsel of gossip.

His progress across the club was halted by a bold dandy attired in gold breeches and a flamboyant orange jacket. The man stepped into his path, slowing Drake's path to the empty table in the far, far corner. Drake held up a hand, shielding his eyes from the offending hues. The candlelight flickered and bounced off the shine of the dandy's satin fabrics. Why, with the seemingly constant rainy days in London, all they needed to do was drag out this fop to brighten the sky.

"My lord—"

"What?"

Drake's dangerous whisper echoed around the still of the room. The gentlemen seated, drinking their traitorous French brandies and placing bets, drew in a collective, audible breath.

The color blanched from the young man's cheeks. "Uh-I-uh… p-pardon me." He scurried off like a rodent being chased by the house cat.

Drake deviated from his path and headed toward the famous betting book. He picked up a pen and scribbled a wager into the infamous log. Slamming the pen into the crystal inkwell, he marched over and at last reached the table furthest from the crowd of gentlemen.

A hesitant majordomo approached. He cleared his throat. "My lord is there something—?"

"A bottle of whiskey," he growled.

With lightning speed, a bottle was procured, along with a tumbler.

Drake picked up the bottle and proceeded to pour a generous amount of liquor into the glass. He tossed it back and welcomed the fiery trail it burned down the back of his throat. His lips twisted up in a grimace. God, it was a foul brew. He'd hated it when he was in Oxford and he hated it even more now. But he'd be damned if he picked up a bloody bottle of French brandy. All in all, the vile stuff would serve the very same purpose. He again reached for the bottle and sloshed liquid to the rim. Before the night was through, he had every intention of getting mind-numbingly foxed.

Just then, his eyes snagged on the copy of the *Times*, resting on the table. The corner of his eye ticked, once, then twice. And because he'd developed a taste for self-torture, he reached for the offending paper and proceeded to skim. There it was. On the front page, in dark bold print were two familiar initials.

Lady E. F.

Why didn't they print the entire bloody names anyways? Every last bugger in the whole bloody kingdom knew each lord or lady mentioned by initials in the scandal sheets. So why stand on ceremony?

They should have out with it already. The paper should come right out and say: *The Earl of Waxham has launched a whirlwind courtship of Lady Emmaline Fitzhugh.*

With fingers that shook, he poured several more fingerfuls into his empty glass. God, he thought he might be sick. He wanted to blame it on the amber brew, then he tortured himself with the excerpt once again. Nausea roiled and it was all he could do to keep from casting up the accounts of his stomach right there in the middle of White's.

Waxham hadn't wasted any time. It had been four bloody days since Drake had signed those damned documents. Four days of regrets. Four days of despair.

In each of the four sleepless nights, he'd railed at himself for signing Mallen's bloody papers. Why hadn't he told the other man to go to the devil?

Because of her. Somewhere along the way, it had all become about Emmaline. Drake didn't merely desire her. He ached for her with a pain-like ferocity. Her happiness and safety meant more to him than even his own. A bitter laugh escaped him. Who would have believed, the emotionless Lord Drake would ever come to care for the same lady he'd spent his life avoiding? Oh, it was the kind of drivel poets wrote about, the kind of nonsense he himself scoffed at.

Until her.

He'd told himself countless times she was better off without him. Sometimes he said the words aloud. Other times he honed in on those words stuck in his mind. Drake willed himself to accept her loss so he could move forward and be free of her sorceress-like hold.

Instead his want for her grew stronger. The feelings swelled each time he read her name.

But this—thoughts of her and Waxham—it was too much. He was strong. He wasn't that strong. He'd rather face down a line of Boney's men than confront this horror.

Drake tortured himself with images of her married to Waxham. Waxham lifting up her skirts, pleasuring her, rutting between her thighs—giving her children. He choked on the sip of whiskey that had been sliding down his throat, nearly gagging on it.

"You look like hell."

Drake didn't glance up. "I'm not looking for company, Sin."

Sin waved off the majordomo who hurried over. "Ah-yes, I assumed as much based on your wager in the books." He hooked his boot around the leg of the chair and tugged it out. "Really, Drake? A wager on which gentlemen would be foolish enough to seek out your company? I took the liberty of having that bet crossed out."

Drake didn't give a damn about the wager he'd put in the books. All he cared about was getting inebriated and tamping down images of Emmaline folded in Waxham's embrace. Emmaline laughing up at the paragon. Emmaline...

Sin snatched the paper from between his tightly clenched fingers. "Ahh, so this is about the lady."

Drake placed his hands on the tabletop and leaned forward, seething. "By the love of God, if you mention her name I will bloody your face."

Sin threw back his head and laughed. "I swear, if I didn't know you since we were mere boys that might alarm me."

How wonderful that Sin could find amusement when Drake was so bloody miserable. "What do you want?"

Sin's smile slipped. He made it a point of tugging his chair directly in front of Drake, effectively blocking him from the voyeurs present. "I want to know you are all right."

"Why, I couldn't be better."

His friend cursed beneath his breath. "Enough with the sarcasm. This is me, Drake."

Drake dragged a hand over his eyes. "What would you have me say? Would you have me lay myself bare before all of Society? It is bad enough having to deal with my father's recriminations."

"Is that why you've taken up here for the past two nights?"

Drake slashed the air with his hand. "Is everything I do known by all?"

Sin shrugged. "At this moment, you are unfortunately the *tons* favorite source of gossip."

Drake threw back the remaining contents in his glass. "To hell with them all."

A frown marred Sin's usually affable countenance. "Nonetheless, you can't go around frightening young pups that have the misfortune of coming near you. It's hardly their fault you drove Emmaline away."

That was the rub of it. He was the maker of his own misery.

"I thought you might prefer the termination of the arrangement," Sin said with quiet honesty.

Drake stared hard at the tabletop. "Damn it to hell, I miss her."

His friend quirked one brow. "Well, that is quite a revelation to come to at this late point."

"Of late, I've come to a whole host of revelations."

Sin leaned forward. "Oh, I'm all ears."

Drake picked up his empty glass and rolled it between his fingers, studying the remaining drops glistening at the bottom of the tumbler and said nothing.

"When you are ready, then."

Sin was a good friend. Just one more person Drake didn't deserve. "If it is all the same to you, I'd like to get myself soused and you're hindering my best attempts."

Holding a hand up, Sin motioned for a waiter. "Another glass and another bottle of your best whiskey."

The uniform-clad servant hurried off, and promptly returned with the requested items.

Sin picked up Drake's bottle and poured two more stiff glasses of whiskey. He raised a tumbler in mock salute. "If you are determined to drink yourself senseless, then as a friend, I must insist on joining you."

"For the love of God man, you're heavy," Sin muttered breathless from the weight of his exertions. He helped guide Drake to the above-floor suites. Drake had flung his arm across Sin's shoulders. "I must admit I am thrilled you've rented rooms here. I don't think I could have managed carrying you to the duke's townhouse."

"Th-that's anufer thing," Drake slurred. "II'm faaaar too old to still reside with my father."

Sin nodded to a gentlemen they passed in the hallway. "That is something easily resolved," he said helpfully.

Drake paused, and forced Sin to a stop. "You know what is naht so easily resolved?"

"What is—"

"Ehh-mmaline. I rather made a mess of thaat situation."

Sin looked at him with a sobering expression. "With a bit of effort, that too can be resolved."

Drake's gut clenched and he swayed on his feet. "Do you truly believe that?" He felt hopeful for the first time in four days. Had it been four days? The days had marched on, interminable in their duration. He fished around his jacket pocket and withdrew his timepiece. The numbers upon the watch blurred before his eyes. "It doesn't have the days?"

Confusion flitted over his friend's face. "Let's get you to your room."

He allowed Sin to lead him along. "I-I saay, you seem faaaar too sober."

Sin snorted. "That is because I didn't drink an entire bottle, my friend. Here we are." Sin fished around for the key Drake had handed him downstairs, then opening the door, led Drake inside the quarters. The space was large enough to serve its purpose; a temporary escape for gentlemen in dire need of temporary quarters.

Winding his way around the front room, Sin steered Drake to his bedchambers. With a grunt he heaved Drake over to the bed.

Drake landed hard and then promptly fell backwards. "Oomph." He blinked up at the ceiling. "The room is spinning. Howww did White's manage such a feat?"

"We shall ask the majordomo tomorrow," Sin promised and, good friend that he was, set to work tugging off Drake's boots.

Drake flung a hand over his eyes. "I don't deserve her, you know. Came back a madman."

Sin paused in his efforts. "I couldn't disagree with you more. But this is not the time to debate the point." Once both boots had been removed, Sin took a seat at the edge of the bed. The mattress dipped under his weight.

"I-I-I'm going to make some changes, maaark my words."

"I certainly hope so. Your first order should be—"

Drake very much did want some guidance on what his first order should be, but he was so damned drunk that he couldn't quite string together Sin's words. And after a bottle of whiskey, he'd at last muted the pain of losing Emmaline to a dull ache.

Closing his eyes, he slid into blessed oblivion.

TWENTY-NINE

My Dearest Drake,
I am a coward. I have not sent you one note in three years. But you
haven't sent me one note either. Are you a coward as well? Or worse, do
you just not care?
Ever Yours,
Emmaline

After two weeks sleeping at his club, Drake moved back home. There were no questions from the Duke of Hawkridge, no articulation of displeasure. Father and son had settled back into the same stilted, uneasy arrangement they'd had since Drake returned from the war.

Drake tugged back the curtains that covered his bedroom window and peered out at the night sky. His finger traced a distracted path across the pane of the window. Clouds billowed across the moon and blotted out all stars in the sky.

As usual, sleep eluded him. This time, demons from the Peninsula were not the ghosts that drifted about his consciousness, robbing him of an undeserving peace. Instead he was possessed by memories of a feisty, courageous lady with joyful eyes, and imaginings of her with another man.

Drake slammed his fist into the ivory plaster wall beside the window.

The violent movement sent the seemingly forgotten drawstring sack tumbling from the edge of the nightstand. His eyes snagged the article lying on the wood floor.

Since they'd parted, he'd not allowed himself to read the notes Emmaline had written to him. The cowardly part of him hadn't wanted to acknowledge there had been a young lady named Emmaline, who'd spent hours of her time writing to him, but had been too shamed to ever send him the notes.

Had he always been an utter bastard where she was concerned?

Drake crossed the few feet separating him from the bag, and snatched it up.

Then with far greater care, he untied the silk sack, and pulled out a large stack of notes that were neatly tied with a blue satin ribbon. The top ivory vellum envelope was addressed to Captain Drake.

Drake returned back to bed and lied down. He propped his head on several pillows. Sir Faithful leapt up onto the bed and claimed the spot next to Drake. He petted the dog. "You, too, want to know what she said, do you, my boy?"

He undid the delicate bow holding the letters together, and pulled out the first envelope. Taking great care, he slipped a finger beneath the fold of the thick vellum and withdrew the note.

He patted Sir Faithful on the head, shook out the parchment, and read her words.

Dearest Lord Drake,

There is something I must share with you. It is dreadful and horrible. And if you were reluctant to wed me before this moment, well then (sigh), I am sure you will never want to wed me now. Are you ready? Dare I even put these words to paper? I cannot dance. There you have it. I tread abominably upon my dance master's toes. I have overheard him speaking with mother. He said he was one broken toe away from finding another assignment.

Having tired of him as a dance master, I ground my heel quite happily upon his foot.

I am awaiting the arrival of my next dance master.

Ever Yours,

Emmaline

Drake dragged a finger along the blank ink, tracing the lines she'd made on the page. Odd that such a long time ago, a much younger Emmaline's hand had stroked the marks on this note.

He set the letter aside and moved to the next. Drake read scores and scores of letters, noting when the tone changed, when the words became the words of a young woman, and no longer a girl who traipsed across the countryside, climbing trees, engaging in mischief with her older brother.

Unlike so many other nights, he willed himself awake. He continued reading until the swell of the bright morning sun appeared on the horizon. Her notes had become a lure he'd been hooked upon, that he didn't want to be freed of.

He reached for the final remaining note.

My Dearest Drake,

I realize you have not read any of my notes—because I failed to send them. There is so much I've yearned to say to you. I've longed to ask why you left to fight. I've longed to ask what flaws are so inherent in my character that you should never have written me. I wonder if you've ever thought of me. Then I wonder if those thoughts are ever pleasant.

I wish you would know I will be a good wife to you. Oh, I might not be biddable and easily controlled, but we will know laughter. When you return, I long to laugh with you.

Since you will never read this, I intend to show you!

Ever Yours,

Emmaline

His eyes slid closed, and he brought the parchment to his nose, inhaling deeply. Except the citrus lemon scent that was hers had long faded.

For fifteen long years he had existed in a world where he was beholden to none, where all he felt, all he knew were his own hurt and disappointments. He had never allowed himself to consider there was any other injured party; a young woman desiring marriage. Instead he had nurtured his anger, kept it close.

He now realized that anger had become a mechanism he'd used to protect himself from the people around him. Emmaline had indeed taught him to laugh again, to feel. She had reminded him he was still human.

It was time he faced life.

He stroked Sir Faithful between the ears and thought about the woman who meant more to him than anyone.

Could he? Should he?

He shoved himself up and rang for his valet to help him into different clothes before starting downstairs. As he walked down the hall, a well-trained Sir Faithful trotted obediently at his heels. The dog came to an immediate stop when Drake halted at one particular room. He rapped on the door and entered his father's study.

"Father."

The Duke of Hawkridge set aside the scandal sheet he'd been reading and removed his monocle. "Come in, come in." He tried to shove an envelope atop the paper.

Drake's eyes narrowed.

His father didn't try to prevent him from picking up the offending document.

He scanned the article and made a disapproving sound. "Really, Father? The scandal sheets?" He threw the paper down upon the desk and took a seat.

His father flushed and made a vague motion with his hand. "What is it, son?"

Drake folded one leg at his knee and tapped a staccato rhythm upon the arms of the chair. Sir Faithful yapped once, and Drake leaned down and scratched him between the ears. "I purchased a bachelor's residence," he said at last.

His father gave a slight inclination of his head. He propped his chin on steepled fingers, but otherwise showed no outward reaction to Drake's pronouncement.

"Are you...certain you are—are...interested in being alone?"

Interpretation being; what will you do when I'm not there to help with the nightmares?

He gave his father a long, assessing look.

For the first time, he looked at the Duke of Hawkridge, and realized his strong, powerful father looked—old. A strip of gray peppered the hair at his temples, and the lines of his face, always firm, had softened. He now possessed wrinkles around the lines of his mouth and the corners of his eyes.

That moment, Drake was shamed as he realized he was not the only one who had been scarred by the war. The Duke of Hawkridge had witnessed far too many of his son's nightmares to remain unaffected by Drake's transformation from man to monster.

Drake held his father's gaze. "It's not your fault, Father," he said.

His father dragged a hand through his hair. The normally steady fingers shook. "What isn't my fault, Drake? The war? The broken betrothal? The nightmares?" he asked bitterly.

"Any of it. The decision to enlist was mine and mine alone."

His father pressed his fingers tight against his forehead and rubbed. "Because of your resentment toward me. I—I am so sorry. More sorry than you can ever know."

Drake swallowed past a swell of emotion. "I believe at one point I did blame you. For years, in fact. It was wrong of me. Childish."

The admission, this sudden absolution his father deserved, was freeing. It had not been his father's fault that Drake had high-tailed it to the Peninsula. Drake had no one to blame but himself. It was also healing to take ownership of the decisions he'd made.

Silence descended upon the room, punctuated by the methodic tick of the clock.

"That blasted betrothal. Seemed like such a good idea at the time," his father muttered. "What a disaster it turned out to be."

Drake flinched. It struck somewhere in the vicinity of his heart, to think of the betrothal as a disaster. "Again, Father, it was only because of me. Given all the decisions I made, I could never bring myself to resent the betrothal." It had given him months of happiness. Filled him with joy.

Sir Faithful nudged Drake's knee. Drake rewarded him with another affectionate stroke. It had brought him Sir Faithful.

He thought of Emmaline and his gut clenched and unclenched at the pain of loss.

If only he had her…

Go to her, woo her.

"You can pursue her on your own," the Duke of Hawkridge said into the quiet.

Drake didn't move. "The nightmares, Father."

"Maybe she can help you."

"I cannot place this burden on her." He had placed enough burdens on Emmaline, he could not, nay would not, add this one. "No matter how much I care for her, no matter how it fills me with rage at the thought of any gentleman courting her, I have to face the reality— I'm a madman."

His father scoffed. "You are no madman. You were affected by what you saw and did. You'd be a madman if you weren't affected by those experiences." He arched a brow. "I made decisions that I felt were in your best interest. How much did you appreciate it? Perhaps you should let Lady Emmaline decide for herself if she would stay and fight these demons alongside you."

Drake lurched to his feet and paced the width of the room. He'd had the same thought each morning upon reading her name in the scandal sheets. But every time he'd stepped a foot out the door, intending to humble himself at her feet, he stopped.

Could he court her? Drake paused mid-stride.

"I have never taken my son as a quitter," his father called from behind his desk.

Drake stiffened.

It felt as though the chains of life that had restrained him all these years were at last lifted. A slow smile formed on his lips. His self-imposed exile was at an end.

THIRTY

My Dearest Drake,
You have returned! I long for the day when we would again meet!
Ever Yours,
Emmaline

Emmaline surveyed the crowded ballroom and upon spying Sophie, squeezed her brother's arm, halting his movements. "I see Sophie." She gestured subtly in her friend's direction.

Sebastian's gaze lingered on Sophie and then he looked back at Emmaline. "You know you do not need to sit with the other wallflowers," he said, a frown on his lips.

Since Emmaline had severed her betrothal, she'd spent her evenings not very much different than so many others—amidst the other wallflowers.

She pinched her brother's arm. "Hush. Sophie is not a wallflower."

He made a non-committal sound. "I'm merely saying—"

"Don't say anything."

Sebastian closed his mouth and proceeded to guide her toward Sophie.

Sophie seemed to notice Sebastian first. Her eyes went wide and a small tremulous smile hovered on her lips before her gaze landed on Emmaline. She climbed to her feet and curtsied. "Em. Your Grace."

Sebastian bowed. "Miss Winters." He turned a wary look on the hopeful wallflowers, who eyed him with a desperate intensity, and beat a hasty retreat.

"Coward," Emmaline muttered for Sophie's ears.

Her friend laughed and claimed Emmaline's hand. Just then, a swell of eager suitors converged upon them. It had been much the same way since word of her broken betrothal had become fodder for the gossips. Emmaline didn't delude herself into believing these gentlemen cared about anything beyond her dowry and a connection with the Duke of Mallen. It might not matter to the other wallflowers who smiled almost gratefully in Emmaline's direction, but it mattered to her.

"May I fetch a glass of punch?" Lord Abbott, one of her more erstwhile suitors, offered a desperate pitch to his voice.

The third Earl of Stanwick puffed out a broad chest, a chest Emmaline highly suspected was compliments of substantial padding provided by his valet. "I said I would fetch the lady punch."

"Oh dear, this has the makings of an all-out fight," Sophie murmured beneath her breath. "Why don't you race and see who brings it back first?" Her suggestion resulted in an exodus of some of the young swains.

Emmaline turned to the expectant crowd of suitors. "Gentlemen, I fear I turned my ankle and will not be dancing any more sets for the remainder of the evening."

The popinjays groaned in disappointment and shuffled off, earning Emmaline censorious looks from her fellow wallflowers.

"Did we ever truly want this?" Emmaline mused.

Sophie's lips twitched. "There must be a happy in-between, no?"

A happy in-between? What exactly would that look like? One would have to actually have a care for one or any of the suitors to be happy, no?

Over the years she'd given so much thought to being courted. She'd dreamed of becoming the recipient of a man's admiration. Oh, she'd hoped it would be her betrothed, but had yearned to know a real courtship. That had been before she'd fallen in love with Drake. Now, every gentleman she met was a pale shadow of his impressive, inspiring figure. Not a single gentleman she'd met had managed to make her heart trip a beat, or set her stomach aflutter with shades of longing.

Only one man thus far had ever prompted such a response in her...and he was gone.

Sophie claimed her hand again. "You look so sad."

Emmaline swallowed painfully. "I ache for just one sight of him. It is as though he's disappeared from Society. I wonder what he is doing. Wonder if he ever has any thoughts of me."

Sophie snorted. "Of course he thinks of you."

A thrum of whispers rose amidst the crowd. Sophie glanced across the ballroom. Her golden brows shot up to her hairline.

"Sophie?"

"Uh, what would you do if you saw Lord Drake?"

Emmaline cocked her head. "Well, I imagine I'll eventually have to see him because we do travel in similar circles."

"Because he's just arrived."

Emmaline's heart quickened and for the first time in weeks, soft joy filled her. She told herself not to search for him, but could no more stop herself from looking about than she could stop breathing.

He stood at the top of the stairwell, greeting Lord and Lady Thompson. Attired in all black and with his halo of golden hair, he may as well have been a fallen angel. He inclined his head in acknowledgement of something Lord Thompson said, before bowing, and pressing ahead. He appeared immune to the hum of whispers, the gaping stares. His intent emerald green gaze swept over the room, searching, searching, searching.

And then finding.

Even with the distance separating them, the hot intensity of his focus as he settled his stare on her scorched her like a noon sun.

"Breathe," she reminded herself. Sophie nudged her in the arm but Emmaline ignored her.

"There is no way a man can look at you the way the marquess is looking at you and not feel *something*."

Aware of the intrusive way in which they were being scrutinized, Emmaline forced herself to look away.

Sophie groaned. "Oh dear, your brother is headed this way."

Sebastian rapidly crossed the room, even as the crowd parted for Drake. "What do you want me to do?" Sophie urged. "Do you want to see him?"

"I do," Emmaline whispered. She heard the consternation in her own words.

Sophie hopped up from her seat and crossed the room, intercepting Sebastian. She held her empty dance card up to his inspection. Her boldness was met with scandalous gasps. His brow furrowed with a blend of annoyance and confusion. Sophie jabbed her finger at the card and showed him an invisible mark. Sebastian directed a pointed glare in Emmaline's direction, before taking Sophie's arm with seeming reluctance and leading her to the dance-floor.

Oh, Sophie. Emmaline's eyes slid closed in gratitude.

"She is a good friend," a quiet voice said, just over her shoulder.

She gasped, a fluttering hand covering her breast, and turned to face her former betrothed.

Drake claimed Emmaline's hand and bent low over it. He placed a slow, lingering kiss on the top of her knuckles, even as his fingers caressed her inner wrist. What he wouldn't give to remove the fabric that separated their skin.

"My lord," she murmured.

With some difficulty, he swallowed around a swell of emotion lodged in his throat. "After all we've shared you might call me by my name."

"You'd have me call you Ashton?" She traced her lips with the tip of her tongue. "In front of a room full of strangers awaiting my misstep?"

"Perhaps not by my given name, then." He'd always quite abhorred the name. "Nor should you worry after the gossips." He glanced around the room and pinned the peering lords and ladies with a collective glare. The crowd immediately redirected their attention. "Is that, better, Emmaline?"

Emmaline's lips twitched but still refused to arc in a full smile. "Would that you could make them all disappear."

He inclined his head. "I shall work on that."

An awkward silence descended. They stood there, studying each other, like two strangers meeting for the first time.

"Will you do me the honor of this set?"

I have wanted to hold you in my arms, since the moment I walked out of your home, out of your life.

She went to place her hand in his, and then pulled it back. "I—I," she stumbled.

His stomach tightened under the bite of rejection. "Forgive me for burdening you," he said lamely. He should turn away. He should—

"Oh no, no," she hurried to reassure him. She motioned down to her slippered feet. "You see, I told the gentlemen I turned my ankle and was unable to dance. How would it appear if I were to suddenly strike out the next set with you?"

A wave of relief washed over him. "That is the reason for your hesitancy?" He laughed; the sound burst from him from a place he'd thought had ceased to exist, a place full of unrestrained hope.

Without allowing her another word on the matter, he commandeered her to the ballroom floor for the current dance—a waltz. He settled his hands on her waist.

"My brother is flaying you to ribbons with his eyes."

Drake arched a brow. "The last person I'm thinking about right now is your brother."

Emmaline looked toward her brother. A small frown marred her lips. She continued to study the glowering duke as he waltzed Miss Winters across the dance floor. "He is not happy."

Drake glanced at the duke and then back at Emmaline. "Really? I'm amazed you can tell. That is the only expression I've ever seen him wear."

She giggled.

Drake's lips twitched at her infectious laughter. "No, really. He must have been born with that terrific glower."

Another giggle escaped her. "He's practiced it since he was a young boy," she said in a conspiratorial whisper.

He nodded somberly. "Of course he has. It is a requisite course for all heirs to dukedoms." Drake narrowed his eyes and studied Emmaline down the length of his nose in his best impression of Mallen's expression.

A gurgle of laughter bubbled up past her lips. "That is a rather impressive rendering."

"Or there is this one." Drake drummed up the disapproving glower his father had directed his way, many a-times when Drake had been a small boy.

"Please, s-s-stop. It isn't seemly if I…" The floodgates opened and Emmaline's giggle became a resounding laugh that earned a multitude of stares from the *ton*. The full, husky sound was hardly the simpering, stifled laugh required of a lady. Instead it conjured thoughts of naked bodies entwined in silken sheets, sated with pleasure.

"Th-they are s-staring again."

Drake arched a brow. "Should I attempt one of your brother's famous ducal scowls?"

Emmaline laughed even harder.

Drake stared down at her. *How did I let you go?* Sheer madness and rash idiocy were the only answers that made any sense. If he'd searched the world two times over, he'd never find a woman like her. And yet, she'd been his since they were mere children.

"I read your notes." He caught her as she lost her footing.

Emmaline had given Drake her notes with the expectation he would read them. That had been at a time when she'd thought she would never speak to him again. But knowing he'd read all her private thoughts, left her feeling exposed.

Now that he was here, she could finally have the answer to the question that had haunted her since he'd walked out of her brother's townhouse and out of her life. "I don't understand. Why did you push me away?" *Why did you give me up?*

His hands tightened on her waist, the heat of his skin warming her even through the soft silk fabric. "If I were a better man I would leave you alone." He nodded towards the eager gentlemen watching from the side of the dance floor. "I would be content to allow you to make a match with one of those more deserving gentlemen. I'm flawed."

She flinched as she remembered her brother had leveled the same charge against Drake. "Don't say that."

He shook his head. A gold strand tumbled across his brow. "No. Listen to me. I need you to understand. The reason—"

"I'd like to dance the remainder of the set with my sister, Drake." A voice snapped.

Emmaline jerked at the sudden appearance of Sophie and Sebastian. Somehow her brother had managed to steer Sophie across the floor and secured a spot right alongside them.

Sophie's eyes fairly glimmered with an apology, as if to say she were sorry she'd been unable to keep Sebastian at bay.

Drat it.

With little ceremony, Sebastian handed Sophie over to Drake so that Emmaline was forced to accept her brother's hand.

Sebastian's eyes had gone glacial. "Stay away."

Drake tore his gaze away from the sight of Mallen waltzing Emmaline away.

"You love her," Miss Winters said, her tone very matter-of-fact.

He blinked. It was one thing for Emmaline to be so brutally direct, it was quite another when it was her dearest friend. "I beg your pardon, Miss Winters?"

Sophie gave a jaunty shake of her curls. "No apologies for loving her. I also love her."

Drake felt as though he'd been spun in one too many dizzying circles. "Uh, n-no...for..." He let the matter rest.

Miss Winters studied him with wide, blinking cornflower blue eyes. She put him in mind of a night owl.

"You really should tell her, you know. The both of you should just end this façade."

Of course, Emmaline would be the best of friends with this opinionated, very vocal creature. "Façade, Miss Winters?"

Sophie pointed her eyes toward the ceiling. "One minute you love her. The next you push her away. The next she is weepy. Then happy. It is enough to exhaust a soul."

"I have never said I loved her," he blurted.

Sophie gave him a wide, knowing smile. "You didn't need to, my lord."

Did he *love* Emmaline? He cared very much for her. He'd missed her when she'd been out of his life. She had brought him so much happiness. But love? Could Miss Winters be correct?

"I am indeed correct." Sophie echoed his unspoken thoughts.

Drake was never gladder for the end of a set. He bowed over Miss Winter's hand. "Will you deliver a message to her? Will you remind her I owe her a picnic?"

With that, he left.

THIRTY-ONE

My Dearest Drake,
Oh, God. My father has died. Where are you? Why have you not come
to me?
Ever Yours,
Emmaline

Lord Sinclair perused the long, pale pink marble foyer. "A bachelor's residence," Sinclair murmured. He fell into step alongside Drake.

Sir Faithful trotted along at their heels.

Sinclair glanced back. "A dog, as well. My, my, you truly are a bachelor."

"Stuff it, Sin," he muttered, leading his friend into his new office.

Drake crossed to the drink cart in the corner of the room and availed himself to a glass of whiskey. He held the bottle up to Sin.

At Sin's nod, Drake poured a healthy amount into a crystal tumbler.

Sin accepted the glass and he and Drake claimed a seat on the set of leather winged chairs.

They drank in companionable silence. Sin polished off his drink before he spoke. "You do know you have set the *ton* on its ear?" He didn't wait for Drake's response, instead rose, and crossed the room, helping himself to another drink.

Drake sipped his more conservatively and absently eyed Sin's movements. "To hell with the *ton*." He waited until Sin had reclaimed his seat. "I want to court Emmaline."

Sinclair sputtered around a mouthful of whiskey. "Lady Emmaline Fitzhugh? As in the same young lady you were betrothed to as a child? The same lady you ran off to war to avoid? The same—"

His hackles went up. "I believe you've made your point."

Sin shook his head. "I don't think I have. After years upon years of complaining about Lady Emmaline, you choose to court her now that she has cut you loose?"

Drake was well aware that courting Emmaline now, after she'd broken off their betrothal, would be met by Society with derision and speculation. The *ton* only knew Drake to be consumed by his own pursuit of pleasure. What they didn't know, what he'd kept carefully concealed, was the madness he battled.

Sin sighed. "So when is this courtship to ensue?"

Drake shook his head. "Not right now. Tomorrow. The day after tomorrow." He raked a hand through his hair. "I don't know. Soon."

Sinclair tapped the edges of his chair.

The rhythmic sound grated until Drake snapped. "You must have something to say."

"I'm certain Mallen won't go for it."

Drake gazed into the depths of his drink wishing he could divine the answers within the swirling amber liquid. "No, no, that is a certainty."

Sin leaned forward in his chair. "What makes you certain the lady will be amiable to your suit?"

Recent memories of last evening's waltz filled him. He could still feel the heat of her skin, still see the smile playing on her lush, seductive red lips, hear her laughter. "Last evening at the Thompson ball—"

Sin slashed the air with his hand. "Yes, yes. I heard all about the Thompson ball. Anyone who is anyone has, in fact. A waltz, however, does not a courtship make." He inched again to the edge of his seat. "As much as I want to see you happy, I don't want to see you hurt again by Lady Emmaline."

Drake tossed back the contents of his glass and growled. He didn't like the way Sin was pinning the state of his unhappiness on

Emmaline. "I was the one responsible for Emmaline's decision to sever the betrothal. Not the young lady."

Sin cradled his drink between his hands, studying Drake over the edge of the glass. "I understand the lady is entitled to her sense of injury. You, however, are my main concern. As far as I'm concerned, you've known enough hurt."

"You're mothering me, Sin."

Sin bristled. "Well, you are in desperate need of mothering."

Drake glanced at a point just over Sinclair's shoulder, unable to meet his eyes. How could Sin ever know that the ache of losing Emmaline was far greater than any physical pain? "I need her."

Sin didn't say anything for a long moment. "Do you...love her?" The word came out halting. Men didn't speak of these things.

Drake grimaced. There it was again. That question. Did he love her?

"I don't know."

Sin held up his tumbler in mock salute. "You'd better have more of an answer for the lady than that."

"I will not lie to her. I want there to be honesty between us."

His friend snorted. "Trust me, when presented with the choice of honesty or love, a lady will always choose love."

In spite of his friend's words, Drake had already made up his mind to share with Emmaline the demons that had held him back. He'd confess to her about the affliction that had haunted him since he'd returned from war. He would, as his father suggested, allow her to decide for herself if it was too much of an albatross.

Still the idea that she might reject him...sweat popped up on his brow. What if it were too much for her? What if she wisely decided he was not worth it?

After all, what had he brought her other than heartache?

"What is it you require of me?" Sinclair asked, his tone, uncharacteristically sober. "You know I will do anything to help you."

Drake reached down and stroked Sir Faithful between the ears. "I need guidance on how to woo a lady." He sat up and then fished around his front pocket. Drake stared at the parchment a moment and then handed it over to Sinclair.

Sin laughed and accepted the parchment. "And you think *I* might be able to help *you*? You, the one recognized throughout Society as being an expert with matrons and debutantes alike?"

Drake shifted in his seat. "That is a gross exaggeration." He nodded to the paper in Sin's hands.

Sin glanced down at the heavily marked sheet with extensive cross-outs and too much ink. His brow furrowed.

"It's a poem."

"Uh, yes, I see that," Sin said.

Drake snatched the sheet back and proceeded to study it. "It's rubbish."

"I take it the poem is for Lady Emmaline?"

It didn't escape Drake's notice that his friend didn't counter his statement about the quality of the poem.

Drake set the paper aside. "No, it's for Mallen. Of course it's for Emmaline."

Sinclair laughed until tears streamed from his eyes.

"So glad you're amused," Drake muttered. "Emmaline wanted to be courted. She deserves to be courted." His eyes went to the impressive bouquet of flowers he'd had delivered earlier that afternoon…to himself. They rested on his desktop, or rather they sat *wilting* on his desktop.

Sinclair followed the direction of Drake's stare. "Uh, they've begun to wilt."

"Yes, yes they have."

Drake had spent last evening and the better part of the morning laboring over a poem. Then, he'd ordered the flowers. He looked over at the buds again. The *dying* flowers. The poem, though rubbish, was finally complete. Who'd have figured it would be so bloody difficult to put words to paper?

Sin cleared his throat. "So when you said you intended to court Lady Emmaline, just not today or tomorrow…that wasn't altogether true."

217

Drake surged from his chair and strode across the room. He shoved back the damask curtains and stared out the window into the dark night sky.

"I don't know how to take the step," he said.

Sin's visage reflected back in the glass pane. He remained seated. "You just...do it, Drake. You tell your brain to tell your feet to move one at a time, and march up Mallen's steps, and demand to see Emmaline. Then you read her your poem." He picked up the poem in question and grimaced. "Well, maybe not this one, per se."

Drake pressed his forehead against the cool window.

Could it be that simple? He glanced over his shoulder at the bouquet of cerastium and the poem still held in Sinclair's hand.

He'd fought a bloody war...how hard could this be? In one of her notes to him, one of the notes that had never been sent, she'd called herself a coward, but it was he who was the coward.

He picked up the dreary looking flowers from his desk.

"You can't go now," Sinclair stuttered.

Drake paused. "Whyever not?"

Sinclair blinked several times. His eyes landed on the ormolu clock on the fireplace mantle. "It is nearly eight o'clock in the evening. Mallen is hosting an intimate dinner party with Waxham. Whyever not, indeed?"

A fiery pit of jealousy flared in Drake's stomach. "Waxham, you say? Why, then I can't think of a better time to pay a visit."

"Mallen's going to give you hell," Sin predicted with a grin.

Drake smiled. "She's worth it." With that, he turned on his heel and marched out of his office. Sir Faithful gave a yap of approval.

Sin hurried after him. "Rude leaving your friend and all. Perhaps you'd like some company along the way? Just to make certain you've thought through everything you are going to say when you interrupt the duke's intimate dinner party."

Drake growled low in his throat. "Stop calling it an intimate dinner party." Intimate was the last word he wanted to come to mind when thinking of Waxham and Emmaline.

He flung back the front door and marched down the steps. Sin trailed after him.

"Not the thing, opening your own doors, you know. Your first order of business really should have been to set up at least a butler and housekeeper. Oh, and of course a chef. Not one of those French fellows that seem all the rage—"

Drake paused mid-stride.

It took a moment before Sin, who'd been prattling on, took note. He looked over his shoulder. "Have you forgotten something? Changed your mind?"

"You do know the last thing on my mind right now is assembling a staff for my new residence? You, of course, remember I am heading out to humble myself before the lady who severed our betrothal?"

"Yes, yes," Sin paused. "In the middle of Mallen's intimate dinner with Waxham."

He growled. "Stop referring to it as…"

"I know, I know, an intimate dinner party. Really, you must do your best to hide that nasty sneer when you march into Mallen's. It will neither win you the lady nor make you a fast friend of the duke."

"I am not looking to make friends with Mallen."

Sin quirked a brow. "I might remind you that you require Mallen's approval just as much as your require the lady's approval."

Damn, he hated it when Sin was right. Which meant Drake needed to win over both Emmaline and the foul-tempered Duke of Mallen. He didn't know which was going to be a greater challenge. And he only had a matter of moments to settle on a course of action.

Sin cleared his throat and motioned to the townhouse in front of them. "Here we are."

Drake stared up at the white façade. "Already?"

"Already."

Apparently, he'd run out of time to develop a proper plan of attack to win over Emmaline and Mallen.

Drake stood rooted to the pavement, and continued to stare up at the elegant white townhouse, its windows aglow with soft candlelight.

He recalled marching up the very same steps as a boy filled with anxiety. He'd been terrified at the prospect of seeing his betrothed. It would appear, in fifteen years, not much had changed in that regard. Only now he feared rejection at her hands.

He glanced down at the sorely wilted bouquet in his hands, and froze. With his free hand, he frantically felt around his jacket.

His frenzied search was met with a beleaguered sigh from Sin, who brandished a scrap of paper and waved it about. "Here it is. I'd rather hoped you'd forgotten about the poem."

Drake took it with a word of thanks, re-reading through the terrible attempt. He grimaced. It really was quite horrendous.

"Ahem," Sin cleared his throat. "I said, ah—"

"I heard you," Drake bit out. He continued to stand there.

Sin tapped a finger to his chin. "I suppose you could always wait until tomorrow, say after the intimate d—"

Without a word, Drake abandoned his friend to the pavement and took the stone steps two at a time.

He'd be damned if he heard the words *intimate dinner party* one more time.

THIRTY-TWO

Dearest Lord Drake,
We returned to the countryside. My brother's friend Waxham joined
us. He devoted an entire morning to helping me clear the weeds from a
bed of flowers. I teased Sebastian, telling him I wish Waxham were my
brother instead of him.
Ever Yours,
Emmaline

With sightless eyes, Emmaline stared down at the carrot and ginger soup placed in front of her. She raised her spoon and absently stirred the parsley sprigs. What an odd soup. Who would have thought to cream carrots and…

"My lady?"

She started and dropped her spoon into the fine porcelain bowl. Liquid splattered the tablecloth made of Spanish lace. Apparently the gentleman had asked her a question.

What did he say? What did he say?

Sebastian drummed his fingers on the tabletop and glared at her. "Emmaline, Waxham asked you a question."

Emmaline fished out the utensil, her gaze fixed on the bowl. Heat stained her neck and flooded her cheeks.

A replacement was quickly brought forward. She cleared her throat and looked over at Waxham. "My apologies, Lord Waxham, I'm afraid my mind was elsewhere."

Waxham favored her with a rueful smile that said he knew she'd been woolgathering. "How was your visit to the hospital?"

221

She took a sip of broth. "The soldiers are always full of such stories. In spite of what they've seen and done, they still are capable of great laughter."

"How could they not be joyful when you are around, my lady?"

Why couldn't Waxham be enough? She'd known him nearly her entire life. He'd toiled alongside her many a summer's morn in her garden. He knew her likes and dislikes. So that *should* be enough? But it wasn't. She wanted the grand passion she knew with Drake. She wanted...wanted...*him*—the man she'd been betrothed to since she'd been a child. Would it always be this way?

"Perhaps I might join you on a visit?" Waxham's words pulled the cloud she'd been floating on from under her, and she tumbled back to reality.

The immediate answer that sprung to her lips, which she tamped down, was an emphatic, resounding, no. The soldiers would be livid if this interloper encroached upon Captain Drake's territory. "Uh-I..."

She dropped her spoon for the second time.

Sebastian caught her gaze and glowered at her. "That would be lovely, is the proper response," he said.

Emmaline accepted yet another utensil, awash with panic.

"Yes, that would be lovely, wouldn't it, Emmaline?" Her mother interjected from the head of the table.

She saw the hard determination in Sebastian's eyes. Noted the silent entreaty in her mother's stare. Observed Waxham's hopeful expression. Suddenly the cloying hands of pressure tightened around her throat. Breathing became difficult. Her whole life she'd been inundated with the wants and desires of everyone else. Since the moment she was born, it had never been about her. Her wishes and hopes had never once been considered.

They might not be aware of it, but Sebastian and her mother had continued to place stringent expectations upon her shoulders, even after the severance of her betrothal.

"That would be—"

A commotion sounded beyond the closed door and the butler, Carmichael's shout filled the hallway and filtered into the dining room. "You must not go in there. I have told you His Grace is not receiving."

The doors flew open with such force that they bounced hard and hit the plaster of the wall. "I am not here to see His Grace."

At sight of the imposing, virile figure in the doorway, Emmaline's spoon clattered again, and this time it plummeted to the floor. She froze. All the breath expelled from her lungs.

Sebastian leapt to his feet. "What is this about, Drake?"

Her mother sat back in her seat and with a wide-eyed stare, took in the tableau.

Drake ignored Sebastian and held up a staying hand as if to stifle her brother's next words. Then, Drake's hot, jade gaze found hers, and caressed her like a physical touch.

She forgot everyone else in the room. Oh, God, he was here. He was, wasn't he? Surely she wasn't dreaming? Just to be sure, she snuck a hand under the table and gave her leg a little pinch.

No, this was real. Very real. The possessive gleam in his eyes heated her like a hot summer sun. Her entire life, she'd longed for him to look at her as he did now; as though she were the only person in the world.

"You owe me a picnic." There was something faintly accusatory in his tone.

Three pairs of eyes swiveled to Emmaline. She opened her mouth to speak but no words emerged. She closed it and tried again. Nothing. She shook her head.

"What's the meaning of this? What is he talking about?"

Emmaline ignored Sebastian's angry questions.

Her brother in turn directed his attention to Drake. "My sister owes you nothing."

An immoveable wall of indifference and coolness, the Marquess of Drake kept a narrowed stare fixed on Emmaline.

Emmaline forced her suspicion out past dry lips. "You lied. You finished *Glenarvon* first, didn't you?"

Drake's lips twitched. "Why am I not surprised you know that, Emmaline?"

"Do not call my sister by her given name," Sebastian said.

Drake took a step forward. "Do you know why you were a wallflower?"

A flood of humiliated heat warmed her cheeks, her chest hitched with pain.

Sebastian kicked his chair backwards with such force it tumbled to the floor. "By God, I will kill you."

"Sebastian, no," her mother cried.

Waxham reached a hand out to capture Emmaline's. He gave it a faint, reassuring squeeze.

Drake's eyes dropped to where her hand rested, entwined with Waxham's. "I asked you a question, Emmaline."

With alacrity in his movements, her brother advanced angrily around the long, wide dining table. "Do not make demands of my sister."

A bitter little laugh escaped her. "I'm sure you will tell me, my lord."

Drake moved across the room, closer to her. "Look at me," he ordered in his Captain's tone.

Emmaline lifted her chin and met his stare.

Drake's throat bobbed up and down. "Because of me. It's because of me that you sat on the bloody sidelines. You are beautiful. And you are vibrant...and the only reason gentlemen didn't flock to your side was because of me." His resounding words carried throughout the room and echoed off the walls.

Emmaline had fallen in love with Lord Drake two times in her life: one being when he'd rescued an old peddler woman on the street, the other being this very moment.

He devoured her with his eyes. "You are beautiful. In every way. I've never deserved you. I never will. Still knowing that, I have come to ask if I might court you?"

She gasped and dropped Waxham's hand.

"No," Sebastian barked.

Drake continued to hold up a single finger to keep an enraged Sebastian in his place.

Emmaline's gaze fell to the bouquet of cerastium Drake held. Tears flooded her eyes and she blinked them back.

Drake saw the direction of her focus. "These are for you."

"The poor buds have wilted significantly," she blurted.

His brow furrowed. "So I've been told."

"They are still beautiful."

A low, animalistic growl emerged from deep within Sebastian's chest, and effectively intruded in the moment she'd shared with Drake. "I've watched enough of this farcical drama. I am having you physically removed. Carmichael, fetch two servants and have Lord Drake thrown into the street," Sebastian said.

The butler hurried to do his master's bidding.

Seeming wholly unaffected by Sebastian's threat, Drake fished around the front of his jacket. He extracted a folded sheet of parchment, shook it out, and held it out for her to see. "I wrote you a poem."

Her eyes went to the scrap in his hands.

A dull flush stained Drake's cheeks. He cleared his throat and began.

"Your eyes and hair are like chocolate.

Warm. Pure. Soothing.

Your smile is like a Christmas morning.

Exciting. Unexpected. Delightful.

Your hand is like…"

Sebastian's groan interrupted Drake's recitation. Her brother shook his head piteously. "For the love of God, that is bloody awful. Spare yourself any further embarrassment."

Tears blinded Emmaline. "Shut up, Sebastian." She silently pleaded with Drake to continue.

Drake's eyes skimmed the paper until he found the spot he'd left off on. "Your hand is like salvation. It saved me."

Warm, salty drops spilled from her lashes and trailed a path down her cheeks. A lifetime ago she'd been a little girl sitting across from a young boy, a prince who'd rescued her from a fall. Years later, when the prince left to fight on the Peninsula, the little girl had been replaced by a whimsical young woman, who'd often ruminated about a moment just like the one she was living in her brother's dining room.

Carmichael arrived with two burly servants from the kitchen.

Well, all of it except for the servants arriving to throw him from the room.

Emmaline shoved her seat back and jumped to her feet. "Don't touch him."

"Remove him," her brother barked.

Drake had battled soldiers who'd been intent on cutting his throat. It would take more than three of Mallen's servants to alarm him. He took a step towards Emmaline.

This was it.

In a room full of witnesses, he who had existed in this shell of himself for the past three years was going to bare himself to this woman who'd come to mean more to him than anyone. It terrified him. Seeing the unfiltered love in her eyes, however, gave him the courage to continue.

"I have wronged you. I have never treated you as you deserved. I have made more mistakes in my life than I can count. My greatest regret has been how horribly I have treated you." He knelt beside her. "You said you wanted a choice. Well, now you have a choice. And I'm asking you to choose me. Choose me, not because you are required to, not because you have no choice. Not because I'm heir to a dukedom. Choose me because you need me as much as I need you."

He set the bouquet down on the table beside her most likely cold soup and claimed her hands in his. He turned them over and studied them. They were so delicate. And shaking. He traced the intersecting lines of her palm with his pointer finger.

"Get your hands off my sister," Mallen shouted.

Drake ignored him. "I don't know if you have it in you to look past all my mistakes, but I ask that you allow me to court you?" He brushed a delicate kiss upon her knuckles. God, he'd missed...

One of Mallen's burly staff members jerked him backward. Drake cursed. He should have been expecting that.

"Don't touch him!" Emmaline cried, appealing to the Duchess of Mallen. "Mother?"

The duchess glared at her son. "This show of force really isn't necessary, Sebastian. For any man to bare his soul, and recite poetry in front of a hostile witness like you speaks volumes of the depth of emotion he has for Emmaline."

"Traitor," Mallen mumbled. He nodded to the two servants, who released Drake.

Drake returned his attention to Emmaline. "It was not my intention to interrupt your meal."

Mallen snorted. "Then what was your intention?"

This time, he did look at Mallen. "My intention is to court your sister."

Sister and brother spoke in unison.

"Yes."

"The answer is no."

THIRTY-THREE

My Dearest Drake,
This will be the last letter I write. It is time for us to meet again.
Ever Yours,
Emmaline

Emmaline had hoped with a night of rest that upon waking Sebastian would be amenable to her picnicking with Drake. Standing before her brother's desk, eyeing his stiffly held form, she now realized she'd been foolishly optimistic.

Sebastian folded his arms across his chest and glared. "I said no."

Emmaline managed a smile. "That seems to be your new favorite phrase."

He dropped his pen on his desktop.

Perhaps sarcasm was not her best tactic. "It is merely a picnic," she reasoned. "There is nothing scandalous about a picnic. Why they are all the rage—"

His snort interrupted her rational explanation. "There is everything scandalous about a picnic when," he proceeded to tick off on his fingers. "One it is with your former betrothed, two, you throw over a fine, respectable gentleman for—"

Emmaline gasped and marched across the room. "How dare you. I did not throw over Waxham. You were the one attempting to bring us together."

A telltale vein pulsated along the edge of his temple, indicating he was doing everything within his power to maintain his self-control. "Drake isn't worth ten Waxham's."

Attempting to diffuse the palpable tension emanating from his rigid form, Emmaline sighed. "I will not debate Drake's worth with you. I love him and more than anything right now, I want to join him in on a picnic. So can't you please, smile at me, pat me on the head, and tell me to go and have a good time? It is not marriage he is asking for." Yet. Hopefully in time. "It is a picnic. That is it. Nothing more."

Sebastian raked a hand through his blonde strands. "Can I think on it?"

"What is there to think about?"

He slashed the air with an agitated hand. "I'm already exerting all my ducal influence to silence as many whispers and speculations as I can. I know you're unaware of the very public censure your actions have earned, but Mother and I are doing our best to save your reputation."

A laugh burbled up from her throat, and spilled past her lips. "Really, Sebastian. You are making far more of it than—" He slammed a powerful fist onto the mahogany desk with a resounding boom. Emmaline jumped.

"Are you really so unaware of how you are being perceived by the *ton*? They say you are fickle. You broke off your betrothal, then allowed Waxham to pay serious court."

"It is your fault—"

"For the love of God, do not say one more time that what happened with Waxham is my fault," he bellowed and then took a calming breath. When he spoke, his words emerged more even. "Waxham cares for you, Emmaline."

All this time she'd assumed Waxham's interest had been borne of nothing other than the connection they shared through Sebastian. A twinge of remorse ravaged her already guilty conscience.

Sebastian groaned. "Damn it, please don't give me that sad little look."

Her chin quavered. "I'm not giving you a sad little—"

"Yes you are. It's the same one you've turned on me since you were a small girl. I'm powerless against it."

She hadn't even known she'd had any such look. But since he seemed very aware of it she quietly pressed her advantage. "Please send me on my picnic outing with Lord Drake with your blessings."

Sebastian cursed softly, obviously noting that he'd tipped his hand. He rubbed his hands over his eyes, agitated. "Fine. The picnic. But do not any time soon, expect me to honor anything else more serious than a picnic."

Emmaline crossed over to his chair. Bending down, she placed a kiss on his cheek. She gave her words all the solemnity she could muster. "It's just a picnic."

"When is this picnic going to take place," he mumbled clearly uncomfortable with her sisterly show of emotion.

"Uh—"

Someone tapped a perfunctory knock at the door.

"Enter," Sebastian called, his expression indicating his annoyance at the interruption.

The butler stood framed in the doorway and bowed respectfully. "The Marquess of Drake awaits my lady in the foyer to escort her on," he wrinkled his nose, "a picnic."

Sebastian's narrowed gaze pinned her to the rug. Carmichael scurried off. "A picnic today. Imagine that. Drake must have amazing hearing and speed to have heard my consent."

Emmaline shifted on her feet, having the sense not to speak.

"What say you, sister?"

She nodded. "His hearing is rather impressive. I shall be off." Turning on her heel, she tossed a wave over her shoulder.

"Remember just a picnic, Em. That is all I'm consenting to."

In spite of Sebastian's earlier protests, Emmaline had been victorious—she had gotten her picnic. Her maid, Grace trailed behind her and Drake as they made their way through Hyde Park. There was something thrilling about turning out the victor in a losing argument against the Duke of Mallen.

"I don't know what to make of that mischievous smile, sweet."

"Perhaps I'm just happy," Emmaline said.

Drake snapped out a blanket and Sir Faithful playfully grabbed a corner and shook it with his teeth. "I know your just-happy smile. That was not it."

Her maid, Grace, rushed forward to assist with the blanket, but Emmaline waved her off. "Grace, I assure you, Lord Drake can handle both Sir Faithful and seeing to the blanket. Why don't you take a short walk?" It was more an order than request.

Her words were met with a loud rip.

"Cease," Drake commanded and the dog immediately sat, and bowed his head.

Grace shot a skeptical look from Drake to Sir Faithful. "As you wish, my lady."

Sir Faithful made one last attempt at tugging the corner of the blanket, but Drake snapped the palm of his hand to the side of his thigh and the dog, dutifully sat at his master's heels, watching expectantly as Drake set the basket down upon the blanket and helped Emmaline to the ground.

"He is a troublesome little thing, isn't he?" She scratched the sensitive spot along the bridge of Sir Faithful's nose.

"Not very little anymore, either." Drake looked at the rapidly growing mutt. "He is, however, true to his name. I would have thought you would find me a pug or Shetland sheepdog," he teased.

Emmaline laughed. "A Shetland sheepdog would have been just the thing. Though after reflecting on the fact you had no sheep, I decided Sir Faithful would do nicely."

He waggled his brows. "Not yet. Perhaps the sheep will come later. How do you feel about becoming the wife of a sheep farmer?"

The image of Drake galloping about the countryside with a Shetland sheepdog, herding a flock of sheep about, was just so ludicrous that she laughed until she developed a stitch in her side.

Then she processed what he'd said.

She tilted her head back and closed her eyes. "I'm dreaming."

The blanket rustled as he sat down beside her. "You are so beautiful," he said. There could be no question of the quiet sincerity of his words.

Never, ever in her life had she before felt beautiful—until that moment. He made her believe she was more than just *tolerably pleasing*, as the papers had labeled her.

"Do you know where I found Sir Faithful?"

Drake scratched the dog under his belly and waited for her answer.

"I visit the soldiers at London Hospital each week. There is a black dog who lives there and wanders the halls. No one is certain what line of dog she is. The soldiers named her Alice. A few months ago, Alice disappeared for three days. For three whole days, the soldiers and nurses were devastated, no one knowing what had happened to the dog. But she returned, and it wasn't long until we realized she was with pups. Sir Faithful is one of those pups." Sir Faithful licked her hand once, twice, and a third time.

"It really should come as no surprise to me that you give your time at the hospital."

Emmaline shifted under the uncomfortable weight of his praise and gave a tiny shrug in response. "It is not a chore to visit the men. Seeing them fills me with great joy." She'd always looked forward to sitting with the soldiers who'd courageously dedicated their lives, who'd risked their physical safety for such a noble cause.

"I imagine you bring them great joy as well." Drake opened the wicker basket and pulled out a thick loaf of bread neatly wrapped in a cloth, along with sliced cheese, and plump red strawberries. He began arranging a dish for her.

Emmaline rested her chin atop her knees and studied his movements. There was something beautifully domestic about his simple actions. She accepted the plate he held out to her with a murmur of thanks. Picking up a piece of bread from her plate, she nibbled at the corner and continued to watch him.

After the way he'd barged in on her brother's dinner party, she'd been at a loss to understand what exactly was her relationship with Drake. The corner of her heart, where she'd buried the dream of being his wife, stirred to life. A man could not humble himself as Drake had in front of her brother, mother, and Lord Waxham, baring his most intimate thoughts, if marriage was not his intention?

Drake plucked a strawberry. He made to pop it into his mouth.

"When you imagine the future, do you see me as your wife?"

For an infinitesimal moment, he paused, before he finally ate the red berry.

A long stretch of silence met her question.

The fine linen of his shirt did little to conceal the heat of his mother's emerald and diamond ring, warm against his chest. Since the moment he'd decided to ask Emmaline to wed him, he'd rehearsed any number of poetic, appropriate speeches, grimacing at the lackluster attempts. However, even the paltry efforts he'd managed, fled.

Drake jumped up and began to pace.

Emmaline cocked her head. "Drake?"

"Hmm?" He continued his path. Back and forth. With as close as he'd come to losing her, Drake would imagine he should have found if not the perfect words, then something suitable.

"Are you all right?"

"Uh-, I...fine. Fine." He stopped abruptly in front of her. With a jerky movement, he leaned down and tugged Emmaline upright.

She pitched forward landing hard against his side. "Oomph."

Emmaline pulled back and eyed him with a healthy dose of concern. "Uh-are we done with the picnic?"

Drake directed his eyes skyward. He needed Cupid's intervention to salvage this sorry, sorry proposal.

Sir Faithful chose that moment to sidle over on his belly, effectively wedging himself between Drake and Emmaline.

Apparently Cupid was otherwise busy.

"The moon is in the sky..."

Emmaline looked up in confusion, and shielded her eyes against the glaring sun high in the cloudless blue sky. "It is? Where?"

"Uh-no, not now. That is to say, it is not in the sky at this precise moment. What I intended to say is…" A black curse fell from his lips. Mayhap Sin was right and he should forget all the nonsense with poetry.

Emmaline's eyes widened the size of saucers.

This was certainly not a proposal for the ages. Frustrated with the debacle he was making out of the moment, he dragged a hand through his hair. "My apologies," he muttered. "What I meant to say is—"

Except those words also eluded him and Drake was once again left with a dry mouth and incoherent thoughts. Who would have imagined he, the otherwise unflappable Marquess of Drake, should find himself bumbling his way through a marriage proposal?

"I need to speak to you about the day your father died." He winced. Hardly the stuff a young lady preferred to hear when a gentleman was asking for her hand. Maybe he should go back to the stuff about the moon and the stars.

"Drake?"

Suddenly the prospect of facing down a line of French soldiers seemed vastly less terrifying than sharing the truth with Emmaline and risking rejection at her hands.

Emmaline slid her hand into his and from the gentle squeeze she gave, found strength and courage. "I don't want to dwell on the past. I—"

As tempted as he was to bury the story that had haunted him since he'd returned from the Peninsula, he would not be able forgive himself if he withheld this truth from her. "No. I need to have out with it." He drew in a deep fortifying breath. "I was coming to see you. I need you to know that." The words were guttural, wrenched from somewhere deep inside him. "I became used to walking during the war. When I returned, I walked everywhere. I was coming to your residence that morning. There was a carriage accident. A broken axle, I suspect. I heard shouts and cries. Something happened to me in that moment. I forgot where I was. I came to hours later, in an alley, not knowing what had happened. That is why I did not go to you the day your father died. And I am sorrier for that than you can ever know."

The only indication Emmaline had heard his confession was the subtle pressure she applied to his hand interlocked with hers. Time crept by. He awaited her rejection, her pity, and what was more, he would understand that rejection.

Her eyes flitted back and forth across his face. "Why didn't you tell me?"

His words emerged on a hoarse whisper. "How could I have shared that with a young lady I barely knew?"

Emmaline rocked back on her heels. "I thought it was because of me. I thought you didn't want to see me." It seemed those words were directed more to herself. "I thought..." She shook her head and gave him a sad little smile. "To think, I took your absence as a personal slight. I believed you were too engrossed with your own merriment, that you couldn't take time to pay your respects. How odd, to now know, you needed me just as much as I needed you.

Drake stared at a point over the crown of her hair. He inhaled the faint scent of lemons, which always clung to her. It represented purity and filled his senses with the heady aphrodisiac of hope. "How many *what ifs* there are. What if you had sent your letters? What if I had written you? What if I had shown up and paid my respects the day your father passed away? What would our life be like at this moment?"

The amount of regret he carried seemed enough to fill the Thames River.

But he had to tell her the whole of it. He could not offer her marriage without the truth laid out between them. Even if the truth could cost him—her.

"I still have nightmares...and as you witnessed, the episodes." He studied his hands a moment. "They come less frequently than when I first returned from the Peninsula, but they are still there. I..." He swallowed. "Fear the war turned me into a madman. The day I visited you in your garden, I put my hands on you and it almost killed me. I cannot make you my wife, without you knowing everything there is to know."

235

She reached a tremulous hand out and with a fleeting caress, stroked his tense jaw. "I wrote you a note. It was about a dream I'd had. The war was over—"

"I was wandering about a field, lost."

"I wrote, if you are lost—'"

"I will help you." He finished and felt his throat bob up and down under the force of his emotion.

Emmaline brushed her lips against his. The soft meeting was like the fluttering whisper of a butterflies wings. It tasted of love.

"I will help you," she promised and brushed back a lock of hair that had fallen across his brow.

Drake pressed his forehead against hers.

He was so close, his toes peeked over the cliff of possibilities, desperately wanting to leap with her. But he'd held back so long, capitulation was far too hard. "I don't want you to be hurt."

Emmaline leaned up on tiptoes and held his gaze. "Oh, you silly man. Don't you yet know, the only way I'm hurt is when I'm not with you? I love you."

Drake dropped his attention to where her hand rested in his. Clearing his throat, he reached into the front of his jacket and pulled out the emerald ring that had belonged to his mother; a ring given in love by his father. And now, if she didn't have the good sense to run the either way, would belong to Emmaline. "Will you marry me?"

Emmaline gasped. "It's a ring," she blurted.

A smile played on his lips. "I hope your answer is yes, because I am fairly certain your brother's answer will be no, and I'd like one yes for the day."

Drake grunted as Emmaline threw herself into his arms. The unexpected movement sent him tumbling backward. She landed on his chest. The ring landed somewhere alongside them.

Sir Faithful jumped up and ran in circles about them, yapping his excitement.

"Yes, you foolish man. A million times yes!"

THIRTY-FOUR

For the third time in Drake's life, he crossed into the Duke of Mallen's office for a meeting that would determine his future. It did not escape his notice how Mallen failed to rise when Drake entered the room. Nor did the stoic man offer any greeting. Instead, he watched Drake with a hawk-like intensity, as if he feared Drake were a thief from the Seven Dials with intentions of absconding with the family jewels.

Which, come to think of it, wasn't too far from the mark.

When it didn't seem as though the duke had any intentions of offering him a seat, Drake motioned to the leather-winged chair in front his desk. "May I?"

Mallen rapped distractedly on the desktop, the first indication of the other man's unease. "As you wish."

Drake settled into the seat and looped his ankle over his opposite knee. He could easily understand Mallen's dogged protectiveness of Emmaline. Though Drake had no siblings, he imagined if he did, that the last thing he'd allow was for his sister to wed a rogue like himself; especially after she'd been hurt by said rogue. In fact, in thinking on it, Mallen had been far more magnanimous than he, Drake would have been. Hell, Mallen would have been justified calling him out.

Mallen's fingers ceased their distracted movements. "Have you come to sit and stare at me all day?" Mallen's words dripped with heavy sarcasm.

Drake shifted in his seat. "No, not at all, Your Grace."

Mallen fixed him with a hard stare. "So, of a sudden, it's Your Grace?"

This wasn't going as Drake had planned. Might as well come out with it. "I've come to discuss your sister," he said evenly.

A muscle ticked at the corner of the duke's right eye. He leaned across the desk. "Oh? To discuss my sister?"

He took a fortifying breath. "I want to ask for her hand—"

"You are either mad, arrogant, or both." Mallen pointed a finger in Drake's direction. "For fifteen years you haven't paid Emmaline any notice. Not until she asked me to sever the arrangement did you decide to court her and that is only after the gossips dragged her name through the scandal sheets. Tell me, why would I ever consent to turning the person I love more than anyone else, over to you?"

"Because I..." Drake tried to force out a suitable response.

But no words emerged.

That was the rub of it—Drake couldn't give one bloody reason Mallen should allow him Emmaline's hand in marriage. Mallen possessed one of the most revered titles in the kingdom and therefore wouldn't be impressed by Drake's status as heir to a dukedom. Nor could Drake drum up one redeeming quality that he possessed to garner the other gentleman's respect.

Nor could he come here and believe that he might erase fifteen years of neglect.

He did know that his only desire was to spend every minute of the rest of his life married to her. That thought consumed him like a conflagration. He wanted her, nay, needed her, and even if it meant spiriting her off to Gretna Green, he was determined to wed her.

"I'm waiting," Mallen said.

No argument would ever be sufficient for the other man.

He settled for honesty. "I need her."

Mallen scoffed. "You need her."

She had become his sustenance. "Yes, I need her like I need water and air to breathe."

The Duke groaned. "Please spare me any further of your meager attempts at poetry."

Drake's collar grew unbearably tight at mention of his recitation the prior evening, and he gave his cravat a tug. In spite of Mallen's scornful words, he forced himself to press on. After all, he hadn't expected to saunter into the Duke's office, request Emmaline's hand, and receive the other man's blessing. He steeled himself. "I'm not being poetic. I need—"

Sebastian swiped the air with an angry hand. "You think I care what *you* need? I care about what she wants and needs. And as her brother, I can say with great confidence that you sir, are not it." Mallen's voice had climbed in volume.

Drake remained quiet. Mallen's tightly coiled frame indicated he was spoiling for a fight. Drake wouldn't give him the satisfaction. To do so, would invite Mallen to toss him out.

The duke slammed his fist on the desktop. "Damn it. Say something."

Uncrossing his leg, Drake leaned forward. He held his palms up. "Listen, Mallen. You don't like me. Which is fine because I don't much like myself. With the exception of a handful of moments in my life, I am hardly proud of who I am. I've got a surly disposition, I've carried on with more widows and opera singers than I can list." He plowed ahead of the Duke's black expression. "I can go on and on. But Emmaline makes me wish I were a better person. More than that, she makes me want to be a better man—for her."

Silence descended, punctuated by the tick of the mantle clock. Mallen scrubbed his hands over his face looking like a man twenty years older. "Damn you and that argument." He dropped his hands and continued to eye Drake with a hard look. "Do you love her?"

Drake paused, frozen by the other man's question. There it was, again. The question—did he love her? Did he love her? He couldn't fathom life without her; knew it would be a desolate existence. Before Emmaline he'd hardly managed a sincere laugh or smile. Having grown up motherless and then living the life of a soldier, he'd never really given much thought to the sentiment.

"That isn't your business."

Mallen jumped up from his seat and stormed out from behind his desk, clearly prepared to argue the point with Drake.

Drake walked over to the duke. Only a hairsbreadth separated them. "Let me stop you, Mallen. It is my intention to wed your sister and I assure you it is her intention to wed me. Emmaline wants your blessing and because of that, I'm asking you to accept my suit. But, I'm going to marry her with or without your approval. Is that understood?"

The door opened and both men spun around at the intrusion.

The duchess stood framed in the doorway. "You will most certainly give your blessing, Sebastian."

"Mother, I am handling this—"

"Poorly," the Duchess of Mallen cut in. She claimed Drake's hands. "So you've finally come to your senses, I see."

He nodded solemnly. "Yes, Your Grace. I've been bewitched by your daughter."

It was the truth, but it was also the right thing to say. A smile reminiscent of Emmaline's played about the duchess's lips. "I wondered when you would at last realize that."

Mallen raked an angry hand through his hair. "If it weren't for my mother and my sister, the answer would be, no."

Drake strove for graciousness. He knew what the capitulation cost Mallen.

Drake nodded solemnly and stretched his hand out. "Thank you."

Finally, Mallen accepted Drake's hand. "Hurt her and I'll kill you."

Emmaline stepped into the room. "Don't be so melodramatic, Sebastian."

The sight of her there in a pale pink creation trimmed in delicate lace, her eyes shining with adoring love and joy, caused Drake's heart to pick up a swift beat.

Mallen threw his arms up. "Lovely, so glad you could join us. Why don't we call in Carmichael and the entire household staff for this meeting?"

Emmaline ignored her brother and glided into the room, coming to a stop before Drake.

He bowed low. "My lady."

"My lord."

He needed to feel her skin against his, needed some kind of assurance that she was real and not the phantom creature who'd visited only in his peaceful dreams. He took her hands in his. "We are to be married."

Emmaline stepped into Drake's arms like it was the only place in the world she belonged—and mayhap it was. He held her close. With a hand that trembled, Drake stroked her cheek. He forgot about Mallen. The duchess. The war became a distant memory. He forgot about everyone and everything, but her and the feel of her soft, slim body in his arms. It turned out everyone else had been right after all. He did love her.

Imagine that.

"Get your hands off my sister." Mallen snarled.

Drake jerked back to reality and placed appropriate distance between him and Emmaline.

"Six months."

He really should have been paying far closer attention to the duke. "I'm sorry?"

"Not as sorry as I am," Mallen muttered. "A six month betrothal—"

Emmaline gasped.

"Don't be absurd," the Duchess of Mallen said.

"Three," Drake countered.

Mallen's jaw set in a hard, unyielding line. "Six months. You waited fifteen years, what is another six months?"

Emmaline set her hands on her hips. "Really, Sebastian?" She looked to her mother for intervention.

"Three weeks," Drake reiterated over the crown of Emmaline's chocolate waves.

"You are mad. Absolutely not. Why, why the planning, the preparation, the scandal—"

The duchess took her son's hand between hers and gave it a reassuring squeeze. "I never took you for one to get weighed down with wedding details."

"Six months is rather a ridiculous length of time, no?" Emmaline argued.

Mallen looked from Emmaline to Drake and then his mother, like something of a caged animal. "I—I..."

THIRTY-FIVE

Ultimately, when faced with the persistent Marquess of Drake, a pestering younger sister, and a displeased mother, the Duke of Mallen had no choice but to agree to speedy nuptials. So it was three weeks later at the Duke of Mallen's country seat in Leeds, with a special license from the Archbishop of Canterbury, Emmaline, escorted by Sebastian, walked down the intimate aisle of the family church to the man who'd upended her world.

They reached the front of the altar and Sebastian continued to stare with his gaze fixed blankly ahead.

She gave his hand a gentle squeeze. "I love you," she whispered.

Sebastian looked down at his sister, and then shifted his gaze over to the Marquess of Drake, who eyed him with an inscrutable expression. "Hurt her and I'll kill you." He placed Emmaline's hand in Drake's and claimed his seat at the front pew.

Emmaline turned a smile up at Drake. "I think he handled that rather well," she whispered.

A startled bark of laughter escaped Drake, causing the select few guests in attendance to erupt into a bevy of curious murmurs.

"If I may?" the vicar inquired, his tone dry. He cleared his throat and continued.

"Wilt thou have this woman to be thy wedded wife, to live together after God's ordinance in the holy estate of Matrimony? Wilt thou love her, comfort her, honor and keep her, in sickness and in health: and, forsaking all other, keep thee only unto her so long as ye both shall live?"

"I will," Drake vowed.

They were just two words, yet somehow they flowed over Emmaline like the faintest caress.

I'm dreaming, she thought, a smile on her lips.

She didn't want to ever look away from the green of his eyes and the emotion she saw there. In him she saw her past; the five-year-old girl with dreams of the thirteen-year-old prince, who'd rescued her up from her knees in her father's office. He represented the hopes she'd carried as a young lady for a love match, dreams that had defied the reality of Society's cold, calculated unions. And now she saw her future—their future. She—

Drake gave a discreet cough.

The vicar looked at Emmaline, with a dark scowl.

...forgot to speak her vows.

"Oh, I missed it." If she weren't standing in a church, in front of her family, a vicar, and the select members who'd been invited to their wedding, she would have cursed. She looked to Drake. His mouth twitched as though he fought back a laugh.

No help there. Emmaline sighed. What had she expected? It wasn't as though he could reclaim the moment for her.

There was a hum of confusion amongst the small crowd.

He leaned in and whispered, "I assure you, my dear, you can still recite the words. You haven't lost the opportunity."

"I will," Emmaline blurted.

Then just like that, after fifteen long years she became the Marchioness of Drake.

The smattering of applause, the flurry of signatures required of them, and the festive wedding breakfast passed in a whirl. At the conclusion of the festivities, Emmaline and Drake started for the carriage.

Drake waved off the groom who rushed forward to help. He held out his arm to Emmaline. "Shall we?"

She placed her fingers along his coat sleeves but then froze. Her brother cut a path through the small throng of well-wishers and walked over to Emmaline and Drake. He stopped in front of them.

The two men stood there. Her brother and husband locked in some silent match of the wills. Emmaline held her breath. Her brother had assented to a match between her and Drake but she wanted so much more than that. She wanted the two of them to forge a friendship. They were the two most important men in her life.

Drake broke the impasse. He held out a hand to his new brother-in-law.

Sebastian's jaw set and for a moment, Emmaline thought he might reject the offer of peace. Then, her brother accepted the gesture. Two strong hands united with a commitment for a truce—an uneasy truce perhaps, but a truce nonetheless.

Emmaline waited until they'd finished and went up on tiptoe. She kissed her brother. "I love you."

Sebastian scratched his jaw, clearly uncomfortable with her public show of emotion. He patted her on the shoulder. "None of that." Then in his typical fashion, Sebastian glared at Drake. "I meant what I said in the church. Hurt her and I—"

"I heard you and would encourage you to do just that," Drake interrupted, his tone solemn.

Sebastian, paused appearing startled by Drake's concession. With a curt nod, he directed his attention to Emmaline. "Here." He thrust a package at her.

Emmaline looked from him to the oddly shaped gift in her hands. "It's a wedding gift."

Emmaline placed one final kiss on her brother's cheek and then Drake made a move to hand her up into the carriage.

"I love you, too," Sebastian blurted.

She winked. "I know."

The doors to the carriage closed and Emmaline leaned her head out the window. She waved at their guests until they were no longer in sight, and then drew laughingly back inside.

Feeling his eyes on her, Emmaline glanced at him. "What?"

"You are so beautiful," he murmured, a husky tone underlying his words.

Her cheeks heated and she dipped her head. Though there was an easy sense of comfort in being with Drake, there was also some awkwardness in the dramatic shift that had occurred in their situation. Her lips tipped at the corner.

"Why the catlike smile, love?"

"I was thinking about all the times when I was a girl that I would practice twining my name with yours. And now you're my husband."

Emmaline settled into his side, burrowing herself close. She stretched her legs out on the seat in front of them. Her movements upset the forgotten gift. It tumbled to the floor.

Drake reached down and rescued the gift, handing it to Emmaline. "I must admit to some curiosity as to what your brother gifted us."

"Me, too," she said, almost hesitant to open the package. With Sebastian one could never be sure. She unwrapped the gift and opened the top of the box to reveal—

A burst of laughter escaped Emmaline.

Drake shook his head in consternation. A bonnet? It seemed a peculiar gift choice.

At that moment, however, he did not want to think of Mallen. Or his rather odd gift habits. Through hooded lids, he studied Emmaline and thoughts of finally making love to her made him harden in anticipation. Playing with the ribbons of her new gift, she seemed impervious to the tension in his tightly coiled body. He reached over and tugged her unceremoniously onto his lap.

A squeak squeezed past her lips.

He tangled his fingers behind her nape, angling her head. "I have been longing to do this all day," he whispered and then brought her mouth to his. It wasn't a chaste meeting of lips. This was a kiss without reservations. It was hot. Demanding. Seeking.

Emmaline twined her arms about his neck and tilted her head back to deepen the kiss. She opened her mouth to his and their tongues collided in a violent exchange. Drake's hands roamed a path over her body, exploring each angle, each curve that had fascinated him since he'd seen her save an old beggar woman in the streets. Aching for more, he held her fast so her center was pressed against his hard shaft.

Emmaline pulled back a little, her eyes clouded with passion. "I want to touch you like you touched me."

Drake groaned, and kissed her again. He shifted her so she was seated astride one of his hard thighs. The fine silk of her ivory gown, rucked up about her legs, leant her an air of wantonness that thrilled him to the core. Just the sight of her made his shaft ache.

He ran his hands over her creamy white thighs. "You are so soft." His fingers trailed higher and higher until he found her center drenched with desire. She was hotter than the sun on a summer day.

A hiss escaped Emmaline's teeth and of their own volition, her hips began undulating.

"Oh, God," she moaned, arching into him. Her moan became a soft, pleading scream. Her head fell backwards. "Drake," she begged.

"That's it," he whispered, his fingers continued to work her.

She cried out in protest when he eased his fingers out of her hot warmth. He set about undoing the fastidious row of pearl buttons along the back of her dress. He lowered the bodice, exposing her to his eyes. Drake closed a hand over a small round breast, fondling it, until she sagged against him. "Perfect," he murmured hoarsely into her mouth. He trailed a finger across a turgid red nipple, and then pressed his lips to the bud.

A small scream escaped Emmaline and she threw her head back, sending her chocolate wave cascading around them like a silken curtain. He continued suckling the sensitive tip of her breast until she was whimpering with incoherent desire.

"Please," she panted.

Drake reached down and released himself from his breeches, at last allowing his aching cock the freedom it craved.

247

Emmaline's unrestrained movements ground to a halt at the sight of his erection. She froze. "You're huge," she said breathless with passion.

A pained, humorless laugh escaped him. He guided her hand to his shaft and encouraged her to explore the swollen length. A groan escaped him, as she wrapped her delicate fingers about him and moved them up and down.

"It feels like satin," she said.

Drake's eyes closed when her emboldened fingers worked him. He couldn't drum up one rationale thought. A guttural groan emerged low in his throat, escaping from some primitive part deep inside him.

As though enflamed by his desire, she moved up and down on his oaken thigh with a frenzy. Her body stiffened, her finger froze on his shaft, and she was coming in waves upon his thigh. Her keening cry rent the quiet of the carriage as she collapsed atop him, fingers still curled tightly about his length.

Drake placed a kiss at her temple, where a faint sheen of perspiration clung to her.

Emmaline glanced up, her eyes clouded with desire. "I want to pleasure you," she said huskily. "Show me." It wasn't a question.

Drake's eyes closed. He wanted to wait. Wanted to wait for the moment she was in his bed, under him, and he was thrusting between her sweet thighs.

"Like this," he instructed hoarsely and showed her the rhythm.

Emmaline watched with wide-eyed fascination as he pumped his hips into her hand, studying the pearly white fluid that leaked from the tip of his shaft.

She squeezed him in her hands, increasing the rhythm, and he sucked in air through his teeth, on a sharp whistle. "God, Emmaline. I'm going to come."

And then he stiffened, and was coming, a stream of milk white seed poured from him, and Emmaline watched through round eyes.

Replete from his exertions and the power of his orgasm, Drake sunk against the cushions and held Emmaline in his arms. He continued to hold her long after she'd fallen asleep just studying her serene, heart-shaped face until his eyes grew heavy. A yawn escaped him. He'd close his eyes. Just for a short while.

THIRTY-SIX

The carriage wheels ground to a jarring halt. Drake's eyes flew open. He made a move to dash his hand across his face and clear the haze of slumber but his hand was caught and he remembered...

His head dropped back slowly into the dark leather squabs of the interior of his carriage and he closed his eyes again on a smile. He must look like a lovelorn pup. Mayhap he was.

They'd arrived at their new home. *Home.* He smiled.

Drake rearranged Emmaline's gown. He tugged the bodice back into place and made quick work of the intricate row of buttons. He dropped her skirts and through it all, his sated wife continued to sleep.

Taking care not to jostle her, Drake shoved the curtain apart, and peered at his townhouse. At the time he'd purchased it, he hadn't allowed himself to imagine the simple things that so many gentlemen took for granted—a wife, a home, children—would ever be his. He believed loneliness was to be the penance required of him for the things he'd done in battle.

Drake let the black fabric fall back in place and shifted his attention to Emmaline. Apparently the gods had, if not forgiven him, granted him this undeserved happiness. They'd sent him down an angel.

A harsh, snorting sound slipped from her slack lips.

He smiled. Apparently, an angel who snored.

Her thick eyelashes fluttered open and closed as she negotiated reality with dream state. There was a sleepy moment of joyful recognition, when her gaze found his and she reached her arms high above her head, arching her back in a contented stretch. She yawned loudly, before closing her eyes, and burrowing into his side.

Then she seemed to realize the carriage had ceased its swaying, rhythmic motion. "We're here, love," he confirmed.

Like a bolt of lightening had struck, Emmaline's body jolted forward and she promptly tumbled to the floor. "I'm a mess," she cried, in a sweetly endearing hoarse morning voice. She glanced down at her rumpled gown and groaned. "It will take just one glance for the staff to know exactly what we've been doing in the carriage."

He didn't debate the merit of that point, and instead reached out a hand to assist her up. She dropped her head into her hands and shook it back and forth, groaning in embarrassment. "I want to stay here all day, buried away in this carriage," she moaned. "I can't meet the staff like this. I look, like, like…"

Drake waited for her to finish her sentence, lips twitching. "Like?"

Emmaline somehow managed to squish his booted foot beneath her slipper. "You are insufferable."

"And you are quite a shrew in the morning, love."

"I am not…" At his pointed smile, she snapped her mouth shut.

He took pity on her frayed state, and quickly helped her up from the floor. He set to work righting her hair, adjusting her gown, and briefly shaking out what wrinkles he could. "There, you're all properly righted. However," he gave her a lingering kiss, "I far preferred you all rumpled and thoroughly loved."

Emmaline accepted his kiss. "You are far too familiar with a lady's ablutions," she charged prettily.

Beneath the light teasing tone, there was a rebuke buried in that quip. The hurt reached Emmaline's wide chocolate brown eyes, spearing him in the heart. He damned himself to perdition.

There was a knock on the carriage door. "We've arrived, my lord," the servant stated from the other side.

Drake ignored him. He took Emmaline's chin between his hands, and urged her to meet his eyes. "I will not lie to you. There were many, many other women."

Emmaline winced.

He raised her knuckles to his lips, caressing them deliberately and delicately with his lips. "From the moment you boldly marched up to me in the theatre, there has never been another woman for me. And there will never be. I pledge this to you."

Her lips pursed in a set line. "There most certainly will not be."

Drake laughed and dropped another kiss on her lips.

A second rap sounded on the carriage door. "My lord, we've—"

"Damn it, I heard you."

Emmaline swatted at his fingers. "Don't be so surly. What His Lordship meant to say was, thank you, he heard you," she addressed the poor servant outside the carriage.

"No it wasn't. I meant exactly what I said," Drake corrected for the servant's benefit.

She rolled her eyes and pulled back the curtains. The servant shuffled back and forth on the balls of his feet.

Emmaline dropped the curtain and leveled Drake with a reproachful look. "Do behave."

"I'll be on my best behavior, love," he whispered, loving the pink blush that stained her cheeks.

He rapped once on the roof of the carriage and the footman promptly opened the door. The young man kept his eyes fixed firmly on the ground.

Drake climbed out of the carriage and held a hand up. Emmaline placed her fingers in his and allowed him to help her down. They proceeded to walk up the steps of their new home.

The staff stood in a small, neat row in the foyer. The housekeeper and butler rushed forward.

"My lord, my lady, welcome. I am Mrs. Brown." The round housekeeper with plump, merry cheeks dropped a small curtsy. "It is an honor, my lady."

A warm smile wreathed Emmaline's face, and the housekeeper fairly preened. Yes, Emmaline had that effect on most people. "Good afternoon, Mrs. Brown. It is so nice to meet you."

The butler cleared his throat and Emmaline directed her attention to the small man. Nearly an inch shorter than Emmaline, he comported himself with stiff, proper decorum. "If we might introduce you to the rest of the staff," he said, his tone laced with disapproval of Mrs. Brown's unfiltered emotions.

Mrs. Brown gave him a pert look, and made a disapproving sound. "Grumpy ole' thing," she said to Emmaline in a loud whisper that carried around the foyer.

Emmaline laughed.

Mrs. Brown beamed and turned approvingly to Drake. "I like her, my lord."

Drake winked. "Which is a good thing, Mrs. Brown, as I've no intention of returning her."

Mr. Smith cleared his throat yet again. "Mrs. Brown."

Mrs. Brown's response was to give the man another disapproving glance. "I heard you, I heard you. No need to be such a Napoleon."

At last, Mr. Smith was ruffled. He propped his hands upon his hips and took a step towards the taller Mrs. Brown. "How dare you, you impertinent bit of baggage. The only reason the Captain agreed to hire you was because—"

Drake gave a sharp clap. "That is quite enough."

Mr. Smith flushed. "My apologies, Cap'n," he muttered, dropping his head.

Drake leaned close to his wife and whispered for her ears alone. "The staff is largely made up of soldiers and their families. I hope it does not offend you, my lady." A sudden uncertainty plagued Drake. He wanted Emmaline to be pleased and knew the servants he'd assembled were a good deal less than conventional.

Emmaline glanced down the line at their rather unconventional staff, her expression inscrutable. Her eyes lingered on the stiff, erect form of Mr. Smith, a military man, and then the gregarious Mrs. Brown, who'd followed the drum. She finally looked at Drake. "I think it is brilliant, husband."

He released a breath.

"Come, my lady, I'm sure you are ready to go above stairs now," Mrs. Brown interrupted.

"You ain't to interrupt. It just ain't done." Mr. Smith couldn't contain himself. His deeply lined cheeks went ruddy at his second uncharacteristic loss of control.

The housekeeper favored him with a wink and a cheeky smile. She took Emmaline by the arm. "Come on, luvvie. Let us get you ready for the captain."

Ten different shades of red colored Emmaline's cheeks as she looked over her shoulder at Drake, as if she were silently pleading with him to rescue her.

He winked.

Emmaline didn't have any choice but to be steered up the staircase, to her chambers. When they entered, Emmaline found her maid. Grace stood removing articles of clothing from Emmaline's trunks.

Grace smiled. "My lady," she greeted with a curtsy.

"Grace," she returned and then her eyes fell to the bed behind Grace, where an elaborate white silk peignoir had been laid out. Her eyes traveled over the delicate fabric adorned with a pearl-encrusted bodice and trimmed with intermittent diamonds. It was stunning.

Mrs. Brown shared a look with Grace. "It will be a fine night for His Lordship. And for my lady, I venture," Mrs. Brown said in a hushed whisper.

Grace laughed, even as Emmaline's cheeks heated with embarrassment. Her maid rushed forward. "Come, come, let me help ready you!"

Mrs. Brown made an approving sound. "If you have any need of me, just ring." With that, she left.

Emmaline allowed Grace to assist her out of her wedding gown and into the silk piece. The smooth silk fluttered over her like the velvety petals of a rosebud, and she shivered as cool fabric met her naked skin. Faintly trembling hands ran along the sides of her nightgown.

She felt...

...naked.

"You are stunning, my lady," Grace murmured. She removed the pins from Emmaline's hair, and began brushing the long brown locks until they fell freely, loosely about her waist.

Emmaline stared at her reflection in the bevel mirror. For nearly the first time in her life she felt...beautiful.

"Is there anything else you require, my lady?"

Emmaline started. "No, no thank you, Grace. That will be all."

Grace dipped a curtsy and slipped quietly from the room.

Emmaline continued to stare at the reflection of the silk clad woman in the mirror, hardly daring to believe it was her own visage. She cocked her head, touching a finger to her lips. Would he find her beautiful? A sharp rap on the door interrupted her musings. Emmaline jumped. She pressed a hand to her chest to try and still the rapid-fire beat of her heart.

"Come," she called, her voice faltering.

Drake filled the open-doorway and a wave of nervousness coursed through her. She made to wipe her damp palms along the sides of her nightgown, but remembered how exquisite the garment was and stopped. "Hullo," she said, breaking the awkward silence.

Drake leaned against the doorjamb and gave her a reverent smile. "You are stunning."

Her mouth went dry, words escaped her. Why couldn't she be seductive and sophisticated, capable of a perfectly naughty smile?

He leveled himself away from the entryway and shoved the door closed with the heel of his boot. "Come, love, you aren't shy around me of a sudden?"

"No," she said a touch too quickly. *Liar. He makes you feel the same way you did when you had your Come Out at Almack's...and look what a disaster that had proven to be.* She took a breath. Painful awkwardness heightened Emmaline's sense of inadequacy. She opened her mouth to fill the void that had engulfed the both of them. "The wedding was lovely. And the flowers from the gardens looked so lovely in the church. We were so fortunate to have sun. The day was just..."

Drake folded his arms across his chest. "Lovely?"

Her mouth snapped shut as he sauntered over to her. His chest rose and fell in a steady, calming cadence. The faint scent of sandalwood clung to his skin.

Silence reigned.

And Emmaline decided she'd had enough of it. "Aren't you going to kiss me?"

Drake's arms fell to his side and his mouth gaped open. Emboldened by his reaction, she took a deep breath, twined her arms about his neck, and pushed up on her tip-toes. "What no answer? Then I suppose I shall just have to kiss you," she breathed against his lips, and then kissed him.

Drake groaned. His hands went to her waist and began roving a course over her silk peignoir, caressing her through the silk garment.

Wordlessly, he swept her into his arms and carried her to bed. He took great care as he lowered her gently down onto the soft mattress and then suddenly, he sat back on his haunches. Rolling his shoulders back, he hastily removed his jacket, and threw it haphazardly to the floor. His expertly tied cravat and white lawn shirt followed.

Drake made quick work of his boots and breeches. In moments, he sat naked before her.

Emmaline's maidenly reservations were replaced with bold curiosity and a woman's desire. The well-muscled wall of his chest was faintly sprinkled with golden curls. Curious to see if the hair was as soft as it looked, she reached out and caressed him.

Like silk.

His breath caught at her touch.

Emmaline's gaze dropped lower. She trailed the tip of her finger along his firm, abdominal muscles, and she stiffened. "Oh my God," she whispered. Thick, jagged scars crisscrossed the lower right side of Drake's stomach. A similar mark marred the upper portion of his shoulder and disappeared somewhere behind his back.

Under the scrutiny of her gaze, Drake tugged the sheet up to conceal his form. "I'm sorry, I shouldn't have...I forgot," he stammered, a wave of humiliated shame fanned out from his stomach. How could he forget? Christ, it was a wonder Emmaline hadn't stormed screaming from the chambers. "I'm hardly the same gentleman I was before the war."

His time fighting Napoleon had left him scarred both inside and out. He'd been humbled to return to England and see the hideous fascination the women he'd bedded had with his disfigurements. To them it had seemed he was nothing more than an oddity, a source of perverse entertainment. To have Emmaline look at him with distress in her eyes did something to him that none of the other women's disgust had ever managed to do. Her horror cleaved him in two.

Emmaline reached out and ran a finger across the scar at his shoulder. She sat up on her knees and she strained to see just exactly where the mark continued; her gaze followed the path all the way across his middle back.

"You are correct, you did not return the same man." She placed a kiss on his right shoulder and proceeded to trail kisses all the way down until she reached the mark. "You came back a better one." Emmaline rested her head against his chest.

Drake knew he was fortunate to have lived when so many had sustained greater wounds, so many had lost their lives. And yet...as shallow as it was, it bothered him to face the imperfections that marred his body and mind, day in and day out. Drake cleared his throat. "I am horribly disfigured."

Emmaline came up on her knees once again, and pressed her form to his. "You are perfection." She smiled and kissed him. "These scars are part of you," she said when she'd pulled away. "And I love every part of you, exactly as you are. Make love to me."

Drake's eyes grew hot and he swore to himself that it wasn't tears but rather passion. "With pleasure, my lady." He proceeded to relieve Emmaline of her gown.

He guided her down so her head met the satiny case of the pillow and trailed a series of kisses along the line of her jaw, down her collarbone, until he found the tip of her breast. He drew the erect tip into his mouth and sucked, alternately sucking and flicking it with his tongue. Emmaline thrashed her head back and forth, her brown, silken waves fanned about them like a curtain.

"Please," she whispered, as her hips undulated with a wild abandon.

Drake responded by placing a hand between her legs and caressing her hot, moist center. Her lids closed and she smartly gave herself over to the feeling of his touch.

His aching shaft swelled, fairly begging to at last be sheathed deep inside her. Moving over her, he propped himself on his elbows and parted her thighs.

She froze at the feel of his manhood pressed against the entrance to her center.

"Easy, love," he whispered into her ear, his words coming out as though he'd run a great distance. "Don't be afraid."

Emmaline reached up and twined her fingers in his golden hair. "I could never be afraid of you."

With that, he slid deeper into her. He closed his eyes and took several, steadying breaths as he willed himself to go slowly. It was bloody torture. He'd longed for this moment since he'd seen her challenge Whitmore in the street with fire in her eyes and outrage on her plump, seductive lips. All he wanted to do was thrust high and deep into her.

She stiffened again and Drake brought a hand between their bodies, fondling her center. Emmaline moaned in response, her head nestling deeper into the feathered pillow beneath her head. Her thighs fell open wider in a sweet invitation.

"That's it, love," he breathed and with a sudden thrust, broke past her maidenhead.

Drake's eyes slid closed as a hiss of breath left his lips. He'd never felt anything like this in his life. Her tightness quivered about his shaft, pulsating, thrumming. She felt like...home.

Emmaline's eyes slid open and a gasp of pain escaped her.

"Just feel, my love." He began to move.

He knew the moment Emmaline turned herself over to desire. She lifted her hips experimentally, then grew bolder. A loud, animalistic groan ripped from his throat.

Her hips picked up rhythm. He increased the depth of his strokes. A scream tore from her and she careened out of control. Her release drove Drake over the edge. He let out a triumphant shout, and poured his seed deep inside her. With a groan, he collapsed atop her.

Taking care not to crush her diminutive figure, he braced himself on his elbows, and placed a kiss on her closed lids.

She murmured something inaudible; a pleased smile played about her lips.

"What was that, love?"

"That was wonderful," she murmured drowsily, and then promptly fell asleep.

Drake rolled beside her, and pulled her into the fold of his arms.

He continued to hold her like that for several hours, not wanting to relinquish this moment of sated peace which had eluded him for years. His eyes grew heavy and he jerked awake as his body tried to pull him into a deep slumber. Drake set her away. He pulled the sheets over her naked form.

Emmaline burrowed into the covers with a contented sigh. He placed one more lingering kiss upon her lips, and went to find his sleep elsewhere.

Drake hovered in the doorway fighting the deep pull to return to her side. He closed his eyes and gripped the sides of the doorway. He could not trust himself to be alone with her—not when he was besieged by nightmares.

With a sigh, he glanced over his shoulder at her, and took his leave.

THIRTY-SEVEN

Emmaline shivered and nestled into the thick blankets, inching to the opposite side of the bed in search of Drake's warmth. It wasn't until she had made her way across the entire bed and hovered at the edge did she realize his spot was empty.

She fought back a yawn and rubbed her eyes. Her gaze landed on the rumpled spot beside her. With a frown, she reached out and ran her fingers over the fabric. Empty *and* cold, she amended.

Where the devil had her husband gone to?

Emmaline pushed herself up on her elbows, and swung her legs over the edge of the bed. A shiver wracked her frame as her feet collided with a thin maroon rug that did little to dull the biting edge of nighttime's cool spring air.

"Drake?" Her gaze did a quick sweep of the room. She folded her arms across her chest to rub warmth into them and walked over to the windows. Emmaline pulled back the curtains. The stars twinkled up in the dark sky like so many gems thrown onto a black blanket. Emmaline looked at the clock on the fireplace mantle.

Two o'clock in the morning.

She retrieved her rumpled silk nightgown and tugged it over her head, and then searched the room for her robe. Finding it on the floor, she picked it up, and stuffed her arms into the sleeves.

Emmaline sank down onto the edge of her mattress and ran her fingers in circles along the coverlet. A strand of hair fell across her eye and she blew it back. Well, blast and damn, Drake had abandoned her on their wedding night. She considered her husband's absence, and tried to work out what it meant. Mayhap he'd left because…because…

She tapped her foot in annoyance. Well, damn and blast again, she couldn't come up with a single, justifiable reason for him to scurry off to….to—wherever it was he'd gone.

And the longer she sat their thinking about it, the more her ire grew. How dare he leave her alone on their wedding night? Emmaline jumped up and with purpose in her steps, crossed to the armoire. She flung the doors open and fished around for a more modest nightgown and wrapper, which she donned in place of the scandalous piece she'd worn for Drake.

Then she set out in search of Drake.

She paused at the door immediately next to her room. Emmaline turned the knob and pushed her way inside. It took her eyes some time to adjust to the darkness of Drake's chambers. When they finally did, she peered around and noted his untouched bed.

So her husband had not sought out his own bed. Which was only slightly more mollifying.

She closed the door on a soft click and then moved down the hall. Generally, all candles would have been extinguished. Yet here, in Drakes home the lit sconces illuminated her way. Eerie shadows danced and flickered off the walls around her and she frowned as a shiver of nervousness stole along her spine.

"Don't be a ninny," she said into the quiet, soothed by the sound of her own voice. Still, she picked up her pace, unsure of her next destination. Emmaline came to a long hall that split into two directions. She paused, chewing her lip.

Well, she wasn't going to find him standing still. Turning down the hallway that would lead her to the rooms on the left side of the townhouse, she approached the first door and poked her head inside. It was a parlor. She wrinkled her nose. A very dark and dreary parlor devoid of feminine frills and adornment. She would see to that.

Emmaline moved to the next door and found what she assumed was Drake's office. It too, was empty. Continuing on, she noted a flicker of a light under the crack of one doorway, and made her way over to it.

She gently turned the handle and pushed it forward. Seated in a leather winged back chair, with his legs propped on a table in front of him, Drake stared off into the flickering flames of the lit fireplace, an open book, seemingly forgotten on his lap. Sir Faithful rested soundly at his feet.

"Drake?"

Drake did not give any indication that he'd been startled by her unexpected appearance. Sir Faithful, however, raised his head drowsily to determine who'd intruded on his sleep, before giving a big yawn and resting his head on his paws.

"He is not much of a guard dog," she said, breaking the thick silence.

He finally spared her a brief glance. "Emmaline." His tone was flat.

Emmaline wet her lips nervously. "You left me." She flinched at the hurt little accusatory edge to her words.

Drake looked away, but not before she glimpsed the blankness in his expression. "I'm not tired."

Was this the same man who'd made sweet love to her mere hours ago? Emmaline cleared her throat. "That isn't possible. After the wedding? Our travels?" *Our lovemaking.*

His jaw set stonily. "I slept in the carriage."

Emmaline sidled closer. "It is past two o'clock in the morning." The fireplace flame danced off the gold lettering of the book on his lap, pulling her attention to that which had drawn him away from her bed.

She started. And then her lips twitched with gloating amusement. *The Castle of Wolfenbach.*

Drake saw the direction of her notice and flushed. He shifted in his seat as though he was a naughty child caught pilfering treats from the kitchen.

"Drake?"

"Yes."

"Are you reading a Gothic novel?"

Drake reached out and before she could anticipate his intentions, he dragged her across his lap and began nuzzling the sensitive spot behind her ear. He trailed his tongue along the skin until she shivered. His skilled fingers inched her modest dressing gown up, higher, and higher, so her naked thighs were exposed to the night air.

She swatted at his fingers. "You didn't answer me."

He proceeded to nibble the corner of her lip. "I think you can see I was," he said on a silken whisper.

She angled her head away from him. "Stop trying to distract me. Apologize."

"I'm trying not to be offended by your lack of interest in my advances, love," he drawled.

"Apologize," she pressed, fighting the allure of his seductive smile.

Drake sighed. "I'm sorry for kissing you..."

Emmaline laughed and took another playful swipe. "Don't be a great lummox. Tell me I was right, and how wonderful a good Gothic novel is."

Drake laid his head back on the leather of the chair and shook his head back and forth. "Are we truly having this discussion now?"

She jutted her chin out. "Yes."

"I still hold your gothic novels are over-dramatic, ridiculous—"

Her gasp quashed his tirade. "You cannot disparage them and then read them clandestinely. It's—"

"May I finish, my lady?"

Emmaline folded her arms across her chest. "Finish."

Clearing his throat, Drake continued. "It is true. Since I stumbled upon you at the Old Corner Bookshop and read *Glenarvon*, I found, to my utter amazement," he muttered beneath his breath, "they do indeed make for occasionally bloody, interesting reading. So, I offer my most humble apologies, my lady. You were indeed correct. A gothic novel can be very entertaining."

Emmaline leaned down and placed a long, slow, lingering kiss upon his lips.

His hand resumed its earlier ministrations, climbing the path of her white thigh, higher, higher, just to the juncture of her thighs, when she swiped at him again.

Drake's hand fell to the arm of the chair. He sighed. "Yes?"

"That isn't all," she reminded him.

Drake's brow furrowed. "It isn't? He resumed his exploration of her body.

"No, it isn't. You left me."

With his fingers, he parted the folds of her womanhood. In spite of her best efforts to the contrary, her body responded eagerly to his touch. With a keening moan, she arched into his hand, writhing helplessly in his lap.

"Stop," she panted, shimmying away from him. She flung the skirts of her nightgown back down into place.

Drake gave a long-suffering sigh. "Must I?"

"I'm not amused, Drake."

A single golden brow arched at her words. "Darling, I'm hard and aching. The last thing I want to discuss on our wedding night is my reading preferences or why I left you."

"Did I do something wrong?"

"Emmaline, I don't think you've done a thing wrong in your life."

Emmaline snorted and roll her eyes. "Oh, I assure you Sebastian would be glad to point out just how wrong you are on that score."

"And I assure you, the last person I want to think about with you sitting on my lap and my shaft hard for you is your brother."

Emmaline laughed. "Fair enough."

Silence fell, and when he didn't seem eager to fill it, she nudged him in the ribs. "I'm waiting."

"I don't sleep well at night, Emmaline." He moved her off his lap and raked an agitated hand through tousled golden hair. "I have nightmares about the war. Sometimes I am violent. I don't feel...comfortable knowing you might be unsafe." The words came out clipped in an emotionless tone. A dry humorless laugh bubbled eerily in his throat. "There you have it. I'm afraid to sleep next to my own wife. What have I become?"

Besieged by a wave of helplessness, Emmaline stood frozen beside Drake's chair not knowing what to do. Or say. The Drake before her was not one she was familiar with. She knew him as the confident, unflappable gentleman, possessed of a wry wit and single-minded determination. This man before her, humbled and hesitant, made her reassess the façade of invincibility she'd constructed around him. With a delicate touch, she reached out and ran her fingers through his hair.

He flinched. "You must know I will not allow you to sleep anywhere but beside me."

Drake made a sound in his throat and turned into her caress. "Emmaline, please do not ask this of me. That day in your garden, when I knocked you down…I thought I would go mad. I would never forgive myself if I hurt you again."

She tapped a finger along his chin. "Don't you see? I'm yours unconditionally. Not only when life is easy." Sinking beside his chair, she knelt at his feet. "I want to be here for you. It is time you let me in. I need you, *all* of you." She framed his face between her hands. "Come to bed."

An inner battle waged within Drake. The devil in him that only cared about how Emmaline made him feel, urged him to pick her up and carry her to bed. Consequences be damned. The practical part that had ruled him since his return from the Peninsula, paraded every time he'd been awakened by demons from his past, through his memory.

Go with her, the devil urged. Perhaps he was a friend of the devil, after all, because he was the one Drake chose to listen to.

Wordlessly he climbed to his feet and swept Emmaline into his arms. He carried her through the silent household, their rapid breaths the only punctuation in the night quiet. That, and the gentle padding of Sir Faithful's paws on the soft carpet as Drake weaved his way down the hallway, up the stairs, and to her bedchamber.

Drake kicked the door shut with the tip of his foot and carried Emmaline to the rumpled bed. He lowered her down and Sir Faithful began to bark noisily. "Hush." The dog sat, tongue lolling out the side of his mouth.

Drake returned his attention to Emmaline.

She eyed the dog. "He is watching us," she said in a hushed whisper.

He didn't pause from his efforts of removing her nightgown and robe, kissing each spot of flesh he exposed. "I assure you, he cannot understand your words, so there really is no need to whisper," he murmured between kisses.

He then devoted his attention to her mouth. Kissing the corner of her lips, he claimed the plump lower bud of flesh between his teeth and suckled.

The world, but for the two of them, ceased to exist.

At least for Drake.

Emmaline cast another nervous glance down when Sir Faithful whimpered.

"He is watching."

In the midst of lowering his head to worship her ruby red nipple, Drake paused. He dropped his head resignedly between her breasts. "He was your gift." Then, he closed his mouth around her nipple.

She cried out in protest when he stopped. He slid down further and further until his head was at the juncture of her thighs. His breath fanned the dark thatch of curls, the hot, musk of her scent drove him to near delirium. He needed to taste her.

Her hand fell to his head, halting his movements. "Yes he was my gift, but..."

Drake paused yet again. "Emmaline."

"Yes," she breathed.

"Be quiet."

At long last, Emmaline forgot about Sir Faithful.

And somehow, after they'd made love, Drake let peaceful sleep overtake him in his wife's arms.

THIRTY-EIGHT

Emmaline laughed. She stretched a hand out to play with the cloying blackness; her other hand gripped Drake's arm as he steered her blindfolded on a winding course through the house. "Are we there yet?"

"Hush," he said, a playful edge infused into his words.

In the time they'd been married, the hard, cynical look Emmaline had come to expect from Drake, had been replaced with tiny lines that creased the corners of his eyes when he laughed. Oftentimes she would awaken in the middle of the night, to watch him as he slept. In his peaceful slumbering's, a boy-like quality clung to him. The tightness around Drake's lips, the firm set to his jaw, disappeared. It was in those stolen moments, she most loved studying him. Arrogant though it was, she loved that she was responsible for his happiness.

Emmaline had expected Drake would continue to go out and visit his clubs. Instead, he'd forsaken all trips to White's and Brooks's and insisted they decline the many invitations for the new Marquess and Marchioness of Drake. They alternated their time between reading gothic novels on the library sofa, and making love—oftentimes also on the library sofa.

Drake guided her to a halt. Carefully untying the length of fabric he'd used to cover her eyes, he removed the fabric. "We're here."

Emmaline blinked to accustom herself to the unexpected ray of sunshine.

Then blinked again.

The garden, walled off by solid brick, was a tangled mess of shrubs, flowers, and weeds. Branches were all twisted up in overgrown ivy weeds had long ago choked off and overrun the rosebushes throughout the space. The area was so vastly different than her mother's well-tended, immaculate gardens.

Taking a long, slow look around…her fingers twitched with the urge to work on the space. Her mind conjured strategies of redesign. It was a blank canvas…and it was hers.

Drake rocked on the balls of his feet. "I purchased the home after seeing the garden. I imagined you working here. If it does not suit, if there is too much to be done, I will gladly bring in as many—"

Emmaline turned and threw her arms about his neck, squeezing tightly. "It is the most amazing gift anyone has ever given me."

Drake took her lips in a slow, lingering kiss. Without a thought for propriety, he scooped Emmaline into his arms and carried her through the gardens, down the hall, up the stairs, down another hall, and into his bedchamber. The bedchamber they'd come to share.

Drake pressed the handle and carried her inside. He shoved the door closed with heel of his boot, and carried her to the bed. His ravaging mouth never broke contact, as he carefully set her down on the edge of the mattress.

Emmaline threw her head back and moaned her disapproval, when Drake pulled his lips away. But he only moved his exploration to her neck, to the line of her bodice. He made quick work of the tiny buttons along the back of her gown. Next, Drake tugged the bodice down, and divested her of her stays and chemise, so that her breasts were exposed to his hot gaze. The cool air, combined with his hungry jade stare made the tips of her breasts tighten painfully.

With breath held, she watched as his lips closed around the bud. A pool of warmth settled at the juncture of her thighs. Drake lowered her to bed, and followed her with his body. His hands expertly worked the hem of her gown up, inching it higher. Her thighs parted for him, urging him closer. He came over her, but Emmaline rolled away. Going up on her knees, she pressed her exposed breasts to the fabric of his blue coat. The rough material against the sensitive skin of her nipples nearly drove her to a fever pitch.

Drake's emerald eyes darkened the color of onyx, his eyes clouded with passion.

"It seems you are in need of release," she purred. She reached between them and through the fabric of his riding breeches, stroked his hard shaft.

"Emmaline, free me," he said his voice scratchy with desire.

"My pleasure, my lord." Emmaline unfastened the buttons at the front flap of his breeches and shoved him down to the mattress. She looked up at him with heavy eyes. "I'd show you pleasure like you showed me last night."

Before Drake could fathom her intentions, Emmaline took him in her mouth.

A hiss escaped his lips at the unexpectedness of her ministrations. He labored to open his eyes so he could view her as she pleasured him. His eyes slid closed. God, she was brilliant with her tongue. "Stop," he commanded. He didn't know how long he could last. The pull of her lips around his length was near torture.

Drake arched his hips upward. Her delicate tongue worked him and a groan ripped from somewhere deep in his chest.

A jerky hiss slipped from between his tightly clenched teeth when she pulled back, but she rucked her skirts above her knees and straddled him. Of their own volition, his hands went to her hips as she eased upon his hard shaft. A sweet, breathy sigh escaped her as she sheathed herself fully.

Emmaline moved upon him in a slow rhythmic motion at first that built into a frenzied movement as she violently rode him.

Drake stroked his palms over the swell of her buttocks. Her body stiffened and she came in long, rippling waves upon him, coating his shaft. With a little moan, she collapsed atop him.

And then, with a guttural cry wrenched from his throat, he spilled his seed deep inside her.

They continued to lay that way; their limbs entangled like old tree branches. The sound of silence filled the room, occasionally punctuated by the tick of the ormolu clock on the oak mantle of the fireplace.

Their efforts had brought the silken waves of her deep brown hair cascading about them. It fanned over them like a satin sheet.

Drake's rapid breath began to slow. "I don't think I'll ever be able to move again."

Emmaline finally picked up her head from his chest and peered at him through sated, heavy eyes. "Was that—?"

"Do not even ask." His lips found hers. He smiled at the pleased expression his words resulted in and pinched her right buttocks. "Don't grow conceited, love."

Emmaline curled into his side and rested her chin on his chest. He felt her smile against his naked skin.

"It's been dreary going through life being adequate at everything. It is nice to know there is something I excel at." She gave a long, exaggerated sigh. "It is unfortunate, others can't know of my skills." Drake pinched her on the buttocks again and she squealed.

"Do not even think about sharing your talents," he growled. He heard the possessive flare in his tone. Just the idea of Emmaline with any other man enraged him to the point that he wanted to find the non-existent bastard and grind his fist into the other man's face.

"Don't look like that."

"Like what?"

Emmaline ran her fingers through his hair. "Like you are capable of murdering a phantom lover. How could I ever desire anyone else?"

Wordlessly he rose over her and gripped her hands within his. He raised them above her head.

Her eyes widened at the feel of his shaft stirring against her belly. "Again?"

"Again."

He proceeded to show her why she could never desire another man.

THIRTY-NINE

A low mewling sound penetrated the thick fog of sleep that had engulfed Emmaline. Her eyes fluttered open as she tried to make sense of the noise that had penetrated her dreamless state. Sleeping against the hard-muscled wall of Drake's chest, she was loathe to move from the warm safety of his arms.

The whimpering increased in volume. Emmaline looked around for Sir Faithful. It took a moment for her eyes to adjust to the lack of light. The ink black of the night sky penetrated the gold gilt curtains which were slightly agape.

Sir Faithful barked.

She peered over the edge of the bed. Sir Faithful paced at her bedside. He emitted a small, quiet moan. "What is it, boy?"

The answering response was a short cry—a very *human* cry, that sent a shivery trail of bumps shooting up her spine. It jerked her attention back toward the bed.

Drake thrashed his head wildly upon his pillow. The golden strands of his hair glistened with so much sweat it was as though he'd been caught in a rainstorm. "No, no, no!"

The despair etched into each line of his slumbering face struck her like a physical blow. "Shh. I'm here, Drake." She took his face between her hands and leaned close to him. "Do you hear me? I'm here." She willed her words to bring him back from the hell that had dragged him by his heels and into this netherworld of horror. But it was unrelenting, unwilling to relinquish its hold.

His body stilled.

A sigh slipped from her lips in the form of a prayer. "Oh thank God, Drake. I—"

"For the love of God, don't do it, man!" Drake screamed into the night, twisting in the covers, which only seemed to heighten his panic.

Emmaline gripped his arm, shaking him gently at first, and then harder. "Please, Drake, please." Tears dripped down her cheeks and merged with his salty mementos of despair.

She scrubbed at her cheeks. Her sadness would do him no good. Emmaline found strength in fury. How dare these demons take him from her? She would be damned if this nightmare stole him from her. They were memories. Hideous, horrible, ugly memories. She, however, was real. She was here. She would not relinquish him to a dream. If he could feel her, if he could taste her then maybe she could rescue him from the memories she'd never be able to see.

"Drake, I am not letting you go. Come back to me. Now!"

His eyes flew open and he stared at her with a blank gaze.

Emmaline swallowed. He was still gone to her.

Drake shouted over and over, the piteous sound reverberated off the walls.

She registered the frantic footsteps outside their chamber. The door opened and then closed with a loud slam.

Emmaline looked to the entryway just as Drake roared. He threw his forearm out and elbowed her in the chin. The force of the blow knocked her over and tangled as she was in the sheets, Emmaline went reeling into the side of the nightstand. She fell from the bed; her hip struck the floor.

A blast of stars danced behind her eyes. Emmaline blinked back oblivion.

Sir Faithful whimpered and lapped her cheek with his coarse, pink tongue. It dragged Emmaline back from the edge of blackness.

"My lady? Are you all right?" Drake's valet's question came as if he spoke down a long hallway.

She couldn't muster the appropriate humility over the impropriety of James viewing her en dishabille. Instead, she motioned to Drake. "Help me." The words came out garbled.

When the valet, rushed to her side, his gaze averted from the sheet draped around her form, Emmaline shook her head. *No, not me. Help me, help him.* "Help him." She forced the words out deliberate, one at a time.

Seeming torn, James hesitated, and then directed his attention to Drake.

Drake's body stilled. Emmaline didn't know whether the nightmare had run its course or whether her husband responded to the familiarity of James' presence but his ragged breaths settled into a smooth, even pattern.

James pulled the coverlet over Drake. "May I be of assistance, my lady?" He very deliberately fixed his gaze on her husband.

"That is all," she assured him. Her head continued to ache, but the dull throb had lessened. "Thank you, James."

He nodded and made to take his leave and then, paused at the doorway, his back to her. "My lady, he is a good man."

"I don't need convincing of Lord Drake's character," she said, gently. She knew more about Drake than anyone suspected. She knew about Valiant and the men he'd saved. "I know he is a good man."

James hesitated, as though there was something more he wished to say, but then bowed. "My lady." He closed the door behind him with a quiet click.

James' exit appeared to have a greater impact than all of Emmaline's pleading.

Drake bolted upright. "Emmaline?"

Drake had to tell his mind that he was safely ensconced in his bedroom and not fighting for his life on the battlefields of the Peninsula.

He looked around the room and frowned. He'd acquiesced to Emmaline's wishes and agreed to sleep with her. Where had she gone?

As if she'd heard his unspoken question, her voice called up to him. "Here."

He peered about and then blinked back a fog of confusion. Why in hell was she on the…A surge of bile climbed up his throat and choked him. Knowing intuitively what he'd find, he leaned over. His fingers gripped the edge of the mattress and he clung to the material object, certain it was all that kept him from tumbling off into madness. Nausea roiled in his gut, nearly overwhelming him with its intensity. *What have I done?*

Drake clenched his eyes tight. He wanted to wail like the beast he was. His greatest fear, a fear now realized, stared up at him.

"Christ," he hissed.

"I'm fine, Drake," she whispered. A faint quaver underlined her words.

His gaze did a sweep of her form and settled on the large knot at her temple. The delicate skin had already begun to turn a purpling-black. It matched the bruise that had begun to form on her cheek.

Drake came off the bed in one fluid motion and dropped to his knees. "What have I done?"

With hands that shook, he inspected the damage he'd caused. He gently probed the lump near her temple. She flinched under his touch and his hands fell to his side. He was a monster. Oh, he'd allowed himself to believe in the weeks since they'd married that he'd begun to improve. He'd assured himself that the episodes were coming less frequently, his sleep less interrupted. He'd attributed it to her, she was his beacon. She gave him strength.

Drake now realized he'd deluded himself. What was worse than his self-delusion was that he'd put Emmaline in danger. Good God, he could have killed her. He abruptly fell onto his haunches, putting distance between him and Emmaline—physical and emotional. Wearily, he dropped his head to his hands.

"Look at me," she said. "Look at me," she repeated when he still didn't acknowledge her.

Forcing himself to look at her, his stomach turned at the sight of her bruised face. "Forgive me?" he pleaded.

Emmaline's lower lip quivered. She reached out a hand and he stared down at her unsteady fingers. "There is nothing to forgive, Drake."

A hollow, mirthless laugh rang from his chest. "There is everything to forgive. I hurt you. I should have never married you."

She flinched. "I love you."

Drake gritted his teeth. "Love is not enough, Emmaline."

Emmaline gasped and it was all he could do to keep from taking her in his arms. He erected an emotionless wall of indifference.

Drake stood and helped her up. He guided her to the edge of the bed. Her full, red lips that would haunt him for the rest of his days parted, as if she intended to speak. "Not another word. We will finish this tomorrow. I am ringing for supplies to tend your—your..." He couldn't finish.

"Drake..."

Drake spun on his heels and rang for a servant. Within moments, knuckles brushed the wood panel of the door and Drake yanked the door open. "I need strips of cloth and water."

The servant bowed and beat a hasty retreat.

Drake took a slow, steadying breath and turned around to face his wife. His body recoiled the same way it had when he'd taken a bullet to the shoulder.

If Mallen could see her, Drake would be a dead man. A black laugh erupted from his lips, the sound eerie to his own ears.

"What are you thinking?" Emmaline whispered.

Drake ignored her. Mayhap that was what he should do. Call for the Duke of Mallen, let the man see his sister, then...his turbulent thoughts were interrupted by a perfunctory knock. In three strides, Drake crossed the room and pulled open the door.

Accepting the items from James without so much as a word of thanks, he shut the door with a quiet click.

Drake closed his eyes momentarily. When he opened them, he trained his gaze on the wood panel of the door. The time of cowardice was at an end. In order to see to her injuries, he had to face her.

Taking a deep breath, he turned around.

With a soft tread, he crossed to the bed and eased the basin of water onto the nightstand. Then, gently, so as to hardly compress the mattress, he sat beside her.

With fingers that shook, he brought the compress to her cheek. He saw her effortful attempts not to flinch and his guilt swelled. "I am so sorry."

Emmaline caught her lower lip between her teeth. "I am fine."

A mirthless laugh escaped him. "Yes, that lump and black bruise on your cheek are just *fine*." He dipped a cloth into the basin. His jerky movements sent water over the sides of the white porcelain, and sprayed the floor.

"You don't need to be so cavalier."

He flung the cloth against the opposite wall and Emmaline flinched. The sopping fabric left a watery trail along the pale blue plaster. "Cavalier? You call me cavalier?" Beset by the hopelessness of it all, he leapt to his feet and began to pace. "This has all been a terrible mistake," he said.

A flash of fury sparked in her brown eyes. "I understand you feel guilty. It is however, unpardonable for you to say such a thing." Fury made her chest rise and fall swiftly, it reddened her cheeks. She stormed across the room and planted herself in front of him. "How dare you say that?" She jabbed a finger at his chest.

Drake dragged a hand through his hair and fixed his stare at a point beyond her shoulder, unable to meet her accusing gaze. Fire fairly leapt in her eyes. Emmaline should be furious…but only with the fact that he'd subjected her to a life of dangerous uncertainty.

"We are not discussing this tonight," he growled. He stepped around her and made his way toward the door. She followed close at his heels.

"You are not to walk away from this discussion," Emmaline said.

He stopped so abruptly she careened into his back.

His spun around and his arms came up instinctively to right her. He steadied her and then dropped his arms by his side. He wasn't fit to touch her. Drake swallowed back a wave of despair. "Good night, my lady."

Drake beat a low, formal bow, and left.

FORTY

The next morning, Emmaline sat on the deep blue velvet sofa in Drake's office. She'd read and re-read the same sentence of the volume in her hands. With a sigh, she set aside his copy of *The Castle of Wolfenbach.*

A bright stream of sunlight angled through the narrow opening in the curtains. Emmaline rubbed a hand over her eyes. She'd not been able to think of anything other than the moment Drake had walked out on her last evening. She had longed to go after him but had not wanted to push Drake when he'd been so clearly vulnerable. Instead, she had lain in bed, counting down the evening minutes until she'd eventually fallen into a restless slumber.

For surely the hundredth time since she'd entered his office that morning, Emmaline consulted the grating clock as it tick-tocked away on the fireplace mantle. Ten o'clock.

Where in blazes was he? He could be at Hyde Park? Why hadn't she thought of the possibility sooner? She should have searched him out. *And what, wander over all of London for her new husband?* Oh, how the gossips would love that story.

On the heel of that thought came the realization that any hint of scandal where she and Drake were concerned would result in an appearance from her far too-overprotective brother. Therefore it was in her best interest to glean his whereabouts before the speculative *ton* did. She pressed her fingers along her temple line and then winced at the painful reminder of last evening.

He'd promised her they would speak in the morning. And instead, he'd left her. She battled down the hurt that tugged at her heart and fed the healthy anger that enlivened her. How dare he lie to her? She was not a child. She was his wife. Drake owed her a conversation.

Emmaline jumped to her feet, and rang for a servant. She paced back and forth until a servant arrived.

"My lady?"

"Will you ask Mrs. Brown to come here?"

The maid dipped a curtsy. "Of course, my lady."

Emmaline rang her hands and walked over to the window. She pulled back the curtain and stared unseeing down into the bustling street below. A fashionably dressed couple caught her notice. With their arms linked, they strolled leisurely down the pavement and seemed unaware of the hurried movements of the strangers around them. The couple wore matching expressions of simple, uncomplicated adoration. An awful niggling of jealousy crept into Emmaline's mind. How she longed for that. Not just for herself, but for her and Drake.

"My lady!" Mrs. Brown's booming voice interrupted her musings.

Emmaline startled and turned to face the housekeeper. "Mrs. Brown, good morning to you. I was wondering if you had happened to see His Lordship today?"

Mrs. Brown's eyes went wide and her big mouth quivered. "I certainly have, my lady." Tears smarted behind the lady's eyes and she dashed a hand across her cheeks.

A panicky fear clawed at Emmaline. Her fingers curled into tight balls at her sides, and she dug her nails into the pad of her palm so hard, she nearly drew blood. "What is it, Mrs. Brown? Is he unwell?"

The normally garrulous housekeeper remained silent, only serving to raise Emmaline's sense of dread. With a determined step, she crossed over to Mrs. Brown and gripped the woman's arm gently, but firmly.

The servant made a choked sound in her throat which added to Emmaline's terror. "He is in your chambers, my lady."

Emmaline dropped Mrs. Brown's arm and blinked. "My chambers?" Drake had in fact been within the townhouse the entire time? Could she have been so foolish as to have missed his presence all morning?

Before Mrs. Brown could reply, Emmaline set out at a near run and flew abovestairs toward her chambers. She entered the room, nearly out of breath from her exertions and stumbled to a halt at the sight of her trunks out. Drake stood in the center of the bedroom with his hands clasped behind his back, directing the packing of her belongings.

"Where are we going?" she blurted.

Drake didn't as much as glance at Emmaline. He murmured something to her maid, Grace, who dipped a curtsy and left. It didn't escape Emmaline's notice how Grace pointedly avoided making eye contact with her. A frisson of unease worked a path down her spine.

As soon as the door closed behind Grace, Emmaline turned her attention to Drake. His intense emerald gaze was trained on her bruised cheek. "Look at me, Drake."

"I am," he said so quietly, she had to strain to hear him.

"I asked, where are we going?" An impenetrable fear kept her frozen, afraid to move from the spot she stood.

"We are not going anywhere. You are going."

His words cut into her like the sting of salt water as it is tossed upon an open wound. Thoughts of the happy couple she'd witnessed mere moments ago flitted through her mind. How very joyous they'd been; their happiness a stark contrast to Drake's own detached demeanor.

God, how she hated those young lovers—even more now. How come they were able to know such happiness when her own life was crumbling down around her like an ancient ruin?

She stuck her chin out. "I'm not going anywhere, Drake." Emmaline hated the quivering timbre of her voice. Damn him for being so indifferent when she read as transparent as a page in a Gothic novel. "How dare you stand before me seeming to be singularly unaffected? You think to send me away like the crumbs on a dinner plate."

The only indication given that he was affected by their exchange was an imperceptible tightening of his jaw. "This isn't a discussion. I'll not have you hurt. As I said last evening, this was a mistake. I have compromised your safety—"

"And as I've said…you are a bloody coward, husband." She spat the curse at him, reveling in the subtle stiffening of his shoulders, the way he flinched at the word. *Good, let him be at least somewhat unbalanced.*

In the end, he retained his calm. "Either way, you cannot remain here."

Emmaline shook her head sadly, her eyes sliding closed. Poor Drake. She thought of all the stories she had learned about him at London Hospital. Thought of all the men he'd considered friends, who he'd left behind. His dog, Valiant.

She took a deep breath. "No."

Unused to having his wishes countermanded, his brow furrowed. "No?

With a cheeky tilt of her chin, she tossed her head. "That's correct. No, as in I'm not—"

He slammed his fist against the wall, the ferocity of his movement caused reverberations that sent the collection of crystal perfume bottles on the delicate vanity clattering.

"Christ, Emmaline. Why are you doing this?" he rasped. "This is the hardest thing I've done—"

"Then don't do it."

Emmaline's words were not a challenge, an entreaty, or demand. Had that utterance been emotional and enraged, it might have fueled his determination to send her packing.

This calm reasoning, however, he was altogether unprepared for. The soft carpet masked her movements and he was unaware of her bridging the distance between them, until he felt her tender touch on the sleeve of his jacket. He couldn't look at her bruised, delicate visage. Could not stare at the damage he'd inflicted with his monstrous hands.

"As long as I've known you, you've turned away from me. Please, stop turning away from me." There was a gentle plea underlying her words, a soft appeal.

Drake pressed the heel of his palms against his forehead. *How could he allow her to remain?* Pure selfishness made him want to move forward with her in his life. Calm reason and logic, however, urged him to send her away.

She, however, was more tempting than a devil among man. "You are not alone, Drake. You do not have to be. I am here. Let me in. I will help you."

How desperately he longed for the presence of someone else alongside him, battling the demons that possessed him. Nay, not just anyone. He longed for her. His brave warrior, who didn't hesitate to put herself in harm's way to help others. First she'd saved the peddler. Now she was attempting to save him. Yet, if he turned to her, what kind of bastard would that make him?

Staring unseeing out at her armoire, he willed himself to confront the demons that tormented his waking and sleeping moments. The specters visited so frequently, he'd begun to lose sense of his own self. He'd been trying so desperately to push the ghosts to a deep, dark corner, and they refused to stay banished. This time, he didn't hold back the memories. Vivid reflections of specific men, and then the other nameless men who visited him each night, paraded through his mind.

Then he knew.

It was guilt he carried. A great sense of blameworthiness that he'd lived when so many others had died. A sense of malfeasance that men had been killed and forever maimed because he'd led them to their death. The confrontation of his own culpability robbed him of the ability to stand. The muscle in his legs turned to nothing and he slid down to the floor, borrowing support from the wall.

And in the light of day, in front of his Emmaline, he did what he'd longed to do for seven long years.

He wept.

Openly. Great big, gasping, noisy tears that wrenched from somewhere deep within him. He felt the flutter of Emmaline's skirts as she dropped to her knees beside him. She took his face between her hands; kissed his tears, kissed his wet lashes.

She stroked a trembling hand across his brow. He leaned into her touch.

Wordlessly, she climbed onto his lap and burrowed deep against his chest.

Drake's lips caressed her temple. "How did I ever get so fortunate as to find myself betrothed to you?" he whispered, his voice ragged.

She tilted her head up and favored him with a bemused smiled. "I suppose we only have our fathers to thank."

Drake gave a rueful shake of his head, remembering that fateful day, when they'd signed the official betrothal contract. A memory tickled the corners of his mind. Recollections suddenly came rushing back to him; he was a boy who'd helped a very young girl to her feet. He caught a strand of her silken brown hair between his fingers. "Brown suits you."

Emmaline's lips tipped up in a tremulously beautiful smile. "I didn't think you remembered."

Drake stroked a hand over her cheek. "I remember it all."

"I'd ask something of you, Drake."

He inclined his head.

"I would that you visit London Hospital. The men would be so pleased to see you. And I think it would do you good, as well."

That was the real motivation behind her request. Somehow, she possessed the insight to know what it had taken him years to realize—in order to be free of the war, he needed to confront it. As long as he ran from the memories, they would continue to haunt him.

The thought of seeing the men who'd shared his hell made him nauseous. His fingers stroked the beloved lines of her face. He was fairly certain there was nothing he could ever deny her. Not even this.

"I will visit with the...men."

Emmaline's expression warmed several degrees. She tangled her fingers in his hair and dragged his mouth down to hers. The kiss she gave him was sweet, soft, lingering.

It tasted like...the future.

FORTY-ONE

The prickling ease of nervousness climbed up Drake's back, around his neck, and nearly overwhelmed him with a cloying panic. He tugged at his cravat.

It did not help.

Where was the nurse who was supposed to meet him? An interminable amount of time had passed since he'd arrived at eleven o'clock. He consulted his timepiece.

Five minutes after eleven.

Mayhap he should leave. He'd simply explain to Emmaline that he'd waited...all of five minutes, and no one had arrived to show him to the respective ward. It might serve him to exaggerate the span of time just a tad. Yes, that was what he'd do. He'd—

A nurse clad in a stark white dress appeared in the main corridor of the hospital. "My lord, it is an honor." She dipped a formal curtsy. "I'm Nurse Maitland."

He lurched forward, the fabric of his greatcoat billowed at the alacrity of his movements. He cleared his throat and inclined his head in greeting. "Nurse Maitland."

Drake reminded himself it was just a visit with men who'd seen and done things not much different than he had. He doffed his hat, and beat the small brim of the article distractedly against his thigh.

"May I show you to the wing Her Ladyship visits?"

He'd rather she show him a way out of the hospital. Drake nodded. "Uh-yes, that would be fine."

"Her Ladyship is a noble, wonderful woman." Either unaware or uncaring of Drake's desire to engage as little as possible in conversation, the woman prattled on and on. "She is always generous and so very kind to the men. They greatly enjoy her visits."

Drake was certain of it. How could Emmaline bring anyone anything other than joy? She had an inherent goodness and warmth that was a tangible force.

"She visits often, I understand," he murmured.

"Oh, yes."

The nurse fell silent; the only sound, the soft click of his boot steps and her serviceable shoes on the hall floor. And yet, now that she'd ceased talking, Drake found himself suddenly eager for more information from the woman. He found a yearning to know more about Emmaline.

Drake cleared his throat. "What—what does the marchioness do on her visits?"

From the corner of his eye, he observed the older woman's smile. "Why, she reads to the soldiers, tells them stories. Brings them floral arrangements and baskets of treats. My lady has visited each week for many years now. I don't know another person more steadfast and pure of heart."

Neither did he.

Where he'd spent the interim years since the war carousing, gambling, and womanizing, she had led a far nobler, far more redeeming life.

"Here we are." She opened a set of double doors and Drake passed through.

In his imaginings of the hospital for returned soldiers, he'd envisioned a drab, dark place with rows upon rows of beds with soldiers lying in stony silence.

With the exception of the rows of beds, none of the images he'd conjured had been correct.

The room, far brighter than he'd imagined resonated with the chatter of men, sharing stories, laughing at ribald jokes. Fresh cut blooms in white porcelain vases had been placed on nightstands beside a number of the beds.

Nurse Maitland saw the direction of his gaze. "My lady's doing," she explained. "The flowers are from her gardens. It does add cheer to the room, wouldn't you say?"

"It does that."

All as one, it was as if the men present registered the presence of an interloper. Seemingly endless pairs of eyes turned in his direction, leveling him with curiosity and suspicion. He thought he'd feel uncomfortable among them, that the sense of failure, which weighed on him would make any meetings awkward. He would not have blamed any one of the men who had served under him and fallen on the fields to feel anything but anger toward him. They would be justified in their feelings.

Drake instead felt a greater sense of belonging than he'd ever before experienced at any club or soiree.

"Cap'n Drake!" One man called, unmindful of Drake's status as lord.

Nurse Maitland made to interject and remind the man of proper address, but Drake silenced her with a brisk wave. "I'm sure there are many other more pressing matters that require your attention. Thank you for showing me to the ward."

The older woman dipped her head. "Please call if I can be of any further assistance."

Drake inclined his head in acknowledgement, and then directed his attention to the soldier who'd called his name.

He moved down the hospital floor and murmured a greeting to the soldiers he passed. Some eyed him with wary curiosity. Others, not knowing he'd fought the same bloody fight they'd fought, eyed him with skepticism, suspecting he was nothing more than another lord doing a charitable service by paying them a visit.

The sight of a reed-thin soldier with a shock of red hair brought his movements to an abrupt halt. From the bright orange hue of his closely cropped hair, to the hue of his skin, even having been in London Hospital as long as he had, the man remained, remarkably—red.

"MacGregor," he called wish a flash of surprise. The young man had fought under him in the Thirty-first Regiment.

"Captain, so very good to see you."

Drake held out a hand to shake Macgregor's, before jerking it back, stunned, forgetting.

Macgregor's gave a shake of his head. "No worries, Cap'n. I forget myself sometimes."

Words escaped Drake. He couldn't imagine there'd ever be a day he woke up or moved through the day forgetting he'd lost not one, but both arms on the battlefield.

"How've you been, Macgregor?" The question sounded lame to his own ears.

The cheerful solider gave a wide, gap-toothed smile. "I've got my hands full, I'm so busy, Cap'n!" He laughed at loudly at his own jest.

Startled by MacGregor's levity, Drake laughed. It felt, good. Better than good, really.

MacGregor nodded in the direction of a chair. "Have a seat, Cap'n?"

Drake eased a chair over out and sat.

He was reminded of the fact that on the battlefield, in the heat of fighting, or on the long treks across the land, social distinctions fell away. During war, it mattered not if your father was a duke or a servant or whether one's family was prestigious.

Upon his return from the Peninsula, Drake's immersion back into Society had battered down all those unchecked relationships he'd forged during war.

When he'd returned to England he'd resumed the life he'd left behind, sometimes wondering if the closeness shared between soldiers had been imagined. This visit to the hospital was testament to a bond that would always be shared.

"I've heard about your pursuits in London, Cap'n."

Drake winced at the reminder of his roguish reputation. Shame filled him. He cleared his throat awkwardly. "I-uh, have since given up my less than noble pursuits."

MacGregor proceeded to launch into a series of questions. They spoke so long, Drake lost track of the amount of time he sat at MacGregor's bedside.

Drake leaned forward in his chair, finally asking the question he'd wondered since he'd sat beside the man. "Tell me, MacGregor, have you been visited by my wife, Lady Emmaline, formerly—"

MacGregor's mouth went slack. "You are married to Lady Emmaline?" A touch of awe underlined the man's words. "*You* are married to *Lady Emmaline?*"

A wry smile twisted Drake's lips. "No need to sound so surprised."

MacGregor ignored Drake's attempt at humor. "My lady's an angel. She..." and for the first time, the easy-going, light-hearted soldier's face darkened. He too, had his black place, Drake realized. Of course he did. They all did.

MacGregor's gaze went vacant. "I actually didn't lose my right arm 'til I returned, Cap'n? Did you know that?"

Drake shook his head. "I didn't." He should have known. There were so many men who'd served with him, served under him. Yet still, he'd owed it to them to know the condition of their welfare.

MacGregor continued. "When I came back, I'd been at my mum's and da's. My da was—is, an inn-keeper. I helped him round there, best as I could," he glanced down at his left arm, "as best as possible with one arm. It was hard at first. I began having pain in my right arm. Mighty painful. An infection set in." His tone was matter-of-fact. "I nearly died. Turns out a bullet I'd taken in my arm had splintered off. Fragment was still there." He shook his head, his expression bemused, as if after three years he still couldn't believe it. "I ended up here. I pleaded with the bloody doctor to leave the arm, to leave the fragment. I told him I'd rather die."

The images painted by MacGregor transported Drake back to the hellish time when he'd returned from the Peninsula. It had been as though Drake had been on a quest; a search for normalcy in his life—a desire to be the same carefree gentleman who'd first gone off to fight. Yet that normalcy had eluded him. The war had been a constant presence. It had dogged his every thought, his every movement. Men like MacGregor, however, had returned from war with not only horrific memories, but physical loss as well.

Drake folded his hands in his lap and looked down at the intertwined digits. "What made you decide to go on?" Did that raspy, barely there whisper belong to him?

MacGregor swallowed and replied on a near whisper. "It was Her Ladyship. It was the first time she visited the hospital. She was so young. She was with the Duke of Mallen. I'd just learned they were going to take my arm. She saw me arguing with the sawbones and rushed over." His lips twitched with remembered amusement. "She yelled at the doctor, cursed the bloody bastard. Oh, he was just doing his job. I know that now...but I'd never heard that in my life. A lady yelling at someone over me. I shut my mouth after that and allowed them to take the arm."

Drake visualized Emmaline at that moment in her life. She would have been seventeen, a girl on the cusp of womanhood. She'd been an avenging angel even then. He could reconcile this story with the brave woman who'd thrown herself between a whip and a peddler woman.

MacGregor interrupted Drake's musings. "You're a lucky man, Cap'n."

"Yes, I certainly am." For whatever reason, the Lord had deemed him worthy of Emmaline. Drake certainly didn't understand it. He'd fought it with everything he was worth. He was, nonetheless, aware of his, for want of a better word, good fortune.

MacGregor nodded down the hall. Drake followed the movement. "Jones was under your command, too, Cap'n. Her Ladyship's very kind to Jones."

Drake took to his feet and patted MacGregor on the shoulder. "It was good seeing you, MacGregor." Surprisingly, he found he meant those words.

"Likewise, Cap'n."

Drake turned down the hall, offering greetings to the men who now watched him with far less suspicion. He heard the murmurs.

"That's Cap'n Drake."

Some of the whispers almost reverent.

Drake wanted to shout that he did not deserve their admiration and praise. He'd been no hero. In truth, they had been far braver, far more courageous, as was evidenced by their stalwart strength even lying in this miserable hospital, forever physically scarred.

He paused by the last bed in the room, neatly situated beside a long column of windows. The man, Lieutenant Jones, who occupied the space stared out the window, at the passersby below on the London streets. In that, Jones surely couldn't help but be confronted by memories of what kept him separated from the world beyond that window pane. Drake suspected he himself would have wanted to be as far away from the window as possible.

Jones shot Drake a sideways glance. "So you married her, finally." There was a reprimand there.

Drake blinked. He'd have to be deaf to not detect the hard edge in Jones' tone. Emmaline certainly did not lack for protectors. She'd done much to earn the respect, admiration, and loyalty of these men.

"Unfortunately for her lady, yes."

A rusty laugh escaped the other man. He motioned to the chair by his bed. Drake slid into it.

"I've been telling her to bring you by." Jones gave him a knowing look.

"Have you?" Drake drummed his fingertips along the edge of his seat. Emmaline hadn't mentioned that. She'd only told him she'd thought it would do him good to see the men who'd fought Boney's forces. He was coming to find, that just like in many other regards, Emmaline had been right.

Jones held out a hand. "It's good seeing you again, Captain."

Drake stared at it a long moment and then shook it.

Why in the world would Jones or MacGregor or any one of them ever want to see him? He'd been no different than any other man on that field…with the exception of the fact he'd at one point been made captain. He therefore could claim the distinction of being responsible for many of them being in the bloody spot they now rested.

Jones must have seen something in Drake, something he perhaps recognized in himself. "It isn't your fault, Captain."

The breath left Drake, and for a moment, a blinding curtain fell across his eyes. He'd seen too much. Taken too many lives. Cost too many men *their* lives.

His voice came out hoarse when he finally spoke. "How can you forgive me?" He made a slashing gesture with his hand to the spot Jones' arm should have been. "How is this not my fault?"

"It isn't your fault a bloody madman took it to his head to try and conquer this world. You were no different than so many of us, Cap'n. You decided to fight for our country. Some of us were luckier than others."

A bark of laughter devoid of mirth escaped Drake. It was hallow and guilt-ridden. "Are any of us really lucky, Jones?" The question burned in his soul.

Jones shook his head slowly. "No, that's a fair point. We've all been touched by that damn war and I suspect it'll always be with us."

Unbidden, Drake's mind went to the nightmares that frequently plagued him. He thought of Emmaline, who'd been leveled by his own hand, the bruise upon her cheek. In his mind he saw the tears wetting his normally unflappable father's cheeks. Would there ever be a time he was not plagued by the hellish memories of those years? He'd hoped that as the months passed, he would begin to forget, that the reminders would fall into the background. Oh, even now there were days when the remembrances were not with him, or were less vivid and gripping. Then suddenly something would happen; a face that reminded him of a fellow soldier, or an unexpected sound, and then his hellish time on the Peninsula would come rushing back.

Drake scrubbed the back of his hand over his face. "Do you ever have nightmares, Jones?"

Jones nodded. "Every day. Sometimes it'll be in the dead of night. Other times I'll be awake, sitting in this bed in the middle of the day and they'll come upon me."

A wave of relief filled him. There was solace in knowing he was not alone—that there were others who shared his struggle. For some time, he'd begun to think he was a madman who belonged in Bedlam. "How do you live with it?" Drake asked on a low whisper.

It was the first time Jones' grey eyes slid away from Drake, out to that window which had earlier consumed his attention. "I came back from the war without my arm. Upon my return, I learned, while in my absence, my wife and son had died of a fever. I wanted to die." He looked back at Drake. "Do you know what kept me alive?"

Drake waited for the other man to continue. He tried to imagine the horror of returning from a war missing a limb, only to discover you'd also lost your wife and child. Jones was far braver than Drake. Drake knew he could never have survived the great losses that had been heaped upon Jones' shoulders.

"Your wife kept me alive. Every week for three years she came and sat beside me. One week I didn't kill myself because I wondered if she'd come back to visit. I told myself she was just a bored lady with nothing to do. Sure enough she came back. Then I made silent wagers with myself, betting how many weeks before she would disappear. The weeks passed, and by then I forgot about killing myself."

Drake's breath caught and lodged in his chest at the realization that this too was a man Emmaline had saved. By her presence alone, she had sustained Jones, pulled him from the precipice of darkness, and given him life. Drake was not very different from Jones. The difference being, Emmaline belonged to him. Her smile, her laughter, filled both his and Jones' lives and for that they both honored her.

It was Drake however, who had the right to hold her, cherish her, love her.

Love her.

God, why had he not allowed himself to acknowledge that thought until this moment? She, who was so free with her love, with her every emotion, deserved so much more than him. She deserved to be told regularly just how special she was.

"She is a remarkable woman," Drake managed to say; forcing his thoughts back to Jones.

Jones tipped his head in acknowledgement. "You know Captain? I lost everything and everyone I loved. You have a reason to live. Trust me. You have your nightmares, we all do. And they're always going to be with us, sir. But as long as you have her you've got something to live for."

Drake felt his throat work. He did have something to live for...
rather he had someone to live for. Someone he needed to see desperately in that moment.

Drake came to his feet quickly. "What are your feelings on leaving
this behind and coming to work for my staff?"

Jones' eyes revealed a gleam of desperate hope, which was quickly
squashed by a dawning sense of reality.

"I am not altogether sure I'd be much help to your staff." Jones'
words were tinged with bitterness.

"I beg to differ, Jones. I have a need of help in my household. I
recall how capable you were with the horses. I'm certain you'd grow
accustomed to adjusting to your changed circumstances."

That gleam of longing reignited in his eyes. Jones fairly licked his
lips, clearly more enticed at the idea of being in the stables, where
he'd always been comfortable.

Jones held out his hand. "It would be an honor, Captain. A real
honor."

Drake accepted the hand in a firm shake. "I'll see the arrangements made and have you sent for." He cleared his throat, suddenly
besieged by a desire to see his wife. "If you will pardon me then, Jones?"
He bowed his head.

"Captain," Jones returned.

Drake took his leave. He needed to see his wife. Emmaline deserved
to hear the words he'd withheld from her. She also deserved his thanks
for bringing him to this place.

His musings were interrupted by the figure of a man who stepped
suddenly into his path.

Drake's feet ground to a quick halt.

The Duke of Mallen arched a dark brow, his expression stony.
"What brings you here?" Mallen drawled.

Drake's jaw set. He'd be damned if he would share something so
personal with this man. He might be Emmaline's brother but he was
no friend of Drake's, and certainly didn't deserve such personal information. He could only imagine what the great, powerful duke would

say if Drake responded with the truth; *Oh, you see, I have frequent night-mares and remembrances of the war. I even occasionally lose control and...*

"None of your business, Mallen." He bit out. "What brings you here?"

Mallen cleared his throat. "I've always had a sense of regret I was unable to enlist and fight. I've felt guilt about the men who lost their lives, risked their limbs, when I was at home, safe and unaffected. I joined the Hospital Board upon my father's passing."

Drake started. He could appreciate what that admission cost Mallen. It would seem he knew his brother-in-law far less than he'd thought. It had never occurred to him the guilt Mallen, and perhaps other lords, would feel for not fighting.

His gaze held Mallen's. "Trust me, you were better off."

Mallen rubbed his chin. "Perhaps."

"Emmaline needed you," Drake said.

"As she did you."

Ah, there it was, the subtle thrust and parry. It would be easy to dislike Mallen...if he weren't so damn loyal to Emmaline. That the other man loved her and hated Drake for having abandoned her all these years, well...it was rather hard to feel any ill-will toward someone who felt that way toward his wife.

"I'm here now, Mallen." Drake sketched a respectful bow. "If you will excuse me, I have to return home." *I miss my wife.*

Drake had nearly reached the entrance.

"Drake," Mallen called out, halting Drake in mid-stride down the hall.

He turned on his heel and waited for Mallen to speak.

"Tell Emmaline to throw out the bonnet I'd given her. Tell her I said her bonnet is just fine."

Drake angled his head. Hell, he'd never figure the other man out. "Certainly, Mallen." With that he left.

There was something he very much needed to tell his wife. Something that had been long over-due—and it wasn't going to be about her bonnet.

FORTY-TWO

Emmaline sat back on her heels and surveyed the overgrown box-woods. She chewed her lip thoughtfully, considering the bushes. A trickle of perspiration dripped from her brow. She removed her bonnet and swiped the back of her hand across the moisture.

Emmaline reached into the front pocket of her apron and withdrew a pair of pruning shears when a warm, wet tongue lapped the salty trace of sweat from her hand.

"Oh you loyal, loyal, boy." Taking a momentary break from her efforts, she sat down with her legs drawn to her chest and proceeded to shower Sir Faithful with some deserved attention.

He made a moaning growl of approval and promptly flipped to his back.

She laughed and scratched the sparse patch of fur on Sir Faithful's underside. "How do you think your master is doing this afternoon?"

Sir Faithful gave a little yelp in response.

"Good, do you?" she answered for him.

Her brow wrinkled. She hoped Drake's time at London Hospital didn't cause him further distress. Emmaline had thought Drake might find kindred spirits in the men who'd come to mean so much to her. She'd prayed Drake might find that which had eluded him for nearly four years—peace.

Emmaline did not delude herself into believing one visit would exact a miraculous transformation over Drake. She worried, however, that he wouldn't want to return to London Hospital. And she couldn't ask any more than that from him. She did not presume to know what his life had been like on the Peninsula. It would therefore, be unfair for her to make requests that could very well cause him greater angst.

She gave Sir Faithful one more pat and then returned her attention to the boxwoods. "My poor forgotten, beautiful dears," she praised them. "You must know you are utter perfection to me. You have not heard that enough, have you?" She clucked her tongue.

"I would say the same to you, my lady."

Emmaline glanced over her shoulder. Drake stood by the wrought-iron bench. He had a riding crop in one hand and beat it against his muscled thigh.

She placed her pruning shears in her apron pocket, and made to rise.

Drake walked over in three long strides, took her hands in his, and guided her up.

She wet her lips. His inscrutable expression gave her little indication of what he was thinking or about his trip to London Hospital. "Drake. How was—?"

He took her into his arms. His lips, a mere hairsbreadth apart from her own, tickled her skin with the faintest trace of coffee. "I love you." He kissed her in the gentlest meeting of lips.

Emmaline's knees went weak, but he caught her to him. His fingers undid the fraying blue satin ribbons of her bonnet. He gave a gentle tug, and then tossed the article aside. It caught a faint spring breeze, and then fell onto a nearby bush.

Emmaline's heart raced with a giddy sense of joy. Oh, she'd known Drake had come to care a great deal for her. What man, after all, would share his poetry and humble himself before a tableside of strangers?

Tears welled in her eyes, and the elegantly white linen fold of his cravat blurred.

Drake's finger traced the fullness of her lower lip, careful not to cause further pain to her bruised cheek. "Do you hear me? I—love—you." He punctuated each word with a kiss.

Emmaline leaned into his caress. "I love you, so much. I think I always have." She had loved him her entire life. There had been the inquisitive five–year-old girl who had loved the boy of three and ten who'd helped her to her feet. She had loved the man who cared so powerfully for his soldiers and a dog named, Valiant.

Drake drew her closer to him, lowering his cheek against the top of her head. He inhaled deep. "I've never deserved it."

Emmaline wrapped her arms about his waist and held onto him tight.

Drake tilted her chin up. "Do you know when I fell in love with you?"

She shook her head.

"I spent the entire ride from London Hospital trying to figure out that very question. Do you know what I realized?"

"What did you realize?"

"There was no one time, Emmaline. There wasn't one particular moment. It was a collection of so many memories and moments with you. When I saw you challenge Whitmore and his crony. The night you approached me at the opera, and then that next morning when you sent around that outrageous note. Or the day I spied you purchasing one of the most scandalous Gothic novels from the Old Corner Bookshop." His throat moved up and down. He fixed his stare at some point beyond her shoulder. "The day I...lost control in your gardens and you just held me...it was the first time I hadn't felt alone since I'd returned from the Peninsula."

Emmaline raised a hand between them and stroked the slight cleft in his chin. His eyes slid closed.

"Emmaline, when I spoke to Jones today, I felt a peace I haven't felt in a number of years. I felt you there with me. Your presence is all over the ward. I fell in love with you as I saw your fresh cut flowers, as I learned of your devotion to the men who'd fought and lost so much."

He returned his dark, moss-green eyes to Emmaline. "You are deserving of that one spectacular moment, a moment when I fell head over heels in love with you, Emmaline. I cannot give you that." His eyes charted an intent path over her face. "I can give you the love I feel that was slowly kindled and cultivated, just like the flowers you tend. I can't—"

297

She placed her fingers over his lips, silencing him. "Do you think I care how you fell in love with me? It is enough that you love me." She stretched up on tiptoes and kissed him. "I love you."

Sir Faithful gave a little bark and scratched a paw on Drake's tan breeches.

Drake turned his attention to the mangy black dog. He had grown significantly since Emmaline had brought him to his life. In spite of his impressive diet, he still managed to appear reed thin.

"Yes, boy, we both love you, as well." He fondly pet the dog between his ears.

Emmaline smiled, and leaned down, to also stroke Sir Faithful.

Drake returned his attention to her. "Do you remember what you asked me the day our fathers signed our betrothal documents?"

Emmaline's mind went wandering down a path fifteen years old. Of course, much of that day had been lost to time but she still remembered so much of it, too. She'd only been a girl of five, after all. Traces of memories had remained with her. She tried to think...

The reminiscence suddenly came to her. "I asked if you wanted to be my husband."

Drake claimed her hands in his own. He brought them to his mouth and lovingly worshipped her knuckles. "I want you to know, Emmaline, that more than anything, I want to be your husband."

Emmaline smiled tremulously. "And I want to be your wife." It was all she'd ever wanted. He was all she'd ever wanted.

He dropped his brow to hers, and rubbed it back and forth. "You are all I ever wanted," he murmured.

And after a forever betrothal, Emmaline at long last had what she'd always yearned for...a forever marriage.

EPILOGUE

Drake stared at the canopy above their bed, and grinned at the cacophony of noise penetrating the night quiet. His wife's snoring stirred the tufts of hair upon his chest, mingling with Sir Faithful's heavy breathing whose chin rested on Drake's ankle.

This time it wasn't nightmares of the past that kept Drake awake. It wasn't even a result of his wife and dog's snores. No. Now, he reveled in the feel of Emmaline in his arms—he reveled in life.

It had been almost a year since they'd married.

Over the months he'd been wed to Emmaline, the nightmares had lessened. Oh, they would still visit him on occasion; when he least expected it. He suspected Jones had been right when he'd said the memories would always, to some extent, be with them. Yet each day it seemed as though they faded in their vividness, in their intensity.

Drake attributed it Emmaline's love.

The support from the soldiers he'd taken to visiting at London Hospital.

And of course, the help of a stubborn mangy black dog, that didn't seem to know his place.

The End

The Sinful Brides features ravishing tales of London's gaming hell rogues—and the women who love them.

THE ROGUE'S WAGER

London, 1821

L ord Robert Dennington, the Marquess of Westfield, has long reveled in the freedom afforded him as the ducal heir. He knows he must someday do right by the Somerset line, but he's in no hurry to give up his carefree existence.

Helena Banbury is a bookkeeper in a gentleman's gambling club, adept at analyzing numbers and accounts but helpless for lack of influence. She's never belonged among the nobility on the gaming hell floors, but neither does she feel completely herself among the men who run the Hell and Sin Club, despite the fact that they are family. The once-illiterate girl from the streets wants more than the gilded walls her protective cage can offer.

When Robert mistakenly enters her chambers one night, Helena is forced out of her predictable life and thrust into the glittering world of Society. Will the charms of the marquess prove more perilous than any danger she ever knew on the streets?

OTHER BOOKS BY
CHRISTI CALDWELL

"To Woo a Widow"
Book 10 in the Heart of a Duke Series

They see a brokenhearted widow.

She's far from shattered.

Lady Philippa Winston is never marrying again. After her late husband's cruelty that she kept so well hidden, she has no desire to search for love.

Years ago, Miles Brookfield, the Marquess of Guilford, made a frivolous vow he never thought would come to fruition—he promised to marry his mother's goddaughter if he was unwed by the age of thirty. Now, to his dismay, he's faced with honoring that pledge. But when he encounters the beautiful and intriguing Lady Philippa, Miles knows his true path in life. It's up to him to break down every belief Philippa carries about gentlemen, proving that not only is love real, but that he is the man deserving of her sheltered heart.

Will Philippa let down her guard and allow Miles to woo a widow in desperate need of his love?

"The Lure of a Rake"
Book 9 in the Heart of a Duke Series

A Lady Dreaming of Love

Lady Genevieve Farendale has a scandalous past. Jilted at the altar years earlier and exiled by her family, she's now returned to London to prove she can be a proper lady. Even though she's not given up on the hope of marrying for love, she's wary of trusting again. Then she meets Cedric Falcot, the Marquess of St. Albans whose seductive ways set her heart aflutter. But with her sordid history, Genevieve knows a rake can also easily destroy her.

An Unlikely Pairing

What begins as a chance encounter between Cedric and Genevieve becomes something more. As they continue to meet, passions stir. But with Genevieve's hope for true love, she fears Cedric will be unable to give up his wayward lifestyle. After all, Cedric has spent years protecting his heart, and keeping everyone out. Slowly, she chips away at all the walls he's built, but when he falters, Genevieve can't offer him redemption. Now, it's up to Cedric to prove to Genevieve that the love of a man is far more powerful than the lure of a rake.

"To Trust a Rogue"
Book 8 in the Heart of a Duke Series

A rogue

Marcus, the Viscount Wessex has carefully crafted the image of rogue and charmer for polite Society. Under that façade, however, dwells a man whose dreams were shattered almost eight years earlier by a young lady who captured his heart, pledged her love, and then left him, with nothing more than a curt note.

A widow

Eight years earlier, faced with no other choice, Mrs. Eleanor Collins, fled London and the only man she ever loved, Marcus, Viscount Wessex. She has now returned to serve as a companion for her elderly aunt with a daughter in tow. Even though they're next door neighbors, there is little reason for her to move in the same circles as Marcus, just in case, she vows to avoid him, for he reminds her of all she lost when she left.

Reunited

As their paths continue to cross, Marcus finds his desire for Eleanor just as strong, but he learned long ago she's not to be trusted. He will offer her a place in his bed, but not anything more. Only, Eleanor has no interest in this new, roguish man. The more time they spend together, the protective wall they've constructed to keep the other out, begin to break. With all the betrayals and secrets between them, Marcus has to open his heart again. And Eleanor must decide if it's ever safe to trust a rogue.

"To Wed His Christmas Lady"
Book 7 in the Heart of a Duke Series

She's longing to be loved:
Lady Cara Falcot has only served one purpose to her loathsome father—to increase his power through a marriage to the future Duke of Billingsley. As such, she's built protective walls about her heart, and presents an icy facade to the world around her. Journeying home from her finishing school for the Christmas holidays, Cara's carriage is stranded during a winter storm. She's forced to tarry at a ramshackle inn, where she immediately antagonizes another patron—William.

He's avoiding his duty in favor of one last adventure:
William Hargrove, the Marquess of Grafton has wanted only one thing in life—to avoid the future match his parents would have him make to a cold, duke's daughter. He's returning home from a blissful eight years of traveling the world to see to his responsibilities. But when a winter storm interrupts his trip and lands him at a falling-down inn, he's forced to share company with a commanding Lady Cara who initially reminds him exactly of the woman he so desperately wants to avoid.

A Christmas snowstorm ushers in the spirit of the season:
At the holiday time, these two people who despise each other due to first perceptions are offered renewed beginnings and fresh starts. As this gruff stranger breaks down the walls she's built about herself, Cara has to determine whether she can truly open her heart to trusting that any man is capable of good and that she herself is capable of love. And William has to set aside all previous thoughts he's carried of the polished ladies like Cara, to be the man to show her that love.

"The Heart of a Scoundrel"
Book 6 in the Heart of a Duke Series

Ruthless, wicked, and dark, the Marquess of Rutland rouses terror in the breast of ladies and nobleman alike. All Edmund wants in life is power. After he was publically humiliated by his one love Lady Margaret, he vowed vengeance, using Margaret's niece, as his pawn. Except, he's thwarted by another, more enticing target—Miss Phoebe Barrett.

Miss Phoebe Barrett knows precisely the shame she's been born to. Because her father is a shocking letch she's learned to form her own opinions on a person's worth. After a chance meeting with the Marquess of Rutland, she is captivated by the mysterious man. He, too, is a victim of society's scorn, but the more encounters she has with

Edmund, the more she knows there is powerful depth and emotion to the jaded marquess.

The lady wreaks havoc on Edmund's plans for revenge and he finds he wants Phoebe, at all costs. As she's drawn into the darkness of his world, Phoebe risks being destroyed by Edmund's ruthlessness. And Phoebe who desires love at all costs, has to determine if she can ever truly trust the heart of a scoundrel.

"To Love a Lord"
Book 5 in the Heart of a Duke Series

All she wants is security:
The last place finishing school instructor Mrs. Jane Munroe belongs, is in polite Society. Vowing to never wed, she's been scuttled around from post to post. Now she finds herself in the Marquess of Waverly's household. She's never met a nobleman she liked, and when she meets the pompous, arrogant marquess, she remembers why. But soon, she discovers Gabriel is unlike any gentleman she's ever known.

All he wants is a companion for his sister:
What Gabriel finds himself with instead, is a fiery spirited, bespectacled woman who entices him at every corner and challenges his age-old vow to never trust his heart to a woman. But...there is something suspicious about his sister's companion. And he is determined to find out just what it is.

All they need is each other:
As Gabriel and Jane confront the truth of their feelings, the lies and secrets between them begin to unravel. And Jane is left to decide whether or not it is ever truly safe to love a lord.

"Loved By a Duke"
Book 4 in the Heart of a Duke Series

For ten years, Lady Daisy Meadows has been in love with Auric, the Duke of Crawford. Ever since his gallant rescue years earlier, Daisy knew she was destined to be his Duchess. Unfortunately, Auric sees her as his best friend's sister and nothing more. But perhaps, if she can manage to find the fabled heart of a duke pendant, she will win over the heart of her duke.

Auric, the Duke of Crawford enjoys Daisy's company. The last thing he is interested in however, is pursuing a romance with a woman he's known since she was in leading strings. This season, Daisy is turning up in the oddest places and he cannot help but notice that she is no longer a girl. But Auric wouldn't do something as foolhardy as to fall in love with Daisy. He couldn't. Not with the guilt he carries over his past sins...Not when he has no right to her heart...But perhaps, just perhaps, she can forgive the past and trust that he'd forever cherish her heart—but will she let him?

"The Love of a Rogue"
Book 3 in the Heart of a Duke Series

Lady Imogen Moore hasn't had an easy time of it since she made her Come Out. With her betrothed, a powerful duke breaking it off to wed her sister, she's become the *tons* favorite piece of gossip. Never again wanting to experience the pain of a broken heart, she's resolved to make a match with a polite, respectable gentleman. The last thing she wants is another reckless rogue.

Lord Alex Edgerton has a problem. His brother, tired of Alex's carousing has charged him with chaperoning their remaining, unwed sister about *ton* events. Shopping? No, thank you. Attending the theatre? He'd rather be at Forbidden Pleasures with a scantily clad beauty upon his lap. The task of *chaperone* becomes even more of a bother when his sister drags along her dearest friend, Lady Imogen to social functions. The last thing he wants in his life is a young, innocent English miss.

Except, as Alex and Imogen are thrown together, passions flare and Alex comes to find he not only wants Imogen in his bed, but also in his heart. Yet now he must convince Imogen to risk all, on the heart of a rogue.

"More Than a Duke"
Book 2 in the Heart of a Duke Series

Polite Society doesn't take Lady Anne Adamson seriously. However, Anne isn't just another pretty young miss. When she discovers her father betrayed her mother's love and her family descended into poverty, Anne comes up with a plan to marry a respectable, powerful, and honorable gentleman—a man nothing like her philandering father.

Armed with the heart of a duke pendant, fabled to land the wearer a duke's heart, she decides to enlist the aid of the notorious Harry, 6th Earl of Stanhope. A scoundrel with a scandalous past, he is the last gentleman she'd ever wed…however, his reputation marks him the perfect man to school her in the art of seduction so she might ensnare the illustrious Duke of Crawford.

Harry, the Earl of Stanhope is a jaded, cynical rogue who lives for his own pleasures. Having been thrown over by the only woman he ever loved so she could wed a duke, he's not at all surprised when Lady Anne approaches him with her scheme to capture another duke's affection. He's come to appreciate that all women are in fact greedy, title-grasping, self-indulgent creatures. And with Anne's history of grating on his every last nerve, she is the last woman he'd ever agree to school in the art of seduction. Only his friendship with the lady's sister compels him to help.

What begins as a pretend courtship, born of lessons on seduction, becomes something more leaving Anne to decide if she can give her heart to a reckless rogue, and Harry must decide if he's willing to again trust in a lady's love.

"For Love of the Duke"
Book 1 in the Heart of a Duke Series

After the tragic death of his wife, Jasper, the 8th Duke of Bainbridge buried himself away in the dark cold walls of his home, Castle Blackwood. When he's coaxed out of his self-imposed exile to attend the amusements of the Frost Fair, his life is irrevocably changed by his fateful meeting with Lady Katherine Adamson.

With her tight brown ringlets and silly white-ruffled gowns, Lady Katherine Adamson has found her dance card empty for two Seasons. After her father's passing, Katherine learned the unreliability of men, and is determined to depend on no one, except herself. Until she meets Jasper…

In a desperate bid to avoid a match arranged by her family, Katherine makes the Duke of Bainbridge a shocking proposition— one that he accepts.

Only, as Katherine begins to love Jasper, she finds the arrangement agreed upon is not enough. And Jasper is left to decide if protecting his heart is more important than fighting for Katherine's love.

"In Need of a Duke"
A Prequel Novella to The Heart of a Duke Series

Years earlier, a gypsy woman passed to Lady Aldora Adamson and her friends a heart pendant that promised them each the heart of a duke.

Now, a young lady, with her family facing ruin and scandal, Lady Aldora doesn't have time for mythical stories about cheap baubles. She needs to save her sisters and brother by marrying a titled gentleman with wealth and power to his name. She sets her bespectacled sights upon the Marquess of St. James.

Turned out by his father after a tragic scandal, Lord Michael Knightly has grown into a powerful, but self-made man. With the whispers and stares that still follow him, he would rather be anywhere but London…

Until he meets Lady Aldora, a young woman who mistakes him for his brother, the Marquess of St. James. The connection between Aldora and Michael is immediate and as they come to know one another, Aldora's feelings for Michael war with her sisterly responsibilities. With her family's dire situation, a man of Michael's scandalous past will never do.

Ultimately, Aldora must choose between her responsibilities as a sister and her love for Michael.

"Once a Wallflower, At Last His Love"
Book 6 in the Scandalous Seasons Series

Responsible, practical Miss Hermione Rogers, has been crafting stories as the notorious Mr. Michael Michaelmas and selling them for a meager wage to support her siblings. The only real way to ensure her family's ruinous debts are paid, however, is to marry. Tall, thin, and plain, she has no expectation of success. In London for her first Season she seizes the chance to write the tale of a brooding duke. In her research, she finds Sebastian Fitzhugh, the 5th Duke of Mallen, who unfortunately is perfectly affable, charming, and so nicely…configured…he takes her breath away. He lacks all the character traits she needs for her story, but alas, any duke will have to do.

Sebastian Fitzhugh, the 5th Duke of Mallen has been deceived so many times during the high-stakes game of courtship, he's lost faith in Society women. Yet, after a chance encounter with Hermione, he

311

finds himself intrigued. Not a woman he'd normally consider beautiful, the young lady's practical bent, her forthright nature and her tendency to turn up in the oddest places has his interests...roused. He'd like to trust her, he'd like to do a whole lot more with her too, but should he?

"A Marquess For Christmas"
Book 5 in the Scandalous Seasons Series

Lady Patrina Tidemore gave up on the ridiculous notion of true love after having her heart shattered and her trust destroyed by a black-hearted cad. Used as a pawn in a game of revenge against her brother, Patrina returns to London from a failed elopement with a tattered reputation and little hope for a respectable match. The only peace she finds is in her solitude on the cold winter days at Hyde Park. And even that is yanked from her by two little hellions who just happen to have a devastatingly handsome, but coldly aloof father, the Marquess of Beaufort. Something about the lord stirs the dreams she'd once carried for an honorable gentleman's love.

Weston Aldridge, the 4th Marquess of Beaufort was deceived and betrayed by his late wife. In her faithlessness, he's come to view women as self-serving, indulgent creatures. Except, after a series of chance encounters with Patrina, he comes to appreciate how uniquely different she is than all women he's ever known.

At the Christmastide season, a time of hope and new beginnings, Patrina and Weston, unexpectedly learn true love in one another. However, as Patrina's scandalous past threatens their future and the happiness of his children, they are both left to determine if love is enough.

"Always a Rogue, Forever Her Love"
Book 4 in the Scandalous Seasons Series

Miss Juliet Marshville is spitting mad. With one guardian missing, and the other singularly uninterested in her fate, she is at the mercy of her wastrel brother who loses her beloved childhood home to a man known as Sin. Determined to reclaim control of Rosecliff Cottage and her own fate, Juliet arranges a meeting with the notorious rogue and demands the return of her property.

Jonathan Tidemore, 5th Earl of Sinclair, known to the *ton* as Sin, is exceptionally lucky in life and at the gaming tables. He has just one problem. Well…four, really. His incorrigible sisters have driven off yet another governess. This time, however, his mother demands he find an appropriate replacement.

When Miss Juliet Marshville boldly demands the return of her precious cottage, he takes advantage of his sudden good fortune and puts an offer to her; turn his sisters into proper English ladies, and he'll return Rosecliff Cottage to Juliet's possession.

Jonathan comes to appreciate Juliet's spirit, courage, and clever wit, and decides to claim the fiery beauty as his mistress. Juliet, however, will be mistress for no man. Nor could she ever love a man who callously stole her home in a game of cards. As Jonathan begins to see Juliet as more than a spirited beauty to warm his bed, he realizes she could be a lady he could love the rest of his life, if only he can convince the proud Juliet that he's worthy of her hand and heart.

"Always Proper, Suddenly Scandalous"
Book 3 in the Scandalous Seasons Series

Geoffrey Winters, Viscount Redbrooke was not always the hard, unrelenting lord driven by propriety. After a tragic mistake, he resolved to honor his responsibility to the Redbrooke line and live a life, free of scandal. Knowing his duty is to wed a proper, respectable English miss, he selects Lady Beatrice Dennington, daughter of the Duke of Somerset, the perfect woman for him. Until he meets Miss Abigail Stone...

To distance herself from a personal scandal, Abigail Stone flees America to visit her uncle, the Duke of Somerset. Determined to never trust a man again, she is helplessly intrigued by the hard, too-proper Geoffrey. With his strict appreciation for decorum and order, he is nothing like the man' she's always dreamed of.

Abigail is everything Geoffrey does not need. She upends his carefully ordered world at every encounter. As they begin to care for one another, Abigail carefully guards the secret that resulted in her journey to England.

Only, if Geoffrey learns the truth about Abigail, he must decide which he holds most dear: his place in Society or Abigail's place in his heart.

"Never Courted, Suddenly Wed"
Book 2 in the Scandalous Seasons Series

Christopher Ansley, Earl of Waxham, has constructed a perfect image for the *ton*–the ladies love him and his company is desired by all. Only two people know the truth about Waxham's secret. Unfortunately, one of them is Miss Sophie Winters.

Sophie Winters has known Christopher since she was in leading strings. As children, they delighted in tormenting each other. Now at two and twenty, she still has a tendency to find herself in scrapes, and her marital prospects are slim.

When his father threatens to expose his shame to the *ton*, unless he weds Sophie for her dowry, Christopher concocts a plan to remain a bachelor. What he didn't plan on was falling in love with the lively, impetuous Sophie. As secrets are exposed, will Christopher's love be enough when she discovers his role in his father's scheme?

"Forever Betrothed, Never the Bride"
Book 1 in the Scandalous Seasons Series

Hopeless romantic Lady Emmaline Fitzhugh is tired of sitting with the wallflowers, waiting for her betrothed to come to his senses and marry her. When Emmaline reads one too many reports of his scandalous liaisons in the gossip rags, she takes matters into her own hands.

War-torn veteran Lord Drake devotes himself to forgetting his days on the Peninsula through an endless round of meaningless associations. He no longer wants to feel anything, but Lady Emmaline is making it hard to maintain a state of numbness. With her zest for life, she awakens his passion and desire for love.

The one woman Drake has spent the better part of his life avoiding is now the only woman he needs, but he is no longer a man worthy of his Emmaline. It is up to her to show him the healing power of love.

Non-Fiction Works by Christi Caldwell
Uninterrupted Joy: Memoir:
My Journey through Infertility,
Pregnancy, and Special Needs

The following journey was never intended for publication. It was written from a mother, to her unborn child. The words detailed her struggle through infertility and the joy of finally being pregnant. A stunning revelation at her son's birth opened a world of both fear and discovery. This is the story of one mother's love and hope and…her quest for uninterrupted joy.

AUTHOR BIOGRAPHY

Christi Caldwell is the bestselling author of historical romance novels set in the Regency era. Christi blames Judith McNaught's "Whitney, My Love," for luring her into the world of historical romance. While sitting in her graduate school apartment at the University of Connecticut, Christi decided to set aside her notes and try her hand at writing romance. She believes the most perfect heroes and heroines have imperfections and rather enjoys tormenting them before crafting a well-deserved happily ever after!

When Christi isn't writing the stories of flawed heroes and heroines, she can be found in her Southern Connecticut home chasing around her feisty five-year-old son, and caring for twin princesses-in-training!

Visit www.christicaldwellauthor.com to learn more about what Christi is working on, or join her on Facebook at facebook.com/christicaldwellauthor and Twitter @ChristiCaldwell.